A KINGDOM
DIVIDED

Also by Alex Rutherford

Raiders from the North

A KINGDOM DIVIDED

Empire of the Moghul

Alex Rutherford

Thomas Dunne Books
St. Martin's Griffin
New York

THOMAS DUNNE BOOKS.
An imprint of St. Martin's Press.

A KINGDOM DIVIDED. Copyright © 2010 by Alex Rutherford. All rights reserved. Printed in the United States of America. For information, address St. Martin's Press, 175 Fifth Avenue, New York, N.Y. 10010.

thomasdunnebooks.com
www.stmartins.com

The Library of Congress has cataloged the hardcover edition as follows:

Rutherford, Alex, 1948–
 A kingdom divided : empire of the Moghul / Alex Rutherford.—1st U.S. ed.
 p. cm.
 ISBN 978-0-312-59701-6
 1. Humayun, Emperor of Hindustan, 1508–1556—Fiction. 2. Mogul Empire—Kings and rulers—Fiction. 3. Mogul Empire—History—16th century—Fiction. I. Title.
 PR6118.U92K56 2011
 823'.92—dc22

2011006910

ISBN 978-1-250-00729-2 (trade paperback)

First published in Great Britain by HEADLINE REVIEW, an imprint of HEADLINE PUBLISHING GROUP, an Hachette UK Company

First St. Martin's Griffin Edition: June 2012

10 9 8 7 6 5 4 3 2 1

SKETCH MAP OF
Humayun's World

Samarkand

Ferghana

Herat

AFGHANISTAN

Kabul R. Kabul

Ghazni

R. Helmand

Kandahar

PERSIA

BALUCHISTAN

Rohtas

R. Jhelum

R. Chenab

R. Ravi

Lahore

R. Sutlej

R. Indus

SIND

Umarkot

KASHMIR

R. Indus

PUNJAB

Sirhind

Panipat   Delhi

R. Jumna

Agra

Gwalior

R. Chambal

RAJASTHAN

GUJARAT

Cambay   Champnir

Surat

R. Ganges

Kanauj

Allahabad

Patna   R. Ganges

Chausa

BIHAR

BENGAL

Main Characters

Humayun's family

Babur, Humayun's father and the first Moghul emperor
Maham, Humayun's mother and Babur's favourite wife
Khanzada, Humayun's aunt, the sister of Babur
Baisanghar, Humayun's maternal grandfather
Kamran, Humayun's eldest half-brother
Askari, Humayun's middle half-brother and full brother of Kamran
Hindal, Humayun's youngest half-brother
Gulbadan, Humayun's half-sister and full sister of Hindal
Hamida, Humayun's wife
Akbar, Humayun's son

Humayun's inner circle

Kasim, Humayun's vizier
Jauhar, Humayun's attendant and later his comptroller of the household
Baba Yasaval, Humayun's master-of-horse
Ahmed Khan, Humayun's chief scout and later governor of Agra
Sharaf, Humayun's astrologer
Zahid Beg, a senior commander
Salima, Humayun's favourite concubine
Suleiman Mirza, Humayun's cousin and general of his cavalry

Maham Anga, Akbar's wet-nurse

Adham Khan, Akbar's milk-brother

Nadim Khwaja, one of Humayun's commanders and Maham Anga's husband

Others

Gulrukh, Babur's wife and mother of Kamran and Askari

Dildar, Babur's wife and mother of Hindal and Gulbadan

Nizam, a water-carrier

Zainab, Hamida's waiting woman

Sultana, Moghul concubine of Raja Maldeo

Wazim Pathan, a retired soldier rewarded by Humayun for his courage

Shaikh Ali Akbar, Hindal's vizier and father of Hamida

Darya, son of Nasir, commander of Humayun's garrison in Kabul

Mustapha Ergun, Turkish cavalry officer

Hindustan

Sultan Bahadur Shah, ruler of Gujarat

Tartar Khan, member of the previous ruling dynasty, the Lodi, defeated by Humayun's father Babur, and a claimant to the throne of Hindustan

Sher Shah, an ambitious ruler of humble origins in Bengal

Islam Shah, Sher Shah's son

Mirza Husain, Sultan of Sind

Raja Maldeo, ruler of Marwar

Tariq Khan, ruler of Ferozepur and vassal of Sher Shah

Adil Shah, Islam Shah's brother-in-law and a claimant to the throne of Hindustan

Sekunder Shah, cousin of Islam Shah and claimant to the throne of Hindustan

Persians

Shah Tahmasp

Rustum Beg, elderly general and cousin of Shah Tahmasp

Bairam Khan, nobleman, military commander and later Humayun's *khan-i-khanan*, commander-in-chief

Humayun's ancestors

Genghis Khan

Timur, known in the west as Tamburlaine from a corruption of Timur-i-Lang (Timur the Lame)

Ulugh Beg, Timur's grandson and a famous astronomer

'If you wish to be king, put brotherly
     sentiment aside...
This is no brother! This is Your
     Majesty's foe!'

From the *Humayunnama* by Gulbadan,
half-sister of Humayun

Part I

Brotherly Love

Chapter 1

Riding the Tiger

The wind was chill. If Humayun closed his eyes he could almost imagine himself back among the pastures and mountains of the Kabul of his boyhood, rather than here on the battlements of Agra. But the short winter was ending. In a few weeks the plains of Hindustan would burn with heat and dust.

Drawing his fur-lined scarlet cloak more tightly around him, Humayun walked slowly along the walls. He had ordered his bodyguards to leave him because he wanted to be alone with his thoughts. Raising his head, he gazed up into clear skies that were splashed with stars. Their intense, jewel-like brightness never failed to fascinate him. It often seemed that everything was written there if only you knew where to look and how to interpret the messages . . .

A firm, light footstep from somewhere behind him disturbed him. Humayun turned, wondering which courtier or guard had been rash enough to disobey their emperor's expressed wish for solitude. His angry gaze fell on a slight, tall figure in purple robes, a thin gauze veil pulled over the lower face, with above it the raisin eyes of his aunt, Khanzada. Humayun's expression relaxed into a smile.

'We are waiting for you in the women's quarters. You said you would eat with us tonight. Your mother complains you spend too much time alone, and I agree with her.'

Khanzada dropped her veil. The tawny light from a torch burning in a sconce fell on a fine-boned face no longer as beautiful as in her youth but one that Humayun had loved and trusted for as many of his twenty-three years as he could remember. As she stepped a little closer he caught the soft fragrance of the sandalwood that burned constantly in jewelled golden saucers in the women's apartments.

'I have much to reflect on. I still find it difficult to accept that my father is dead.'

'I understand, Humayun. I loved him too. Babur was your father, but don't forget he was also my little brother. He and I went through much together and I never thought to lose him so soon . . . but it was God's will.'

Humayun looked away, unwilling for even Khanzada to see the tears gleaming in his eyes at the thought that he would never see his father, the first Moghul emperor, again. It seemed incredible that that strong, seasoned warrior, who had led his nomadic horsemen down through the mountain passes from Kabul and across the Indus to found an empire, was dead. Even less real was the thought that only three months ago, with his father's eagle-hilted sword Alamgir at his waist and the ring of his ancestor Timur on his finger, he himself had been proclaimed Moghul emperor.

'It's so strange . . . like a fantasy from which I keep expecting to wake.'

'It's the real world and you must accept it. Everything Babur wanted, everything he fought for, had one purpose only – to win an empire and found a dynasty. You know that as well as I – weren't you fighting at your father's side when he crushed Sultan Ibrahim Lodi at Panipat to claim Hindustan for the Moghuls?'

Humayun said nothing. Instead he looked up once more at the sky. As he did so, a shooting star sped across the heavens and vanished, leaving not even a trace of its fiery tail. Glancing at Khanzada, he saw that she had seen it too.

'Perhaps the shooting star was an omen. Perhaps it means my reign will fizzle out ingloriously . . . that no one will remember me . . .'

'Such self-doubt and hesitancy would anger your father if he were here now. Instead he would have you embrace your destiny. He could have chosen one of your three half-brothers as his heir, but he selected you. Not just because you are the eldest – that has never been the way of our people – but because he thought you were the most worthy, the most able. Our hold on Hindustan is precarious – we have been here only five years and dangers press in from every side. Babur picked you because he trusted not just in your courage, which you had already demonstrated on the battlefield, but also in your inner strength and your self-belief, your sense of our family's right to rule, which our dynasty must have to survive and prosper here in this new land.' Khanzada paused.

When Humayun did not reply, she raised her face to the light of the torch and ran her finger down a thin white scar extending from her right eyebrow almost to her chin. 'Do not forget how I got this, how when I was young and your father had to abandon Samarkand to the Uzbeks I was seized by their chieftain Shaibani Khan and forced to submit to him. He hated all who, like us, have the blood of Timur. It gave him pleasure to humiliate and degrade a princess of our house. I give thanks that I never despaired all the time I was a captive in his *haram* . . . never forgot who I was or that it was my duty to survive. Remember that when another woman attacked me and stole some of my beauty, I wore this scar as a badge of honour – to show that I was still alive and that one day I would be free. After ten long years that day came. I re-joined my brother and rejoiced to see him drink to my return from a vessel made from the skull of Shaibani Khan. You must have the same self-belief, the same strength of character, Humayun, as I had.'

'Such courage as yours is hard to emulate, but I will not fail my father or our house.'

'What is it, then? You are young, ambitious . . . you were eager for the throne long before your father fell ill. Babur knew; he spoke to me of it.'

'His death was so sudden when it came. I left so much unsaid. I didn't feel ready to be emperor . . . at least not so soon, nor in such a way.'

Humayun let his head drop. It was true. His father's final moments still haunted him. Summoning the last of his strength, Babur had ordered his attendants to dress him in his royal robes, seat him on his throne and call his nobles to him. Before the entire court, in a weak voice but firm in his resolve, Babur had ordered Humayun to take Timur's heavy gold ring, engraved with the head of a snarling tiger, from his finger, saying, 'Wear it with pride, and never forget the duties it imposes on you...' But Babur had been just forty-seven, still in his prime and far too young to hand on his fledgling empire.

'No man, not even an emperor, can know when he will be called to Paradise and in what manner. None of us can predict or control fully the course of our lives. Learning to live with the great uncertainty of mortality as well as the other vicissitudes of fortune is part of growing to adulthood.'

'Yes. But I often think there is more we can do to understand the underlying patterns behind our lives. Events that appear random may not be. For example, Aunt, you said just now that my father's death was God's will, but you're wrong. It was my father's will. He deliberately sacrificed himself for me.'

Khanzada stared. 'What d'you mean?'

'I've never revealed to anyone my father's last words to me. Just before he died, he whispered that when I was sick with fever a few months earlier, my astrologer, Sharaf, had told him that he'd read in the stars that if he wished me to live he must offer up what was most precious to him. So falling on his face he offered God his life for mine.'

'Then it was indeed God's will – God accepted the sacrifice.'

'No! Sharaf told me that all he intended was that my father should offer up the Koh-i-Nur diamond – not his life. But my father misinterpreted his words . . . It seems overwhelming that my father loved me so much, saw me as so important to the future of our dynasty that he offered his own life. How can I live up to such faith in me? I feel that I don't deserve the throne I once so hungered for. I fear that a reign that began in such a way will be tainted . . .'

'Such thoughts are absurd. You search too hard for patterns of cause and consequence. Many a reign begins in loss and uncertainty. It is up to you to make sure by your own actions that yours doesn't end so. Any sacrifice Babur made was done through love for you and trust in you. Remember also he did not die immediately – you recovered and he lived eight more months. His death at that time might well have been pure coincidence.' Khanzada paused. 'Did he say anything else to you in his last moments?'

'He told me not to grieve . . . he was happy to go. He also made me promise to do nothing against my half-brothers, however much they might deserve it.'

Khanzada's face tautened. For a moment Humayun thought she was about to say something about his brothers, but instead, with a toss of her small, elegant head, she seemed to think better of it.

'Come. That's about enough of these musings. The cloth is spread in the *haram*. You must not keep your mother and the other ladies waiting. But Humayun . . . one last thought. Don't forget that your name means "fortunate". Fortune will be yours if you will be strong in mind as well as in body and seize it. Banish these foolish self-doubts of yours. Introspection may become a poet or a mystic but it has no place in the life of an emperor. Grasp with both hands what fate – and your father – have bequeathed you.'

With a last look up at the sky that showed him that the moon was now obscured by cloud, Humayun slowly followed his aunt towards the stone staircase that led down to the women's apartments.

• ◆ •

Prostrating himself before Humayun in the emperor's private chambers some weeks later, Baba Yasaval, his usually blunt, ebullient master-of-horse, looked strangely nervous. As the man rose again and looked up at him, Humayun noticed that his skin seemed stretched unnaturally tight over his wide cheekbones and a pulse throbbed at his temple.

'Majesty, if I might speak to you alone?' Baba Yasaval glanced at the guards positioned on either side of Humayun's low silver chair. It was an unusual request. Security dictated that the emperor was seldom on his own – even when he was in the *haram* guards were always near at hand, ready to turn an assassin's blade. But Baba Yasaval, who had fought loyally for Humayun's father, could be trusted.

Humayun dismissed his guards from the chamber and beckoned Baba Yasaval closer. The man approached but hesitated before speaking, scratching his stubbly scalp which, to remind him of the old ways of his clan, since arriving in Hindustan he had taken to shaving, except for a single lock of coarse, greying hair that swung like a tassel.

'Baba Yasaval, speak. What is it you wish to tell me?'

'Bad news . . . terrible news, Majesty . . .' A sigh that was almost a groan escaped Baba Yasaval's lips. 'There is a plot against you.'

'A plot?' Humayun's hand instinctively reached for the jewelled dagger tucked into his yellow sash, and before he knew it he had risen to his feet. 'Who would dare . . . ?'

Baba Yasaval bowed his head. 'Your half-brothers, Majesty.'

'My brothers . . . ?' Only two months ago he and they had stood side by side in the courtyard of the Agra fort as the gilded cart drawn by twelve black oxen and bearing their father's silver coffin departed on the long journey to Kabul, where Babur had asked to be buried. His half-brothers' faces had been as marked by grief as his own and in those moments he had felt a rush of affection for them and a confidence that they would help him complete the task their father had left unfinished: making the Moghuls' hold on Hindustan unassailable.

Baba Yasaval read the incredulity and shock on Humayun's face. 'Majesty, I speak the truth, though I wish for all our sakes that I did not . . .' Now that he had started, Baba Yasaval seemed to take courage, becoming again the tough warrior who had fought for the Moghuls at Panipat. His head was no longer bowed and he looked unflinching into Humayun's eyes. 'You will not doubt me when I tell you that I have this information from my youngest son . . . he is one of the conspirators. He came to me just an hour ago and confessed everything.'

'Why should he do that?' Humayun's eyes narrowed.

'Because he fears for his life . . . because he realises he has been foolish . . . because he knows his actions will bring ruin and disgrace on our clan.' As he spoke these last words, Baba Yasaval's face creased as he struggled to contain his emotions.

'You have done well to approach me. Tell me everything.'

'Scarcely a fortnight after His Majesty your father's coffin left for Kabul, the princes Kamran, Askari and Hindal met in a fort two days' ride from here. My son, as you know, serves Kamran, who offered him great rewards to join the plot. Hot-headed young fool that he is, he agreed, and so heard and saw everything.'

'What are my brothers planning?'

'To take you prisoner and force you to break up the empire and yield some of your territories to them. They wish to return to the old traditions, Majesty, when every son was entitled to a share of his father's lands.'

Humayun managed a mirthless smile. 'And then what? Will they be content? Of course not. How long before they will be at each other's throats and our enemies begin to circle?'

'You are right, Majesty. Even now, they can't agree amongst themselves. Kamran is the real instigator. The plot was his idea and he persuaded the others to join him, but then he and Askari came almost to blows over which of them was to have the richest provinces. Their men had to pull them apart.'

Humayun sat down again. Baba Yasaval's words rang true. His half-brother Kamran, just five months his junior, had made no secret of his resentment that while he had been left behind to govern as regent in Kabul, Humayun had accompanied their father on his invasion of Hindustan. Fifteen-year-old Askari, Kamran's full brother, would not have been hard to persuade to join in. He had always followed worshipfully where Kamran led despite being both bullied and patronised by him. But if Baba Yasaval's account was accurate, now he was almost a man Askari wasn't afraid to challenge his older brother. Perhaps their strong-willed mother Gulrukh had encouraged them both.

But what about his youngest half-brother? Why had Hindal become involved? He was just twelve years old and Humayun's own mother, Maham, had brought him up. Years ago, distressed at her inability to bear any more children after Humayun, she had begged Babur to

9

give her the child of another of his wives, Dildar. Though Hindal had still been in the womb, Babur – unable to deny his favourite wife – had made Maham a gift of the child. But perhaps he should not be so surprised at Hindal's treachery. Babur himself had been just twelve when he had first become a king. Ambition could flare in even the youngest prince.

'Majesty.' Baba Yasaval's earnest voice brought Humayun back to the present. 'My son believed the plot had been abandoned because the princes could not agree. But last night they met again, here in the Agra fort. They decided to bury their differences until they had you in their power. They plan to take advantage of what they call your "unkingly desire for solitude" and attack you when you next go riding alone. Kamran even spoke of killing you and making it appear like an accident. It was then that my son came to his senses. Realising the danger to Your Majesty, he told me what he should have confessed weeks ago.'

'I am grateful to you, Baba Yasaval, for your loyalty and bravery in coming to me like this. You are right. It is a terrible thing that my half-brothers should plot against me, and so soon after our father's death. Have you mentioned this to anyone else?'

'No one, Majesty.'

'Good. Make sure you keep it to yourself. Leave me now. I need to consider what to do.'

Baba Yasaval hesitated, then instead of departing threw himself on the ground before Humayun. He looked up with tears in his eyes. 'Majesty, my son, my foolish son ... spare him ... he sincerely repents his errors. He knows – and I know – how much he deserves your wrath and punishment, but I beg you, show him mercy ...'

'Baba Yasaval. To show my gratitude to you not only for this information but for all your past services I will not punish your son. His actions were the indiscretions of a simple youth. But keep him close confined till all this is over.'

A tremor seemed to pass through Baba Yasaval and for a moment he closed his eyes. Then he rose and, shaven head bowed, backed slowly away.

As soon as he was alone, Humayun leaped to his feet and seizing

10

a jewelled cup flung it across the chamber. The fools! The idiots! If his brothers had their way, the Moghuls would quickly return to a nomadic life of petty tribal rivalries and lose their hard-won empire. Where was their sense of destiny, their sense of what they owed their father?

Just five years ago Humayun had ridden by Babur's side as they swept down through the Khyber Pass to glory. His pulses still quickened at the memory of the roar and blood of battle, the odour of his stallion's acrid sweat filling his nostrils, the trumpeting of Sultan Ibrahim's war elephants, the boom of Moghul cannon and the crack of Moghul muskets as these new weapons cut down rank after rank of the enemy. He could still recall the ecstatic joy of victory when – bloodstained sword in hand – he had surveyed the dusty plains of Panipat and realised that Hindustan was Moghul. Now all that was being put at risk.

I'll not have it – this *taktya, takhta*, 'throne or coffin' as our people called it when we ruled in Central Asia. We're in a new land and must adopt new ways or we'll lose everything, Humayun thought. Reaching inside his robe for the key he wore round his neck on a slender gold chain, he rose and went to a domed casket in a corner of the chamber. He unlocked it, pushed back the lid and quickly found what he was seeking – a flowered silk bag secured with a twist of gold cord. He opened the bag slowly, almost reverently, and drew out the contents – a large diamond whose translucent brilliance made him catch his breath each time he saw it. 'My Koh-i-Nur, my Mountain of Light,' he whispered, running his fingers over the shining facets. Presented to him by an Indian princess whose family he had protected in the chaos after the battle of Panipat, it possessed a flawless beauty that always seemed to him the embodiment of everything the Moghuls had come to India to find – glory and magnificence to outshine even the Shah of Persia.

Still holding the gem, Humayun returned to his chair to think. He sat brooding and alone until the sound of the court timekeeper, the *ghariyali*, striking his brass disc in the courtyard below to signal the end of his *pahar* – his watch – reminded him that night was falling.

This was his first major test, he realised, and he would rise to it. Whatever his personal feelings – at this moment he'd like to take all of his half-brothers by the neck in turn and throttle the life from them – he must do nothing rash, nothing to show that the plot had been betrayed. Baba Yasaval's request for a private audience would have been noticed. If only his grandfather Baisanghar, or his vizier Kasim, who had been one of his father's most trusted advisers, were here. But the two older men had accompanied Babur's funeral cortège to Kabul to oversee his burial there. They would not return for some months. His father had once spoken to him of the burden of kingship, the loneliness it brought. For the first time, Humayun was beginning to understand what Babur had meant. He knew that he and he alone must decide what to do, and until then he must keep his own counsel.

Feeling the need to calm himself, Humayun decided to pass the night with his favourite among his concubines – a pliant, full-mouthed, grey-eyed young woman from the mountains north of Kabul. With her silken skin and breasts like young pomegranates, Salima knew how to transport his body and patently enjoyed doing so. Perhaps her caresses would also help clear his mind and order his thoughts and thus lighten the road ahead, which seemed suddenly and ominously dark.

Three hours later, Humayun lay back naked against a silk-covered bolster in Salima's room in the *haram*. His muscular body, scarred as befitted a tested warrior, gleamed with the almond oil she had teasingly massaged into his skin until, unable to wait a moment longer, he had pulled her to him. Her robe of transparent pale yellow muslin – a product of Humayun's new lands where weavers spun cloth of such delicacy they gave it names like 'breath of wind' or 'dawn dew' – lay discarded on the flower-patterned carpet. Though the pleasure Salima had given him and her response to him had been as intense as ever and Humayun had relaxed, his mind kept drifting back to Baba Yasaval's revelations, re-igniting his anger and frustration.

'Bring me some rosewater to drink, Salima, please.'

She returned moments later with a silver cup inlaid with roundels of rose quartz. The water – chilled by ice carried down in huge slabs from the northern mountains by camel trains – smelled good. From a small wooden box beside the bed, Humayun extracted some opium pellets and dropped them into the cup, where they dissolved in a milky swirl.

'Drink.' He raised the cup to Salima's lips and watched her swallow. He wished her to share his pleasure, but somewhat to his shame he also had another purpose in doing so. His father had nearly died when Buwa – mother of his defeated enemy Sultan Ibrahim – had tried to poison him in revenge for the death of her son. Since then, Humayun had been wary of anything untasted by others . . .

'Here, Majesty.' Salima, lips lusciously moist with rosewater, kissed him and handed him the cup. He drank deeply, willing the opium that in recent weeks had helped blunt his grief and lessen his anxieties to do its work, uncoiling softly through his mind and carrying him to pleasurable oblivion.

But maybe tonight he had taken too much or was expecting too much of its soothing powers. As he lay back, portentous images began forming in his mind. The gleaming blue domes and slender minarets of an exquisite city rose before him. Though he'd been too young to remember his brief time there, he knew it was Samarkand, capital of his great ancestor Timur and the city his father had captured, lost and yearned for all his life. From Babur's vivid accounts, Humayun knew he was standing in the Registan Square in the centre of the city. A crouching orange tiger on the soaring gateway before him was coming alive as he watched, ears flattened, lips drawn back over pointed teeth, ready to spit defiance. Its eyes were green as Kamran's.

Suddenly, Humayun felt himself on the tiger's back, wrestling it with all his strength, feeling its sinewy body twist beneath him. He gripped hard with his thighs, smelling its hot breath as, arcing its body and swinging its head from side to side, it fought to dislodge him. Humayun locked his legs yet tighter around the animal and felt its flanks writhe and plunge anew. He would not be thrown off. He leaned forward, sliding his hands beneath its body. His fingers encountered flesh that was soft and smooth and within it a warm, rhythmic pulse, the source of its life force. As he began to grip harder, to press and to thrust, the beast's breath came in jerky, rasping gasps.

'Majesty . . . please . . .'

Another, weaker voice was trying to reach him. It, too, was gasping for breath. Opening his eyes and looking down through his dilated pupils, Humayun saw not a wild tiger but Salima. Her body, like his, was running with sweat as if the moment of climax were approaching. But though he was indeed possessing her, his hands were grasping the soft flesh of her breasts as if Salima were the ravaging beast he was fighting to subdue. He relaxed his grip but continued to thrust harder and harder until finally they both climaxed and collapsed.

'Salima, I'm sorry. I should not have used you in such a way. I felt thoughts of conquest mingling with my desire for you.'

'No need for sorrow – your love-making filled me with pleasure. You were in another world and I was willingly serving you in that world as I do in this. I know you would never intentionally hurt me. Now make love to me again, this time more softly.'

Humayun gladly complied. Later, as he lay back exhausted and still dazed by opium, *haram* attendants came to sponge his body with cool scented water. Finally, wrapped in Salima's arms, he found sleep. This time he dreamed of nothing at all, waking only when the soft light began shafting through the latticed window of the room. As he watched the strengthening rays play over the carved sandstone ceiling above him, he knew what he must do. His battle of wills with the tiger had told him. He was the ruler. He should not always be gentle. Respect was won by knowing when to be strong too.

• ◆ •

'Majesty. Your orders have been carried out.'

From his throne on its marble dais in the audience chamber – the *durbar* hall – with his courtiers and commanders positioned around him in strict order of precedence, Humayun looked down at the captain of his bodyguard. He already knew what had happened – the officer had come to him soon after midnight – but it was important that all the court should hear it and witness the scene about to take place.

'You have done well. Tell the court what occurred.'

'As Your Majesty instructed, I and a detachment of guards arrested your half-brothers last night while they were feasting in Prince Kamran's apartments.'

As a collective gasp went up around him, Humayun smiled inwardly. He had chosen his time well. Since Baba Yasaval's warning he had kept safely within the fort. Then a week ago a consignment of red wine from Ghazni, the finest the kingdom of Kabul could produce, heady and rich, had arrived by mule train – a timely gift from his mother's father, Baisanghar. Knowing Kamran's love of wine, Humayun had presented some to him. As he had guessed, Kamran's invitation to all his brothers to join him in drinking it had not been long in coming. Humayun himself had declined it graciously but Askari and even young Hindal, not yet of an age to enjoy drinking but doubtless flattered to be in company with those who did, had hurried eagerly to the party. With all three together and off their guard, the opportunity for decisive action had been perfect.

'Did my brothers resist?'

'Prince Kamran drew his dagger and wounded one of my men, slicing off part of his ear, but he was soon overcome. The others did not try to fight.'

Humayun's gaze swept the faces before him. 'Some days ago, I received word of a plot. My half-brothers intended to kidnap me and force me to relinquish some of my lands – perhaps even kill me.' His courtiers looked suitably shocked. How many were play-acting, Humayun wondered. Some, at least, must have known of the conspiracy, even tacitly acquiesced in it. A number of the tribal chieftains who had accompanied Babur on his conquest of Hindustan had never adjusted to their new home. They disliked this new land with its featureless, seemingly endless plains, hot, gritty winds and drenching monsoon rains. In their hearts, they longed for the snow-dusted mountains and cool rivers of their homelands over the Khyber Pass and beyond. Quite a few would have welcomed an opportunity to collude with the conspirators that would enable them to return home richly rewarded. Well, let them sweat a bit now . . .

'Fetch my brothers before me so that I can question them as to their associates.'

The silence was absolute as Humayun and his courtiers waited. At last, the sound of metal chains scraping the stone slabs of the courtyard beyond the audience chamber broke the silence. Looking up, Humayun saw his brothers enter in a stumbling line, half dragged along by the guards. Kamran was first, his hawk-nosed, thin-lipped face showing nothing but disdain. He might have shackles on his legs but the proud carriage of his head showed he had no intention of pleading. Askari, shorter and slighter, was another matter. His unshaven face was creased with terror and his small eyes looked beseechingly at Humayun from beneath his dark brows. Hindal, at first half hidden behind his two elder brothers, was gazing about him, his young face beneath his tangle of hair blank rather than fearful, as if what was happening were beyond him

As the guards stepped back from them, Askari and Hindal, though hampered by their chains, prostrated themselves full length on the ground before Humayun in the traditional obeisance of the *korunush*. After several moments' hesitation, and with a contemptuous half-smile Kamran did the same.

'On your feet.'

Humayun waited until all three had struggled to stand. Now that he could study them more closely he saw that Kamran had a dark bruise on the side of his face.

'What have you to say for yourselves? You are my half-brothers. Why did you scheme against me?'

'We didn't . . . it's not true . . .' Askari's tone, shrill and nervous, was unconvincing.

'You're lying. It's written on your face. If you do so again, I'll have you put to the torture. Kamran, as the eldest, answer my question. Why did you seek to betray me?'

Kamran's eyes – green as their father Babur's had been – were slits as he looked up at Humayun on his glittering throne. 'The plot was my idea – punish me, not them. It was the only way to redress the wrong done to us. As you yourself said, we are all Babur's sons. Doesn't the blood of Timur flow through all our veins? And through

16

our grandmother Kutlugh Nigar the blood of Genghis Khan as well? Yet we have been left with nothing except to be your lackeys, to be sent hither and thither according to your whims. You treat us as slaves, not princes.'

'And you behave – all of you, not just you, Kamran – like common criminals, not brothers. Where is your sense of loyalty to our dynasty, if not to me?' Glancing up at an intricately carved wooden grille set high in the wall to the right of his throne, Humayun caught the flash of a dark eye. Doubtless Khanzada and probably his mother Maham were observing him from the little gallery behind it where the royal women, unseen themselves, could watch and listen to the business of the court. Perhaps Gulrukh and Dildar were also there, waiting in trembling anticipation for the sentence he was about to pronounce on their sons.

But now that the moment had come, Humayun felt strangely reluctant. Even half an hour ago he had been so certain what he would do – ruthless as Timur, he would order Kamran's and Askari's immediate execution and send Hindal to perpetual imprisonment in some far-off fortress. Yet looking down at the three of them – Kamran so arrogant and defiant, Askari and young Hindal plainly terrified – Humayun felt his anger ebbing. Their father had been dead only a few months, and how could he ignore Babur's dying words? *Do nothing against your brothers, however much you think they might deserve it.* Just as in love-making, there was a time to be rigorous and a time to be gentle.

Stepping down from his throne, Humayun walked slowly over to his brothers and, starting with Kamran, embraced them. The trio stood before him, swaying slightly, expressions confused as they searched his face for the meaning of his actions. 'It is not fitting that we brothers should quarrel. I do not wish to spill the blood of our house into the earth of this new land of ours – it would be a bad omen for our dynasty. Swear your loyalty to me and you shall live. I will also give you provinces to govern which, though part of the empire, you shall rule as your own, subject only to me.'

Around him, Humayun caught sounds first of astonishment and then of approval rising from his courtiers and commanders, and pride flooded through him. This was real greatness. This was truly how an emperor should act – crushing dissent but then showing magnanimity. As he embraced his brothers a second time, grateful tears shimmered in Askari's and Hindal's eyes. But Kamran's green ones remained dry, and his expression was bleak and unfathomable.

Chapter 2

An Impudent Enemy

The morning sun was glinting gold on the breastplates of the two tall, white-turbaned bodyguards who preceded Humayun across the courtyard of the red sandstone Agra fort, past the bubbling fountains into the high-ceilinged *durbar* hall. Making his way across the pillared hall which was open to the cooling breezes on three sides, and moving through the assembled ranks of his counsellors who prostrated themselves in formal salutation at his approach, Humayun ascended the marble dais in the centre of the room. Here, gathering his green silk robes around him, he seated himself on his gilded, high-backed throne. The two guards, hands on their swords, positioned themselves just behind the throne, one at either side.

Humayun signalled his advisers to rise. 'You know why I have called you together today – to discuss the presumptuous posturings of Sultan Bahadur Shah. Not content with his rich lands of Gujarat to our southwest, he gave refuge to the sons of Ibrahim Lodi, Sultan of Delhi, whom my father and I with your magnificent help deposed. Proclaiming his family ties to them, he began assembling allies around him. His ambassadors insinuated to the Rajputs and the Afghan clans that our empire is more illusion than reality. He derided it for being only two hundred miles wide even though it extends a thousand miles from the Khyber. They dismiss us as mere barbarian raiders whose rule will be as easily blown away as the morning mist.

19

'All this we knew and held as beneath our contempt but this morning a messenger – exhausted by riding through the night – brought news that one of Bahadur Shah's armies, led by the Lodi pretender Tartar Khan, has raided across our borders. Scarcely eighty miles west of Agra, they captured a caravan bearing tribute from one of our Rajput vassals. Of this much I am certain. We will not tolerate such disrespect. We must and will punish the sultan severely. What I have summoned you here to discuss is not whether we should crush him, but how best to do it.' Humayun paused and looked around at his counsellors before continuing.

Suleiman Mirza, a cousin of Humayun and general of his cavalry, was the first to speak. 'Bahadur Shah will not be easy to defeat. To do so we must look to our strengths. Unlike when your father conquered Delhi, we have more men, horses and elephants than our enemy. The animals are well trained and the soldiers loyal. The prospect of the booty from Bahadur Shah's overflowing vaults will reinforce their appetite for battle. But there is another difference from when the Moghuls came to Hindustan. This time, both sides will have cannon and matchlock muskets – not just us. The sultan has used the taxes he imposes on the pilgrims setting out across the high sea on the *haj* to Mecca and on the traders from distant lands who throng his ports of Cambay and Surat to buy many cannon and matchlocks and to entice experienced Ottoman armourers to work in his foundries. We can no longer rely on the very presence of our artillerymen to turn every battle for us. They will still be important, but we need to change our tactics once more.'

'Yes, easily enough said, but what does it mean in practice?' asked Baba Yasaval, tugging at his tassel of hair.

'Combine the tactics of His Majesty's father Babur in his youth with those of his last battles,' answered Suleiman Mirza. 'Send fast raiding parties of cavalry and mounted archers into Gujarat to hit Bahadur Shah's forces wherever they find them and then disappear again long before he can concentrate his armies against them. Leave him guessing where our main attack will come but all the time advance our main column with the artillery and elephants steadily into his territory.'

Though most of Humayun's counsellors nodded, Baba Yasaval asked, 'But what should our main army's specific objective be?'

'Why not the fortress of Champnir, deep in the forests of Gujarat?' said Humayun. 'It contains Bahadur's greatest royal treasury. He will not feel able to yield it to us. He will be forced to attack to relieve it from our besiegers.'

'Yes, but how will we combat his threat to the rear of our besieging force?' said Suleiman Mirza.

This time it was Baba Yasaval who answered, eyes now gleaming at the thought of action. 'We have the advantage of time. We can dig in our guns so they can fire at both the fortress and the relieving columns, and we can position our armies to fight a battle on two sides. If Bahadur Shah tries to lift the siege he'll get a nasty surprise.'

'You speak soundly,' said Humayun. 'I will myself lead the first of the raiding parties to cross into Gujarat. If Bahadur Shah hears – as he will – that I am in the field myself, it may confuse him further as to our real objectives. Suleiman Mirza, I look to you and Baba Yasaval to make the preparations. The council is now dismissed.'

With that Humayun rose and with his two bodyguards once more in front of him slowly made his way back across the courtyard to his quarters. Once there he asked Jauhar, his cup-bearer and most trusted attendant – a tall, fine-featured youth whose father had been one of the commanders of Babur's bodyguard – to summon his astrologers to join him in an hour or so to calculate the most auspicious time to begin his campaign. His battle plan had been decided quickly. The reassurance that he had the support of the astrologers' star charts and tabulations in the timing of his invasion would be valuable to his own confidence as he began his first campaign as emperor as well as to the morale of his army.

In the meantime he would visit his aunt Khanzada to seek her wise advice on his choice of officers for his expedition and, even more important, to discuss with her his views on another question. Was it safe while he was away on campaign to leave his half-brothers in their various provinces – Kamran to the northwest in the Punjab, Askari in Jaunpur to the east and Hindal to the west in Alwar? Might they use the opportunity to rise against him? Should he give them

21

commands in his army and take them with him so he could keep an eye on them?

The reports reaching him from their provinces gave no outward reason for concern, particularly in the case of Hindal and Askari who regularly wrote back in punctilious detail on their administration and remitted their taxes in full, sometimes even ahead of time. Kamran too sent in the due proportion of his province's revenues, even if his reports were infrequent and brief. Occasionally an official, dissatisfied with his progress at Humayun's court, had gone to Kamran's province to try his luck there. Sometimes there had been rumours that Kamran had been assembling a larger army than he strictly needed for his province, but these had usually proved groundless or justified by the need to put down some petty rebel or other.

Yet Humayun couldn't quite rid himself of the feeling that Kamran would not abandon his ambitions so easily and might only be biding his time, ready to exploit for his own benefit any misfortune of Humayun's. So be it. He would ensure he suffered none to allow Kamran such an opportunity. In any case, perhaps he had misjudged Kamran and, together with Hindal and Askari, he had learned his lesson and was grateful as he should be for Humayun's mercy. He hoped it was so. Just in case it was not, he needn't move against Bahadur Shah until his grandfather Baisanghar was back in Agra. He and Humayun's vizier Kasim had after their return from Kabul set off on a tour of inspection of the imperial treasury in Delhi from which they would return in a few days. Then Humayun would appoint Baisanghar regent in his absence. He could safely trust his grandfather – and Khanzada and Kasim too – to keep an eye on his troublesome half-brothers.

They would also watch over his mother. Since Babur's death Maham seemed to have lost the little interest she'd ever had in the affairs of the world. Though proud her son was emperor, she never questioned him about his plans or offered him advice as Khanzada did. When he was with her, all she did was speak longingly of the past. But perhaps, in time, she would see that it was the future that must occupy him now.

• ◆ •

Humayun looked down from a sandstone escarpment on to a long column of Bahadur Shah's men who, oblivious of his presence, were throwing up clouds of dust as they snaked along the riverbank four hundred feet below. At this time of year – early March, two months after he had left Agra – the river was mostly dry with only a few pools of water remaining in the deepest parts of its bed. Along the banks an occasional palm tree provided a touch of green. Humayun could see squadrons of cavalry to the front and rear of the column with divisions of infantry and a large baggage train in its middle.

Unable to suppress a smile of triumph, Humayun turned in his saddle to speak to Jauhar, who was accompanying him on the campaign as one of his *qorchis* – his squires. 'We have them, Jauhar. Our scouts have done well in gathering information and leading us here. The Gujaratis have no suspicion of our presence. Now gallop back the mile to where we left the rest of our men. Order them to ride along the top of the escarpment, keeping far enough from the rim to avoid being seen from below, until they reach that point a mile or so ahead where the slope becomes gentle enough for us to swoop down to attack our enemies. I and my bodyguard will meet them there.'

Jauhar nodded and moved off. As Humayun turned with his bodyguard back from the lip to make his own way to the rendezvous point, he felt the same mixture of apprehension and excitement as he always had before battles, but also a greater weight of responsibility than ever before. Previously his father, even if not present on the immediate battlefield, had approved the overall plan of campaign and it had been his father's throne – not his own – that had been at stake. The thought caused a cold shiver to run through Humayun and he halted his men for a moment. Was he sure – as sure as he could be – that his plan was a good one – that he had spent enough time checking and re-checking each detail to leave as little as possible to chance? As he pondered this, he saw two large brown hawks soar seemingly effortlessly from beneath the escarpment high into the cloudless blue sky as the hot air bore them upward on outstretched wings. Suddenly he remembered the eagles he had seen at the battle of Panipat which had proved such a favourable omen. Surely these

23

birds would prove so too as he struck the first blow in his conquest of Gujarat.

Throwing off his doubts and uncertainties, Humayun reached the appointed meeting place for the rest of his forces. As soon as they were all assembled, Humayun quickly gave orders for the attack to be conducted in two waves. The first, after galloping down the steep slope, would envelop the rear of the enemy column. The second would encircle the vanguard, exploiting its confusion as it halted and tried to turn round – as it would be bound to do – to assist the rear. Drawing his father's sword Alamgir, Humayun kissed its jewelled hilt and shouted to his men, 'Fill your minds with warrior spirit and your lungs with heroes' breath. We fight to defend our newly won lands. Let us prove to these presumptuous upstarts that we have not lost our ancient reputation for courage.' Then, waving his sword above his head, Humayun signalled the charge and with his bodyguard about him kicked his black stallion down the slope to the attack.

As they raced down the hill, stones and red dust flying around them, he could see in front of him the Gujarati column halt as the men turned in his direction to see what the noise was. Taken completely by surprise the Gujaratis hesitated and then began to react only slowly as if for them time was almost standing still, fumbling for their weapons and looking around in panic for their officers to see what their orders were. One black-bearded man was quicker than the others, dismounting and trying to pull his musket from its thick cloth bag tied to his saddle.

Humayun turned his horse towards the musketeer and, gripping his sword in his right hand, ducked low to his horse's neck as he urged his mount on, all thoughts of command and destiny banished from his mind by the visceral instinct to survive, to kill or be killed. Within moments he was on the man, who was still struggling to prime his musket. Humayun slashed at his bearded face and down he went, blood pouring from his wound, beneath the hooves of the attacking cavalry. Humayun was well into the enemy column now, cutting and slashing as he rode. Suddenly he was through, pulling up his snorting, panting horse as his men rallied around him.

Immediately he had enough men, Humayun charged back into the column a second time. A tall Gujarati cut at him with his curved sword, striking his breastplate and knocking Humayun back in the saddle. As Humayun struggled to control his rearing horse, the Gujarati rode at him again and, over-eager to finish his victim off, aimed a swinging sword cut at Humayun's head. Humayun reacted instinctively, ducking under the blade which hissed through the air just above his helmet. Before the Gujarati could recover, Humayun quickly thrust Alamgir deep into his abdomen. As the man dropped his sword and clutched the wound, Humayun coolly and deliberately struck at the back of his opponent's neck, almost severing his head from his shoulders.

Glancing about him, Humayun saw through the billowing red dust that the Gujarati column was disintegrating. Some of the horsemen were galloping away in panic. Others in the middle of the column were, however, offering stouter resistance, defending the wagons which presumably contained the baggage and the cannon. Humayun knew that even if he captured them, he would not be able to carry off any cannon because they would slow down his force whose entire purpose was fast raiding. However, he could disable them. With the blood of battle thumping in his veins and yelling to his trumpeter to sound the order to follow him, Humayun immediately charged towards the baggage wagons.

Suddenly he heard the crack of a musket – then of another. Some of the Gujarati musketeers had got their weapons into operation and were firing from the cover of the baggage carts. One of the horses galloping ten yards from Humayun was hit, falling headfirst into the dust and catapulting its rider into the ground where he lay twitching a moment before the horses of his comrades following behind kicked and tossed him beneath their hooves, extinguishing any life lingering in his body.

Humayun knew that he must reach the wagons before the musketeers could reload. Waving Alamgir once more, he kicked his horse on and almost immediately was among the carts. He cut at one musketeer who was endeavouring with shaking hands to ram the metal ball down into the long barrel of his musket with a steel

25

rod. Struck across his face, the man collapsed, dropping his weapon. The enemy had had no time to pull the wagons into any defensive formations and so Humayun's men, who had quickly joined him, found it easy to surround and subdue the defenders of individual wagons. More of the Gujarati cavalry galloped away and the infantry and camp followers were also fleeing as fast as they could.

Resistance was at an end – at least for the present. However, Humayun knew that his force was considerably outnumbered and that when the Gujarati officers realised this, they would try to re-group and attack him. Therefore there was no time to waste. Humayun ordered a detachment of his cavalry to pursue the fugitives, cutting down as many as they could but riding no more than a couple of miles before returning to form a loose defensive perimeter. He gestured to other men to investigate the contents of the wagons. They went at it with a will, throwing off the heavy jute covers to reveal six medium-sized cannon and their powder and shot as well as bundles of new spears and five boxes of muskets.

'We'll take all the muskets. Empty the boxes. Strap bundles of the muskets to the saddles of some of the spare horses. Fill the cannon barrels with as many linen bags of powder as they will take and then run a trail of powder along the ground to those rocks over there. We'll ignite the powder from behind them,' Humayun said.

A quarter of an hour later the work was complete. Humayun despatched most of his men to a safe distance but remained with a few of his bodyguards to oversee the destruction. He gave the honour of firing the powder to a tall young Badakshani who, taking the flint box, struggled nervously to get a spark. When eventually he succeeded, the powder flame went sputtering across the ground. For a moment it seemed that it was going to die as it skirted a small rock but then it was away again. Almost immediately there was a massive bang followed closely by five others. The charges had exploded in each of the cannon barrels.

When the debris and dust had settled Humayun, still half deafened by the blast, could see that four of the barrels were split and peeled back, much like the skin of a banana. Another had disintegrated completely. The barrel of the sixth was cracked – just enough,

Humayun thought, to render it useless. His men had soon returned and were searching the remaining baggage wagons for booty. One had found some silks, another was jamming his dagger into the lock of a casket, trying to force it in search of jewels.

Then Humayun saw one of the cavalrymen he had detached to form the perimeter defence galloping towards him. 'The Gujaratis have re-grouped, Majesty. They are forming up to attack, now they have seen how few we are.'

'We must be away. Trumpeter, sound the retreat. We'll go back up the escarpment. They won't follow. They'll know it would be death to give us the opportunity to attack them as they struggle up.'

Twenty minutes later, Humayun looked down from the sandstone escarpment on to the wreckage of the column around which the Gujaratis were now milling. His men had got away safely except for a foolish few who, mesmerised by the prospect of loot, had lingered too long investigating the contents of the baggage wagons. Among them, Humayun reflected sadly, had been the young Badakshani who had been brought down by an arrow in the back as he galloped too late for the escarpment. The bolt of embroidered pink silk tied to his saddle had unravelled, streaming out behind his riderless horse.

• ◆ •

There it was – beyond the tall palm trees and the pale tangerine sand the glinting ocean reflecting the light of the midday sun with such an intensity that Humayun was forced to shield his eyes with his hand. After his successful raid on the enemy column he had despatched half his force of three thousand men back to the main body of his army, which was beginning its slow advance from Moghul territories towards the jungle fortress of Champnir with all the equipment and provisions required for a siege.

Humayun himself, together with a picked body of fifteen hundred horsemen, had penetrated even further into Gujarat, disrupting and defeating enemies wherever he found them. He had succeeded, he was sure, in leaving them uncertain and confused as to the main thrust of his army, just as he had planned. His quest for a caravan reported by captured Gujaratis to be carrying military supplies and trade goods towards the port of Cambay had brought him to the sea. Humayun was glad that it had. He called Jauhar to his side. 'Pass the order that we will rest and refresh ourselves beneath the shade of the palms during the midday heat while our scouts search for the caravan. It cannot be far off now. Indeed, from what we learn Cambay itself should be no more than ten miles or so northwest up the coast. Give orders for pickets and sentries to be posted so that we cannot be taken by surprise.'

As Jauhar turned with the message, Humayun nudged his black horse forward through the palms, whose long, pointed, dark green leaves were rustling in the breeze coming off the sea, and on into the soft sand. Here, Humayun jumped down. Stopping only to discard his boots, he walked out into the sea, conscious that he was the first of his family ever to do so. The water slapping against his lower calves was refreshingly cool. Again shielding his eyes, he gazed out to the glittering, sparkling horizon. There he thought he could make out the shape of a ship – presumably one of those trading with Cambay. What kinds of goods were they carrying? What kind of people? What else lay beyond the horizon, beyond even Arabia and the holy cities? Was there new knowledge to be gleaned there? Were there new enemies or were there simply barren lands or an infinity of ocean?

A shout from Jauhar interrupted Humayun's solitary contemplation. 'Majesty, your officers wish to consult with you. Will you take food with them? You've been watching the sea for some time and the waters are rising around you.' It was true. The little waves were now splashing Humayun's knees before retreating. Reluctantly he turned his mind away from the metaphysical speculations he found so beguiling to present-day practicalities and made his way to where the officers waited, sitting cross-legged under a scarlet awning beneath the palms.

Ten minutes later, his chief scout Ahmed Khan, a wiry turbaned man of about thirty from the mountains of Ghazni, south of Kabul, was standing before him, sweat running from his brow down his cheeks into his thin, brown beard. 'The caravan is no more than five miles off, travelling along a road about a quarter of a mile inland on the other side of that thick belt of palms fringing the coast. It is about four miles from the town of Cambay, which is hidden from our view by that low promontory over there.'

'We will ride along the beach itself on the other side of the palms and ambush them as they reach Cambay. God willing, we may even be able to force our way into the port if the gates are opened ready for the caravan's entry.'

Only five minutes later, Humayun was galloping along the edge of the sand with his bodyguard grouped close around him. In less than an hour they had crossed the rocky promontory and from the continuing cover of the palms Humayun could see the masts and sails of the ships lying in the port of Cambay or at anchor outside it. The caravan, including loaded, swaying camels and pack elephants as well as mules and donkeys, was trudging slowly towards the open main gate in the mud wall surrounding the settlement. The wall itself did not look too high – perhaps only double a man's height. The caravan's escort, about four hundred men in total, were riding on either side of it but appeared indolent, heads bowed in the midday heat with their swords in their scabbards and their shields on their backs.

Riding back to the main body of his men, Humayun yelled, 'Charge now. Take them by surprise. Try to panic the camels and elephants. That should disrupt the Gujarati escort.' Even as he spoke, Humayun kicked on his black horse, which was already flecked with creamy sweat, and soon he was galloping full tilt with his men out through the palms, over the half a mile of stony, sandy ground separating him from the caravan and the port's gate. At his command, some of his most expert archers took their reins in their teeth and standing in their stirrups loosed off a volley of arrows towards the caravan just as its escort realised that they were under attack. Some of the arrows wounded one of the elephants which with several shafts embedded in its leathery skin turned, trumpeting in pain, across the path of some of its fellows, scattering them.

A camel fell with a low snort of pain, shedding its load as it subsided to the sand, its large, padded feet flailing futilely in the air. Another, with a black-feathered arrow piercing its long neck, galloped off towards the sea. Almost immediately, Humayun and his men were riding through the thin line of the escort, slashing at them as they went. Some Gujaratis fell under the first weight of the charge. A few were cut down as they tried to rein in their horses and turn to face the unexpected onslaught. Most simply bent low to their horses' necks and urged the beasts towards the shelter of the still open gates of Cambay.

Humayun and his bodyguard followed. Humayun galloped as hard as he could after what looked like an officer who was fleeing with two of his men. Hearing Humayun close behind, the officer turned and seeing his danger tried to grab his shield to protect himself. Before he could do so, Humayun's sharp sword cut deep into his thick, muscular neck just above his chain mail coat and he fell, rolled over several times and was still.

In moments, Humayun was in the gateway to Cambay. Hauling his horse round to avoid an overturned table from which some frightened tax or customs officials must have fled only moments earlier, he was soon out into the small square behind the gatehouse. Here it seemed a market had been in full swing. The stalls had been quickly abandoned, bags of bright-coloured spices pushed to the dust in panic, corn spilled to the ground where it mingled with orange lentils and rivers of milk from an overturned barrel. There was no sign of soldiers. Like the caravan's escort, Cambay's defenders seemed to have no appetite for a fight. The few stallholders that were left — mostly white-bearded old men or dark-clad women — were prostrating themselves faces to the sand before their attackers.

'Find the barracks. Imprison any soldiers you find there. Take what you can from the warehouses and ships. Burn the rest. Don't overburden yourselves. We must depart before sundown. When they learn of our attack on Cambay, the Gujaratis will be alarmed enough and uncertain enough of our whereabouts to feel unable to concentrate their forces when they hear of the threat to Champnir. We ourselves must hasten to re-join our main column attacking that fort. It is there we will win the decisive victory that will make Gujarat ours.'

Chapter 3

The Spoils of War

'Jauhar, bring me some of that lime juice and water – what do the Hindus call it? *Nimbu pani*? It's refreshing in this heat.' Humayun was standing in his large scarlet command tent in the middle of his fortified encampment outside the fortress of Champnir. Through the raised flaps, he could see its massive stone bulk at one end of a two-mile-long rocky outcrop which rose above the scrubby jungle trees whose leaves were turning brown and gold as the summer heat dried them.

Humayun had joined the siege six weeks ago. As he had first discussed with his council, his officers had fortified their own position with barricades and cannon on both sides so that they could not only beat off any sorties by the besieged but also repulse the relieving force they had been so certain would arrive. It hadn't yet and scouts still reported no sign of its approach. Bahadur Shah was said to be in the highlands on the southern border of his lands. Perhaps he trusted in the strength of the fortress and its garrison as sufficient to see off Humayun and his army.

If so, he'd been right so far, Humayun mused. He and his commanders had tried everything but without success. Their cannon had pounded the thick stone walls, but many of the artillerymen had been picked off from the fortress's battlements as they struggled to man the guns. Even on the one occasion when the gunners had succeeded in breaching a small portion of the walls, the Gujaratis had shot down Humayun's men with their muskets as they tried to scramble through and over the rubble. Those who had survived to struggle back had reported there was an inner wall from the protection of which the Gujaratis had been able to fire their bullets and arrows to repulse them. At other times, the Gujarati cannon, well protected by stone embrasures, had been able to break up frontal attacks even before the Moghuls could get close enough to the walls to place their scaling ladders.

Blackened and bloated bodies of dead Moghul warriors littered the ground before the fortress walls giving off the sickly-sweet smell of putrescence and attracting clouds of purply-black flies which had multiplied and now clustered throughout his camp. So many men had been killed in trying to rescue wounded comrades or to recover the bodies of the dead that Humayun had had to forbid such attempts except under cover of night and even then there had been more casualties.

Jauhar's reappearance with his drink broke into Humayun's thoughts. As he drank the cooling liquid he looked out once more and saw that dark clouds were piling the afternoon sky. They would get darker and even more numerous as the monsoon approached. The rains would provide the defenders with water and make Humayun's attacks even more difficult. They might even bring disease to his camp.

'Jauhar, when do the local people say the rains come hereabout?'
'Mid-July, Majesty.'

Humayun stood, his mind made up. 'We must complete our business here before then. Our frontal attacks are not working. We need to find an alternative and soon. I will go out with the leaders of our scouts tomorrow to see if we can identify any weaknesses in their defences the Gujaratis may have overlooked.'

· ◆ ·

Humayun was sweating profusely beneath his chain mail as he rode along the southern side of the rocky outcrop on whose eastern tip the seemingly impregnable fort of Champnir stood. Added to his physical discomfort was a feeling of acute frustration. He and his scouts had already spent five hot hours in a fruitless reconnaissance of the northern side and were already over halfway down the southern. Every time he or a scout had thought they had spotted a vulnerable point where his men might make an ascent it had ended in an overhang impassable to climbing soldiers. Once a scout had got three-quarters of the way up a cleft in the rock wall before he fell backwards, arms flailing, when a single musket shot cracked out, revealing that there was indeed a defensive post concealed in one of the folds of the cliff.

'Jauhar, give me some water,' Humayun said, wiping his sweating face with a cotton cloth. 'Quickly boy,' he snapped as Jauhar fumbled at his saddlebag.

'Sorry, Majesty, the ties are entangled.'

'As quick as you can then,' Humayun said more softly, conscious that his anger was inspired not by the boy's ineptitude but his own frustration at failing to locate an attack route. 'We'll dismount and rest for a little under the shade of those trees over there on that small hill.'

Wearily Humayun turned his horse towards the copse five hundred yards away. But as he rode up the gentle slope and dismounted, he realised that the higher elevation and a new direction of view gave a completely different perspective. He was able to see that above the trees was a deep cleft in the rock which seemed to run all the way to the top. Perhaps a waterfall ran down it in the monsoon but at the moment it looked dry. Thirst and frustration forgotten, Humayun called his chief scout Ahmed Khan to him.

'Do you see that fissure over there? What d'you think? Could it be passable?'

'I'm not sure, Majesty, but it looks promising. I will go and investigate.'

'Before you go make sure that the rest of our men are under cover of the trees. We don't want them spotted . . . and good luck.'

'Thank you, Majesty.' Ahmed Khan took a pair of leather boots from his saddlebag. Their thick soles had extra leather bands sewn across them for better grip. Pulling them on, he set off the half-mile or so to the cliff. After five or ten minutes he was lost to view in the scrubby bush and straggling trees. Then Humayun made out a figure climbing the cliff. Sometimes it disappeared but reappearing seemed to make good progress. Then it went out of sight entirely for a while. When Humayun next saw the scout he was much lower down. Humayun paced to and fro, waiting for his return, fearing that the last few yards had proved impassable but hoping they had not. Half an hour later Ahmed Khan was back on the tree-covered hill. His hands were grazed in places and the knees of his baggy pants were torn. By the uneven way he was walking his left boot seemed to have lost some of its leather banding but he was smiling broadly.

'There appear to be no defenders. It's not too difficult to get within forty feet of the top but those last few feet are very awkward with very few footholds. For a mountain man like me it should be possible to get up one of the narrow clefts, putting feet against one side and back against the other. But it would be impossible for many, particularly when encumbered by weapons. However' – and here he smiled again – 'the rock is fissured and soft enough for those going first to drive metal spikes into the cliff to make a kind of ladder for the less skilled to climb.'

'I give thanks to God and to you for your bravery and skill. We will return tomorrow night with five hundred picked men. While our main forces make a frontal attack to occupy the defenders, we'll make the climb and get into the fortress from the rear.'

· ◆ ·

Under the pale light of the moon, Humayun with Ahmed Khan at his side climbed up through the scrubby trees towards the fissure. The loose, smooth stones and pebbles beneath their feet confirmed that this was the dry bed of a stream and that a waterfall from above did indeed feed it during the rains.

Impatient as always to be in the thick of the battle, Humayun had disregarded the advice of Baba Yasaval that he should stay at the centre where he could better direct the action, and decided to accompany Ahmed Khan and ten of the best climbers among his bodyguard on the mission to drive the spikes into the rock. He knew he was as agile as any of them and that by going among the first party he would encourage the remainder of his five hundred men. The knowledge that their emperor had already made the climb himself meant that in honour they could not fail to follow.

All was going well. They had tethered their horses a considerable way off and taken advantage of every scrap of cover and every occasion the scudding clouds had concealed the moon to get to this point undetected. Just in front, through the overhanging branches, Humayun saw the head of the streambed and the dark cliff rising above it. He motioned Ahmed Khan and the ten men who would climb with them to gather round him.

'My destiny and that of the empire as well as all our lives are at stake in this attempt. There are great risks but also great rewards if we succeed, as, God willing, we will. Now, check that you have your bags with your equipment safely secured and any weapon you wish to carry well tucked in. We want nothing dropped to reveal our position or to harm those following behind.'

Humayun had left his sword Alamgir with Jauhar, who was to follow among the remainder of the force. He had dressed simply in dark clothes like the rest of his men but tied to a leather thong around his neck was Timur's ring. Just before he began the ascent he took it out and kissed it. Then they were off, Ahmed Khan in front searching for the hand- and footholds he had used the previous day and signalling to Humayun, close behind now, to follow. Although occasionally they dislodged a few small stones, sending them tumbling down to the ground below, Humayun hoped any sounds they were making would be masked by the booms that were now resounding from his camp as his cannon heralded the frontal attack that was to serve as a distraction.

Within twenty minutes, the two men were at the base of the final fissure. Looking upwards Humayun realised how difficult it would be to climb. The rock seemed worn smooth by the initial rush of the waterfall and the cleft was just too wide to brace the back comfortably against one side while climbing up the other with the feet. The spikes that Ahmed Khan – resting on a ledge that could only be two feet wide – was pulling from the satchel slung across his body and pushing into the dark sash around his waist would be essential. Humayun began to unpack his own hammer.

'Majesty, the first ten feet looked the smoothest yesterday. I will brace myself in the cleft and you must climb over me using my limbs as steps to get into a position to drive in the first spikes.'

Humayun nodded and Ahmed Khan crammed himself into the rocky fissure. Humayun then put a foot on Ahmed Khan's tensed thigh and pushed himself up until he could perch on Ahmed Khan's shoulders. Reaching up above his head, he felt along the surface of the rock until he detected a small crack. Pulling his hammer and a foot-long spike from his belt, he drove the spike into the rock, each clang of the hammer seeming to the anxious, sweating Humayun to echo alarmingly around the fissure. However, there was no movement from above and soon the spike was in. Humayun tugged at it and finding it firm used it to move up half off Ahmed Khan's shoulders to locate a place for the next spike.

Again it went in well and, supporting himself mostly on the spikes and partly by bracing his back to the rock, Humayun climbed up, finding another foothold. And so it went on as, sweating and breathing hard, the two men made it to about ten feet from the top where to their consternation a rocky outcrop seemed to bar their way. However, tugging at Humayun's clothes in a way he would never normally have done, Ahmed Khan gestured through the gloom to a thick length of jungle creeper hanging over the lip and dangling down about six feet to their right.

'Majesty, I think I can reach it and use it to climb the final distance, hitting in spikes as I go, but I must be the one to make the attempt as I am lighter than you and – pardon me, Majesty – to do so I must use you as my ladder.'

Humayun nodded and gripping the last spikes tilted his body to the right. Soon he felt Ahmed Khan's foot on his left shoulder, then it slipped painfully against his neck and suddenly it was gone. Ahmed Khan was swinging from the creeper, thumping spikes in to provide a route round the overhang to the top. Then he was up, waving down to Humayun to follow which he did, resisting the temptation to close his eyes as he manoeuvred out and around the overhang.

Then he too was on top. Panting so heavily that he could scarcely speak, Humayun whispered, 'Thank you, Ahmed Khan. I will remember your courage.'

In half an hour enough men had climbed up, driving in more spikes and using ropes to rig makeshift ladders to make it easier for those following to form an advance party to move towards the fort. Humayun addressed the first hundred or so gathered around him. 'Remember we must make no noise and therefore rely on our old silent weapons – the bow and arrow and the sword – and on our bare hands to kill any enemy we find. Once inside, I will instruct the four of you who carry trumpets and drums to make the pre-agreed signals to alert our forces attacking from the front that we are inside so they can redouble their efforts. Now let us move forward.'

Advancing through the bushes, the men crept more than half a mile before the vegetation thinned out and allowed them to make out about a thousand yards in front of them the rear wall of the fortress – much lower than those at the front and sides and with no sign of guards. Crouching and taking advantage of the cover of the few remaining bushes and the darkness as some large clouds drifted over the moon, the men ran across the intervening ground to squash themselves against the walls, any sound they made more than blotted out by the noises of battle coming from the front of the fort. Some of the men had brought ropes with them and, at an order from Humayun, Ahmed Khan seized one and began to climb up the wall at a corner where it turned almost at right angles to follow the contours of the land. Within seconds, he had scrambled to the top using the same techniques as he had in the fissure and thrown down his rope for others to follow. Soon several other men had climbed up and more ropes were hanging down.

Humayun himself was quickly on the smooth battlements, peering along them to see whether there was a guardhouse. Yes, there was one – about a hundred yards away. Suddenly its door opened and six men appeared with torches – presumably a skeleton guard left behind while the others rushed to bolster the troops on the front wall which judging from the noise and commotion was now under full assault. The guards moved towards the wall to look down and, as they did so, Humayun ordered his men carrying bows to shoot as fast as they could before the guards could raise the alarm. Almost immediately there was a hiss of arrows and the six men were hit, two falling headfirst from the walls they were looking over and another drumming his legs on the stone battlements in his death throes. The other three were at once still.

Humayun led the charge towards the guardhouse. As he reached it, another Gujarati who had been hiding inside sprinted out, making for a covered staircase only ten yards away leading to the courtyard below. He was too near it for there to be time to loose off arrows before he disappeared beneath its protective roof. Humayun ran after him, arms and legs pumping, and reached the top of the staircase to see that the guard had descended most of its twenty or so stone steps. Without pausing to think, Humayun leaped from the top step on to the guard, knocking him down to the bottom. Both men were winded but the guard was the first to his feet and attempted to run on. Humayun scrambled after him and catching him by the ankle brought him to the ground once more. Summoning all his skill as a wrestler to pin the wildly struggling man beneath him, Humayun succeeded in closing his fingers round his neck and started to squeeze the life out of him until he heard the man's breath rattle in his throat and threw the limp body aside. Humayun's men were surrounding him again.

'We now have at least four hundred men,' Ahmed Khan gasped. 'What next?'

'Get as far to the front of the fort as we can before we are detected.'

Ahead, the men could see the flashes of the cannon and hear their boom and the crack of muskets as well as all the cries and screams of battle. Smoke was drifting across the courtyard, in particular through a large gateway in the opposite wall. This must mean that the gate gave directly on to the main part of the fort where the defenders were concentrated, Humayun thought. 'Get our men to the gate, half on each side, and then we'll sound our drums and trumpets to alert our fellows attacking the front wall before we charge into the enemy's rear,' he ordered. The command was quickly passed on and at Humayun's signal his men rushed to the gateway. Peering round the corner of the gate, Humayun could see through the billowing smoke cannon positions on the front wall and also defenders firing and pouring burning pitch and oil on to his own men attacking below.

'Trumpeters and drummers, give the signal and keep on doing so. The rest of you, follow me!' As the instruments sounded out, Humayun rushed through the gateway. Once through, the first volley from his archers took many of the Gujaratis in the back, the whole crew of one cannon falling together. Turning in surprise and confusion, some tried to fight back. Others seemed to lose heart and ran into the shelter of the buildings.

'Make for the main gatehouse. Kill the defenders and open the gates to our troops.'

Humayun's men rushed to obey, one of his trumpeters at their head, still sounding his call. However, from behind a pile of his dead comrades, a Gujarati fired an arrow which caught the trumpeter in the throat, and as he fell his last breath bubbling with blood produced a weird scream from his instrument. Nevertheless, Humayun, with Ahmed Khan and at least fifty men at his side, were in the gatehouse killing or putting to flight its defenders. Soon they were winching open the gates. Once they were even a quarter open, the Moghuls began to pour through. Seeing them do so, most of the remaining defenders threw down their arms but a few took refuge in an inner keep and maintained steady fire on Humayun's men, several of whom fell, mortally wounded.

'Get our men under cover. We need not risk more casualties. The fort is ours. Bring me the most senior of the Gujaratis we've captured.'

Soon, a tall, balding officer with blood running from sword-slash wounds to his arms and legs was dragged before Humayun and pushed to his knees. 'I am not a barbarian,' Humayun told him. 'I will not spill blood unnecessarily. You will go to those in the keep and tell them resistance is useless. If they surrender now I swear on the Holy Book that I will spare their lives. If they resist, all will die, including those I have already captured.'

Humayun saw the fear and alarm in the man's eyes. He believed him and should convince his fellows.

'Now go. You have ten minutes in which to bring an answer.'

Humayun ordered his men to hold their fire while the officer limped over to the keep. Recognising him, the defenders swung open the heavy metal-studded oak door and he disappeared inside. After five minutes he re-emerged and crossed to Humayun's troops. 'They will surrender provided they can leave with their personal weapons.'

'Agreed', said Humayun and immediately a great surge of relief travelled through him. He had been victorious in his first campaign as emperor. 'We have won a great victory. Take care of our wounded. Then start the search for the treasure vaults.'

◆

'We still can't find the entrance to the vaults, Majesty,' one of his officers told Humayun thirty-six hours later. 'May we put some of the captured Gujaratis who remain to the torture?'

'No. I promised on the Holy Book they could depart unharmed and under safe conduct. We need to secure the treasure — but there are other means to get information from people than torture. Tell Baba Yasaval to throw a feast for the most senior of the captured Gujaratis on the pretext of honouring their bravery. Then when many toasts have been drunk and the alcohol has loosened their lips, bring the conversation round to the subject of treasure and see what you get from them that way.'

Towards midnight that same day, Baba Yasaval staggered up to the door of the apartments temporarily occupied by Humayun. Even though his gait was unsteady and his eyes were unfocused, a broad smile creased his face. 'May I speak to His Majesty?'

A few moments later, he was admitted to Humayun's presence. 'I'm sure I know the answer, Majesty. I've spent much of the night dining and carousing under the stars in the courtyard with the Gujarati officers. As he drank deeply of the rich red wine of Ghazni, one of them — Alum Khan by name — relaxed and became ever more garrulous, confiding titbits of gossip about the Gujarati royal family and his fellow officers. When I thought the moment right, I slipped in a question about the treasure. Startled, he did not betray the location in words but I noticed his eyes flash across to one of the marble pools and he became flustered.

'Instinctively I knew that the pool had something to do with it so I questioned him further about it. You know – how long it had been there, its depth, its construction, how often it was drained and refilled. With each question he became ever more agitated as he stammered unconvincing and contradictory answers. I am sure the entrance to the vaults is concealed beneath that pool.' Baba Yasaval stopped, seemingly exhausted by the effort of forcing himself to speak so coherently after his drinking.

'You've done well. We'll drain the pool and excavate beneath it as soon as it is light. Now go and lie down before you fall down.'

Early the next morning, amid the raucous cawing of green parrots from the jungle surrounding the fortress, Humayun, with a somewhat pale and bedraggled Baba Yasaval at his side, watched as a team of labourers naked but for their white loincloths formed a chain to empty the pool with their leather buckets. Then, clambering down, they began to prise up one by one the marble slabs forming its lining before heaving them on to the poolside where others took them and piled them carefully in the courtyard.

As the first slabs were moved there was, to Baba Yasaval's obvious consternation, nothing to see beneath them but reddish sandy earth. Then, as Humayun paced impatiently along the poolside, Baba Yasaval shouted, 'Look, Majesty! Those four slabs towards the centre have indentations and chips around their sides. They've been lifted before.'

'You're right,' Humayun replied. 'Remove them.'

As soon as the crowbars were inserted the slabs came up quickly and as the sweating labourers lifted them, Humayun saw part of a wooden trap door emerge beneath them.

'That's it! Your instincts were right, Baba Yasaval, I'm sure. What a reward I will give you to compensate for that sore head.'

Jumping down on to the pool bottom, Humayun himself tugged at the trap door. It came up easily to reveal several shallow steps leading to a low, iron-studded door secured with a large metal lock.

'Give me a crowbar,' he ordered. Taking it, he pushed its tip into the lock and using all his force levered it apart. Swinging the door open, he bent his head and entered. In the half-light he caught the glint of gold. As his eyes adjusted he saw that the floor was piled with thick gold ingots and open chests of what looked like gems. There seemed to be several other chambers radiating off the first. Humayun shouted for torches and as servants brought them he saw that the chests indeed contained sapphires, rubies, emeralds and other glittering stones and that there was more booty in the other chambers including silver dishes and drinking vessels and ornately decorated weapons and armour. He would have more than enough to reward his faithful and brave warriors.

'Remove all the gold, jewels and other valuables. Have them guarded well and their number recorded. Tonight we will feast and share our spoils.'

In the late afternoon, servants and soldiers alike worked hard. Their first task was to construct a low wooden platform in the centre of the courtyard from which Humayun could address his troops and distribute their share of the booty which was piled under guard at the back of the dais. Then they rigged additional awnings around the courtyard using all the fabrics they could find, whether wool, cotton or mere jute, whether bright reds or purples or duller duns and greens, whether elaborately patterned or plain. Beneath them they improvised low wooden tables and around them scattered all the cushions, blankets and mattresses they could find for the banqueters to recline upon. They fashioned rough stands for torches and placed them where they were least likely to get knocked over as the revelries got wilder as they inevitably would.

As they were completing their work, their appetites were whetted by the smell of cooking wafting from the nearby field kitchens. Sheep were roasting on spits, men were stirring spices into bubbling vats of vegetables, more skilled cooks were combining sugar, yoghurt, rosewater and spices in smaller copper pots to make sweetmeats. Probably more important to the mind of many of the soldiers who, in common with Humayun and most of his courtiers, were good Muslims but could not convince themselves that the consumption of alcohol was entirely sinful, all the supplies of drink from the fortress and Humayun's own baggage train – including the red wine of Ghazni that had been the downfall of Alum Khan – were being assembled in whatever containers were available.

An hour after sunset, when the bats were swooping through the warm, velvet darkness and the noise of insects was at its height, two of Humayun's trumpeters put their lips to their six-foot-long brass instruments. Then, as their reverberations stilled the voices of officers and common soldiers alike, Humayun appeared from the main door of the fortress clad in a tunic and trousers of gold-coloured material over which he was wearing a coat of gold chain mail found in the treasure chambers. To the continuing sound of the trumpets and the heavy beat of the large military drums from the battlements above, Humayun advanced through the ranks of his soldiers to the low dais and slowly mounted it, followed by his most senior officers, and stood before the assembled treasure. Motioning the trumpeters and drummers to be silent he addressed his men.

'Tonight we celebrate the successful end to our campaign in Gujarat. Everywhere we have defeated those of our enemies brave enough to face us. Sultan Bahadur Shah has not even dared to do so, hiding in the most remote corners of his realm like the cowardly rat he is. Yet we have conquered his lands and behind me you see all the piles of his treasure we have made our own. First let us give thanks to God for our victory.'

'*Allah akbar*, God is great,' came the instant response from the ranks.

'Before we feast let me share some of this treasure with you. Each senior officer has been ordered to bring his shield to this assembly. Shortly you will see why. It is not for fear of sudden attack – our enemies are well scattered and demoralised – but to carry off rewards for himself and his men. Officers, advance with your shields. First you, Baba Yasaval.'

The shaven-headed Baba Yasaval walked forward and bowed low before Humayun.

'Take your shield from your back and place it upside down on the ground.'

Baba Yasaval did so.

'Servants. Pile it with gold and silver bars and top it with jewels.' The servants brought forward the precious metals and gems, glinting and glittering in the torchlight, and heaped them on the shield. 'Now carry it away, Baba Yasaval, with my heartfelt thanks, and if you're still too weak from drinking get your men to help!'

The burden would have been far too great for any man, young or old, hungover or not, and a smiling Baba Yasaval bowed his head, his hand on his heart, and motioned to his men to assist. As together they bore their treasure off, Humayun signalled to the next officer, a tall pale Afghani, to mount the stage and the process was repeated. All the time the cries of 'Glory to Humayun, our emperor, our *padishah*' increased. As he acknowledged the acclaim, both hands held high above his head, Humayun smiled. He had been successful in his first campaign as emperor. Like his father before him, he had brought himself and his men glory and booty. Life was good – long might it continue so.

Chapter 4

In the Balance

The monsoon rains were falling so hard that the courtyards of the Agra fort were awash. The heavy drops bounced off the paving stones and drowned the fountains that should have been bubbling up. Clothes were beginning to mildew and in the imperial library anxious scholars were at their annual task of trying to protect from the damp the manuscripts brought to Hindustan by Babur. Among them were Babur's own diaries, which Humayun had ordered his librarians to store in a specially made metal box with a tight-fitting lid to protect against the moist air and the ceaseless swarms of insects. In the room where the box was kept, a fire of camphor wood was kept constantly burning during the monsoon to dry the air.

Late last night, oblivious of the pouring rain, Humayun had returned to Agra in triumph from his conquest of Gujarat. The gold, silver and jewels that remained, even after rewarding his men, had already been piled in the imperial treasure houses. Except, that was, for a few items that Humayun had kept back – a silver belt set with pearls that he would enjoy fastening around Salima's supple waist, a carved jade cup for his mother Maham, and for Khanzada a double-stranded necklace of rubies and uncut emeralds set in gold that had reputedly adorned the throats of generations of royal women of Gujarat. Unlocking an enamelled casket he drew it out, admiring once more the fiery brilliance of the rubies counterpointed by the dark green emeralds.

Still holding the necklace, Humayun made for his aunt's apartments. He knew the details of the campaign would interest her but he also wanted her advice. As he entered, he saw that Khanzada was reading and that sitting by her side, head also deep in a book, was his eleven-year-old half-sister Gulbadan. The child's eyes – a dark tawny like her mother Dildar's and her brother Hindal's – gazed up at him, bright and curious.

Khanzada rose at once and taking him by the shoulders kissed him on both cheeks. 'Welcome back, Humayun. You conquered as I knew you would . . . Every report of your progress filled me with pride.'

'I have a gift for you.' Humayun opened his hand and let the ruby and emerald necklace trickle through his fingers. Gulbadan edged closer for a better look, but Khanzada seemed to hesitate before taking the jewels and holding them up to the light. 'They're beautiful, but they're too fine for me . . . I am no longer young. Keep them for your wife when you take one.' She returned the necklace to Humayun, closing his fingers over it before he could argue and gestured him to sit by her. 'Gulbadan – leave us. But come to me again tomorrow – there is a Persian poem I want to show you.'

As the girl closed her book and walked slowly away, Khanzada looked after her. 'I've grown fond of her since her mother's death last year – she's a clever child and notices everything.'

'As you did at her age? My father often told me nothing escaped you.'

'He flattered me.'

'I don't think so, and it's for that reason that once again I come to you for advice. I learned many things during my campaign against Bahadur Shah. My victory proved to me that I can inspire men to follow me in battle and confirmed to me that I am a good warrior. . . . Many more fights lie ahead of me and I don't fear them – indeed I'm eager for them if they help me make our empire more secure . . .'

'You're right. You've proved you are a leader of men. That you are fearless. So what is worrying you?'

'As I travelled back to Agra, I often thought to myself, when the tensions and excitement of battle are over, what then? I know how to be a warrior, but do I really understand how to govern and keep an empire? How to behave when sitting on my gilded throne, surrounded by counsellors, sycophants and suppliants, all eager for my attention to their requests or problems? Sometimes I just wish to banish them all and be with Salima or one of my other concubines, or go out hunting.'

'That is only natural for a young man, but you must resist such temptations. A ruler must be alive to what is going on around him and sensitive enough to sniff out discontent before it ferments into rebellion. You will learn just as your father learned. It wasn't easy for him either. He was much younger than you when God gave him a throne but he became a great ruler. Read his diaries – you will find what you seek in their pages, born of hard experience and blood . . .' Khanzada paused, then smiled a little sadly. 'If Babur were here with us now he would tell you to be vigilant about those you allow close to you at court . . . Take care to whom you give power, trust few. Always ask yourself the question why – Why is this man advising me to do this? What will he gain if I agree? What will he lose if I don't? Will he be grateful for what he is given or think it is due to him as of right?'

'I think I understand much of this. It's almost as if a ruler's watchword must be suspicion. It grieves me it must be so, but my half-brothers' rebellion has taught me to be less trusting and more on guard, even with members of my close family who I thought would be my natural allies. But what about my subjects, the ordinary people I see only as suppliants or on a royal progress but whose loyalty I must have?'

'You will always be remote to them. What matters is not how you really are but how they perceive you. You must appear to them whenever you can and when you do you must be like the sun to them, too bright to gaze upon. They must believe in your power to protect them . . . and in your power to punish any who defy you. Remember how our ancestor Timur dazzled his people not only by his conquests but by his magnificence. The palaces and mosques he built in Samarkand, the fabulous wealth he displayed and distributed, were as important as his victories in stamping his footprint for ever upon the earth.'

Humayun rose and walked slowly over to the casement. The rain was easing and a few pale shafts of sunlight were penetrating the sullen grey sky. His aunt was right – he must not begrudge the time and effort he expended on court politics. He must give his people not only victories but also pageants and spectacles . . . They must see him not as a man but as an image of perfection and power.

'Humayun – look at this . . .'

Turning, he saw Khanzada undoing two silver clasps on the carved ivory covers of a large book that one of her attendants had brought her. Resting it on a sandalwood stand, she began to turn the pages, frowning as she scanned the lines until, finding what she wanted, she gave a nod of satisfaction.

'While you were away, I ordered some of Sultan Ibrahim's household documents to be translated into our tongue. To our eyes the court customs of the rulers of Hindustan seem strange – bizarre even – but they deserve careful study. For example, it's written here that every year, on the anniversary of his accession, Sultan Ibrahim was weighed at a public ceremony and an equivalent weight of silver, food and fine cloth was distributed to his courtiers and the people according to their rank and merit. Why shouldn't you do something similar? Bind your subjects high and low to you by showing them your wealth and power – and your generosity. See – the ceremony is described in precise detail . . .'

Coming close to Khanzada, Humayun read over her shoulder. At first, the description of the elaborate ritual of the weighing ceremony made him smile. No wonder the Moghuls had smashed through Sultan Ibrahim's armies at Panipat if the sultan had indulged in such things. It seemed soft, unmanly, to dish out wealth that had not been earned through hard combat and blood. How much better in the immediate aftermath of victory to pile his warriors' shields with booty . . .

His lip curled a little with contempt. The Moghuls hadn't conquered Hindustan to rule as its past kings had done. But Khanzada's eyes, fixed intently on his, made him pause and as he did so his certainty wavered. Perhaps his reactions were still those of a nomadic warrior from the Asian steppes . . . But he was in Hindustan now and must learn to change. Khanzada could be right. A king's power did reside in his ability to awe and reward as well as to conquer on the battlefield. There might indeed be something in these old ceremonies. Perhaps he should adopt some of Sultan Ibrahim's customs but build on them to create new spectacles . . . new magnificence . . .

Humayun put his hand on Khanzada's shoulder. 'Again you have shown me what I should do . . .'

• ◆ •

Humayun looked at his reflection in the burnished mirror held up by Jauhar. His robes were of pale blue brocade encrusted with gold embroidery and gems glittered on his fingers and around his neck. He smiled, pleased with the image he presented, encased in his finery. In fact, the only pieces of jewellery that mattered to him were the Koh-i-Nur diamond, his Mountain of Light, that mounted in gold was pinned to his breast, and – even more so – Timur's gold ring on the middle finger of his right hand. The ring was Humayun's talisman – its virile, elemental strength a constant reminder of how much he had to live up to, how much he had yet to accomplish . . .

Humayun signalled that he was ready to proceed to the great audience chamber of the Agra fort. To the blast of two long-stemmed bronze trumpets and cries of 'Padishah salamat', 'All hail the emperor' he entered the many-pillared durbar hall where his leading subjects – his officers of state, his commanders, his courtiers and the Hindustani rajas who had acknowledged his supremacy – were waiting. As they prostrated themselves, touching their foreheads to the ground, they looked in their bright robes like a field of flowers tossed down by a sharp gust of wind.

'You may rise.'

The scent of rosewater, cascading down a tiered fountain at the far end of the hall into a marble pool carved into the shape of a lotus leaf, mingled with the spicy incense smoking in four tall golden burners shaped like slender-legged cranes with rubies for eyes. Beneath Humayun's feet, the carpets of red and blue spread over the stone floor felt thick and soft as he advanced slowly towards the green velvet, gold-fringed canopy erected over a raised platform on which stood giant golden scales – two great saucers, their edges set with lozenges of pale pink quartz rimmed by pearls, suspended by gold chains from a stout wooden frame.

Directly in front of the scales was the largesse to be weighed against him – carved ivory boxes of unset gemstones, gilded wooden trunks filled with silver and gold coins that had each taken eight men to carry into the chamber, bales of pashmina goat's wool so soft and supple a length six feet wide could pass through a tiny golden ring, rolls of silks in rainbow colours and brass trays piled with spices.

Humayun surveyed his audience, grouped around the front and sides of the dais, among them his grandfather Baisanghar and his white-bearded vizier Kasim. The two elderly men were watching him approvingly and for a moment Humayun thought of Babur whose early reign they had also guided . . . but this was not a moment for grief and regrets but for pomp and ceremony. He had an imperial pronouncement to deliver.

'Nine years ago I fought by my father's side at the battle of Panipat. God granted us a great victory and a new realm. It was also God's will that my father did not live long to enjoy what he had won. This is the third anniversary of the reading of the *khutba* proclaiming me Moghul emperor of Hindustan. My empire is still young but it will grow . . . indeed it will become great, surpassing that of the Persian shah or the Ottoman sultan. The Moghuls' magnificence will blaze like the noonday sun, blinding those who dare gaze into its heart. Already, I have shown my power to defeat those who threaten our borders. Bahadur Shah and the Lodi pretender Tartar Khan skulk in the mountains and their once great wealth now fills my treasuries. But you who are loyal to me and to my house, you will share in the glory and the riches, starting today.' Humayun nodded. 'Kasim, let us proceed.'

Just as they had carefully rehearsed, Kasim gestured to the trumpeters who delivered a further long blast that reverberated around the chamber. Humayun approached the scales. Stepping on to one of the golden saucers, he felt it dip to the floor beneath his weight. At a clap of Kasim's hands, attendants began to pile box after box of gems on to the other saucer until slowly, to the sonorous beating of drums, Humayun began to rise off the floor. When, finally, the scales were in equilibrium, the trumpets sounded once more.

Opening a book bound in red leather, Kasim began to read. 'His Imperial Highness, Humayun, has in his infinite generosity decreed that these gems be shared among his courtiers and loyal subjects who are listed here.' Slowly, portentously, he intoned name after name. Humayun saw the smiles of gratification – greed even.

And so it went on. Next Humayun was weighed against the bags of gold and silver to be distributed as a further reward to his commanders and then against the silks, brocades and spices to be sent to leading officials and subjects in other cities and provinces. Finally he ordered grain and loaves to be distributed among the poor as a reminder that the emperor thought not just of his rich and important subjects but of all his people.

By the time it was all over and the roars of thanks and acclamation had died down, Humayun's head was aching. Court ceremonial – the messages it conveyed – was essential to the dynasty. He understood that now, and that he must find further ways to awe his people, but he was relieved to return to his own apartments and throw off his heavy robes. As his attendants dressed him in a simple tunic and trousers and Jauhar locked away his jewels, he felt a need to be alone, to have time to think. He'd go out for a ride along the banks of the Jumna where the air would be cooler than the stifling atmosphere here in the fort. Perhaps on his return he would visit the sweet-scented *haram* and one of his beautiful young concubines who inhabited it.

'Majesty, Her Highness Gulrukh begs a word with you.' A soft, oddly accented voice interrupted his thoughts. Turning, Humayun saw a dark-eyed young man with luxuriant black hair curling down to his shoulders. Humayun did not recall seeing him before. He looked no more than about twenty and was slender and supple. His arms – left bare by his embroidered scarlet waistcoat – were smoothly muscled.

'What is your name?'

'Mehmed, Majesty.'

'And you serve my stepmother?'

Mehmed's amber eyes flickered. 'Yes, Majesty.'

'Where are you from?'

'The Ottoman court in Istanbul. I came to Agra with my master, a spice merchant, but when he departed I remained to seek my fortune here. I have been lucky enough to find favour with Her Majesty.'

What did Gulrukh want? She seldom troubled him. Indeed, since the death of his father and his half-brothers' conspiracy he'd barely seen her. Never before had she asked him to go to her. Unsettled by her request, Humayun reluctantly decided to postpone his ride. It would appear courteous to go to her straight away, and the sooner he went, the sooner he'd find out what it was about. 'Very well; take me to your mistress.'

Humayun followed Mehmed out of his chamber, across a courtyard and up a flight of stairs that led to the suites of rooms overlooking a flower-filled garden where the senior royal women – except for Khanzada who preferred to live in another part of the fort – had their apartments. As befitted her status as Babur's second wife and mother of two of his sons, Kamran and Askari, Gulrukh's apartments were grand. As they reached the silver-inlaid mulberry wood doors outside them, attendants swung them open and Humayun entered.

'You are kind to come so quickly', said Gulrukh in her rich, warm voice – easily the most attractive thing about her – as she came towards him. 'I did not expect such an honour.'

Two years older than his own mother, Gulrukh was in her early forties but her sleek plumpness made her look younger. Kamran – sinewy as a mountain cat with slit-like green eyes – had inherited his looks from Babur, not from her, Humayun thought. But Gulrukh's small black eyes – fixed intently on his face – were just like Askari's.

'Please – won't you rest?' She gestured towards a red silk bolster and Humayun sat back against it.

'I've never spoken of it to you because I was ashamed, but my sons' folly in plotting against you caused me much distress. Your father – may his soul rest in peace in Paradise – chose you as his heir and it was not for anyone to challenge. Believe me – I knew nothing of their rash and childish scheming. When I heard what they had done I was terrified. I thought you'd have them executed. I was about to come to you to plead for their lives. But then I heard of your generosity – how you had raised them up and forgiven them and appointed them to govern wealthy provinces . . . I have long wished to have this conversation with you because I wished to thank you as a mother. I chose today because it is the third anniversary of the start of your reign. I thought it auspicious and also I wanted to congratulate you. You have been emperor only a short while but already you've achieved much.'

'I trust my brothers have learned their lesson and that they are finding fulfilment . . .' Humayun shifted uneasily against the bolster, embarrassed and anxious to be gone. But, as he suspected, Gulrukh had more to say. She moved closer, her hennaed fingers clasped over her breast.

'I have a favour to ask of you though I hardly dare . . .'

Was she going to ask him to recall Kamran and Askari to court? Humayun felt a flash of irritation as he waited for her to go on.

'If you grant my wish it will give me much pleasure.' Gulrukh was seemingly undisturbed by his silence. 'To celebrate your victory over Gujarat, I wish to hold a feast for you. Your mother and aunt and the other royal women will also be my guests. Let me do this for you and I will know that you have truly forgiven my sons and that harmony has returned to Babur's family.'

Humayun felt himself relax. So that was all she wanted – no tearful pleading about her sons returning to Agra . . . just a celebration. He bowed his head, signifying his acceptance of Gulrukh's request, and after a final exchange of graceful courtesies left her.

Abandoning thoughts of his ride, he decided instead to visit his mother. As he made for Maham's apartments, he passed what had been Dildar's rooms. He had been very young – only ten or eleven – when Babur had given Hindal to Maham. All he remembered was his mother calling to him to look at the baby she was holding in her arms. 'See, you have a new brother,' she had said. Puzzled,

53

Humayun had stared down at the bawling infant that he knew was not his mother's but another woman's . . .

At the time he'd dismissed it from his mind. Growing up in Kabul, learning to fight with a sword and fire off thirty arrows a minute and play polo had been what mattered. Only later had he come to realise that giving Hindal to Maham had been one of the few acts of weakness of his father's life – albeit done out of love.

What good had it done? It had soothed Maham's grief but it had nourished discord within the family. In the early years she had jealously guarded Hindal, keeping him away from Dildar. But as Hindal had grown older and learned who his true mother was, inevitably he had turned from Maham. Perhaps that was why, young as he was, Hindal had joined Kamran and Askari's plot against him. Perhaps it was his revenge for that day when he had been torn from Dildar's arms.

What of Dildar herself? What would have been in her mind all those years? At least she had had Gulbadan to console her . . . But when she was born, had Dildar feared that Maham would try to take her also? Humayun shook himself. He would never know. Dildar was dead now. Maham never spoke of these things and he was reluctant even to ask Khanzada. The world of women could be a dark and difficult place. In comparison the world of men with all its battles and conflicts, where disputes could be settled with fists or the slash of a blade, seemed cleaner and easier.

• ◆ •

Beneath an almost golden moon, the courtyard which Gulrukh had chosen for her party was lit by the soft radiance of hundreds of wicks burning in pools of scented oil in copper bowls or *diyas*. Against one wall of the courtyard was a large tent – conical in shape like those of the Moghuls' homelands. But instead of the sturdy sticks locked together to withstand the shrieking winter winds and covered in thick felt, Humayun could see that the framework was of slender silver rods covered with flowered silk. The silk was caught back on each side by pearl-sewn ribbons so the entrance was half open to the warm night air.

Two of Gulrukh's women led him to the tent where she was waiting, wearing a robe of dark purple and a shawl of the same colour, shot through with silver thread, that covered her head and shoulders. But her young attendants were dressed in semi-transparent muslins. As they moved in the flickering light, Humayun caught the curve of slender waists, firm breasts and voluptuously rounded hips and buttocks. Jewels flashed in their navels and their dark hair was interwoven with white jasmine flowers in the Hindustani fashion.

'Please . . .' Gulrukh indicated a low, velvet-covered chair. As Humayun took his place, one of her women knelt before him with an enamelled golden ewer of cool, sandalwood-scented water while another brought a cotton cloth. Humayun held out his hands and the first attendant let the water flow over them. Slowly, caressingly, the second dried them.

Puzzled, Humayun looked around for his mother and Khanzada and the other royal women, but apart from Gulrukh and her servants, they seemed to be alone.

'I thought a smaller, less formal celebration might be more to your taste,' Gulrukh said. 'I am your only hostess but hope you will pardon my deficiencies.'

Humayun sat up a little straighter in his chair, eyes watchful. What was Gulrukh doing? As she must know, he'd accepted her invitation only out of courtesy – nothing more – yet she seemed to be trying to turn the occasion into something intimate. For a moment he feared she might be trying to seduce him, either herself or through her attendants.

'I have prepared a surprise for you.'

Humayun looked around, half expecting to hear the clash of cymbals and bells and see the usual line of undulating dancing girls or tumbling jugglers, acrobats and fire-eaters that were the staples of court entertainment. Instead, a willowy form emerged from the shadows to his right. As the figure came towards him, Humayun recognised the pale face of Mehmed. The Turk knelt before Humayun and held out a goblet of what looked like red wine.

'What is it?' Humayun ignored Mehmed and turned to Gulrukh.

'A special blend of heady opium from south of Kabul and the

red wine of Ghazni, mixed by my own hand to a recipe handed down within my family. Sometimes – when he was weary – I made it for your father. He said that it transported him . . .'

As Humayun gazed at the dark, almost purple liquid, a series of images flashed through his mind – of Babur, high with joy after victory on the battlefield and calling for opium to take him to yet further heights . . . He'd seen the ecstasy on his father's face, heard his delighted murmurings. Of course, he was no stranger to opium himself. It had numbed his grief at his father's death. Later, he'd discovered the sensual languor that a few pellets dissolved in rosewater could induce and that heightened the pleasures of love-making. But seldom had he been as completely transported as Babur had seemed to be.

'Do you wish to send for your food taster first?' Gulrukh asked. But before Humayun could answer, she stepped forward, took the goblet from Mehmed and raised it to her own full lips. Her plump throat quivered as she swallowed and Humayun saw her raise her hand to catch a few beads of liquid that had trickled down her chin and then delicately lick her fingers clean.

'Majesty, drink. It is my gift to you . . .' Humayun hesitated then took the goblet, still three-quarters full, and raising it to his lips took a sip. The wine tasted of something fiery – Gulrukh must have spiced it to mask the faint bitterness of the opium. Humayun drank again, this time more deeply, and felt a soft warmth start to spread through his body – first down his throat, then to the pit of his stomach. After a few moments, his limbs were beginning to grow heavy. A delicious, irresistible lethargy was taking possession of him and Humayun gave himself up to it like a weary man who sees a soft bed laid ready for him and cannot wait to lie on it.

He swallowed what was left in the goblet. His eyes were already half closed as he felt soft hands take the cup from him, raise him out of the chair and guide him to a soft mattress, where they laid him down. Someone placed a cushion under his head and gently wiped his face with scented water. It felt good and he stretched luxuriously. Soon his body began to feel as if it was dissolving into nothingness. He could no longer feel any part of it but what did it matter? His spirit – the very essence of who he was, not the prone, earth-bound creature he had once been – seemed to be streaming up into the star-splashed heavens that were suddenly opening up before him.

Released from his body, Humayun felt himself soaring like a comet. Beneath him, he could make out the waters of the Jumna flowing dark as Gulrukh's cup of wine beneath the battlements of the Agra fort. Beyond in every direction stretched the flat, seemingly limitless plains of Hindustan, the warm darkness pierced, now here, now there, glow-worm like by the dung fires burning in the villages of his new subjects. Stretched on their simple beds beneath the acacia and banyan trees outside their mud-baked houses, they were dreaming the dreams of people whose lives were governed by the seasons, when to sow and when to reap, and whose greatest worry was the health of their bullocks and how they would pull at the plough.

As his spirit flew onwards, Humayun could see the sun beginning to rise. A pool of orange light was seeping over the rim of the world bringing warmth and renewal. And what was that he could see beneath him now in the pale apricot glow? – the palaces, towers and grandiose royal tombs of the great city of Delhi, once capital to the Lodi sultans but humbled by the Moghuls. Still Humayun's unleashed spirit flew on, leaving the heat and dust of Hindustan behind. Below him now were the chill waters of the Indus. Beyond lay the bleached, bone-hard hills and twisting passes leading to Kabul and on towards the hard, diamond-bright peaks of the Hindu Kush, gateway to the Moghuls' ancestral homelands on the plains of central Asia. What a long way they had travelled. What glories they had achieved. And what marvels still awaited . . . To what new heights could they ascend with the help of visions such as these? Above Humayun's still exultantly soaring spirit the sky glowed like molten gold, embracing the entire world.

Chapter 5

The Tyranny of the Stars

'I have decided to change how I govern. The imperial court is not as I would wish it.'

Humayun's counsellors, sitting cross-legged in a semicircle before his gilded throne, stared in surprise. He saw Baisanghar and Kasim exchange puzzled glances before returning their attention to him. No matter. Soon they would understand the wonderful ideas that had come to him in his opium-induced dreams when, released from the everyday obligations of ruling, his thoughts seemed to flow with a crystal clarity. Everything that had been revealed to him had a purpose. Everything he had dreamed was indeed written in the stars . . .

Humayun raised his right hand and his astrologer Sharaf, a thin, elderly, beak-nosed man dressed in sweeping brown robes, stepped forward holding a heavy leather-bound volume in his thickly veined hands. With a grunt of relief, he laid it on the white marble table inlaid with images of the planets that Humayun had had placed before his golden throne.

Humayun rose and leafed through until he found the page he was seeking. There in the hand of his ancestor, the great astronomer Ulugh Beg – Timur's grandson – was a chart depicting the celestial movements of the planets and the stars. As he stared at the delicate drawing, the heavenly bodies seemed to start moving in stately progress, slowly at first but then gathering momentum so that they appeared to be chasing one another. He blinked and looked again and the page was still . . . It must be the effect of the opium he had taken last night. The now familiar concoction mixed for him by Gulrukh and carried to his apartments by Mehmed must have been especially potent. He'd not woken until the sun was a spear's length above the horizon and had chided Jauhar for not rousing him earlier on a day when he would reveal his insights.

Suddenly Humayun became conscious of the eyes of his counsellors watching him intently. He'd almost forgotten they were there. He drew himself up. 'You know I have studied the never-ending motion of the planets and stars as did my ancestor Ulugh Beg. After much thought I have concluded that we can go beyond his researches and that the star charts and tables and the records of events long past, when interpreted with the aid of learned astrologers and one's own power of pure thought, can provide a framework for living and even for ruling.'

By his counsellors' expressions, Humayun saw they still had no idea what he was talking about. But then how could they? They had not seen what he had seen when – set free by Gulrukh's potions – his mind had travelled through realms they could not begin to imagine. But they were about to learn of the great improvements he planned to make to his government.

'I have come to realise that we can learn from the planets and the stars. Under God Almighty they govern us, but like a good master they can also teach us. Henceforward, I will only deal with certain matters on the days the stars designate as auspicious for them . . . and I will dress appropriately. The stars tell us that today, Sunday, is governed by the sun whose golden rays regulate sovereignty. Therefore on Sundays, clad in bright yellow, I will deal with affairs of state. On Mondays – the day of the Moon and of tranquillity – I will be at leisure and wear green, the colour of quiet reflection. On Tuesdays – the day of the planet Mars, patron of soldiers – I will devote myself to matters of war and of justice. I will wear the red raiment of Mars, the colour of wrath and vengeance, and dispense both punishment and reward with lightning speed. Treasurers with purses will stand ready to reward any I deem worthy while guards in coats of mail and blood-red turbans will stand, axe in hand, before my throne to punish culprits instantly . . .

'Saturdays – the day of the planet Saturn – and Thursdays – the day of the planet Jupiter – will be devoted to religion and learning, and Wednesday – the day of the planet Mercury – will be a day of joy when we will make merry and wear purple. And on Fridays, dressed in blue like the all-embracing sky, I will deal with any matter. Any man or woman – no matter how humble or poor – may approach me . . . All they need do is beat the Drum of Justice that I have ordered be set up outside my audience chamber.'

Humayun paused again. Kasim, who had been recording his pronouncements in his ledger, seemed to have halted in mid-sentence while Baisanghar was pulling with the fingers of his left hand at the metal hook that many years ago had replaced his severed right hand. The rest of his counsellors looked stunned by his pronouncement but they would come to accept his insights. In the mechanical movements of the stars and planets everything was in its properly ordained place. And that was exactly how the government of a great empire should be. Everything must be done in the appropriate way and at the appropriate time . . .

After a minute or two Humayun continued slowly, his tone flat and formal. 'I have also decided to reorganise my offices of government according to which of the four main elements – fire, air, water or earth – dominate them. The Office of Fire will be responsible for my armies. The Office of Air will deal with matters of the imperial kitchen, stables and wardrobe. The Office of Water will be responsible for everything to do with the rivers and canals of my empire, for irrigation and for the imperial wine cellars. And the Office of Earth will deal with agriculture and grants of land. And all actions, all decisions, must be taken in accordance with the guidance written in the stars to ensure everything is done in the most auspicious way . . .

'And you – my counsellors and courtiers – you will also have your place in this new structure. The stars tell us there are three classes of men. All of you, my nobles and officials and commanders, are Officers of State. But there are two other classes essential to the well-being and health of the empire – Good Men, which includes our religious leaders, philosophers and astrologers, and Officers of Pleasure who are the poets, singers, musicians, dancers and artists who beautify and embellish our lives, just as the stars decorate the sky. Each of these three classes will be divided into twelve ranks and each rank will have three grades – high, middle and low. In due course I will inform you to which rank and grade I have assigned you ... Now, leave me. I have much to think upon.'

Alone in his audience chamber except for Sharaf, Humayun again examined the star charts of Ulugh Beg, losing all sense of time as one hour flowed into the next. Not till the sun was beginning to sink, sending purple shadows creeping over the Agra fort, did Humayun lift his eyes from the pages. As he returned to his apartments a yearning for the dark opium-infused wine that unleashed his soul again welled up inside him and he walked more quickly.

'Kasim, I did not realise how many hours had passed.' Humayun rubbed his eyes and pushed himself upright from where he had been slumped on a purple-silk-covered divan. It was embroidered in gold thread with a network of stars and Humayun believed that, lying on it, he thought more deeply. 'Are the council still assembled? What about the envoy from my governor in Bengal?'

'The council broke up a long time ago. As for the envoy, you had already postponed your meeting with him several times because you did not consider the days well suited to such discussion and once – forgive me for mentioning it, Majesty – when you banished him from your presence for entering the audience chamber by the wrong door, thus rendering a discussion that day too inauspicious. The season for travel down the Jumna and the Ganges to Bengal is coming to an end and he could wait no longer. Therefore Baisanghar and I took the great liberty of offering guidance on your behalf on the level of taxes to be imposed and the number of troops to be raised. He went aboard his boat and the anchor was weighed two hours ago.'

For a moment Humayun felt anger that the two old men had usurped his authority.

'Majesty, we can of course send another boat after him if you disagree with what we said.'

Kasim must have sensed his annoyance, thought Humayun. He'd been unjust. The envoy was both garrulous and tedious. He had delayed his audience with him deliberately, sometimes using excuses which seemed trifling even to himself. Humayun spoke softly. 'I'm sure that when I hear in the morning what you and Baisanghar suggested I will agree, Kasim. Now leave me to rest and relax once more.'

Kasim seemed reluctant to do so, shifting from foot to foot and fiddling with a golden tassel on his robe. Then he made his mind up and spoke. 'Majesty, you know for how long I have loyally served you and your father.'

'Yes, and I appreciate it.'

'Therefore may I take advantage of my years of experience to proffer you some advice? Majesty, you indulge in opium. Your father enjoyed it too, as well as wine and *bhang* – marijuana.'

'So?'

'Some of us have more tolerance of such things than others. Even when I was young, *bhang* could prevent me from working for days so I abstained from all such potions despite your father's urgings. Perhaps they have more effect on Your Majesty than you realise.'

'No, Kasim. They help me to think and to relax. Is that all you've got to say?'

'Yes, but please remember even your father did not indulge every day, particularly when he had important business to transact.' As Kasim bowed and turned to leave, Humayun saw an expression of deep anxiety on his lined face. His concern was genuine. It had cost the self-effacing, reticent old man much to make his little speech. Humayun could not be angry with him.

'I will give thought to your words, I assure you.'

· ◆ ·

Humayun looked with satisfaction at the huge circular carpet woven in silk blue as the sky that attendants were unrolling before his throne. The series of circles – outlined on the carpet in red, yellow, purple and green chain stitch and representing the planets – were placed exactly as he had ordered. He would reward the weavers well for their skill and the speed with which they had brought his 'Carpet of Council' to life.

The idea had come to him only a month ago during a particularly vivid dream – indeed his drugged sleep after drinking Gulrukh's opium and wine seemed to be growing ever more marvellous and revelatory. One of the stars had actually seemed to speak to him, telling him to make such a carpet so that – when advising him – his counsellors could stand on the planet most appropriate to the business in hand. He had had the weavers work on the carpet in secret, taking it in turns so that the looms were moving every hour of the day. He had not spoken of the carpet to anyone except Sharaf – not Baisanghar, nor Kasim nor even Khanzada. Let it be a surprise to them as it would be to the rest of his council, whom he'd summoned to join him here.

Before long his counsellors were assembled. As it was a Wednesday, their robes, like Humayun's, were a bright purple and their sashes orange. Humayun smiled to see their curious glances fall on the shimmering circle of pale blue spread out before him. Baba Yasaval was scrutinising it in frank puzzlement.

'I have summoned you here to see this wondrous carpet. It represents the sky above us. These circles are the planets – see, here is Mars and Venus and Jupiter – and, over here, we have the moon. When you have something you wish to say to me, you must stand on the appropriate circle. For example, if you wish to speak to me of army matters, you must stand on Mars. That will help the planets to guide you . . .'

Humayun looked around but suddenly found the faces of his counsellors hard to distinguish – was that Kasim, forehead wrinkled in thought, over there? . . . He couldn't be sure . . . everything around him seemed a little blurred. Maybe his eyes were weary from studying the star charts or straining into the heavens when, at night, he climbed to the battlements of the Agra fort to contemplate the stars.

But after a moment everything slid back into focus. Yes, that was Kasim watching him thoughtfully and there was Baba Yasaval looking nonplussed, perhaps unable to comprehend the power of the carpet's symbolism. But what about Asaf Beg? He seemed to be laughing – a disdainful curl to his lip – as he surveyed Humayun's carpet. His expression as he raised his face to look full into Humayun's seemed more than a little mocking. Anger ran like a flame through Humayun. How dare this ignorant petty chieftain from Kabul make fun of his emperor?

'You there!' Humayun rose and pointed a trembling finger towards Asaf Beg. 'You are impudent and you will pay for your disrespect. Guards – take him into the courtyard outside and give him fifty lashes. Think yourself lucky, Asaf Beg, that you are losing only the skin off your back and not your head.'

There was a collective gasp followed by shocked silence. Then a voice spoke. 'Majesty . . .'

Humayun swung round, determined to tolerate neither contradiction nor criticism, but saw that it was Kasim who had spoken. At the real concern showing again on the face of the man whom he trusted and who had served both his father and himself well, Humayun's rage began to ebb. At the same time he realised his breathing was ragged, his pulse was racing and his forehead was beaded with sweat.

'What is it, Kasim?'

'I'm sure that Asaf Beg meant you no disrespect, Majesty . . . I beg you to reconsider.'

Asaf Beg, pale and with no trace of a smile now on his wide mouth and usually cheerful face, was gazing pleadingly at Humayun. To be publicly flogged would bring terrible shame on him and all his clan, Humayun knew. He also recalled Asaf Beg's bravery in battle. He was already regretting his action.

'Kasim – you speak well, as always. Asaf Beg, I pardon you. But do not test my patience again or you will not find me so merciful.' Humayun rose – the signal for his council to disperse which they seemed to do more quickly than usual. As he sat down again Humayun found himself shaking. The carpet had lost its lustrous charm. It was growing late. Perhaps he should return to his apartments to rest. But as he entered them, he was surprised to find Khanzada waiting for him.

'What is it, Aunt?'

'Dismiss your attendants. I must speak with you alone.'

Humayun gestured to his servants and to Jauhar to leave. The double doors had barely closed behind them before she began. 'I witnessed what happened at the council meeting from behind the *jali* screen. Humayun . . . I had not thought it possible . . . first you behaved like a man in a trance and then like a lunatic . . .'

'My council do not always understand that what I am doing is for the best, but you should. It was you who first taught me the value of display to a ruler – you who suggested the weighing ceremony and encouraged me to use ritual as an aid to governing . . .'

'But not to the exclusion of humanity or reason . . .'

'Under the tutelage of the stars I have devised new patterns and new procedures. Government will become simpler. If my counsellors and advisers follow my guidance the tedium of time spent in the audience chamber will be reduced, leaving me free for the further exploration of the unplumbed depths of the heavens.'

'Forget the stars. You're obsessed with them and are losing your hold on reality. I've tried to warn you before but you wouldn't hear. Now you must or you risk losing everything you've striven for – everything your father achieved . . . Humayun, are you even listening to me?'

'Yes, I am.' But Khanzada was wrong, he was thinking . . . only in the patterns of the stars and the planets could he find the answers to other questions that had long fascinated and tormented him. Whether everything was somehow predestined by the heavens? Whether his father's early death had been part of some greater plan? How much of a man's destiny rested in his own hands? How much was preordained, like the position and the family into which he had been born and the responsibilities and privileges that flowed from it? And how could he know . . . ? An old Buddhist monk whom he had visited in his youth in the monk's solitary retreat by one of the great statues of the Buddha – cut into the cliffs of the Bamian Valley a hundred miles west of Kabul – had told him that, given the precise date, time and place of his birth, he could foretell not only the course of his life but as what animal he would be reincarnated in the next. The idea of reincarnation was nonsense to him, but what of the rest? Of one thing he was already sure – that with the star charts and tables and records of events long past that he spent so much time studying and that in his opium-fuelled dreams came alive for him, he could create a framework for living and ruling and was already well along the way to doing so.

'Humayun! Won't you even answer me?'

Khanzada's voice seemed to be coming from far off and as he stared at her she seemed to diminish in stature, becoming a little doll animatedly waving her arms and waggling her head. It was almost comic.

'You smile when I speak of the danger you are in . . .' Khanzada's firm grip on his arm, the sharpness of her nails digging into his flesh, brought him back to reality. 'You will hear me out. There are things that must be said . . . that perhaps only I can say . . . but remember I speak only from love.'

'Say what you wish.'

'Humayun, you spend your days fuddled with opium. You used to be a ruler, a warrior. What are you now but a dreamer, a fantasist? I never thought I'd have to say these words to you . . . but a leader must be strong, he must be decisive. His people must know that they can look to him at all times. You know that. How many times in the past have you and I not discussed such things? Now you seldom visit me . . . And when I look around the court, I see expressions of fear and uncertainty and hear uneasy laughter behind your back. Even to those who've known and served you long and loyally – like Kasim and Baba Yasaval – you've become like a stranger. They no longer have confidence in your judgement. They never know how you will react – whether you will approve their actions or whether you will be angry. Sometimes they can get no coherent guidance or direction from you for hours . . . even days . . .'

Never before had Khanzada spoken to him in this way and he felt resentment stir. 'If you or my courtiers disapprove of my decisions and of how I choose to govern my empire, it is because you do not understand. But in time you will come to see that everything I'm doing is for the best.'

'Time is not on your side. If you do not rule as you should, the eyes of your nobles and commanders will turn to your half-brothers – to Kamran in particular. Think, Humayun. He's only a few months younger than you and has already proved himself an able warrior and a strong governor of his province. Babur's blood and Timur's too flows through his veins just as it does through yours. You know he is ambitious – ambitious enough to have already plotted against you. You have no reason to think he won't do so again. Hasn't it occurred to you to wonder why Gulrukh has insinuated herself into your favour, why she plies you with that brew of hers? Instead of gazing into the infinite mysteries of the stars it better befits an emperor to peer deep into the minds of those around him. Remember what I once told you . . . always to look for the motive. Gulrukh could never encourage open revolt against you in favour of Kamran and Askari . . . how much cleverer and more subtle of her to undermine you gradually with opium. And as your powers weaken and fade and your subjects begin to despise the ruler they once admired, what would be more natural than for them to turn to one of her sons? Remember also the fate of Ulugh Beg. When he – like you – became obsessed with the stars and what they could tell him about the purpose of life, one of his sons had him murdered and took his throne.'

'You speak out of anger and jealousy. You resent the fact that I have taken your thoughts on ceremony and, with the stars' aid, improved them beyond your narrow comprehension. You resent my not needing you as I once did, that I am a grown man who takes his own decisions and has no need of the advice of women – not yours, nor Gulrukh's nor any of you . . . You should know your place – all of you.'

Khanzada's gasp told him how much he had hurt her, but she needed to be reminded of certain things. Much as he loved and respected her, he, not she, was emperor and he would decide how he would rule.

'I have done my best to warn you. If you choose not to listen there is no more I can do . . .' Khanzada's voice was low and measured but he could see a vein throbbing in her temple and that her body was trembling.

'Aunt . . .' He reached out to touch her arm but she turned away and making for the doors flung them open herself. Calling to her two women who were waiting for her, she hurried away down the torch-lit corridor. Humayun stood for a moment in silence. He'd never quarrelled with Khanzada before, but what he'd said had been necessary, hadn't it? The stars and their messages could not be ignored. A man – even one as powerful as an emperor – was as nothing compared to the seemingly never-ending cycles of movement of the stars within the fathomless universe. If he followed their signs his reign would surely prosper.

And what his aunt had said about Gulrukh . . . that was also wrong. Of course, like all those at court she wanted the emperor's good will. Maybe she hoped that by pleasing him she'd secure favours and privileges for her sons, his half-brothers Kamran and Askari . . . but that was all. The mind-expanding journeys on which Gulrukh's dark, opium-laced wine took him were her gift to him and he would not, could not give them up . . . not when they were bringing him ever closer to unravelling the mysteries of existence.

• ◆ •

'Let whoever is striking the drum approach. Today is Friday – the day when I am ready to dispense justice to even the most humble of my subjects.' Humayun smiled as he sat on his high-backed throne. This was the first time in the six months that it had been sitting outside his audience chamber that anyone had struck the great ox-hide drum to demand justice of the emperor. At the beginning the sound had been faint and uneven and for a moment had seemed to stop entirely. Then Humayun had heard it again. Whoever was beating the Drum of Justice seemed to have taken courage. The booms had grown louder and more frequent. He'd known this moment would come just as – in time – his ministers would accept the reforms he was making. Even old Kasim, standing so solemn-faced by the side of his throne, would acknowledge he'd been right.

The footsteps of six of his blue-turbaned bodyguards rang on the stone floor as they marched out to the courtyard. When they returned, a young Hindu woman in a red silk sari with a red *tilak* mark on her forehead was with them. Her long dark hair was streaming unbound over her shoulders and her expression was both nervous and determined. The guards brought her to within ten feet of the throne and she knelt before him.

'Rise. The emperor is ready to hear your request,' said Kasim. 'You may be assured that you will receive justice.'

The woman glanced uncertainly at the glittering, bejewelled figure of Humayun on his throne as if she could not quite believe she was in his presence. 'Majesty, my name is Sita. I am the wife of a merchant in Agra. My husband deals in spices like cinnamon, saffron and cloves. A week ago he was returning to Agra with a small mule train carrying goods he had purchased in the markets in Delhi. Two days' ride from here – near our holy Hindu city of Mathura – he and his men were attacked by dacoits who robbed them of everything they were carrying – even stripping the clothes off their backs. The dacoits were about to ride away with the mules when a party of your soldiers came riding by. The soldiers killed the dacoits but instead of restoring his goods to my husband they jeered at him. They said that he was bleating like a sheep and that was how he deserved to be treated. Cutting the ropes with which the dacoits had bound him, they made him run naked and barefoot over the hot sand, chasing him on horseback and mocking and pricking him with the tips of their spears. When finally they had tired of their sport, they rode off leaving him lying exhausted and bleeding in the dust. And with them they took all my husband's mules with their precious cargo of spices . . .'

Sita's voice was trembling with anger and indignation but she raised her chin and looked Humayun squarely in the face. 'I seek justice for my husband. He is a loyal subject of Your Majesty and no longer young. Your soldiers should have protected not abused him. Now he is lying at home covered in festering wounds inflicted by them . . .'

Kasim stepped forward, ready to question the woman, but Humayun waved him back. The soldiers' behaviour reflected on his dignity. He must be like the sun to his subjects. His light and warmth must fall on them all but this poor merchant had been cast into the darkness . . .

'What more can you tell me of these soldiers? Do you know their names?'

'My husband said that one of them called their leader Mirak Beg and that he was a tall, broad man with a broken nose and a white scar disfiguring his lip.'

Humayun knew Mirak Beg – a rowdy, hard-living chieftain from Badakhshan who had marched with Humayun and his father to invade Hindustan. He had distinguished himself at Panipat, leaping from his horse on to the back leg of a war elephant and hauling himself up the beast to kill enemy archers who'd been firing arrows at Humayun's men from the howdah on its back. But past bravery was no excuse for present crimes. Mirak Beg must answer for his lawlessness.

'If what you have told me is the truth, I will give you justice. Go home now and await my summons. Kasim – find Mirak Beg and bring him before me as soon as possible.'

Rising, Humayun rushed from the audience chamber. He felt sick. His head was aching again – these sharp stabbing pains behind his eyes were becoming more and more frequent and so too were the tricks his eyes were playing, making it hard for him to focus. He needed more wine and opium to soothe away the pain, relax his mind again and free him from the mundane obligations of the court.

• ◆ •

Dressed in blood-red robes as befitted Tuesday, the day governed by the planet Mars, Humayun looked down at Mirak Beg's defiant face. Though hauled into the audience chamber in chains, he was somehow managing to maintain his usual swaggering air. His dark eyes were fixed on Humayun's face and he seemed not to have noticed the executioners standing ready with their freshly oiled axes or the dark red blood staining the Stone of Execution – the giant slab of black marble that had been placed to the right of the throne and on which four of Mirak Beg's wildly struggling men had just had their right hands chopped off and the stumps cauterised with red-hot irons. The smell of their burning flesh still filled the air, even though they had been led out.

71

'I have left you till last, Mirak Beg, so that you could witness the punishment meted out to your soldiers. Though they did wrong and have paid the price, you, as their leader, bear the responsibility for their shameful acts. You have freely admitted your guilt but that will not save you . . . Your acts have put a stain on my honour that only your death will cleanse. What is more, you will not die by the axe. The means of your execution will fit your crime. Woman – come closer.'

Humayun gestured to Sita, the spice merchant's wife, who wrapped in a dark blue sari was standing to one side. She had not flinched from watching the amputations and now she would see true imperial justice, Humayun thought. The punishment he was about to pronounce on Mirak Beg had come to him in his dreams and its appropriateness pleased him. It would come as a surprise to all – he had not even told Kasim or Baisanghar, both standing by the throne and, like the rest of his courtiers, dressed in red as he had commanded.

'On your knees, Mirak Beg.' The chieftain looked almost surprised as if until now he'd not believed Humayun would kill him. The white scar on his upper lip almost disappeared as the blood seemed to drain from his face, which now had a waxy sheen. He licked his lips, then, finding his courage again, spoke out firmly for all to hear.

'Majesty . . . I fought for you at Panipat and later in Gujarat . . . I have always been loyal to you. All I did was seek some sport with a fat, cowardly merchant. That does not merit death. I and my men are warriors, yet since Gujarat you've given us no fighting . . . no conquests . . . you spend your time eating opium and gazing at the stars when you should be leading your armies. That's what we came from our homeland for . . . that's what you promised us . . . the sound of our horses' hooves pounding on the earth as we rode from victory to victory . . .'

'Enough!' Raising his hand, Humayun signalled to the two executioners. They put down their axes and one of them picked up a small sack that had been placed against a nearby pillar. Then, as Humayun's guards held Mirak Beg by the shoulders, one of the executioners went behind him, wrenched back his head and forced his mouth open. The other man dug his hand into the sack. Humayun could smell the sharp tang of the coarse-ground turmeric and pepper as he took a fistful of the bright yellow powder and crammed it into Mirak Beg's gaping mouth.

Mirak Beg at once began to choke. His streaming eyes bulged from his head as a second, then a third fistful was rammed through his open jaws down into his throat. His face was purpling now and strings of yellow saliva were dribbling from his tortured mouth while mucus streamed from his nostrils. Desperately he fought to get free of the strong arms holding him down and to struggle to his feet, kicking out with his legs like a man being hanged.

From all around Humayun heard gasps. Kasim had turned away and Baisanghar too was averting his gaze. Even Sita was looking shocked, one tightly curled hand raised to her mouth and her eyes round. A few more seconds and it would be over. For one last time, Mirak Beg forced his streaming eyes to open and for a moment they looked directly into Humayun's, and then his body went still.

Humayun rose. 'The punishment has fitted the crime. And so will all who transgress my laws suffer.' Stepping down from the dais on which his golden throne, his *gaddi* – draped in red velvet to mark the day of Mars – stood and flanked by his guards, Humayun made his way out of the room. For a few seconds there was silence, then behind him he heard a babble of voices as his courtiers once more found their tongues.

It was early evening now. Above the darkening Jumna, a sliver of moon was already rising, casting its silver light upon the riverbank where oxen and camels were drinking their fill. He would visit Salima. He had done so less often recently, absorbed in his opium dreams. At the thought of her soft, golden-hued body, he smiled.

Salima was lying on a silver brocade divan while one of her waiting women traced intricate designs on her slim feet with henna paste. All she was wearing was the jewelled belt Humayun had chosen for her from the plunder he had captured in Gujarat.

That campaign seemed so long ago now – like something from another life. Into his mind came Mirak Beg's accusing words 'You've given us no conquests . . . You spend your time eating opium and gazing at the stars.' Mirak Beg had deserved to die, but perhaps there had been some truth in his accusations. What would his father have said about the way he was governing, even about the amount of opium he was consuming? Perhaps, as Kasim and Khanzada had urged, he should use less of the drug to enable him to devote more time to those around him. But things had changed, hadn't they? The Moghuls' wild, nomadic days were over. He was the ruler of an empire and it was no one's business but his own that he was finding new ways of ruling, new sources of comfort and inspiration. The stars whose radiance was brighter even than the Koh-i-Nur would not let him down.

Nor would Salima. As her women hurried from the room, she rose from her couch. Slowly, caressingly she began to loosen his red robes, running her fingers over the hard muscle of his arms and shoulders beneath the soft silk. 'My emperor,' she was whispering. He wound his hands in the long black hair spilling over her bare breasts and pulled her to him, hungry for the pleasures they would enjoy until – at last – with salty sweat running down their bodies they would collapse exhausted against one another.

A few hours later, Humayun was lying by Salima's side. A soft breeze was blowing through the open casement and a pale light was already rising in the eastern sky. Salima murmured something and then, turning her silken hip to his, returned to her dreams. But for some reason, sleep had eluded Humayun. Each time he'd closed his eyes, he saw Mirak Beg's distorted, choking mouth foaming with yellow spittle and his panic-stricken eyes half bursting from his head. He should have taken some of Gulrukh's wine to banish these disturbing images but that was in his own apartment. Nevertheless, he could still ease his restless mind. Reaching for the gold locket studded with amethysts hanging from a chain around his neck, he extracted some opium pellets and, pouring water into a cup, swallowed them down. The familiar bitter taste caught at the back of his throat but then the drowsy, languorous warmth began to steal through him. With his eyelids at last growing heavy, Humayun stretched out. The soothing sweetness of the sandalwood oil with which Salima loved to anoint her body filled his nostrils and he began to drift into sleep.

But only moments later – or so it felt to Humayun – he heard a female voice urgently calling his name.

'Majesty . . . Majesty . . . a messenger has come.'

Dazed, Humayun sat up. Where was he? Looking around he saw Salima, sitting up now beside him and pulling on a pink silk robe to conceal her nakedness. But it wasn't her who'd woken him. It was one of the *haram* attendants, Barlas – a squat woman with a face wrinkled as a walnut.

'Forgive me, Majesty.' Barlas was averting her gaze from his naked body. 'A messenger has come from the east, from your brother Askari, with news he says is urgent. Even though it is early, he requests an immediate audience and Kasim ordered me to wake and tell you.'

Humayun's unfocused eyes stared at Barlas as he tried to take in what she was saying, but the opium had made him slow. 'Very well. I will return to my apartments. Tell Kasim to bring this messenger to me there.'

Half an hour later, back in his own quarters, dressed in a simple purple tunic and having splashed his face with cold water, Humayun looked at the man whose arrival had caused him to be roused from his rest. The messenger was a tall, slight man still with the dust of the road on his sweat-stained clothes. In his eagerness to speak to Humayun he almost forgot the ritual obeisance until reminded sharply by Kasim. As soon as he was back on his feet, he began. 'Majesty, I am Kamal. I serve your brother Askari in Jaunpur. Reports reached us there of a great rebellion led by Sher Shah. Your brother waited until he was certain they were true then sent me to warn you.'

Humayun stared. Though Sher Shah controlled large lands in Bengal, this grandson of a horse trader would surely never dare to threaten him. He had pledged himself to Babur as a vassal of the Moghuls. Yet ambition often pushed men to rash acts. It might be ominous that he had assumed the name 'Sher', which meant 'tiger'. Perhaps by doing so he intended to throw down a direct challenge to the true dynasty of the tiger – the Moghuls. Humayun glanced down at Timur's ring, but with eyes still dilated by opium he could not focus on the snarling image of the tiger etched into its surface.

After a moment Humayun returned his attention to the messenger. 'Tell me more.'

'Sher Shah is claiming large Moghul territories for himself. He has also declared himself leader of all Hindustani resistance to the Moghuls and has vowed to free Hindustan of every prince of the house of Timur. Even the proudest chieftains have become his retainers. Here – I bring you a letter from your brother which tells you everything that has happened – how far Sher Shah has advanced, how many chieftains have declared their support for him . . .' The man held out a camel-skin pouch.

'Give it to my vizier. I will read it later, when I have rested.'

The man looked startled but at once handed the pouch to Kasim.

'Kasim – see that this man is given food and water and lodgings in the fort.' But Kasim too seemed to be looking at him strangely. He didn't understand that there was no point in rushing to take action. Later – when his mind had cleared – Humayun would think what to do. 'Go now. Leave me in peace.'

As the doors closed behind Kasim and the messenger, Humayun glanced out through the casement. The perfect orange disc of the sun was rising into a cloudless sky. The red sandstone of the fort glowed as if it were about to burst into flame. Humayun rubbed his eyes and signalled to his attendants to lower the woven grass *tatti* screens to block out the relentless brightness that was making his head throb. The news of Sher Shah was bad and he must respond, but first he must sleep and to do that needed something to soothe his mind. He went over to a carved rosewood cabinet, unlocked it and took out a bottle of Gulrukh's wine. This would help, wouldn't it? He pulled out the stopper but then remembered that he would need a clear head later in the morning to decide what to do about Sher Shah. But perhaps it wouldn't really matter if the decision waited until the afternoon. He poured some of Gulrukh's mixture into an agate cup. A few minutes later he was drifting softly away but almost at once some sort of commotion again intruded into his dreams.

'Raise the *tattis* and leave me alone with the emperor,' came an angry female voice. 'Humayun.' Now it was shouting his name and

76

seemed to be drawing closer. 'Humayun!' He sat up with a gasp as a deluging mass of cold water brought him back to consciousness. Forcing his eyes open he saw Khanzada standing by the side of his bed, an empty brass ewer in her hand and eyes full of anger.

'What d'you want?' Humayun gazed at her stupidly, uncertain whether she was real or some sort of hallucination.

'Get up. You are a warrior – an emperor – but I find you lounging here in the dark in a drugged stupor like a *haram* eunuch at a time when your empire is in danger . . . I have just learned of the arrival of Askari's messenger and of the news he brought. Why haven't you summoned your council immediately?'

'I will when I am ready . . .'

'Look at you!' Khanzada seized a mirror set with rubies and thrust it before him. Reflected in the burnished surface he saw a pallid face and dark, distant eyes with dilated pupils and deep, almost purple bags beneath them. He continued to stare, fascinated by the features that seemed so familiar, but Khanzada ripped the mirror from his hand and flung it against the wall, causing the metal to buckle and several of the rubies to fall from their mounts. They lay on the floor like drops of blood.

Kneeling before him, Khanzada took Humayun by the shoulders. 'Opium is destroying your mind . . . You do not even recognise yourself in the mirror, do you? Do I have to remind you who you are . . . do I have to tell you of your bravery and the battles you won on your father's behalf and of your destiny and duty to the Moghul dynasty? Have you forgotten everything that made you – us – the descendants of Timur – who we are? I've tried to warn you before that you are losing your grip on reality but you would not listen. Now I must force you to. The same blood that runs through your veins flows through mine also. I fear nothing except the loss of everything your father – my brother – fought and suffered for.'

What was she saying? Suddenly she let go of him and, leaning back, hit his face with the full force of her right hand. Again and again she struck – first the right and then the left side of his face. Tears were streaming down her cheeks.

'Be as you once were. Be the man your father made his heir,' she was shouting. 'Abandon this cocoon of ritual and opium that is alienating your nobles and compromising your ability to rule. You are a warrior like your father. Stop worrying about what the stars say and whether you can live up to Babur, just do it!'

She had stopped striking him but the stinging pain was clearing the fog in his mind. The words that – when she had first begun speaking – had seemed to have no meaning were beginning to make some sense. Round and round in his mind they went and with them images of the past that they conjured – the visceral excitement he had always felt in the heat of battle or wrestling with his nobles or galloping out to the hunt with Babur. That whole, vibrant, physical world to which he had once belonged . . .

'Give up the opium, Humayun . . . it is destroying you. Where are you keeping it?'

Kasim's gentle words of warning began to come back to him from many months ago when Kasim and Baisanghar had given advice in his stead to the envoy of his governor in Bengal. If he had talked to the man himself might he have caught some nuance or given some guidance that might have prevented Sher Shah's rebellion? Or perhaps Sher Shah had somehow come to learn of his lack of interest in what happened in Bengal. Humayun's hand went slowly to the locket around his neck. Unclasping it, he handed it to Khanzada. Then, equally slowly, he walked over to the still open cabinet where he kept Gulrukh's opium-infused wine. As he reached inside for the bottle, the dark, almost purple liquid inside glinted. It had brought him so much pleasure, so much knowledge . . . revealed so much to marvel at. Could it really be the destructive force that Kasim and Khanzada claimed?

'My father took opium . . .' he said slowly, turning the flask.

'Yes, but not like you . . . Babur never let it control him or dictate his actions. He never neglected his trusted band of comrades, his commanders and his courtiers in its favour. But in you it has enslaved an emperor. You have become addicted . . . just like the man who cannot taste a cup of wine without wanting to empty the entire wineskin. You must give it up, Humayun, or it will destroy you. You will lose the empire your father gained. Renounce opium now before it is too late.'

Still he gazed at the liquid in the bottle with all its hidden secrets and delights. But then he looked up at Khanzada's face, still wet with tears, and saw how strained she looked and how afraid. And he knew that that fear was for him and for the dynasty of which she was a part and for which she had suffered. Slowly the realisation that she was right, that Kasim was right, that all the others who had expressed concern were right, penetrated the opium fumes in his mind. He must be strong – strong within himself. He had no need of outside props. Suddenly more than anything he wanted to regain Khanzada's respect, her approval. The thought of how he had treated her and his closest advisers in recent months made him ashamed.

'Give me the bottle, Humayun.'

'No, Aunt.' Going to the casement, he poured the liquid away to splash on the ground below; then, flinging the bottle after it, he heard the faint, fragile tinkle as it shattered. 'I will tell Gulrukh that I will accept no more of her drugged wine. I swear to you, on this ring of Timur, that however hard it may be I will take no more opium or wine. I will send her to live with one of her sons. And I will prove anew to myself and to you that I am worthy of my father's trust.'

Khanzada took his face between her hands and kissed him. 'I will help you conquer this addiction. Opium has such a grip that it will not be easy. You are a great man, Humayun, a great leader – I have always known that – and you will become a greater one.'

'And I have always known that you are my most trusted confidante.'

'And now?'

'Stay with me while I send for the messenger and question him again. I want you to hear what he says. If it is true, I must prepare immediately for war.'

Later that day, Humayun sat on his throne. Before him were his courtiers and commanders. As he had ordered they were no longer dressed in clothing matching the planet governing the day – neither was he. Khanzada was right. The rituals he had imposed had brought neither harmony nor strength to his court. He must win the respect and allegiance of his nobles in other ways. And one of those would be by victory in the field.

'You have all heard the news brought by the messenger Kamal. Sher Shah's invasion of Moghul territories is an affront to our honour that I will not tolerate. As soon as the army is ready, we will ride against this upstart. And when I have finished with Sher Shah I will trade him into slavery, just as Sher Shah's ancestors used to trade a worn-out horse to the knacker's men.'

As Humayun finished speaking, a great roar went up around the audience chamber that in recent months had fallen so silent. Humayun's commanders were clashing their swords on their shields in the age-old tradition of their people and their deep voices were taking up the chant, 'Mirza Humayun, Mirza Humayun', that proclaimed him of Timur's blood. Humayun glanced up at the grille in the wall to one side of his throne behind which he knew Khanzada would be watching and listening, and smiled. All would be well. The Moghul emperor was leading his armies to war once more. However lacking in the arts of peace he might have proved, he had demonstrated his skills as a general, hadn't he?

Part II

In the Eye of the Tiger

Chapter 6

The Water-Carrier

An hour after dawn, Humayun made his way from his private chambers out through the courtyards of the red sandstone Agra fort with their marble pools and splashing fountains, through the high gateway and on to the parade ground where his army was drawn up. He was dressed for war with an etched silver breastplate set with rubies on his chest over a coat of silver chain mail. His father Babur's eagle-hilted sword, Alamgir, was in its sapphire-encrusted scabbard at his side. On his head was a domed helmet, again decorated with rubies and with a tall peacock feather set in gold waving from its peak.

As he emerged from the iron-studded gate and progressed towards the stand at the centre of the parade ground where his imperial elephant – the usual conveyance for emperors and generals on ceremonial journeys – was waiting, he saw that the vanguard of his troops had already raised so much pink-grey dust as they marched out that the sun was only a pale, beige disc, all the intensity of its glare lost. The large grey elephant was on its knees with its great gilded red-canopied howdah securely positioned on its back and its two drivers or *mahouts* standing by its head. His senior officers were grouped in order of rank on either side of the elephant. After accepting low bows of greetings from each of his commanders Humayun paused to address them.

'Bear this message to your men from me. Our cause is just. We go to recover what is ours from this ill-bred, upstart usurper. How can anyone who has seen our army doubt that it is the greatest in history and invincible? Bid the men be of good cheer. Victory and its comrades, fame and reward, will accompany us.'

The officers bowed once more and placing one foot on the crouching elephant's knee Humayun climbed into the howdah and sat on a small gilded throne. He was followed immediately by two of his bodyguards and by Jauhar. At a sign from Humayun to the *mahouts* they too mounted and, positioning themselves one behind the other on the elephant's neck, whispered instructions into its large ears. The obedient great beast rose slowly and gently to its feet and Humayun gave orders for the trumpets to sound the signal for his elephant and those bearing his generals to move off. As they advanced to take their place in the column they passed the artillery – large cannon with bronze barrels nearly twenty feet long mounted on four wheels, some pulled by teams of up to fifty oxen, others by six or eight elephants. Smaller cannon were on carts also drawn by oxen.

Next Humayun moved along the serried ranks of his cavalry – first the mounted warriors from his father's homelands, Tajiks, Badakhshanis, men from the Kyrgyz mountains and Ferghana Valley, as well as those of Afghanistan. Theirs were the strongest horses, still bred from those they had brought from the steppes. Theirs too, he believed, was the strongest loyalty to the Moghul dynasty. After them he saw the orange garb of some of his Rajput vassals. Eager as all Rajputs were said to be for battle, these imposing, black-bearded men beat their swords on their small, round, studded shields in martial greeting as Humayun passed.

As he saluted each contingent in turn, Humayun reflected that victory would indeed surely be his. He had a quarter of a million soldiers – far more than Sher Shah. He had at least ten times more cannon and – as he had proved during his campaign in Gujarat – he himself was an able general blessed by fortune. Therefore he had granted the request from his aunt Khanzada to accompany the army on the march and to bring with her his bright-eyed, quick-witted half-sister Gulbadan. Amid such a protecting host they would face no more danger than at Agra, which he was leaving in the loyal and capable hands of Kasim and his grandfather Baisanghar. He would be glad of his aunt's experienced advice but also of her support should he ever feel the temptation to lose himself in opium once more. She would not permit it.

He had also allowed himself the luxury of taking with him Salima and three of his other favourite concubines. His renunciation of wine and opium had only served to increase his appetite for the soft, sensual pleasures of the *haram*. The three young women he had chosen – Melita of the flexible, wanton body from Gujarat, the voluptuous full-lipped, full-breasted Mehrunissa from Lahore and witty, puckish and inventive Meera from Agra itself – were each, like Salima with her supple body, soft mouth and agile tongue, in their different ways experts in the arts of love. What relaxation amid the stress of preparation for battle they would bring him, what pleasures in his victory. The women would ride in curtained howdahs on sedate elephants and be guarded by the most trusted of his bodyguard.

◆

Just after the time of the midday meal six weeks later, Humayun's chief scout Ahmed Khan approached his scarlet command tent, erected as usual in the very centre of the camp. Here Humayun was relaxing on a gold brocade mattress topped with maroon cushions, a cooling sherbet in his hands as he listened to the soft cadences of Jauhar's flute. As Ahmed Khan entered, Humayun signalled to Jauhar to cease playing.

'What is it, Ahmed Khan?'

'Majesty, despite exploring for fifty miles around our camp we were unable to detect any sign of Sher Shah's armies. However, we came upon a small landowner in his mud fortress about forty-five or so miles to the southeast of here. He claimed to be a vassal of Sher Shah but one who feared that his master had overreached himself in rebelling against you. He had not therefore hurried to join Sher Shah's army. He told us that to his knowledge Sher Shah was at least another fifty miles away beyond the point at Allahbad where the Jumna and the Ganges meet. He said he would be happy to accompany us here to tell you what he knew. We took him at his word and brought him, blindfolded of course to prevent his seeing anything of the direction of our camp or the strength of our army. We arrived just an hour ago and I have arranged that he should be given food while I discovered whether you wished to speak to him.'

'You've done well. Bring him to me in half an hour.'

Exactly thirty minutes later, Ahmed Khan – well aware of Humayun's penchant for precision – was back. Behind him, between two well-armed guards, was a short, slightly stout, dark-skinned man of about forty, dressed all in dark green with a turban of the same colour. Unprompted, he bowed low before Humayun.

'Who are you?'

'Tariq Khan, *takhaldar* of Ferozepur.'

'And you're a vassal of Sher Shah?'

'Yes – and he has always been a good master to me . . . but above all I am a loyal subject of yourself, my ultimate overlord, Majesty. Sher Shah has been foolish to rebel.'

'Insolent and disrespectful, insulting the rightful order, you mean to say . . . But what do you know of his whereabouts and intentions?'

'His armies did not pass directly through my own territories but they did traverse those of my cousin twenty miles to the north of mine. He said Sher Shah's army was small – no more than eighty thousand men. My cousin paid his respects to him in his camp. He told me Sher Shah seemed shocked that he had provoked you to action with such a vast army. He told my cousin he would not fight if he could negotiate a peace with you under which he retained his lands as your vassal once more.'

'Did your cousin learn anything of his future movements?'

'One of Sher Shah's scouts indiscreetly told my cousin's vizier that they were heading for the low-lying jungles and marshes of Bengal where – if they had to fight – they might be better able to withstand your might.'

'Before I discuss what you have said with my council, have you anything else to add?'

'Only that should Your Majesty wish to test Sher Shah's resolution by offers of peace, I am prepared to accompany any emissary you send and undertake to bring him safely to Sher Shah's camp and into his presence.'

'I will consider this. Now, Ahmed Khan, blindfold him once more and keep him in close but comfortable confinement in your headquarters. Jauhar, summon my council to meet me here an hour before sunset. In the meantime ask Salima to join me.' In the heat his lust rose quickly, Humayun thought, and twice as often as in the cool. She would know how to slake it and clear his mind to concentrate on the discussions ahead.

Salima, as always, did her work well. When his council assembled, Humayun felt relaxed, almost ready to purr like some great tiger, as he addressed his advisers. 'You have heard about Tariq Khan and his reports that Sher Shah is headed deep into the jungles of Bengal to avoid confronting us and that – regretting his presumption – he may be amenable to negotiations for peace. What do you think?'

'There's no question we have the stronger army. Let us simply find and destroy him,' said Baba Yasaval, his lock of grey hair swinging from his shaved head as he looked around at his fellow commanders.

'But wait,' said Humayun's cousin Suleiman Mirza. 'If we have the stronger army and we trust in our men's loyalty, what do we lose by delaying long enough to send an ambassador? They'll be back in plenty of time for us – if needed – to advance again before the monsoon arrives in two months.'

'It's still better to crush him now.' Baba Yasaval was adamant. 'Making an example of him will deter other rebels.'

'But we will lose troops and time we could spend in other campaigns to enlarge our empire. I've always hankered to ride south across the Deccan Plateau to the diamond mines of Golconda,' said Suleiman Mirza.

'I agree,' said Yunus Pathan, one of Humayun's best generals, quietly. 'Sher Shah is said to be an able administrator and Bengal is a rich, fertile province. If we kill him and his chief courtiers, we will need to spend time setting up new structures and appointing new officials. If we reach an agreement with him from our position of strength we can use him and his administration to raise taxes quickly to pay for our armies and reward our troops, and move on to Golconda.'

Humayun pondered. Yunus Pathan's words were persuasive. Besides, being magnanimous was the mark of a great ruler. Humayun rose. 'Suleiman Mirza, go with Tariq Khan and a small escort to locate Sher Shah and offer him peace, provided he comes and makes full obeisance and compensates us richly for our time and expense and above all for the disgraceful insult he has shown us.'

• ◆ •

But Sher Shah did not respond immediately. Weeks passed while he procrastinated, sending profuse apologies for delay and repeated requests to be permitted to send messengers to consult allies before finally agreeing to any terms. So it was that in mid-summer 1539, Humayun was sitting after dinner in Khanzada's tent placed near his own in the very middle of his vast encampment covering more than four square miles near the settlement of Chausa in Bengal. Humayun had had the camp erected on low hillocks overlooking the muddy flood plain of the Ganges delta. Outside, the night was hot and the smoke from the camp fires rose vertically into the still air. Inside the tent, whose sides were down to protect the women from prying eyes, the air was stifling. Despite the best efforts of Khanzada's attendants to trap them using bowls of sugar water or to crush them with their fly swats, mosquitoes buzzed ceaselessly. Humayun, sweating profusely, occasionally felt their sharp bite on his exposed flesh and slapped futilely at his small attackers.

'What is it, Humayun? You've hardly spoken all through the meal,' Khanzada asked.

'I'm worried that Sher Shah is playing me for a fool, that I've allowed too much time to pass by. Suleiman Mirza and Tariq Khan assure me that on each visit he has been courteous and humble and seems sincere but I am no longer certain. Was I wrong to trust so entirely in Tariq Khan? What if he was planted by Sher Shah in an effort to gain himself time?'

Khanzada rose and paced for a moment or two, face grave in the

88

golden glow of the wicks burning in their pools of oil in the saucer-shaped brass *diyas*.

'I think you're right to be suspicious. Victory doesn't always go to the strongest but sometimes to the most wily. You have advanced many miles down the Ganges over these last nine weeks, ready to meet Sher Shah either in battle or in council, but each time he has moved further off, using trifling excuses that he's exhausted the food in the region or that there's an epidemic of fever he must avoid.'

'True. Latest reports are that his main army is still thirty miles away along the Ganges.'

'What will you do?'

'Accept no more excuses, set deadlines for Sher Shah and if he doesn't meet them I'll attack. But I'm concerned that these jungles and marshes are ill-suited to the easy passage of my cannon and large forces of cavalry.'

'Then have the courage to retreat to better terrain. Or else consider bypassing Sher Shah's forces and occupying his cities . . .' A single crash of thunder interrupted Khanzada's words. It was followed by the rapid pattering of rain on the tent roof.

'The monsoon can't have broken – it's too early.'

'Nature's rhythms are not always bounded by man's calendars.'

'If it is the monsoon, we must definitely seek out better ground. But it's late and it'll be time enough to decide in the morning when we know if the rains are continuing. The camp is too high above the river for there to be any danger of flooding in the meantime.'

Several hours later Humayun was lying asleep on his back, his arms spread wide, his perspiring muscled body naked beneath the thin cotton sheet. He had taken a long time to fall asleep, listening to the rain which seemed to be growing heavier rather than slackening. Now he was dreaming he was back in the Agra fort, moving towards his concubines' quarters where for some reason he knew they would be bathing beneath rosewater fountains. He felt his body harden with desire and his legs thrashed beneath the thin sheet as in his dreams he quickened his steps, eager to reach his women. Suddenly a female scream penetrated deep into his imaginings. A rising crescendo

of male and female voices followed. One cried, 'To arms! Hurry –
no time to put armour on. Reinforce the perimeter.'

Struggling to full consciousness, Humayun realised the voices were
real. Raiders must have got as far as the women's quarters. Tying a
robe about him and reaching for his father's sword, he stumbled
from his tent. It was still raining hard and his bare feet slipped in
the wet mud. Peering through the heavy, slanting raindrops and
desperately trying to adjust his eyes to the darkness, he ran towards
Khanzada's tent.

As he got nearer he made out by the steely flashes of the almost
constant sheet lightning a tall, female figure – Khanzada. Her right
hand was raised high above her head and in it was a curved sword.
As he watched, she brought it down across the face of an assailant
who was trying to subdue her. The man fell to the ground where
he lay writhing in pain. By the next lightning flash, Humayun saw
that his aunt's sword had slashed open the man's face all down one
side, bloodily exposing his jaw and teeth. He also saw that – unknown
to Khanzada – another attacker was behind her. He held not a sword
but a large scarf which he was about to throw over her head and
to pull tight around her neck. Humayun shouted a warning.

Suddenly realising the danger, Khanzada pulled her arm back and
elbowed the man in the throat but he did not fall and continued
to try to tighten the cloth. By now Humayun was near enough to
launch himself upon her assailant and, grappling with him, to force
him to the ground. For a moment they struggled in the glossy, oozing
mud, each grasping for advantage. Then Humayun succeeded in
pushing his right thumb into his opponent's left eye and pressing
hard he felt the eyeball burst liquidly beneath the force. The man
instinctively relaxed his grip as the pain ran through him, and
Humayun took Alamgir and thrust it deep into his opponent's groin,
leaving the man screaming and bleeding into the muddy puddle in
which he lay dying.

Although the noises of battle still reached Humayun's ears from
around the distant perimeter of his camp, by now his bodyguards
seemed to have subdued the rest of the men who had attacked the
women's quarters. There had only been about twenty or so. All had

worn dark clothing and seemed to have penetrated the heart of the camp by stealth while a stronger force assaulted the periphery. Only one remained alive.

Running over to him where he was held, arms pinioned and on his knees, by two guards, Humayun, face contorted with rage, grabbed the man by the throat, hauled him to his feet and pushing his own face into his screamed, 'Why did you do this? No honourable enemy attacks women. Their lives should be protected by all, whatever the circumstances. Our religion demands it, as do all the moral decencies. You will die anyway but if you speak it will be quick – if you do not it will be long and lingering and so exquisitely painful you will beg for the death that is so slow in coming.'

'We did not intend to kill the women but to kidnap them, particularly your aunt. Tariq Khan told us she was with you and the story of her capture by Shaibani Khan is well known to all. Sher Shah said if we took her you might be prepared to come to terms to spare her a second ordeal.'

So Tariq Khan had indeed betrayed him. In his anger and dismay at his own stupidity, Humayun tightened his fingers around the prisoner's throat and placing his thumbs on his Adam's apple twisted his neck until he heard a crack and the death rattle bubble through the man's throat. Throwing the body aside, he ran – bare feet again slipping in the mud – back to Khanzada. She was standing sword still in hand looking surprisingly composed while the rain streamed down her face and reduced her long greying hair, unbound for sleep, to a series of rats' tails.

'I am sorry not to have protected you better – are you injured?'

'Not at all. I think I have proved I too am of Timur's blood, like you and my brother Babur. When the attack came, I felt anger and outrage, not fear. I knew I must protect Gulbadan and your young concubines. I told them to collapse the tent poles and to remain hidden in the material until they were sure the danger had passed. Look over there. They're just emerging.'

Sure enough Humayun could see through the pouring rain Salima crawling from beneath the vast, enveloping folds of the tent, followed by young Gulbadan and the other women. Humayun embraced

Khanzada and as he did so he realised that, now the immediate danger was over and the hot blood of battle was ebbing from her, she was beginning to shake.

'Send Ahmed Khan to me, Jauhar, and find out if we can still launch boats on the Ganges. If so, have several prepared as fast as the sailors can so that my aunt, sister and concubines can be rowed upriver to safety. Make sure an escort is readied too. Go now.'

Almost immediately Jauhar had left, Ahmed Khan ran up.

'How is our perimeter withstanding these attacks?' asked Humayun.

'Well, Majesty. After their fierce initial assault in which they made severe inroads, the enemy seemed to hold back for a while as if waiting for something.'

'To learn the success of their raid on the women's tents . . .' muttered Humayun. 'They won't keep back for long. But it might give us enough time to prop up our defences.'

'Majesty. The passage upriver is clear. We've boats ready and a double crew of rowers for each,' the breathless returning Jauhar broke in. 'A strong detachment of cavalry is mounted and ready to ride along the north bank to accompany them.'

Humayun turned to Khanzada. 'Aunt, you must go now. I trust in you to protect yourself and the other women. I appoint you to command the boats. Jauhar, tell the soldiers and sailors that however strange they find it to obey a woman's commands, they must do so or face my wrath.'

'They will have no need of Jauhar's words,' said Khanzada's determined voice. 'They will obey Babur's sister. We will meet again when you have your victory. Bring me the head of that slippery-tongued traitor Tariq Khan, and Sher Shah bound to serve as my latrine cleaner.' With that she turned and swiftly picked her way over the mud to Gulbadan and the other women, then led them towards the riverbank, soon disappearing into the rain and gloom.

How brave she was, Humayun thought. How strong the blood of Timur ran in her slight and no longer youthful body. He had been foolish, oh so foolish, to trust in Tariq Khan and to believe in Sher Shah's crafty delaying answers. Why hadn't he questioned their motives more rigorously? Had he been too content to relax into the pleasures of the *haram*? Now he must redeem his lapses of mental concentration by his physical courage and use it to inspire his men to victory.

'Ahmed Khan, get further reports from our defences. Jauhar, bring me my armour, then saddle my horse.'

In the quarter of an hour it took Humayun to ready himself fully for battle, it had begun to grow light. Several of his commanders, led by Baba Yasaval, had joined him. 'The situation is serious, Majesty. Sher Shah is attacking with renewed force. We cannot move the cannon into firing positions. Look over there.' Following the direction of his officer's pointing arm, Humayun saw a number of his artillerymen lashing a double team of oxen yoked to one of his largest bronze guns in an attempt to turn it to face the enemy threat. But however hard they were hit, however much they were cajoled, the great beasts stumbled and slipped in the mud, sinking ever deeper into the quagmire. When the men added their own weight to that of the animals, they too could make no impression, some simply falling full length in the churned brown mud.

'Majesty, it's the same with all the guns,' said Baba Yasaval.

'I believe you. Besides, the downpour is such it'll be difficult for either the gunners or the musketeers to keep the gunpowder dry or light their fuses. We must rely on our bravery in close combat with the old weapons of cold steel. We still have many more men than our enemies. Get the officers to marshal them in the best defensive positions they can improvise. Use the wagons and tents as barricades ...' Humayun paused and then – still conscious of the perilous position of his aunt and the other women and that it was his complacency and naive gullibility that had exposed them to danger – commanded, 'Send another strong detachment of cavalry – ten thousand men including half my own bodyguard – back along the riverbank to add to the protection of the royal women.'

'But we need them here, Majesty.'

'Don't question my orders. It's a matter of honour to save them.'

Baba Yasaval did not argue further but despatched a messenger with the instruction.

'Now, Baba Yasaval, where will my presence help the most?'

'Over there to the northwest, Majesty. Enemy cavalry broke through our pickets and attacked our infantry while they were still in their tents and killed many before they could defend themselves. Some ran away. Only by rushing reinforcements of Badahkshanis and Tajiks into position have we been able to hold the line, and even then only some distance back from our original perimeter.'

'To the northwest then.' Humayun mounted his black stallion and, with the half of his bodyguard that he had not sent to protect the women around him, made his way over to the northwest defences as fast as he could. In the muddy conditions the horses sometimes sank up to their hocks. When one rider tried to push his mount too hard, it stumbled and fell, fracturing a hind leg which had stuck in the mud.

Approaching the area of his camp which had become the front lines, Humayun saw that his commanders had got howdahs on to a dozen war elephants and brought them forward. Protected by the canopies of the howdahs from the seemingly unceasing rain some of his musketeers had actually succeeded in priming and firing their long-barrelled weapons and bringing down into the mud a few of Sher Shah's attackers. Taking a little heart from their success, small bands of his infantry were firing volleys of arrows from the cover of overturned baggage wagons and forcing Sher Shah's men, in turn, to shelter behind five of Humayun's large cannon which they had overrun in their first assault.

As he reached the forward position, Humayun shouted to his men. 'Thank you, my brave soldiers one and all. You've blunted the enemy's attack. Now it is time to recover our great cannon. To allow Sher Shah's rabble to carry them off would be a dishonour. I will lead you. Elephant drivers advance. Musketeers, shoot down more of those insolent rebels for me.'

Humayun waited impatiently for the elephants to begin to move forward. Eventually they did so, lurching through the mud and making the howdahs on their backs sway so much that it was difficult for the musketeers to steady their weapons to shoot accurately. Humayun waved his horsemen forward too. As they approached the captured cannon, Humayun saw a group of Sher Shah's gunners run from the shelter of one of the largest bronze cannons towards a beige-coloured tent belonging to Humayun's infantry that had apparently remained standing after his men had retreated. Suddenly these gunners pulled away the front of the tent to reveal a sixth captured cannon that they had somehow managed to drag inside the tent and to get dry enough to fire. Immediately an artilleryman, who had been hidden within the tent, applied a light to the fuse.

With a loud bang and lots of billowing white smoke, the ball flew from the cannon's mouth, hitting the foremost of Humayun's advancing elephants squarely in its great domed forehead. Mortally wounded, the elephant at once fell sideways, dislodging its howdah and throwing the musketeers, arms and legs flailing, to the ground. The elephant behind panicked and ran forward, squashing one of the fallen musketeers into the mud beneath its feet. As he struggled to regain control of his charge, which had its head back and grey trunk raised and was trumpeting in fear, one of this elephant's two drivers also tumbled from its neck but the other held on and seemed to be succeeding in restraining his mount.

However, by now all Humayun's attention was on the cannon which had fired the shot. The gunners were frantically trying to reload it. They had taken a linen bag of powder from the metal chest which had kept it dry and succeeded in ramming it down the cannon barrel. Two of them were struggling to lift a metal cannon ball, ready to roll it down the barrel after the powder, when Humayun reached them. Bending low from the saddle of his black horse, Humayun's first stroke with Alamgir almost severed the arm of one of the men lifting the ball. He fell to the ground together with the cannon ball, blood spurting from his wound. Humayun cut at the face of the other man but the gunner got his arm up to protect it. Nevertheless, his arm was badly gashed and, turning, he began to run. He had got no more than a couple of paces before Humayun's sword caught him in the flesh at the back of his neck, above his chain mail and below his domed steel helmet, and he too crumpled to the ground. By this time Humayun's bodyguard had killed or put to flight the remainder of the enemy gunners and his musketeers were dismounting from the elephants.

'Good work. Order the remaining infantry to advance to protect the cannon. Our success will give them renewed confidence. I must return to the centre of the camp.'

With that, Humayun turned his horse, which was already blowing hard from its charge through the clinging mud, towards his scarlet command tent. Visibility had much improved as the rain, which had slackened during his attack on the guns, had by now almost ceased. From the centre he would be able to direct a further strengthening of his position, Humayun thought.

However, he had covered scarcely half the distance to his tent when Jauhar galloped up. 'Majesty,' he gasped, 'Baba Yasaval asked me to beg your presence on the far southwestern perimeter. A large force of Sher Shah's cavalry is attacking along the bank of the Ganges. They have already broken through our front lines and the vanguard are deep among our makeshift secondary defences.'

Immediately Humayun pulled the head of his black horse round and the willing beast, responding to his urging, began to pick up pace towards the west past the neat lines of tents hastily abandoned by Humayun's men as they had rushed earlier to repel the unexpected attackers. He was followed by Jauhar and his bodyguards.

Very soon Humayun could hear increasing cries and sounds of battle and then, breasting a low rise, he looked down on the wide, muddy banks of the Ganges and a scene of chaos. Several bands of Sher Shah's cavalry had breached his front line and his own cavalry were trying to encircle them or drive them back. Other mounted officers, waving their swords, were encouraging groups of his infantry forward to fill gaps in the defences but they seemed to be having only limited success. Indeed some of the infantrymen were fleeing towards the rear, throwing down the small round shields and the long spears with which they were armed.

Most ominously of all, only a mile or so from his wavering defences another large force of Sher Shah's cavalry was forming up to launch a further attack. At their centre was a knot of bright flags and pennants and to Humayun it seemed obvious that Sher Shah was there, ready to lead this charge in person finally to overwhelm his enemies.

'We've only got a short time to prepare to confront them, Jauhar. Where are Baba Yasaval and my other commanders?'

'When I left to find you, Majesty, Baba Yasaval was a little further along this rise with some of his junior officers. But he told me the situation was so perilous that he could not wait for your arrival but would straight away lead an attack on some of the enemy cavalry that had already broken through. Isn't that his yellow flag at the head of those riders over there, driving that group of our enemy before them?'

'You have good eyes, Jauhar. Get a message to him to bring as many men as he can detach to meet me by that cluster of grey tents over there. Send further messengers to summon any other officers who can break off from the action to lead their men there too. We'll meet Sher Shah's advance head on. The ground around those tents looks firm enough for us to be able to get up enough speed to do them some damage with the weight of our initial charge.'

Only ten minutes later Humayun had a number of his officers around him. He was saddened how many including Baba Yasaval – who was helmetless and had a bloody, yellow cloth wound around his head – were wounded, and even more how many were missing. 'Where is Suleiman Mirza?'

'Dead, Majesty, killed by a spear thrust as he attempted to fight off cavalry.'

'And Ahmed Khan?'

'Badly wounded. In the very first minutes of Sher Shah's attack while he was inspecting the pickets two arrows hit him in the thigh. Some of his men found him weak from loss of blood and got him over to the opposite side of the Ganges along with other wounded. They're being cared for by the men you stationed there.'

'We must manage without these brave officers, trusting in our own courage and in our destiny.'

Looking round, Humayun saw that his commanders had assembled a sizeable force, perhaps as many as five thousand riders, to confront Sher Shah's next attack which, from the increasing movement amongst his opponents' ranks, would not be long delayed.

'As soon as Sher Shah's lines advance, so too do we. Make for the centre where I believe he will ride himself. If we can kill or capture him, his men will become demoralised. Despite our losses the day will be ours . . .'

Moments later, Sher Shah put his cavalry into motion, galloping increasingly quickly towards Humayun's defences. Humayun took Alamgir from its jewelled scabbard and waving it above his head yelled, 'Charge! Let it be a matter of honour to die rather than to retreat.'

Soon his whole force was galloping as fast as the mud and puddles would allow. Humayun's tall black horse, despite its previous efforts, kept him at the head of his troops, closing fast with his opponents who were themselves racing forward, weapons extended, shouting 'Tiger, Tiger' in celebration of their leader, Sher Shah.

All his thoughts now concentrated on the coming fight, Humayun bent low over his stallion's neck and kept its head aimed at the very centre of Sher Shah's galloping ranks where he saw a black-bearded man in bright steel armour on a white horse shouting encouragement to those around him as he rode. It could only be Sher Shah himself. Humayun pulled on his reins once more to bring him directly into Sher Shah's path. Within seconds the two lines clashed. Humayun slashed at Sher Shah with Alamgir but the sword slid harmlessly off his steel breastplate and in a moment the press of forces had separated them.

Suddenly, Humayun thought he saw the traitorous Tariq Khan mounted on a brown horse and wearing his familiar dark green beneath his armour. Humayun urged his own mount towards him. Although hampered by the disorganised mass of wheeling, rearing and snorting horses with their riders slashing and striking at each other, Humayun reached the green-clad man. It was indeed Tariq Khan.

'Tariq Khan, your life is forfeit. Face me and die like a man, not the slippery snake you are.' With that, Humayun struck at Tariq Khan but his opponent quickly got his shield up and deflected the blow and at the same time swung wildly at Humayun with his double-headed steel battleaxe. Humayun leaned back in his saddle and the axe only hissed through empty air but Humayun thrust Alamgir deep into Tariq Khan's unprotected armpit, exposed as he made his axe-sweep. With a cry of pain Tariq Khan dropped the axe and, as blood poured from his armpit staining his dark green clothing, he seemed to lose control of his brown horse which carried him off into the mêlée. Moments later, Humayun saw him fall, sliding backwards from the saddle of his rearing mount to be trampled into the muddy ground beneath the hooves of other horses. So perish all traitors, thought Humayun.

Looking round, he realised most of his bodyguards had lost touch with him, but shouting hoarsely to the few who remained to follow he turned his own black horse, now covered with white, frothing sweat, towards where he calculated Sher Shah's charge might have taken him. As he pushed forward, a riderless horse, blood streaming from a deep sword slash to the rump, crashed into the right flank of his own, knocking it off course and for a moment painfully trapping Humayun's mail-clad thigh against his saddle. Then, neighing shrilly, it careered away, veering straight across the path of one of Humayun's remaining bodyguards. The bodyguard's horse stumbled and fell, throwing its young rider over its neck on to the ground. He lost his domed helmet on impact, rolled over two or three times and then lay still.

Regaining control of his horse once more, Humayun urged it towards where the fight seemed the most intense. Suddenly thunder crashed overhead and immediately rain began to fall again in torrents, heavy drops splashing into puddles and dripping from the rim of Humayun's helmet before running down into his eyes. He removed his leather gauntlet and raised his right hand to brush the rain away and clear his vision. But his action prevented him from seeing two dark-clad riders dashing towards him until they were almost upon him. When he did, he swerved away from the first but could not prevent the sharp sword of the second slicing into the exposed flesh of his hand and wrist and sliding down into his forearm, pushing back his chain mail and penetrating deeper as it went on. His black horse carried him away from his assailants, who failed to turn quickly enough in the mud to pursue him.

Bright scarlet blood was streaming from Humayun's wounded

right arm and hand and flowing down and through his fingers, coating Timur's ring. He tried to untie his cream neck cloth with his left hand to use it to staunch the wound but he could not. His numb right fingers could scarcely keep a grip on his reins. He began to feel light-headed and white flashes started to appear before his eyes. Through them he could just about make out that there were none of his men around him. The situation was bad but surely he was not destined to end like this? Defeat was not inevitable. He must get back to his men to rally them. Humayun tugged at the reins with the last of his strength, trying to turn his tired, blowing horse in what his blurring mind imagined was the direction of his remaining men. He kicked the horse's sides to urge it on, then slumped forward on to its black neck, clinging to its mane with his left hand as the last remnants of his consciousness deserted him.

◆

'Majesty.'

Humayun's opening eyes throbbed with bright light and he half closed them again. The glare was the same when he tried again. Slowly he realised he was lying on his back staring up into the midday sun.

'Majesty.' The same voice came again and a hand tentatively shook his shoulder. He was no longer wearing armour or chain mail. Where had it gone? Was he captured? He turned his clearing head towards the voice and slowly a nut-brown face came into focus, a concerned, anxious expression on its small features.

'Who are you?'

'My name is Nizam. I'm one of the water-carriers in your army.'

'Where am I?'

'On the banks of the Ganges, Majesty. I was gathering water from the river in my leather bottles to take to your soldiers when I saw your black horse coming slowly towards me from the direction of the battle a mile or so from here, with yourself slumped over its neck. When it got nearer the horse's knees buckled and it collapsed. As it did so, you slid to the ground.'

'Where is the horse now? Where are my men?'

'The horse is over there. It is dead, Majesty, from exhaustion I think, even though it had many small wounds and a larger one to its rump.'

Feeling a little stronger, Humayun raised himself on his left elbow and there indeed was his black stallion no more than twenty paces away lying neck outstretched, tongue lolling. Clusters of green-black flies were already forming around its mouth and nostrils and on its many wounds.

'And my men?'

'Mostly they retreated east down the riverbank closely followed by Sher Shah's force who struck many from their saddles. Some crossed the river where it is low, about a quarter of a mile from here, to the opposite bank where some of your troops still are.'

'Was I not pursued?'

'No. And it's difficult to see this particular place because of the banks and mud spits, so no one has come since. Do you wish to drink, Majesty?'

'Please.' Instinctively Humayun tried to extend his right arm for the bottle. It was stiff and numb. Remembrance of the fight and his wound came back to him. His arm felt bandaged. Looking at it he realised that it was – with the same cream neck cloth he had himself failed to untie, and there seemed to be something like a flat pebble bound against the worst of his wound.

'Help me to drink.'

Nizam took the stopper from one of his large water bottles, which seemed from its size and shape to have been made from the skin of an entire small goat. Supporting Humayun's head, Nizam poured a little into his mouth. Humayun drank quickly, then asked for more. With each gulp he felt life returning to him.

'Did you bind the wound?'

'Yes, Majesty. I have often watched the *hakims* at work after battles and one told me that a small flat stone was good to keep pressure on a cut to stop the loss of lifeblood.'

'It clearly worked. You've done well. How did you know I was your emperor?'

'By your tiger ring and your jewelled sword. I've often been told of them in the camp.'

Humayun was fully conscious now and sitting up realised that he did have both the ring and his father's sword Alamgir, which either he or Nizam had put back into its scabbard.

The midday sun was beating down, causing the wet ground to steam in an eerie semblance of morning mist. Scrutinising his saviour, Humayun saw that Nizam, who was wearing only a rough black cotton tunic, was small, skinny and mud-streaked – probably no more than thirteen or fourteen years old. Nevertheless, he could easily have stripped Humayun of his possessions and run but instead he had loyally stayed with him. Humayun realised that – although defeated as he surely had been – he still deserved his birth name of 'Fortunate' bestowed on him by his father Babur. One defeat was of little matter. Babur had suffered many setbacks. 'It is how you deal with them,' he remembered Babur saying. Then Humayun's head swam again. Pulling himself back to the present, he knew that his first task must be to re-join his army.

'Where are the nearest of my soldiers, Nizam?'

'As I told you, those on this side of the river have mostly retreated far off. But there remain many on the opposite shore – see.' Nizam pointed across the steaming, muddy banks and over the main branch of the Ganges. There Humayun made out a large group of horsemen.

'Are you sure they're mine?'

'Yes, Majesty. The detachment over there has been joined by many from this side.'

Nizam must be right, thought Humayun. He had been wise to take the precaution of stationing a force on the opposite bank to prevent Sher Shah from bypassing his army, crossing the river and attacking him from the rear.

'I must join them.' As he spoke, Humayun scrambled to his feet but his legs shook under him and he again felt dizzy.

'Lean on me, Majesty.'

Humayun gratefully put his left arm on Nizam's bony shoulder. 'Help me down to the river so that I can swim across.'

'But you are too weak. You will drown.'

'I must make the attempt. It would be a great dishonour to be captured.'

Nizam's eyes glanced around and alighted on his two large goatskin water bottles and he looked up into Humayun's face. 'Can you stand for a minute alone, Majesty? I think I have the answer.'

Receiving a nod from Humayun, he ran over to the bottles and pulling out the rough stoppers emptied them. Then, to Humayun's surprise, he took the larger of them, placed the filling hole to his lips and began to blow, dark eyes bulging and thin cheeks puffing out with effort. After some moments, Humayun saw the skin begin to inflate and soon it became taut and full of air. Nizam inserted the stopper and brought it over to Humayun. Then he swiftly blew up the second and, tapping it playfully, smiled. 'That should do. We must hurry, Majesty. Soon Sher Shah's men will be dispersing to look for booty on the corpses of their enemies. I've hidden your armour so that it won't catch the light, but they're bound to inspect the whole shore.'

'I know, but first help me to my brave horse. I must check he is dead or else put him out of his misery. He has served me well.' An inspection quickly satisfied Humayun that the black stallion was indeed dead. Then, leaning on Nizam's shoulder, he slowly picked his way across the hillocks and flats towards the river. He fell at least twice but on each occasion Nizam – already burdened by the inflated water bottles – hauled him to his feet. After ten minutes' struggle, the pair reached the Ganges. Nizam passed the water bottles to Humayun.

'Thank you, Nizam. Now be gone and save yourself.'

'No, Majesty, I will accompany you or else you will drown.'

'Help me off with my boots then,' said Humayun, half sitting, half collapsing on to the bank. Soon Nizam had tugged the heavy boots off and, being all the time barefoot himself, helped Humayun into the water.

'Swim with your legs and your good arm, Majesty. Try to keep one bottle under your right arm and the second beneath your chin. I will help direct you.'

Slowly they succeeded in reaching what to Humayun seemed the middle of the river. His right arm was stinging intensely from contact with the water but the pain had cleared his mind. He mustn't die – it wasn't his destiny – and he kicked harder with his feet. Nizam had clearly been brought up on the water and was pushing and pulling at Humayun to keep him headed for the far shore. A few minutes later, they were only five yards from the south bank when Nizam suddenly became frantic, legs thrashing at the water and arms pulling at Humayun. 'It's a crocodile, Majesty – he must have scented your blood. I saw the snout not far off. Hurry!'

Humayun took another two strokes and, as he put his feet down, soft mud oozed beneath his toes. Summoning his last reserves of strength he staggered, dripping and breathless, from the water, Nizam at his side.

'We must get further up the bank, Majesty.'

With Nizam's help Humayun stumbled another ten yards. From this place of relative safety, he looked back to see the crocodile's amber eyes and snout breaking the surface near the shore. As he watched, the reptile turned and slunk sinuously away into deeper water. Perhaps it had been too small to finish him off but he was glad not to have to find out.

'Majesty, I will find some of your officers, tell them of your plight and ask them to send people to bring you back to your army. Then I must swim back across the river – I need to find my father. He is one of the cooks in your field kitchens and I haven't seen him since Sher Shah's first attack.'

'But you did not mention him till now?'

'I knew it was my duty to help you.'

'You must return to me so I can reward your bravery and your loyalty.'

'No, Majesty – I must find my father,' Nizam replied, his small face set.

A strange thought came into Humayun's head. Impulsively he blurted it out. 'You have been a prince among water-carriers. When I am back in my capital, come to me and you shall sit on my throne and be a true king, giving orders for an hour or two. Whatever you command shall be done.'

Nizam looked puzzled then smiled hesitantly and stammered, 'Yes, Majesty,' before turning and running swiftly over the undulating muddy banks of the Ganges in the direction of Humayun's remaining forces.

Chapter 7

A Promise Kept

Humayun looked around at those of his officers who had re-joined him in his makeshift headquarters twenty miles up the Ganges from Chausa, the site of the battle two days previously. Suleiman Mirza was of course dead and Humayun had taken part in the mullahs' solemn prayers for him and the other fallen. Baba Yasaval was there, however, bandaged more heavily than Humayun himself. So too amazingly was Ahmed Khan, his face pale and drawn above his stringy brown beard. His wounded thigh was strapped and he was leaning on a stout wooden crutch.

Only a few minutes after Nizam had left Humayun on the banks of the Ganges a detachment of his cavalry had reached him. The *hakims* had washed and stitched together the sides of the long, deep wound in his hand and forearm, dressed it with ointments and bound it in fine muslin bandages but he had refused their offer of opium to deaden the pain. He needed more than ever to think clearly. He was pleased to find he could still move his fingers but the wound sometimes felt hot, sometimes numb, and stung unbearably every time it caught against anything. But above all, he was glad to be alive. He had suffered a major defeat but was determined to recover his lost lands just as his father Babur had done when he'd faced adversity.

'Ahmed Khan, what are Sher Shah's latest movements?' he asked.

'He hasn't moved beyond Chausa. He and his men are dividing the contents of our treasure chests and attempting to extricate our cannon from the muddy banks of the Ganges before its waters rise so far that they cover them. Like us, they have lost many men. Others will probably slip off home once they have their booty.'

'You're sure of all this, Ahmed Khan? You failed to warn previously of the imminence of Sher Shah's attack.'

'Yes, Majesty.' Ahmed Khan lowered his head and paused before continuing. 'Like many others I was deluded into thinking that Sher Shah wanted peace. Although I sent out scouts, perhaps I did not send out enough. And perhaps they themselves were not vigilant enough . . . and then there was the weather . . . and the speed of movement of Sher Shah's—'

Humayun held up his hand to halt Ahmed Khan's self-exculpation. Wittingly or not he had been trying to transfer some of the burden of responsibility for what had happened on to the loyal and badly wounded Ahmed Khan. But that was unfair. He was the emperor, the sole commander, the final arbiter in decisions. He had been tormenting himself as he lay on his bed, kept awake by the pain and itching of his wound, as to how he had let this defeat happen. Had he been too trusting, too ready to hear what he wanted to hear without, as Khanzada always urged, seeking the motive? He had been complacent, that he knew, but had his military strategy also been flawed? However, he must not brood too much on the past but rather put the defeat behind him and make sure it did not happen again. Of one thing he was certain. His resolve to rule had grown in the face of setbacks.

'I did not mean to criticise, Ahmed Khan, but make sure we keep as many scouts out as possible on both sides of the river. Have we heard from the troops accompanying my aunt and the other royal women?'

'At least good news from them. They are making excellent progress despite the monsoon and expect to reach Agra in seven or eight weeks.'

'Good.' Turning to Baba Yasaval, Humayun asked, 'What were our losses?'

'Grievous, Majesty. Over fifty thousand men are dead or severely wounded, or have deserted, and we've lost at least that number of horses, elephants and baggage animals. We were able to bring off only a few of the cannon and those were mainly small ones. We lost a good part of the war chest as well as other equipment too.'

'I feared as much. We need time to re-equip and to recruit. We must send ambassadors to reassure our allies before any unwise seeds of rebellion or defection germinate in their minds. Like Sher Shah, we're in no position to renew the conflict immediately. Instead, we should continue our march back along the Ganges. There is no shame in such a retreat if it is a prelude to victory, as we must ensure it is.'

· ◆ ·

Although the rain had ceased and the sun was now shining brightly, producing rainbow effects in the bubbling fountains, the courtyard before Humayun's *durbar* hall, his audience hall, in the Agra fort was still wet and glistening. It was four months since the ill-fated battle at Chausa. Humayun had stationed his main army one hundred and twenty miles south of Agra to block any unexpected advance by Sher Shah while he himself had returned to his capital to rally more allies.

More bad news had greeted him on his arrival in Agra. Bahadur Shah the Sultan of Gujarat and his allies the Lodi pretenders had taken advantage of his preoccupation with Sher Shah in Bengal to re-emerge from their hiding places in the highlands and drive out Humayun's governors and their few men from Gujarat's strongholds. Recognising that he could not fight a war on two fronts, Humayun had sent Kasim, his vizier and veteran of so many perilous ambassadorial missions for his father Babur, to Gujarat to negotiate a peace deal. Humayun would return autonomy to Gujarat provided the sultan nominally at least recognised him as his overlord.

A week ago, a tired, dusty but smiling Kasim had dismounted from his horse and told Humayun that the sultan had agreed to his proposals. And there had been other encouraging developments, Humayun reflected as he moved across the courtyard towards the *durbar* hall where his courtiers and commanders were waiting. His half-brothers had sent small contingents of troops from their provinces, together with promises of much larger contributions. There was no sign – as yet at least – of Kamran and his other half-brothers using his misfortunes to attempt a rising against him, rather Sher Shah's revolt seemed to have brought them together. All would yet be well, Humayun comforted himself, and a half-smile crossed his face.

'Get back. Do not dare approach His Majesty.'

Humayun turned to look behind him where the shout had come from. A tall, black-turbaned guard was gripping a small, struggling figure firmly by the wrists.

'He told me to come – that I could sit on his throne for an hour or two.'

'Have you been touched by the sun? Don't be disrespectful – you'll get yourself flogged at best, crushed beneath the elephant's foot at worst.'

Humayun looked closer at the wriggling figure with the determined voice. It was Nizam, the water-carrier who had saved his life.

'Release him.' The guard did so and Nizam dropped to his knees before Humayun, head bowed.

'You may stand, Nizam. I remember well how you helped me from the battlefield of Chausa and across the Ganges. I also remember how you asked for no reward and – to show my gratitude – I did say that for a short while you could sit on my throne and that any command you gave would be carried out.' Humayun's guards and the courtiers including Kasim and Baisanghar who had been escorting him to the *durbar* hall were exchanging surprised glances but he ignored them. 'Fetch a fitting robe for our temporary emperor,' he ordered Jauhar, who returned a few minutes later with a red velvet robe and a gold-tasselled sash of the same material.

Nizam himself was gazing round the flower-filled courtyard and fountains bubbling with rosewater. His self-confidence seemed to have deserted him and as Jauhar approached him with the robe he recoiled.

'Courage, Nizam.' Humayun patted the youth's shoulder. 'To have your dearest wish fulfilled isn't always easy.' He took the robe

110

from Jauhar and himself helped Nizam into it, fastening the silver clasps at waist and right shoulder and tying the sash around Nizam's slight frame. There should have been something comical about the sight of the shock-headed young water-carrier in the velvet robe, but Nizam drew himself up and the carriage of his head had a dignity.

'Let us proceed.' Humayun nodded to the two drummers stationed outside the *durbar* hall, who at once began to strike with the flats of their hands the tall ox-hide drums resting on their lapis lazuli inlaid golden stands, announcing the coming of the emperor.

'Come Nizam, let us go together – you the emperor of the hour, I the emperor born to carry the burden of leadership to the grave.'

Humayun and Nizam led the procession into the *durbar* hall where Humayun's courtiers and commanders were waiting. As they approached the throne, Humayun stopped and pushed Nizam gently forward. To a huge gasp of surprise, Nizam slowly mounted the throne and, turning, sat down.

Humayun raised his hands for silence. 'I acknowledge before all my court the bravery and loyalty of this youth, Nizam the water-carrier, in saving my life after Chausa. I promised Nizam that for a short while he should sit on my throne and make whatever pronouncements he wished. He has already shown himself honourable and will not, I know, abuse the power that I have put into his hands. Nizam – what are your wishes?'

Humayun was intrigued. What would Nizam ask for? Money, jewels, land? He must know that his life – and that of his family – need never be the same again. It felt good to be able to grant Nizam's wishes.

'Majesty . . .' Nizam's voice from high up on the throne sounded reedy and thin. As if he'd realised it, he tried again. 'Majesty.' This time his young voice rang out, true and clear. 'I have just two commands. That I receive a grant of a small parcel of land near the Ganges where I can grow crops and that the tax on all water-sellers be rescinded for a year.'

Humayun heard some open sniggers. Even Kasim's usually serious, ascetic face seemed in danger of twitching into a smile, but Humayun himself was touched by Nizam's modest requests. He was not seeking to enrich himself excessively like so many at court.

'It shall be as you command.'

'Then I am ready to descend the throne.' Nizam got up and, relief etched on his small features, stepped lightly down, holding his robes clear of his feet to avoid tripping. Looking at him Humayun realised he had witnessed real courage. What must it have cost Nizam to come to court to ask Humayun to honour his promise? For all he knew, Humayun might have forgotten all about him or been angered by his presumptuousness. Just as the guard had yelled at the struggling boy he might well have paid the price of a flogging or even death for his temerity in calling an emperor to account.

Humayun now mounted the throne. 'As emperor again I too have orders to give. These are that Nizam the water-carrier also be given five hundred gold coins and that the grant of land should be sufficient to support him and all his family in comfort.' Humayun watched as the small figure, with one backward glance at him, was escorted from the *durbar* hall.

Later that day, with all business done and the pale moon just beginning to rise and the first cooking fires alight, Humayun climbed to the battlements of the Agra fort. He had dismissed his guards and wished to be alone with his thoughts for a while. His love of solitude which to Babur had seemed such a vice in a ruler had never entirely deserted him. Neither had his fascination with the machinations of the stars. Though he curbed such feelings, as he knew he must, they were still there – far stronger than any longing for Gulrukh's concoction of wine and opium.

His father had once spoken to him of the tyranny of kingship – and he had been right. In some ways, was being a ruler any better than being a poor man? At least Nizam, dipping his water bottles into the Ganges, was his own man. It wasn't easy to bear the burden of the future of a dynasty, yet he knew he would never wish to abandon such a sacred charge.

Night had fallen around him while he mused. It was time to return to his apartments where Jauhar and his attendants would be spreading the evening meal – the plates of lamb, buttered rice and root vegetables of the Moghuls' homelands and the spicy dishes of Hindustan with their saffron and turmeric, intense as the sun which burned by day above the plains of his new empire. By the light of a blazing torch mounted on the wall, Humayun made for the three flights of steep stone steps that led back towards his apartments. Still lost in his thoughts he descended the first flight then, about to round the corner to descend the second, he paused at the sound of voices.

'I thought the emperor had cured himself of his madness. We put up with months of his lunacy . . . all that rubbish about days of Mars and days of Jupiter and that stupid carpet with the planets. I'm surprised we were allowed to piss when we wanted . . .'

'That smelly little peasant should never have got near the *durbar* hall, let alone have sat on the imperial throne,' said another voice after a pause. 'If the emperor had wanted to reward him, a copper coin and a goodbye kick would've done. I hope this isn't the start of some fresh insanity. With Sher Shah's armies pressing nearer we need a warrior, not a dreamer.'

'The emperor is a fighter – no one is braver in the field . . .' said a third man. His voice was deep and sounded older but – as with the others – Humayun didn't recognise it.

'Well let's hope he remembers that's what he's there for. Babur was a real man – that's why I rode from Kabul with his invasion force. I didn't leave everything behind for a fanciful star-gazer I can't trust . . .'

'But he's already won great victories . . . remember Gujarat and how we . . .' the deeper voice went on, but as the men began to move off Humayun couldn't catch the rest.

Their words had angered him. He'd been tempted to leap out and confront them but there'd been justice in some of what they'd said. Doped with opium and living in a twilight world he had lost touch with his commanders and courtiers and let his people down. But they were wrong about Nizam. He had given Nizam his word and had kept it. That was the action of an honourable man. To do otherwise would have damned him in the next life, if not in this . . .

• ◆ •

'First, what do we know of our enemy, Ahmed Khan?'

Humayun was seated once more in his scarlet command tent with his military council around him. He had arrived at his army's camp, a hundred and twenty miles south of Agra, the previous evening to renew the war against Sher Shah.

'The news, Majesty, is not good. After burying his dead, Sher Shah returned slowly to Kakori, the town he had used as his forward command centre. Here, ten weeks ago, he held a great parade to celebrate his victory. To the beating of drums a detachment of his elite cavalry riding beneath their purple pennants led the way. They waved to the crowd who cheered them at the tops of their voices. Sher Shah had succeeded in getting most of the bronze cannon he captured from us out of the Ganges mud and back into working order. These came next in the parade, pulled through the streets by some of our elephants which he'd rounded up. They were followed by ranks of our prisoners, forced to march in chains. According to one of our spies who got close disguised as a sweetmeat-seller, some were limping or had their wounds bandaged with dirty cloths. Others had raw, weeping sores where the chains bit into their flesh. All were gaunt and hungry-looking and held their eyes on the floor. The spy said the crowd yelled obscenities at them, jostled and pelted them with rotting rubbish and even lashed out at them with sticks.

'They in turn were followed by further detachments of Sher Shah's rejoicing troops and at last by Sher Shah himself riding high in a gilded howdah atop a tall elephant which had its tusks painted with gold leaf and its large saddle cloth, which reached down to the ground, embroidered with pearls and jewels. When the procession reached the main square of the city, Sher Shah dismounted to take his place on a great dais covered in purple cloth.

'Here he distributed further gifts of our captured treasure to his chief supporters and granted assignments of our captured lands to them, and even gave them groups of our wretched prisoners to serve as slaves in their fields and quarries. Then, further shame to say, many of our former allies and vassal rulers came forward dressed in their ceremonial finery. They happily prostrated themselves in the dirt before Sher Shah to be pardoned and rewarded with positions in

114

his army and promises of further bounty when you were defeated. They were followed by ambassadors from the rulers of the Deccan states such as diamond-rich Golconda who, seeing the opportunity to enrich themselves further from our weakness, promised aid to Sher Shah and were in turn gratified by grandiose assurances about portions of our land to be ceded to them.

'Finally, to another loud blaring of trumpets, one of the most important of your former vassals – the Raja of Golpur – came forward and joined by many of Sher Shah's commanders fell to his knees before Sher Shah. Together they begged him to accept the title of emperor – *padishah* – obsequiously and traitorously assuring him he was much better suited to hold it than ever you were. Twice Sher Shah refused with self-deprecating statements that all he sought was to help those suffering your oppression. He sought neither power nor reward for himself. However on the third occasion, beseeched in ever more flattering and vainglorious terms – the hyperbole of their words knew no limits – he accepted, saying, "If it is your settled wish, I can but agree. I promise to rule wisely and give justice to all." Then a crown of gold set with rubies – held ready all the time; the whole thing was stage-managed, his initial refusals merely for show – was placed on his head by the Raja of Golpur and three of Sher Shah's officers. All present prostrated themselves before him, traitorous noses pressed to the earth.

'Later that night, Sher Shah staged a grand pageant. By the flaring light of torches young warriors from each of the states and clans now allied to him performed martial exercises before Sher Shah as he sat beneath a canopy of gold cloth on a tall, straight-backed gilded throne. A snarling tiger was carved into it, just above where Sher Shah's head came. It had two large rubies for eyes which – I am told – glowed fiercely in the dark. Then after the performance was completed each in turn bowed low before the so-called emperor and he sprinkled their perspiring shaved heads with saffron, ground pearls, musk and ambergris as betokening the riches and sweet success he would make adhere to them and to the factions they represented.

'The following day being a Friday, in the city's main mosque –

crowded to bursting point with Sher Shah's commanders – the mullah too proclaimed Sher Shah emperor by reading the sermon – the *khutba* – in his name and traitorously and blasphemingly assigning to Sher Shah all your lands whether already occupied by him, as in Bengal, or far beyond his reach in Afghanistan and the Punjab. The next day, Sher Shah marched out to renew his advance upon us. With his new allies, his armies now number near two hundred thousand.'

'Where is he now?'

'About a hundred miles away, advancing slowly towards Agra.'

'And Baba Yasaval, what of our own armies? Has the re-equipment progressed well?'

'Yes, the armourers have done good work. Our men have new weapons. The foundries have blazed red fire day and night to produce more cannon. The horse brokers have supplied us with sufficient animals to re-mount our cavalry – even if some are not as big and strong as those bred on the steppes of our ancestral homelands.'

'And how about the promises of further detachments of troops by our allies and by my half-brothers too?'

'Here the news is less good. Several of our allies have procrastinated, citing the monsoon or local rebellions as reasons for delay in despatching troops or for only sending small detachments. Your younger half-brothers Hindal and Askari have, however, fulfilled and in the case of Hindal exceeded their promises, but your eldest half-brother Kamran has sent from the Punjab only a small detachment of two hundred and fifty cavalry, albeit mounted on fine horses. In response to our promptings for further assistance he will give no clear timescale and hints he must hold some troops back in case you suffer further reverses.'

'But that is the certain way to ensure that we do suffer further defeats,' Humayun snapped but then stopped himself from saying more. It would do no good to criticise his half-brother publicly. Yet his commander's words chimed with his own private correspondence with Kamran. His half-brother had delayed responding to messages and – when he did reply – although suitably bellicose in his hostility to Sher Shah, he was noncommittal about despatching troops to serve under Humayun's command. Instead, Kamran had offered to lead all his men to join the fight himself. He must have known that Humayun had to refuse, since to accept would be to leave the Punjab without a governor and without troops to keep order. Kamran seemed to be playing a waiting game, more anxious to preserve his personal position than to recover the lost provinces of their father's empire if it meant adding to Humayun's glory rather than his own.

'I will write to my half-brother. But how many men can our commanders deploy now?'

'A hundred and seventy thousand, Majesty.'

'So for the present Sher Shah's forces outnumber us?'

'Yes, Majesty. Until reinforcements arrive from your brother Kamran and others.'

• ◆ •

Humayun felt a soft, warm evening breeze on his cheek as, not far from the settlement of Kanauj on the Ganges, he looked from his command position on a sandstone ridge dotted with scrubby bushes and the occasional stunted tree towards the opposite ridge where, if his scouts' reports were correct, Sher Shah's army would emerge the next morning. Briefly, the breeze reminded Humayun of the gentle winds of summer in his birthplace, Afghanistan. At the recollection a half-smile crossed his face only to be driven away by the ever-present knowledge that the two months since his military council had brought nothing but bad news.

Sher Shah's advance had continued, slow but relentless. That was perhaps only to be expected but what Humayun had not anticipated was the defection to Sher Shah of Hanif Khan, Raja of Moradabad, one of Humayun's most senior cavalry commanders now Suleiman Mirza was dead, together with fifteen thousand of his men, all drawn from Hanif Khan's feudal lands to the east of Delhi. Just after his desertion, Sher Shah – in an obviously pre-arranged move – had attacked a fortified town on the Ganges which had previously been under the command of Hanif Khan. Demoralised by Hanif Khan's desertion, the few thousand of Humayun's troops who had remained loyal had put up little resistance and the town had soon surrendered, clearing the way for Sher Shah's advance. Humayun could scarcely blame these troops. Instead he reproached himself that he had devoted insufficient time to understanding the characters and ambitions of those around him – a mistake he would avoid in future.

Equally troubling to Humayun had been reports of what was happening to his rear. There had been a rising in favour of Sher Shah in Hindal's province of Alwar which, Hindal wrote, he'd only been able to put down with difficulty. Other rebellions had broken out among Hanif Khan's vassals in the mountains near Delhi and Humayun had had to detach troops to suppress them who should have been training in preparation for joining his army.

Worst of all had been the letter he had received from Kamran. While still pledging his loyalty to Humayun and the dynasty and his opposition to Sher Shah, he had questioned his brother's military strategy in moving further east to confront Sher Shah two hundred miles and more beyond Agra. He had proposed instead preparing either Agra or Delhi for a siege and allowing Sher Shah to waste his strength in futile attempts to breach their great walls. Kamran had used his 'disquiet' as a pretext for refusing to send further troops, insisting that he had to hold them back under his own command to serve as a second line of defence if Humayun's flawed strategy failed, as Kamran thought it had every chance of doing.

'Majesty, Baba Yasaval is waiting to accompany you to review your troops.' Jauhar broke into Humayun's reverie. He was holding the reins of Humayun's tall brown horse.

'Very well.' Humayun turned and mounted the horse to join Baba Yasaval a little further along the ridge. As the two men moved off, Humayun asked, 'What are our scouts' latest reports? Is there any change?'

'No, Majesty. Sher Shah has encamped about two miles beyond the ridge opposite and from the sight and sound of the preparations being made in his camp tonight, it seems he will indeed attack tomorrow.'

'Has the work been completed on the defensive earth ramparts I asked to be constructed halfway up this ridge?'

'Yes, Majesty – you will see as we make our tour of inspection.'

'Good. From the ramparts' protection we should be able to blunt Sher Shah's attack with cannon and musket fire as well as our archers' arrows rather than charge headlong into a costly hand-to-hand engagement.'

'But we'll need to get in close, Majesty, if we are to vanquish rather than just avoid being vanquished.'

'Of course. Once we've reduced Sher Shah's numerical advantage and his men are nearing exhaustion we'll sally out and destroy them. I want no half-measures either. It's just the timing of our attack I want to control carefully.'

By now, they were riding along the red earth of the ramparts. His men had worked well in the heat with their picks and shovels in the four days they'd been encamped here, athwart the route to Kanauj and the Ganges. The piles of earth and stone were six feet high everywhere and in most places ten. They stretched all along the mid section of the ridge which ran roughly north to south.

'Who am I to reward or promote during this review, Baba Yasaval?'

'We have chosen three men, Majesty. A wounded Afghani from south of Kabul named Wazim Pathan who fought well in one of the skirmishes as Sher Shah advanced. He saved one of his officers at the cost of losing his own right hand and part of his lower arm. We have a bag of silver coin for him to take with him as he makes the long journey back to his village. The second is a junior officer from Lahore who showed great bravery in fighting off an ambush by Sher Shah's men on one of our equipment convoys. We have a jewelled sword for you to present to him as a reward. The third man you know well – young Hassan Butt from Ghazni. As you requested, he is to be given a greater position in the cavalry.'

The troops chosen for Humayun to review were drawn up a little distance from the ramparts near where oxen and elephants had laboured to get his cannon into position. Humayun rode up and down the ranks of cavalry, some of whose horses, restless from standing in the heat, were tossing their heads or pawing the ground, and then on past the straighter lines of foot archers, infantry and gunners to a position in the centre where a dais had been erected. Those to be rewarded or promoted were called forward. A tear formed in the eye of the wounded Wazim Pathan, who was grey-haired and looked much older than many of Humayun's troops. As he took the red velvet bag of coin in his remaining hand, he stammered, '*Padishah*, thank you. I will be able to hold my head up high in my village and be able to pay dowries for my daughters.'

'You deserve all the respect you obtain,' said Humayun. The officer from Lahore smiled with pride as Humayun handed him the sword. So too did young Hassan Butt, as usual wearing his pale blue turban, when before the whole army Humayun announced his appointment to command an elite band of cavalry.

While all three men returned to the ranks, Humayun spoke to the troops assembled before him. 'Tomorrow we expect to fight Sher Shah and his men. Even though his armies are strong, his cause is weak. The throne of Hindustan is mine by right as the son of Babur and the descendant of Timur. Sher Shah is the son of a horse dealer and the descendant of nameless bastards. Let us fight so well that by tomorrow evening he will lie in a traitor's grave and even then occupy more of this land than he is entitled to. Never forget the justice of our cause. Remember that all I ask is that you fight as bravely as the men I have just rewarded. I swear to you I will attempt to outdo them myself.'

Chapter 8

Blood and Dust

Taking no chances that Sher Shah would again surprise him by a night-time attack as he had at Chausa, Humayun had had his men awake and standing to, ready for action, three hours before dawn. But no attack had come and breakfast was now long over and the cooking fires doused. The morning was clear and even at around nine o'clock the heat was building up as Humayun, dressed for battle, paced once more along the ridge. His scouts had reported that Sher Shah had started to advance about an hour ago and should soon approach the ridge opposite.

They were right. Only a few minutes later Humayun made out the first purple pennants topping the ridge. Then he saw one mail-clad rider, then another, then hundreds. Sher Shah's vanguard of elite cavalry was deploying in the position Humayun had anticipated under the orders of a tall figure whose breastplate and helmet glinted in the morning sun. It was too far off to distinguish who it was but Humayun assumed – hoped, even – that it was Sher Shah. He wanted to take Sher Shah on in personal combat once more to prove he was the better fighter and to see his enemy bleed into the dust. But he knew that like his men he must fight the temptation to risk all on one sudden desperate onslaught.

A quarter of an hour later, Humayun saw the tall figure wave his sword to put the first ranks of his horsemen into motion. To Humayun there seemed about five thousand of them as they came galloping down from the ridge, yelling and shouting with their purple banners streaming behind them. They appeared, as Humayun expected, to be going to assault head-on his makeshift ramparts, constructed halfway up the ridge on which he stood.

Already Baba Yasaval had given orders for Humayun's artillery to open fire and the first of Sher Shah's horsemen were crumpling under the impact of shot. Through the white cannon smoke now swirling around the valley below, Humayun watched others fall from their horses, struck by arrows or musket balls. Among them was one of the banner-carriers who, as he fell, lost his grip on the staff. His purple banner was blown into the path of another rider, becoming entangled with his horse's legs and bringing animal and man to the ground. A moment or two later, Humayun saw to his intense surprise that rather than charging full tilt straight at his positions, the horsemen were dividing. Some were riding for one end of his line of earth ramparts and the others for the opposite end. They were attempting an encircling movement, seemingly prepared to take the inevitable casualties from Humayun's gunners and archers as they swerved across his front line.

Moments later, Humayun saw from the corner of his eye another large force of Sher Shah's cavalry appear, galloping over the low saddle joining the two ridges at their northern end and clearly preparing to attack his less well-defended flanks.

'Jauhar, send a messenger to tell Baba Yasaval to divert some squadrons of cavalry to repulse the attack over the saddle from the north. I will gallop across to lead them myself.' Without waiting for confirmation from Jauhar that he had heard, Humayun waved his leather-gauntleted hand to his bodyguard to follow and kicked his brown horse to a gallop along the crest of the ridge. After a few hundred yards the ground began to fall away towards the saddle and Humayun could see that some of Sher Shah's cavalry had already succeeded in getting behind the northern extremity of his ramparts. His musketeers and archers were firing back at them from the cover of rocks. Then, as he watched, one group of archers turned and, dropping their bows, ran towards the rear, only for Sher Shah's cavalry to catch up with them. Slashing from their saddles they struck at the archers' backs, sending most of them sprawling to the ground.

If only foot soldiers would learn that it was impossible to run from cavalry, thought Humayun. It was not only more honourable but safer to stay behind cover and make a fight of it. Hearing the sound of horses' hooves behind him, he turned in the saddle to see the detachment of horsemen he had requested from Baba Yasaval. They were on a converging path with his own and within a minute and scarcely reducing their speed they had joined up with Humayun's bodyguard and they were all galloping as one unit.

'Charge! We must throw the enemy back before he can bring up his own infantry to consolidate his position on our flanks. Aim to separate the attackers into small groups. They'll be easier to surround and kill that way.'

As Humayun's men galloped down the slope towards the fighting, a band of mounted archers rode out from Sher Shah's cavalry. They fired a volley of arrows towards Humayun's riders before quickly wheeling to return to the protection of their companions. The arrows hissed through the morning air and some of Humayun's cavalry slackened their pace to lift their shields to protect themselves. Several horses fell, shedding their riders and in turn bringing down others, further disrupting the impetus of the charge. However, Humayun urged his men on, yelling to those around him, 'Ignore these pinpricks, we'll be among them before they can fire again.' Then from his left he heard another noise – the crackle of musket fire from behind a jumble of rocks and boulders. Sher Shah must have had some of his musketeers ride with the cavalry.

Hassan Butt, the young commander Humayun had promoted the previous day, was among the foremost in the charge, easily distinguished by his pale blue turban and the white horse he was riding. Hit in the head by a musket ball, the horse fell instantly and Hassan Butt crashed from the saddle, arms flailing, and rolled over several times on the stony ground. Almost incredibly he then struggled to his feet. The last Humayun saw of him before the main force of his charging cavalry engulfed him, he was waving his sword encouraging his fellows onward.

Humayun had no time to think more about his bravery since he was himself now among Sher Shah's horsemen. Swerving to avoid the swinging flail of one warrior on a black horse, he made for a tall man who was mounted on a ginger horse and wearing a steel breastplate – surely an important officer. Two of the riders around the man instantly turned their horses towards Humayun who, ducking low, avoided their sword strokes and struck one of them – a small, bearded man with a pock-marked face – a glancing blow to the shoulder which made him drop his weapon.

Quickly Humayun urged his horse alongside the officer. The man cut at Humayun with his long curved sword but at close quarters was unable to put sufficient force into his swing for the sword to penetrate Humayun's breastplate. Nevertheless, the strength of the stroke knocked Humayun sideways and his horse carried him away. Quickly regaining his balance, Humayun pulled on the reins to turn his mount again and attacked the officer head on. The man raised his metal shield to parry Humayun's first sword stroke but was too slow in getting the heavy shield down to prevent Humayun's second catching him in his side where it was unprotected by his breastplate. He was not wearing chain mail so the sword bit deep into muscle and rib cartilage. As the officer instinctively dropped his shield and grasped at his wound, Humayun slashed again, this time across the man's throat, nearly severing his head, and the officer fell from the saddle.

Bent on vengeance, another of the officer's bodyguards next engaged Humayun, wielding a two-headed axe. He was soon joined by a second and then a third, both with long, double-edged swords. Humayun held them off, wheeling his nimble brown horse and parrying their blows but suffering a minor wound to his cheek from a sharp sword, until some of his own guards galloped up to assist him. Before long, two of his attackers were stretched on the stony earth, cut down by Humayun with sword strokes to head and neck. The third had dropped his sword and was fleeing, blood from a spear thrust to his thigh inflicted by one of Humayun's guards pouring down his saddle and staining his horse's light coat.

'We have driven off most of Sher Shah's cavalry. His musketeers and archers are pulling back too,' a breathless officer reported.

'Good. Establish our archers and musketeers among the boulders where those of Sher Shah were. Turn over some of those baggage wagons to make extra barricades and get some of the guns pulled round ready to fire if Sher Shah tries another flank attack.'

As his men went to work, pushing and straining at the large wooden baggage carts to topple them and bringing up oxen to move the cannon, Humayun rode towards a point a few hundred yards away on the ridge where he could get a better view of the battlefield and ponder his next move. On reaching it, his decision was made for him. Sher Shah's horsemen had broken through the middle of his line of earth ramparts about three-quarters of a mile away and his own men were retreating before them.

'What happened?' Humayun demanded of a short, dark officer on a brown and white horse who was leading a party of about fifty tough-looking Badakhshani archers forward.

'I am not certain, Majesty, but I was told that after Sher Shah's first attack surprised us by dividing to encircle the ends of our lines, he ordered a second wave of horsemen to gallop down the ridge in close formation to assault the very centre of our ramparts, a position which was weakened – as he knew it would be, I am sure – by our withdrawal of troops to protect the flanks. So fierce was their charge that they overwhelmed our remaining defenders and drove deep into the very centre of our camp. Baba Yasaval sent orders for us to advance to help defend the position he has established over there, around the base of that outcrop.'

Looking in the direction of the officer's pointing arm, Humayun saw a great mêlée of horsemen and could just make out Baba Yasaval's yellow flag. 'I trust in the bravery of you and your men. We will drive Sher Shah back. I will summon my mounted bodyguard and precede you into the fight.'

'Majesty.'

Humayun turned and, beckoning his bodyguards to follow, galloped back up the rise of the ridge towards the outcrop where the fighting was centred. As he rode, he could see more and more of Sher Shah's men pouring through the undefended breach in his earth ramparts and joining the battle around the outcrop. As he got nearer, he

125

encountered a small group of his own foot soldiers who were running away, abandoning positions which had not yet even come under direct attack. Reining in his horse he shouted to them to return, that all was not lost – but they ran on, eyes fixed and fearful, heading for Kanauj and its crossings over the nearby Ganges.

Only a minute or two later, Humayun was on the edge of the heaving mass of men and of horses around the outcrop. He saw a loose horse gallop away with part of its intestines protruding from a great cut to its belly. Several bodies lay sprawled on the ground, attackers and defenders indistinguishable in death. Baba Yasaval's soldiers seemed to be slowly yielding ground and being forced back against the steep side of the outcrop but Humayun could still see Baba Yasaval's yellow flag flying in the middle of the fight. Immediately he charged towards it, leaving his bodyguards to follow as best they could.

Humayun's brown horse stumbled on the mangled body of one rider whose skull had a great bloody cleft in it but Humayun was a good horseman and the beast was nimble and recovered, carrying Humayun further into the press. He struck one of Sher Shah's cavalry from the saddle with a single stroke of his sword Alamgir, wounded the horse of a second in the neck, causing it to throw its rider before, collapsing to the ground with a severed windpipe, it brought down another horseman who had been preparing to attack Humayun from behind. Humayun was now what seemed only twenty or so yards from Baba Yasaval. Spying a gap, Humayun pressed forward towards his commander through riders too deeply engaged in fighting each other to notice him.

As he did so, Humayun saw that in fact Baba Yasaval had only about a dozen of his men around him. Three or four of them had lost their horses and Baba Yasaval and their comrades were trying to protect them as they held off Sher Shah's more numerous attackers. At that very moment, however, one of their assailants – a large, purple-turbaned man with a bushy black beard armed with a long lance – kicked his horse towards one of the dismounted men who was becoming separated from the rest. Despite getting his shield up in front of him to ward off the lance tip, the man was unable to withstand the weight of the charge which knocked him off his feet. He tried desperately to roll away from under the hooves of his attacker's horse towards his companions but, as he did so, the purple-turbaned horseman pulled back his lance and taking deliberate aim skewered him through the belly before any of Baba Yasaval's other soldiers could intervene. Quickly twisting his blood-tipped lance out of the body, the purple-turbaned man – surely an officer – retreated back into the mass of his fellows. The whole incident had taken less than a minute, during which Humayun had pushed through to Baba Yasaval's side.

'Majesty, where are your bodyguards?' Baba Yasaval broke off from waving his own men back into tighter formation. Humayun suddenly realised that none of them had succeeded in following him through the press and that Sher Shah's fighters now completely filled the small corridor through which he had come. They had almost surrounded himself and Baba Yasaval and his men, cutting them off from either help or retreat.

'Baba Yasaval, we must keep as close order as we can to protect ourselves and each other until either more of our warriors arrive or we can identify a break-out route. If we keep our backs to the wall of the outcrop our rear at least will be protected.'

Humayun and Baba Yasaval waved their other soldiers together, but as they attempted to obey, three of Sher Shah's riders surrounded a horseman and one of them knocked him from his mount with a swinging flail. One of the fallen man's companions kicked his own horse forward to try to save him only to be killed instantly by a stroke from a two-headed battleaxe which caught him by his Adam's apple and decapitated him. Another of Sher Shah's men meanwhile despatched the man knocked from his saddle by the flail. At the same time, the purple-turbaned officer separated another of Baba Yasaval's unhorsed men from his protectors and stuck him in the groin with his lance. The wounded soldier's legs and heels thrashed against the ground for about a minute and then he lay still.

There were now only nine men left with Baba Yasaval and Humayun, two of whom were unhorsed and another badly wounded in the head. Then, the purple-turbaned officer waved Sher Shah's riders in for the kill as Humayun and his soldiers retreated until they were only a few yards from the side of the outcrop. At this point it was almost twenty feet high and nearly sheer, clearly impossible to ride up on a horse and offering no obvious route for a climber on foot.

One of the nine men with Baba Yasaval was a young trumpeter whose smooth-skinned face had as yet no need of the barber. He still had his instrument strapped to his back. Baba Yasaval shouted to him, 'Sound your trumpet so we may get help. The rest of you protect him while he does so.' The trumpeter succeeded in taking his three-foot-long trumpet from his back and putting it to his lips. However, at first no sound came and the youth looked at Baba Yasaval in alarm and panic.

'Calmly, boy,' said Baba Yasaval. 'The excitement and fear of battle have dried your mouth. Cough and try to wet your lips with your tongue.'

The youth obediently coughed and licked his lips before trying again. This time, the full sound issued from the trumpet's brass mouth – the rallying call of Humayun's men.

'And again, boy, and again!'

Three more of Humayun's riders had been killed in valiantly providing protection for the young trumpeter before suddenly the purple-turbaned officer swerved his black horse towards the trumpeter and with his long lance caught the boy in his right armpit, exposed as he kept the trumpet to his lips, unhorsing him. He was killed by a further stab of his assailant's lance as he lay on the ground.

Humayun, seeing another of Sher Shah's horsemen ride towards one of the two remaining men who were on foot, kicked his own horse to meet the rider's charge, blocking his path to his target. As the man pulled hard at his reins to guide his mount round Humayun, Humayun cut at his wrists severing one of his hands, causing the rider to lose control and be carried away into the mêlée. Humayun extended his hand to the man on foot to pull him up behind him on his horse. But as he did so, a spear thrown by an unknown assailant pierced the soldier's chest and another spear hit Humayun's horse in the neck. It staggered and collapsed, blood pouring from the wound.

Humayun slipped from the saddle and, as the purple-turbaned officer kicked on to attack him, ran back towards the steep face of the outcrop, zigzagging sharply to put the rider off his aim with his deadly lance. Coming close to the rock face, Humayun realised it was indeed impossible to climb, at least with an assailant armed with a long lance close behind. So Humayun turned at bay, with Alamgir in his right hand and a foot-long, serrated-edged dagger drawn from his belt in his left. Pivoting on the balls of his feet so that he could dart this way and that once the officer attacked, Humayun waited.

The officer charged seconds later, his lance tip pointed at Humayun who left it until the very last moment to jump aside. Thwarted, the officer swerved and turned to try again. As he did so, Baba Yasaval – now unhorsed too and bleeding from a deep sword slash to his face – ran in front of Humayun and, as the officer charged, struck at his horse. He succeeded in bringing the animal down but at the cost of taking its rider's lance full in the abdomen. Humayun ran forward towards the purple-turbaned man who, although winded by his fall from his horse, was quickly on his feet with sword drawn to parry Humayun's first blow with Alamgir. He managed to fend off the second blow too but while he did so, Humayun struck with the dagger in his left hand, striking the man in the throat and twisting the dagger's jagged blade as it entered to cause fatal damage. The officer's warm blood spurted all over Humayun's hand.

'Majesty, we heard the trumpet,' a voice came from above on top of the vertical outcrop. Humayun glanced up. Some of his men – from the cast of their features and the colour and cut of their orange clothes members of the army of one of his Rajput vassals – had succeeded in getting on top of the outcrop and were peering over the edge. As Humayun turned again to face his attackers – he seemed to be the only survivor of those trapped beneath the outcrop – one of the Rajputs fired a black-shafted arrow, felling the horse of one of Sher Shah's men. A second arrow wounded another man in the leg. The rest of Humayun's attackers recoiled as if to consider their next move. In the few seconds while they did so, the Rajput archer uncoiled his orange turban from around his head. He threw one end of the material, which was about ten feet long, over the edge of the outcrop where it hung blowing slightly in the breeze about a foot above Humayun's head.

'Grab hold of my turban cloth, Majesty. I will pull you to safety.'

Humayun hesitated and looked around him. Baba Yasaval was still lying where he'd fallen, slumped against the steep side of the outcrop. His helmetless head with its grey stubble was down on his chest and trickles of blood were still seeping from his nostrils and the corners of his lips and dripping down on to his breastplate. His arms were by his side but his legs were splayed and the lance still protruded from his abdomen. He was surely dead and Humayun could see no sign of life in any other of his men.

Any moment now his attackers would close in again to finish him off, Humayun realised. His duty to both his destiny and his dynasty was to save himself. Transferring Alamgir to his left hand, he reached up with his right and grasped the orange turban cloth tightly. Immediately he felt the material tauten and as he scrambled with his feet against the stone rock face for added impetus he began to rise. Suddenly, his attackers, seeing that he was about to escape, rushed towards him.

Humayun slashed awkwardly at the foremost of them with Alamgir in his left hand but the cut went home, the sharp blade slicing into the man's forehead as he looked upward, almost detaching a flap of skin and causing blood to pour down into his eyes. At the same time, Humayun felt the air move close to him as a Rajput from above threw his battleaxe at the next attacker, catching him in the muscle of his upper arm, and he too fell back. A third hesitated for a moment and that hesitation allowed Humayun to scramble and pull himself over the edge and on to the top of the outcrop. He scarcely noticed that the scar tissue on his right forearm and hand had opened up under the pressure imposed on it as he had been pulled up and was now bleeding profusely.

'Majesty.' The Rajput who had thrown the turban cloth spoke urgently as he helped Humayun to his feet. 'We have a fresh horse for you. Everywhere your men are retreating. Unless you too ride quickly away you will be captured or killed.'

Looking round, Humayun realised that he had indeed only two

choices – to retreat to fight another day or die in battle. However much the latter appealed to his warrior's honour, he felt that life and ambition still burned bright within him and that fate had better in store for her fortunate son than a futile if courageous death. He must live.

'Let us ride and re-group as many of our forces as we can.'

Chapter 9

Brothers

The hot, still air, already heavy with the moisture that in a week or so would begin to pour from the skies, was oppressive. Beneath his chain mail and fine-woven cotton tunic, sweat trickled down Humayun's back. His face too was beaded with it. Impatiently he wiped it away with a face cloth only to feel the salty drops immediately re-form. The drumming of his bay horse's hooves as he galloped back towards Agra, bodyguards ahead and a detachment of cavalry including his loyal orange-clad Rajputs behind him, seemed to pound out a bitter message. Defeat and failure. Defeat and failure. The words echoed around his head but even so he could scarcely believe what had happened.

The troops he had hoped to re-assemble had melted away. Some had returned to their own provinces but more had deserted to Sher Shah's advancing armies. That they should believe the son of a low horse trader could overthrow the Moghuls . . . the enormity hurt more than a physical wound, but even worse was the thought that, for all his courage in battle, he had allowed it to happen.

Where was his good fortune now? At Panipat, Hindustan had dropped like a ripe, juicy pomegranate into the Moghuls' outstretched hands. The ease with which he had defeated Bahadur Shah and the Lodi pretenders had made him think his dynasty invincible. Perhaps he hadn't understood the nature of his new empire – that rebellion was endemic. However many insurrections he quashed, however many rebels' heads he struck off, there would always be more. Inspired by Sher Shah's success, enemies were now menacing him from the west and south as well as from the east.

In his frustration, Humayun slapped his gauntleted hand so hard against the pommel of his saddle that his startled horse skittered sideways, tossing its head and snorting, almost unseating him. Gripping hard with his knees he managed to steady it, then relaxing the reins leaned forward and patted its sweating neck to reassure it. Anyway, with luck he and his advance party should be in Agra before nightfall. Though it would be another week, maybe longer, until the rest of his army – the artillery wagons, baggage carts and thousands of pack beasts – reached the city, he would have a little time to consider his next move. According to his scouts, Sher Shah had halted his advance, at least for the moment, not moving far beyond Kanauj. Perhaps he too was taking stock . . .

In fact it wasn't till after midnight that Humayun's exhausted horse carried him through the dark streets of Agra, along the banks of the Jumna and up into the fort. The kettledrums above the gatehouse boomed out into the night as, by the orange light of torches flickering in sconces high on the walls, he rode up the steep ramp into the courtyard. A groom rushed to take the reins as Humayun lowered his weary body from the saddle.

'Majesty.' A dark-robed figure moved forward. As it came closer, Humayun recognised his grandfather, Baisanghar. Normally so strong, even forceful, his face looked haggard, for once showing every one of his seventy-two years and it told Humayun immediately that something unforeseen and unwelcome had occured.

'What is it? What's happened?'

'Your mother is ill. For the past six weeks she has complained of a pain in her breast so sharp that only opium can bring her relief. The *hakims* say they can do nothing for her. I wanted to send messengers to you but she insisted I should not distract you from your campaign . . . yet I know she longs to see you. It's all that has kept her alive . . .'

'I will go to her.' Hurrying across the stone flagstones towards his mother's apartments, Humayun no longer saw the red sandstone fortress around him. Instead, he was a boy again in Kabul – galloping his pony through the grassy meadows, firing arrows from the saddle at the straw targets Baisanghar had set up and already rehearsing wildly inflated stories of his skill and daring with which to impress Maham.

As he entered his mother's sickroom, the soothing smell of frankincense filled his nostrils. It came from four tall incense burners set up around her couch in which the golden crystals of resin were smouldering. Maham looked very small beneath the green coverlet, the skin on her face paper thin, but her large, dark eyes still had their beauty and they warmed as they rested on her son. Humayun bent and kissed her forehead. 'Forgive me – I come to you with the sweat and dust of the journey still upon me.'

'My beautiful warrior . . . Your father was so proud of you . . . he always said you were the most worthy of all his sons, the most fit to rule . . . Among his last words to me were, "Maham, although I have other sons, I love none as I love your Humayun. He will achieve his heart's desire. None can equal him."' She touched his cheek with her dry hand. 'How is it with you, my son, my emperor? Have you defeated our enemies?'

So they had kept the news of his reverses from her, Humayun thought with relief. 'Yes, Mother, all is well. Sleep now. I will come to you in the morning and we will talk again.' But Maham's eyes were already closing and Humayun doubted she'd heard him.

Khanzada was waiting for him in the antechamber. She looked drawn – Humayun guessed she had spent many hours by Maham's bedside – but her face lit at the sight of him. 'I gave thanks when I heard you had reached Agra in safety,' she said as he kissed her cheek.

'I must speak with the *hakims* . . .'

'They have done what they can. We even sent messengers to consult Abdul-Malik, knowing how his skill saved your father when he was poisoned. Though he is old and half blind, his mind is still clear. But when told of the symptoms he said nothing could be done except to ease Maham's pain.' Khanzada paused. 'She was waiting for one thing only – to see you again, Humayun. Now she will die happy . . .'

Humayun looked down at Timur's ring on his battle-scarred hand. 'I lied to her just now . . . I told her I had conquered our enemies. But as she looks down on me from Paradise I will make her proud – I swear it . . .' Without warning, he felt tears running down his cheeks.

Two days later, Humayun was one of the four men carrying the sandalwood coffin containing his mother's body, washed in camphor water and wrapped in soft woollen blankets, down to the Jumna where a boat was waiting. A bright, flower-filled garden – one of several planted by his father Babur on the far bank of the river and now coming to maturity – would be her resting place. Humayun glanced at Baisanghar, walking beside him. Despite his age he had insisted on accompanying his daughter on her final journey. How stooped and frail he looked – no longer the warrior who had hazarded his life to help Babur capture Samarkand.

An even deeper melancholy took hold of Humayun – not only grief at Maham's death but a sense that many of the certainties of his youth were crumbling. All his life he'd been a pampered prince, brought up to expect great things as of right, confident of his place in the world. Never before had he felt so insignificant, so vulnerable to the buffeting of others' actions. Never before had he felt it so difficult to control his destiny.

As he and the other coffin bearers reached the riverbank, Humayun raised his face to the heavy grey skies. Without warning, the rain began to fall, at first in large, fat drops but soon in a ceaseless sheet that drenched his dark mourning robes. Perhaps the rain was a sign, sent to cleanse him of his doubts, to tell him that though some things must end, there could always be a fresh beginning for a leader who never despaired in the face of grief or adversity but kept his belief in himself and in his ultimate triumph.

• ◆ •

Humayun looked around at his counsellors, like him dressed in the mourning that custom demanded they wear for forty days. Maham had been dead for only fourteen of those days but if the alarming reports reaching him were accurate, little time was left for observing the courtesies to the dead.

'You're certain, Ahmed Khan . . . ?'

'Yes, Majesty', responded his travel-stained chief scout. 'Sher Shah is advancing fast with an army at least three hundred thousand strong. I saw the vanguard with my own eyes just five days' ride east from here.'

'This matches other reports that have been coming in, Majesty,' said Kasim. 'Despite the start of the rains, Sher Shah is making good progress.'

At least Sher Shah hadn't caught up with his retreating army, Humayun thought. The main force had reached Agra safely nearly a week ago though many had deserted along the road. 'So he means to attack us here in Agra . . . How many troops do we have left?' Humayun turned to Zahid Beg, the tall, thin officer he had made his commander-of-horse in place of Baba Yasaval.

'Around eighty thousand including the returning forces from Kanauj, Majesty, but the number diminishes every day . . .'

Raising his head, Humayun looked down the length of his audience chamber to the courtyard beyond. The rain had ceased temporarily and in the shafts of sunlight the red sandstone glowed. This fortress had been the Moghuls' greatest stronghold ever since they had swept down to conquer Hindustan. Last night before retiring into the pleasures of the *haram* he had stood on the battlements with his astrologer, Sharaf, and together they had gazed into the night sky. But Sharaf had been unable to find any messages written there – or in his charts and tables. Was the silence of the stars God's way of showing him that he and he alone must find a way of saving his dynasty. . . ?

'Ahmed Khan's news confirms what I had already feared. We have no choice but to retreat from Agra,' Humayun said at last. There was an audible gasp.

'Abandon Agra, Majesty?' Kasim looked shocked.

'Yes. That is the only way.'

'But where will we go?'

'Northwest, to Lahore. That will buy us time and I will be able to summon more troops from Kabul – the clans there will welcome a chance for some plunder . . .'

A long silence followed then Baisanghar spoke. 'Many years ago when I was still young and with Babur in Samarkand, we faced an enemy – Shaibani Khan and his numberless Uzbeks whom we knew we could not defeat. The only alternative to retreat was the death of thousands of our people. Babur, with the courage and foresight that made him so great, understood that. Though it grieved his warrior soul to yield Timur's city to the barbarian Uzbeks, he knew he must . . . Just as we must leave Agra . . .'

Humayun looked down. Baisanghar's words were the truth. But what he hadn't said was that, as part of the bargain, Shaibani Khan had demanded Khanzada as a wife and Babur had been forced to yield her up. For ten years she had endured life in the *haram* of a man with a visceral hatred of Timur's descendants who had enjoyed trying to break her spirit. He had failed. Whatever happened, he, Humayun, would make sure that no such fate overtook her again.

'We are retreating, not running away. Though we will ride out tomorrow morning at dawn, everything must be done in an orderly fashion . . . Kasim, assemble the officers of the imperial household and ensure that they and their servants carry out my commands swiftly and without question. The contents of the royal treasuries in Agra must be transferred into strong boxes. Anything else of great value must also be packed to go with us – I will leave Sher Shah nothing that will help him. Zahid Beg, prepare our troops. Tell them that we are riding to Lahore to join our forces coming from Kabul. And make sure all our muskets and all the ammunition are securely loaded on to bullock carts and the cannon made ready for travel. Say nothing, do nothing to suggest defeat or flight or that we are in any way afraid of Sher Shah.'

Humayun paused and looked around. 'And you, Ahmed Khan, choose your fastest and best young riders to carry letters to my half-brothers with orders to leave sufficient troops to hold their provinces but to join me with the rest at Lahore. I myself will write the letters and mark them with the imperial seal so my brothers are in no doubt it is the emperor who commands them. Now hurry, there is little time . . .'

Humayun neither slept nor visited the *haram* that night – there was too much to attend to. In any case the hours of darkness were punctuated by the frequent arrival of scouts bringing fresh and ever more disquieting news of the progress of Sher Shah's advance troops. If they maintained their present pace, their vanguard could reach Agra in as little as three or four days' time, Humayun calculated.

Even before the sky was lightening to the east, the first detachments of Humayun's army, pennants streaming in the warm breeze, were moving out, their task to secure the route ahead. Once word spread that he was leaving Agra, the populace might become restive and dacoits might take the chance for some mischief. The task of Humayun's vanguard – in their burnished steel breastplates and mounted on fresh horses from the imperial stables – was to impress them with a show of power. And he was still powerful, Humayun told himself. He still had nearly eighty thousand men under arms – far more than he and his father had had at Panipat.

Looking down from his apartments into the courtyard below, he saw the royal women and their attendants preparing to climb into the carts and litters that had been prepared for them. They would travel in the heart of the column, with guards positioned around them in a protective cordon, and to the front and rear would be further lines of specially assigned cavalry. But Humayun had ordered that Khanzada and his half-sister Gulbadan should ride close to him on one of the imperial elephants. Salima, still his favourite concubine, would follow behind on another.

Behind the women would come the baggage wagons with all the equipment for the imperial camp – the tents and mobile bath houses, the cooking pots and other utensils necessary for the four-hundred-mile journey northwest. And, of course, the imperial treasure in the huge iron-bound travelling chests whose intricate locks required four separate silver keys – each in the keeping of a different official – and a fifth golden key that was hanging from a chain around Humayun's neck. Humayun was glad that before first marching out to face Sher Shah he had had the foresight to order his treasure in

139

Delhi to be sent to Agra for safe keeping. With his own money and gems and what he had captured from Bahadur Shah, he should have more than enough funds to recruit and equip a new army to match Sher Shah's.

At the very end of the line would come further ranks of cavalry and foot soldiers, including some of his best archers, so skilled they could fire forty arrows a minute. And strung out all around the column and out of sight for much of the time would be Ahmed Khan's scouts, ever watchful for trouble.

Two hours later, mounted on the long-legged, muscular bay stallion that had carried him so swiftly back to his capital after the disaster at Kanauj, Humayun himself rode slowly down the ramp of the Agra fort. Beneath his jewelled helmet, his eyes looked straight ahead. This was no time for backward glances or nostalgic thoughts. This was only a temporary setback and soon – very soon, if God so willed – he would return to claim what was his. Yet there was still one thing he must do before departing. Riding down to the riverbank, he dismounted and boarded the small boat waiting to carry him across the Jumna to Maham's grave. Arrived at the simple white marble slab, he knelt and kissed it. 'Sher Shah is a man of our own faith,' he whispered. 'He will not violate your grave and one day I will return to you. Forgive me, Mother, that I cannot observe the forty days of mourning, but the fate of our dynasty is in the balance and I must strain every nerve and sinew to defend it . . .'

• ◆ •

The rains that had fallen almost daily since they had left Agra seemed to be easing and – just as Humayun had hoped – though Sher Shah had seized Agra, he had not pursued him further. According to Humayun's spies, the *khutba* had been read in Sher Shah's name in the mosque of the Agra fort, proclaiming him once more *Padishah* of Hindustan, and he was now holding court in the pillared audience chamber. Well, let the usurper enjoy his moment of glory – it would be brief.

He and his column were making good progress, Humayun reflected – usually twelve or thirteen miles a day, perhaps more, as they travelled northwest over the flat, featureless terrain. If they could continue at this pace they should reach Lahore within a month. So far they had suffered no serious attacks. As the Moghul column passed by villages, the people seemed afraid to come close, watching the passing ranks of soldiers and wagons from the safety of the sodden fields or peeping from their thatched, mud-brick houses. All that moved were hollow-ribbed dogs and scrawny, yellow-feathered chickens.

There had been only one attack on his column. One evening in a rapidly falling dusk made darker by a veil of drizzle, a band of dacoits had fallen on a baggage cart carrying spare tents and cooking equipment that had become bogged down and separated from the main column. It had been some hours before its absence had been spotted and Ahmed Khan sent scouts to search for it. They had found the drivers' sodden bodies lying with arrows in their backs and the wagon gone. But even in the darkness, the thieves and the stolen wagon had not been hard to track. By the time the first fires of the day were flickering into life, Ahmed Khan's men had brought the dacoits, trussed like fowl for market, into the camp. Humayun had immediately ordered their heads to be cut off and cemented into a pyramid of stones as a sign that he would permit no lawlessness among his subjects.

Neither would he tolerate it amongst his troops. Though not of his blood, these Hindustanis were his people – his subjects – and he would not have it said that he allowed his men to pillage them at will. He'd given strict orders that there was to be no looting and had already had six soldiers flogged, spread-eagled across wooden frames in front of their comrades, for stealing a sheep and a seventh executed for raping a village girl.

All the same, as he passed the village temples with their carved stone bulls garlanded with marigolds, and their statues of bizarre gods – some multi-armed, some part man, part elephant – he couldn't help wondering whether he'd ever understand fully the land to which fate and a hunger for empire had brought the Moghuls. His own god was single, indivisible and all-powerful and it was sacrilege to attempt to create his image. The Hindu gods seemed legion and

141

in their voluptuous bodies and sinuous limbs more suggestive of earthly delight than eternal salvation.

Sometimes as he rode, Humayun discussed his thoughts with Khanzada and Gulbadan, speaking with them through the pale pink silk that covered their swaying howdah, fastened with gold chains to the back of one of his best elephants. The practical Khanzada didn't share his curiosity about the religious practices of his Hindu subjects – why they venerated stone *yoni* and *lingams* – representations of the female and male sexual organs – why their priests daubed their foreheads with ashes and why they wore a long cotton thread suspended over their right shoulder.

Yet Gulbadan seemed not only fascinated by these infidel practices but also knowledgeable about them. Of course, Humayun reminded himself, she'd been just a very young child when brought from Kabul to Babur's capital of Agra. She'd grown up in Hindustan and had few if any memories of the Moghuls' mountainous homelands beyond the Khyber Pass. Among her nurses would have been Hindustani women – *ayahs* they called them – who would have explained their religious rituals to her. When times were calmer, he might do well to spend time with Gulbadan, to try to understand more about his subjects.

• ◆ •

Humayun's column continued to pass on through a seemingly quiescent land until Lahore at last rose before them. Though the city had no surrounding walls to protect it, the ancient royal palace, built centuries ago by Hindu rulers in the heart of the city, looked solid and strong as Humayun dismounted in front of it. Still better was the news that his half-brothers had already arrived and were awaiting him within. In his darker moments he'd wondered whether they would obey his order but they had . . . even Kamran.

He was surprised how eager he felt to be with them. What would they be like now? He'd not seen any of them since that bleak time after Babur's death when they had plotted against him. Now, more than ever, he was glad he'd been merciful to them – not only because with his dying breaths Babur had asked him to show them compassion but because he needed his half-brothers and they surely needed him. Sher Shah was a threat to them all as Moghul princes. If Babur's sons could unite, they could drive Sher Shah back into the festering marshes of Bengal whence he'd come. But more than that, it might also be an opportunity for them to start again, re-forging the bonds not only of blood but of affection that should never have been broken. Was it foolish to hope that they also might wish to heal the wounds of the past?

As soon as it was growing light next morning, Humayun summoned his half-brothers to his apartments. Kasim, Zahid Beg and a weary-looking Baisanghar were present as Kamran, Askari and Hindal entered and Humayun embraced them one by one, appraising each with a frank curiosity that matched their own as they stared back at him. When he'd last seen them over six years ago, Askari and Hindal had been youths and Kamran, just five months younger than himself, little more. Now they were all men.

Kamran's eyes – that vivid green just like their father's – flickered above a nose that was still hawk-like, indeed even more so. It had clearly been broken – perhaps in a fall from his horse or in a skirmish – and the *hakims* had failed to set it properly. That was not the only change – Kamran had broadened out. His sinewy shoulders and thick biceps bulged beneath his yellow tunic. Askari had altered less. Though his face looked longer and narrower than Humayun remembered and he now wore a clipped black beard, he was still slight. He was also at least half a head shorter than Humayun or Kamran. As for Hindal, Humayun would not have recognised him at all. Dildar's son – Gulbadan's brother – had grown so much. Taller than any of his brothers by at least four inches and thickly muscled, he looked far older than his eighteen years, an impression reinforced by a scar across his right eyebrow beneath his unruly brown hair and by his deep, resonating voice as he greeted Humayun.

Politenesses over, Humayun motioned his half-brothers to sit in a semicircle around him with Kasim, Baisanghar and Zahid Beg and got immediately to the point. 'I am glad to see you. It has been a long time since we were all together. You know why I

143

summoned you here. This is a council of war and the fate of every one of us – of our entire dynasty – rests on the results. In the past we have had our differences but we are all four the sons of Babur. Timur's blood runs in all our veins and we must unite against the danger that presses in around us. As you know, Sher Shah at the head of three hundred thousand men has occupied Agra, our capital . . .'

'It is regrettable that your campaigns against him did not prosper,' Kamran said quietly. 'It seems that for once your stars misled you.'

Humayun flushed, his hopes of harmony shattering as Kamran spoke. 'I shed my own blood fighting Sher Shah's armies and many good men died – men like Baba Yasaval. Had you sent the help I requested, I could have defeated Sher Shah, and those brave warriors who fell around me might still be living . . . '

'I offered to come at the head of all my troops but you declined . . .'

'Because I did not wish to see your province left undefended.'

'But I warned you against riding so far east to confront Sher Shah – I advised you to prepare for a long siege in either Agra or Delhi. Secure within the walls and well stocked with provisions, you could have bled Sher Shah dry and used some of your other forces to attack him from the rear. But as always you did not heed my advice . . .' Kamran persisted with what seemed to Humayun a half-sneer on his face.

'And as always your loyalty to me is dubious . . . like sand in the hourglass it is already trickling away . . . I see it in your treacherous eyes . . .' Humayun was on his feet. In their boyhood he had always been the better fighter and wrestler. He'd thrashed Kamran a thousand times and would do so again . . . Kamran too had leaped up, his hand reaching for the jewelled dagger in his dark purple sash.

'Majesties . . .' Baisanghar's calm voice brought both of them to their senses. Humayun felt shame that he had allowed Kamran to provoke him. They were not boys sparring in Kabul but Moghul princes facing a deadly and common danger. Kamran too seemed to have regretted his reaction. His hand moved away from his sash and, eyes lowered, he sat down again. Askari and Hindal were also looking down, as if making clear that they wanted no part in this spat between Babur's two eldest sons.

'As always, Baisanghar, you are the voice of reason.' Humayun too seated himself again. 'What is past is past. What matters is the future. Our father struggled nearly his whole life – from the time he was twelve years old – to found an empire. God guided him to new lands, far from our ancestral home, and it is our sacred trust not to lose what he fought for. That is why I summoned you here – so that we four could decide how to fulfil that trust . . . And because our greatest strength, our greatest safety, lies in unity.'

His half-brothers nodded and Humayun began to breathe more easily. 'Zahid Beg, outline our military thinking to my brothers. I would welcome their opinion.'

As Humayun sat back against a large brocade cushion, his master-of-horse began to summarise the strategy that Humayun with his advice and that of Baisanghar had drawn up.

'Majesties,' Zahid Beg began, bony face grave, 'we cannot know Sher Shah's intentions but at present he seems occupied in consolidating his position – he has brought his armies a long way westward from Bengal so he needs to secure more supplies. Also, he risks rebellion to his rear from the lawless tribes who inhabit the swamps of the Ganges Delta. That means that we have at least a little time before he feels secure enough to pursue us here from Agra . . . if indeed he means to, and that is not certain. We must use that time to recruit. We've already sent to the governor of Kabul for reinforcements. Once they arrive, our position will be immeasurably stronger and our options greater.'

'Can we pay these recruits?' Askari asked, his small black eyes intent. 'Or do we expect them to fight for us on the promise of booty alone?'

'We have funds – from the imperial treasuries at Agra but also Delhi,' Kasim replied.

'And till they arrive . . . ?' asked Kamran.

'We will use the time to provision and reinforce Lahore,' said Humayun. 'It is unfortunate the city is unwalled, but we are protected to the north by the Ravi river and can dig defensive trenches and position our cannon and musketeers to west, south and east. The palace itself is strongly built. We could defend it for some time while awaiting fresh forces.'

Kamran's green eyes flickered but he said no more.

'How many troops have you brought with you, Majesties?' Kasim opened the mulberry wood covers of the book in which for as long as Humayun could remember his vizier had kept notes of important matters. Unstoppering the little jade inkbottle hanging from a chain around his neck and dipping in his quill, Kasim waited.

'I have brought five thousand horsemen, including one thousand mounted archers,' said Askari, 'and also five hundred spare horses.'

'My force numbers about three thousand cavalry and five hundred foot soldiers,' said Hindal. 'All good men.'

They all looked at Kamran. 'I came with only two thousand cavalry. After all, you warned me some weeks ago against leaving my province undefended in case of attack . . .' His tone was almost too much for Humayun – Kamran's province was the largest and richest of all and the farthest from Sher Shah's armies and he could easily have spared many more than two thousand without placing it in jeopardy, but Humayun forced himself to swallow his anger. For a moment the only sound was the scratching of Kasim's pen, then the vizier looked up. 'So, Majesties, with the addition of these extra men, that brings our strength up to around ninety thousand.'

'We must do everything we can to keep them here – I don't want them disappearing home . . .' Humayun said.

'The way to avoid that is by promising them action and booty soon. Given that the women and the treasure are safe here in Lahore, we should march out now against Sher Shah – surprise him . . .' Kamran replied.

'Yes,' agreed Askari eagerly, 'Kamran is right. Wouldn't that be best?'

'It would be reckless,' Humayun replied. 'You forget how vastly he outnumbers us. To stand any chance of a decisive victory we would need to take our artillery. That would not only slow us down but give time for news of our approach to reach him. I do not understand you, Kamran. You criticised me for riding to confront

146

Sher Shah instead of allowing him to besiege me in Agra or Delhi but now when I suggest fortifying Lahore against him, you urge me to ride to battle against him . . .'

'The circumstances are different. But plainly you don't want our views. You just want to tell us yours,' Kamran said with a sulky expression. 'I have nothing further to suggest.'

Catching his grandfather's warning look, Humayun this time resisted the temptation to let Kamran provoke him. Instead, he turned to Askari and Hindal. 'Kamran is mistaken. I do want to know your thoughts.' They remained silent, perhaps inhibited by the tension between their elder brothers. Regret mingled with frustration seeped through Humayun. It shouldn't be like this. He was ready to forget the past but it didn't seem his half-brothers, his flesh and blood, were as willing.

However, after a moment, Hindal spoke. 'Zahid Beg spoke of options once the reinforcements from Kabul reach us. What are they?'

Humayun answered. 'I am expecting at least fifty thousand men. I have sent orders that if we are already under siege here in Lahore, they are to attack the rear of the besieging force. But if they reach us before Sher Shah has advanced far from Agra — as I hope — we will have sufficient men to be able to attack Sher Shah's advancing army on the flanks. He will have the advantage of numbers but we will have those of speed and horsemanship that have always served us well against our enemies. So you see, Kamran, I am ready to take the initiative against Sher Shah — only we can't do it yet . . .'

Kamran shrugged and silence fell again. Humayun rose. 'Let's talk again when we've more news of Sher Shah's intentions and of the progress of our reinforcements from Kabul. But tonight let's feast — it is a long time since we were all together. We must show the world that despite present adversities Babur's sons are united.'

Hurrying down the corridor leading to his apartments, Humayun passed the doors leading to the women's quarters. Somewhere within would be Gulrukh whom he had been told had travelled to Lahore with Kamran. Predictably it was with her elder, more ambitious son that she had chosen to live after he himself had banished her from his court. Would she be seeking to influence her sons and if so, how? It would be a good opportunity. Humayun wondered whether he had been wise to bring his half-brothers together again. Maybe it was foolish to think there could ever be real trust, real unity between the four of them – ambition, rivalry, would always get in the way. And could he blame them? In their place wouldn't he feel resentment against the brother who had inherited everything? He would have to have all of them – and Kamran in particular – closely watched and at any sign of disloyalty he would act. With enemies at the gates he could not tolerate an enemy within.

Suddenly Humayun decided to visit Salima. Her warm, fervent embraces would banish troubled thoughts as he lost himself in physical pleasure. He smiled and quickened his pace.

· ◆ ·

'Majesty, Sher Shah's vanguard is on the move from Agra towards Lahore.' Jauhar's voice cut into Humayun's disturbed dreams. He struggled to wakefulness to see Jauhar's anxious face lit by the flickering light of the candle he was holding in his right hand. 'Ahmed Khan begs to see you at once. He would not even wait for first light. One of his scouts is with him. He has been on the road these past six days and just returned.'

Humayun sat up, splashed his face with water from a brass bowl on a wooden stand by his bed and wrapped a green silk robe around him. A few minutes later, Ahmed Khan and a sweat-soaked scout swaying with fatigue were before him.

'You are certain Sher Shah is on the move?'

'Yes, Majesty. Hear what my scout says.'

The scout stepped closer. 'I would stake my life on it. I waited until from what I saw with my own eyes and heard with my own ears I was absolutely sure and then I rode for Lahore, pausing only to change horses along the road.'

'How many men?'

'It's hard to estimate but by the great dust they were raising on the road, many thousands of cavalry, Majesty.'

'And Sher Shah himself?'

'Still in Agra according to what I heard. But soon he will ride out too, I am sure of it. Before I left, I saw a great baggage train being assembled on the riverbanks beneath the Agra fort – pack mules, oxen and camels without number and hundreds of elephants. Sher Shah's own tents with their purple awnings were being loaded on to carts.' The scout's drawn, filthy face relaxed visibly now his task was accomplished.

As soon as he was alone, Humayun sat cross-legged at his low table. Any further discussions with his brothers would be fruitless. Over the past few days, Askari and Hindal had had little constructive to suggest, preferring to listen to their elder brothers spar. Kamran had continued to argue for confronting Sher Shah and Humayun to insist that without many more men such a strategy would fail, reminding Kamran he'd already fought and lost two great battles against Sher Shah. Since then his enemy had grown stronger while he had grown weaker. This was not the time to seek another head-on confrontation.

And all the while, something he had once read in his father's memoirs had kept returning to Humayun's mind. *If you cannot defeat your enemy by force of arms, do not despair. Find other ways. A sharp, well-oiled double-bladed axe is a fine weapon but so is a finely honed mind that can find a subtler path to victory . . .*

After thinking for a while, Humayun began to write. 'Sher Shah, you seek to take Hindustan from me though it is mine by virtue of my blood descent from Timur. Meet me in single combat and let us settle this dispute for ever. But if you will not fight me, let us at least agree a truce to prevent further bloodshed while we seek other ways to settle our differences.'

Taking a stick of dark red sealing wax, Humayun stuck the end into the flame of a candle and watched the wax soften, then begin to drip ruby droplets like beads of blood. Taking the stick out of the flame, he held it over the bottom of the letter, until a small wax pool had collected. Then, turning his right hand over, he pressed Timur's gold ring hard into the wax to leave a perfect impression of a snarling tiger.

An hour later, Humayun watched two of Ahmed Khan's men

gallop out of Lahore to seek out Sher Shah and deliver his letter. Sher Shah would never agree to personal combat – only a fool would accept such a challenge – but the idea of a truce might tempt him. Stories – admittedly not much more than rumours – brought by travelling merchants suggested discord between some of Sher Shah's commanders. If there was even a speck of truth in them, Sher Shah might welcome a pause to help him re-establish his authority. If so, it would buy Humayun a little more time. There was still no sign of the troops he had summoned from Kabul and probably wouldn't be for at least several more weeks. Every day he could delay Sher Shah would help . . .

Seven days later – an ominous sign of how close Sher Shah now was to Lahore – Humayun had his answer. It was Kasim who brought it to him in his apartments. Strangely there were two letters – one in Sher Shah's bold, ungraceful hand and bearing his seal and the other rolled up in a piece of bamboo that – according to what the scouts had told Kasim – Sher Shah had insisted must also be delivered to Humayun.

Humayun read Sher Shah's letter first. *I have conquered Hindustan. Why should I fight you for what is already mine? I will leave you Kabul – go there.* But there was more: *Why expect to keep an empire when you cannot even command your own family's loyalty? Your brother Kamran is willing to betray you. But I want nothing to do with any of you Moghuls except to see your heads roll in the dust where they belong. I have written to your brother rejecting his offer – just as I reject yours – and telling him I would inform you of his treachery.*

Humayun took the bamboo tube and pulled from it a piece of yellow parchment. Unrolling it, he immediately recognised Kamran's spiky writing. It was his letter to Sher Shah. "'My brother denied me my birthright,'" he read aloud in a voice trembling with anger. "'If you, Sher Shah, will leave me the Punjab and the Moghul lands to the north including Kabul to rule as my own, I will deliver Humayun to you or – if you prefer – slay him with my own hand, I swear it.'"

Kasim picked up Kamran's letter from the floor where Humayun had let it fall and re-read it, face creasing in shock as he took in

Kamran's arrogant, murderous words. Humayun himself strode to the doors and flinging them open shouted, 'Guards, bring my brother Kamran to me immediately. If he resists, overpower and bind him.' He had suspected his brothers might intrigue against him but never that one of them would be so lost to what he owed to the dynasty to offer to betray him to an outsider. Humayun paced his chamber, watched by a silent and anxious Kasim, until at last one of the guards returned.

'Majesty, we cannot find him. We went first to his apartments but he was not there. Then we searched the rest of the fort – we even sent into the women's apartments to see whether he might be with his mother, Her Highness Gulrukh, but she was not there either . . .'

Humayun and Kasim exchanged glances. 'Send me the officer in charge of guarding the main gate – quickly, man!'

A few minutes later a nervous-looking officer was ushered before Humayun.

'Have you seen any of my brothers today?'

'Yes, Majesty. This morning Prince Kamran and Prince Askari went out riding. They have not yet returned . . .'

'And their mother Gulrukh and her women?'

'They too left the palace in a litter. The *begam* said she wished to call on her cousin, the wife of the chief treasurer of Lahore, in her palace in the north of the city.'

Humayun swore. Doubtless she was already with her sons and their troops and they were all hurrying to get beyond his reach. The temptation to ride in pursuit was almost overwhelming but that was exactly what Sher Shah would hope he would do. His enemy had played his hand well, on the one hand giving Humayun evidence of his brother's duplicity and on the other giving Kamran reason to fly. But he would not fall into the trap so artfully set for him by neglecting Sher Shah's threat and immediately pursuing Kamran and Askari to pit brother against brother in battle.

Revenge must wait.

Chapter 10

Flight

Humayun twisted in the saddle. It was thirty-six hours since he had abandoned Lahore to Sher Shah. Behind him streamed his remaining troops, only some fifteen thousand men – many had deserted. Beyond them straggled for miles a desperate mass of humanity half choking in the hot dust, their possessions loaded higgledy-piggledy on carts, donkeys and mules.

Only four days ago a group of travel-stained merchants – so terrified that they'd abandoned their mule trains and goods along the way – had galloped into Lahore, yelling to whoever would listen that Sher Shah was threatening to put the city to the sword. A few hours later, a messenger had arrived from Sher Shah himself. The letter he was carrying was simple and to the point. Sher Shah was indeed threatening to destroy the city and slaughter its people – but only if Humayun refused to withdraw from it.

The decision to quit Lahore just as he had been forced to yield Agra was a terrible humiliation. But Sher Shah commanded vast armies that – if the reports reaching Humayun were true, and there was no reason to doubt them – outnumbered his own forces by twenty to one, perhaps more. Despite the trenches and fortifications he had ordered to be dug, without city walls to protect it any attempt to defend Lahore against such an overwhelming force was doomed, even if the troops he had summoned from Kabul could reach him in time.

After only a few hours' reflection, Humayun had ordered his commanders to prepare to evacuate Lahore. As the news had spread, the citizens had refused to believe that with Humayun gone, Sher Shah would keep his word to spare them. There had been panic. From one of the citadel's stone towers, Humayun had watched people pouring from their houses, clutching cloth-wrapped bundles of their most precious belongings and gripping the hands of small, screaming children. A few carried old people on their backs. Soon the narrow streets had become clogged with handcarts and wagons drawn by stumbling animals. Under the pressure of fear ordinary citizens had lost their reason and become a crazed and callous mob, desperate only to get away and save themselves. Shops had been looted and the weak and frail elbowed and pushed aside, some falling to be trampled and crushed underfoot. It had been like witnessing the end of the world.

The panic and chaos had grown yet worse as the boom of massive explosions had begun to reverberate in the citizens' ears, coming from the great parade ground near the palace where Humayun had ordered the destruction of his largest bronze cannon, which would be too slow and cumbersome to take with him. Teams of straining oxen had dragged the guns out on to open ground where Humayun's gunners, their naked torsos dripping with sweat, had hastily stuffed their barrels with powder and – after fixing long cotton fuses – ignited it, sending fragments of hot, twisted metal into the air.

Snatching his thoughts back to the present, Humayun glanced to his left at the powerful figure of Hindal riding on a great cream-coloured stallion at the head of his own small entourage. Immediately on hearing of Sher Shah's message, Hindal had sought Humayun out and sworn on their father's name that he had known nothing of Kamran's and Askari's defection. Since childhood Hindal had never been good at concealing his emotions and seeing his half-brother's shocked face and incredulity at what Kamran and Askari had done, Humayun had believed him. Later, calm reflection had told him his instincts had been correct. Otherwise, why would Hindal have remained in Lahore and risked retribution? Also, Kamran and Askari were full brothers. Hindal – like Humayun himself – was only their half-brother, so the ties of blood and honour were weaker. As if sensing Humayun watching him, Hindal turned his head and gave him a brief smile. It was good that Hindal had chosen to stay with him, thought Humayun. Perhaps amid the present danger to their dynasty at least two of Babur's sons could form an enduring bond and draw strength from it.

In the last desperate hours before abandoning Lahore to his rapidly advancing enemy, Humayun had embraced Baisanghar and bidden him farewell, perhaps for the last time. It had been hard to part from his grandfather and even harder to convince the old man he must go north with a detachment of troops to secure Kabul for Humayun. Again and again Humayun had had to argue that Kamran and Askari might take advantage of his plight to try to seize the kingdom, that he no longer had confidence in his governor there who had been so tardy in sending reinforcements and that Baisanghar was one of the very few he could trust unreservedly to hold it for him.

This was true, but there was another reason too why Humayun wanted his grandfather to go north, although he could not have admitted it to Baisanghar. Though the warrior spirit still burned within him and his mind was clear, he was old — eight years older even than Kasim — and losing his physical stamina. He'd be safer as well as more useful in Kabul rather than draining his small remaining stock of strength accompanying Humayun on the long, perhaps dangerous, journey he had decided on: six hundred miles southwest down the Ravi and Indus rivers to Sind. The Sultan of Sind, Mirza Husain, was of Humayun's blood — his mother was Babur's cousin — so he was honour bound to receive Humayun. But would honour mean any more to Mirza Husain than it had to his half-brothers with whom his ties of blood were so much closer?

Eventually, Baisanghar had given way, persuaded by the logic of Humayun's arguments. However, Khanzada and Gulbadan had been harder to deal with and this time it was Humayun who had conceded defeat. His aunt and half-sister had refused to accompany Baisanghar. 'I have earned the right to decide my own fate,' Khanzada had insisted quietly. 'All the years I suffered in Shaibani Khan's *haram*, I told myself that if I survived never again would I lose control of

155

my life, my destiny, even if death was the only alternative. And the destiny I choose is to go with you, nephew.' Gulbadan had remained silent throughout this speech but Humayun had noticed how tightly she was gripping Khanzada's hand and how determined was her expression. When Khanzada had finished speaking Gulbadan too had made clear her wishes to accompany Hindal and Humayun.

In his heart Humayun was glad they were with him. They were riding close by on sturdy brown ponies, followed by their attendants and the wives and daughters of some of his and Hindal's commanders, including Zahid Beg's wife, also mounted on ponies. Speed was vital and this was no time for more decorous modes of transport, concealed from the common gaze behind the curtains of litters or howdahs. Nevertheless, the small group of women was closely guarded by the most trusted of Humayun's bodyguards and well hidden from prying eyes beneath voluminous garments, their hair bound up and concealed by tight-fitting caps. Above the cotton face cloths that protected them from the wind and the choking dust only their eyes were visible.

There should have been a further pair of eyes — grey ones — to gladden his soul, Humayun thought. Before finally quitting the Lahore palace he had paid a brief visit to the newly dug grave in the garden where Salima had been buried only two days before. She too would have wanted to go with him — he was sure of it — but a sudden fever contracted just as news came of Sher Shah's ultimatum and with chaos rising all around had claimed her life within twenty-four hours of its onset. In the last minutes of her sweating delirium, her staring, unfocused eyes had not recognised him or seen the tears in his eyes as he held her small hand in his own larger one and watched as her last breaths fled from her body. He would miss her so much. Since he had abandoned Gulrukh's opium-laced wine and even more since his defeats at the hands of Sher Shah, Salima had become ever more important to him, providing an all-consuming physical relief from his mental doubts and daily cares and responsibilities.

But there was no time now for grief or for reflections upon the fragility of human existence. All the time as he rode Humayun kept returning to the same question. Had he done the right thing in abandoning Lahore? The answer, though, was always the same. Faced with an imminent bloodbath – the massacre of so many thousands of innocent citizens – he'd had no choice but to order his forces to retreat across the broad wooden bridge that spanned the Ravi river north of the city. As soon as his men were safely over, he'd had the bridge destroyed to hinder Sher Shah's troops from pursuing him. The camp followers had had to cross as best they could, scrambling aboard fishing- and ferry-boats.

But Sher Shah had as yet made no attempt to pursue Humayun who, after a day and a half almost constantly in the saddle, was now forty miles clear of Lahore. With each passing mile and hour he became more and more convinced that he would be given time to re-group. It was also good that those cannon he had been able to bring with him – dragged to the Ravi river by bullocks – had been safely loaded on to rafts to be floated downriver under the care of Humayun's gunnery commander and his men. Their orders were to wait for the rest of the army to catch up at Multan, two hundred miles southwest of Lahore. He was well provided with muskets, powder and shot as well as with treasure in coin and gems which he could use to pay his forces and buy provisions for them as they journeyed to Sind. Perhaps things were not as bleak as they seemed.

But gazing up into the bleached, cloud-streaked skies, Humayun saw two vultures, circling doubtless above some dead or dying creature. At Panipat – just before the Moghuls' great victory – he had seen eagles wheeling above the battlefield. From noble eagles to filthy, ill-omened devourers of carrion . . . Was that a symbol of how his fortunes had declined? Humayun plucked an arrow from the gilded leather case hanging across his back and, unstrapping his double-curved bow from his saddle, sent an arrow hissing through the hot air. It found its mark. Swiftly he drew another arrow but as he looked up, eagerly seeking his second target, all he saw above him was an empty sky.

'Majesty, my scouts report a small band of riders still some three or four miles off but galloping quickly towards us,' Ahmed Khan said, reining in his horse.

'God willing, it's the messenger I sent to Mirza Husain, returning with an escort. But just in case, halt the column and order the men to take up defensive positions around its perimeter. Post extra guards around the women and the treasure.'

'Yes, Majesty.'

With luck, the arduous six-week trek from Multan, where he had rendezvoused as planned with his gunners and cannon, and then along the Indus would soon be over and he could plan how to regain the initiative against Sher Shah. Humayun strained his eyes towards the western horizon where the great, blood-red sun was sinking rapidly. Soon, he could make out a cloud of dust rising from among the spindly trees and tumbled rocks ahead and then the horsemen themselves – about thirty of them – led by a cavalryman whose steel helmet glinted in the last rays of sunlight. As the horsemen reined in, Humayun saw that the messenger he had despatched with letters to Mirza Husain nearly two weeks ago was indeed among them. The leading rider removed his helmet, dismounted and made obeisance.

'Greetings, Majesty. Mirza Husain, Sultan of Sind welcomes you to his lands. He awaits you at a camp just ten miles from here. He denied himself the honour of greeting you in person because he wished to assure himself that all was ready for your reception. I – the captain of his bodyguard – and my men will escort you there.'

Dusk had fallen by the time Humayun saw the orange light of camp fires through the dark silhouettes of the trees. The only time he had seen Mirza Husain was many years ago when the sultan had come to Kabul to pay his respects to Babur and he'd no memory of what he looked like. The tall, straight-backed man waiting in the centre of the camp, hand on breast and dressed in magnificent red robes with a tightly wound golden turban on his head, was therefore a stranger to him.

'Welcome, Majesty. Your arrival honours my kingdom.'

'Your hospitality is most welcome, cousin. My brother and I thank you.'

Mirza Husain was a good-looking man if a little fleshy, Humayun thought as the ritual exchange of courtesies continued. Before he let himself run to fat he must have been a good fighter. He recalled Babur's stories of how Mirza Husain had consolidated and enlarged his kingdom, even taking land from his neighbour to the south in Gujarat, Bahadur Shah. While Humayun had been fighting in Gujarat, Mirza Husain had sent messages of support but had offered no troops. Neither had Humayun asked his cousin for any. Confident of victory, he'd had no wish to share Gujarat's rich booty any more widely than he'd needed to.

'Everything is ready for your reception, Majesty. Special quarters have been prepared for the women, near your own, and rows of tents erected for your soldiers. Tonight you must rest. I have ordered food to be brought to you. Three days from now, when we reach my palace at Sarkar, we can talk of former times.'

And of future ones, Humayun thought to himself. He needed Mirza Husain's help if he could be persuaded to give it. But of course the courtesies must be observed . . .

That evening, lying back on a brocade-covered bed in his own tent, Humayun felt himself begin to relax for the first time since leaving Lahore. He had brought his family and his remaining forces to safety. God willing, soon he would be riding to battle again.

• ◆ •

Sixty hours later under a blazing sun, with Mirza Husain on one side and Hindal on the other, Humayun rode into the fortress palace of Sarkar, set within thick walls on a high rocky promontory overlooking the sea. Above the gatehouse, two banners fluttered in the clear air – the scarlet red of Sind and by its side the brilliant green of the Moghuls. The palace, approached up a short, steep ramp leading up from the gatehouse, was a golden-stoned building constructed around three sides of a courtyard.

Installed in opulent apartments covering almost the entire middle floor of the palace's west wing, Humayun summoned Hindal and

Kasim. He wished to confer with them alone without the listening ears of his own attendants, apart from Jauhar whom he trusted with his life and who was standing on guard by the door.

Humayun gestured Hindal and Kasim to be seated. The vizier lowered himself with difficulty. The hardships of recent weeks had taken their toll. Kasim looked even thinner and more stooped than before. Humayun waited while his old counsellor settled himself before speaking. 'Though for courtesy's sake I've not yet said anything, Mirza Husain knows very well why I have come – that I want his help against Sher Shah. Soon, though, I must raise the matter and wish to be prepared. Have you yet managed to glean anything of his thoughts or intentions from those around him, Kasim?'

'I may have learned something of what is in his mind . . .' Kasim said cautiously. 'People reveal more than they realise if you are a good listener . . . I've been told that when Mirza Husain first read your letter asking him to receive you, he was thrown into great consternation. He has no desire for his kingdom with its prosperous merchants and harbours crammed with cargo dhows from Arabia to be drawn into a conflict. He even fears you mean to take his kingdom from him . . .'

'Then why did he welcome us here? He could have made excuses,' asked Hindal.

Humayun grunted. 'He had little choice. He is our cousin and I think that means something to him. Also, despite my reverses I am an emperor intending to recover my lands and, when I do, well placed to reward him and to further his ambitions. Mirza Husain knows this. And unless he wished for an open breach he could not bar his doors against me. But whatever is in his heart and mind, I must plan our next steps. Has any further news reached us of Sher Shah's movements these past three days?'

'None, Majesty,' said Kasim. 'From what little we can glean from travellers and others, he has still not moved beyond Lahore.'

'And what news of Kamran and Askari?'

'No one knows where they are at present, Majesty. According to some rumours they have withdrawn northwards up the Kabul river to Badakhshan – but as I say, Majesty, those are only rumours . . .'

Humayun frowned. 'Sometimes I wonder whether Kamran wasn't playing an even deeper game than I realized, and Sher Shah also. What if the whole business of Kamran's offer to betray me and Sher Shah's rejection of it was a subterfuge by the pair of them to draw me out of Lahore so their forces could fall on mine and destroy them?'

'It's possible, Majesty,' said Kasim. 'We cannot discount it.'

'I also keep wondering how much Askari knew of Kamran's plans. Did they scheme together to betray me to Sher Shah or did Askari flee with Kamran because he thought I would never believe he hadn't been implicated?'

This time Hindal answered. 'I'm sure Askari did know. He always follows where Kamran leads. I do not speak from malice but because I have reason to know – I was once the same.'

'I suspect you are right. Unlike Kamran, Askari's weak and he stands in awe of his elder brother,' said Humayun. 'Consequently, his treachery hurts me less. In my boyhood it was Kamran – almost my equal in age – that I played and hunted and sparred with. Though we often argued – sometimes even fought – for a while we were close . . . almost like full brothers. That he should desire my death brings me almost as much grief as anger . . .'

A knock on the door interrupted him and he fell silent as Jauhar swung the well-oiled rosewood doors open to see who was there. Humayun heard low voices conversing outside, then Jauhar reappeared.

'Forgive me, Majesty, but Mirza Husain has sent his vizier with a message.'

'Admit him.'

The vizier, slight and fine-boned with a direct, intelligent gaze, made an elaborate obeisance. 'Pardon me, Majesty, for disturbing you but Mirza Husain begs that you and your brother will honour him with your presence at a feast tonight.'

'Of course.' Humayun nodded graciously. 'We would be pleased to attend and thank Mirza Husain for his hospitality.'

The vizier bowed and withdrew.

As soon as the doors were closed again, Hindal smiled. 'A good sign, don't you think? Mirza Husain can't do enough for us . . .'

'You may be right, but he may be trying to placate us with small things while seeking to deny us what we really want . . . let us see . . .'

That evening, as a hazy, pink dusk was falling, drums began to beat softly. Humayun and Hindal followed the attendants sent by Mirza Husain into the palace's central wing and up a long, shallow staircase strewn with jasmine petals and lit by wicks burning in *diyas* filled with scented oil. At the top of the stairs, Humayun and Hindal passed through a carved marble doorway into an octagonal chamber ablaze with light from giant silver candelabras and torches burning in gilded sconces on the walls. Rugs gleaming with gold thread covered the floor while the walls were hung with richly coloured brocades decorated with strings of pearls and coloured glass globes. Directly ahead was a dais draped in silver cloth and piled with cushions.

As Humayun and his brother entered, musicians struck up. A smiling Mirza Husain advanced towards his cousins. Hanging necklaces of frangipani blossoms around their necks after the Hindustani custom, he led them to the places of honour on the dais. Once they were comfortably seated, he clapped his hands and a succession of bearers entered through a side entrance, each carrying a golden dish upon his shoulder piled with food – pomfret fish steamed in banana leaves or simmered in creamy coconut sauce, sides of roast deer, haunches of spiced lamb, aubergines delicately smoked and pureed, fluffy rice cooked with split peas and hot bread stuffed with sultanas and dried apricots.

'Eat, Majesty, eat, and you, Prince Hindal. Eat, my cousins, you are my honoured guests. See, the food is good . . . Tell me what dishes tempt you and I myself will be your food taster. You have no reason to fear while under my roof . . .'

'I thank you, cousin. And I have no fear.' To secure his cousin's help, Humayun knew he must indeed demonstrate trust. Without hesitating, he took a piece of hot bread and wrapping it around a chunk of fish began to eat. 'The food is indeed good.'

Later, as Humayun lay against his cushions, Mirza Husain clapped his hands and three girls entered the room through a side entrance and bowed low before him, eyes downcast. Then, simultaneously striking their tambourines with their palms and stamping their feet on the floor causing the bronze bells around their ankles to clash, they began to dance. One was tall and slender, the other two shorter and more voluptuous. Their short, tight bodices left their midriffs bare. The swell of their hips and buttocks was emphasised by the diaphanous pale pink silk of their voluminous trousers, which fastened round their waists with gold cord that ended in pearl tassels. Watching the girls whirl before him, for a moment Humayun imagined he was back in the Agra fort, his empire intact and nothing to concern him but the quest for yet greater glory and which concubine to choose for his night's pleasure.

At a wave of Mirza Husain's bejewelled hand, the girls ran off. Attendants cleared the dishes and others brought new ones – platters of ripe fruits stuffed with marzipan, delicate almonds covered in silver leaf. But something else was shining amongst them. Looking more closely, Humayun saw that the sweetmeats rested on a bed of gems – rubies, carnelians, emeralds, turquoises, pearls of many shapes and hues and glowing golden cat's-eyes.

'These are my gift to you, cousin.' Mirza Husain selected a ruby and held it out to Humayun. 'See the quality of this gem.'

Humayun took the stone from him and examined it. 'You are gracious and generous.'

'I have sent other gifts to your commanders – jewelled scimitars, daggers, bridles and gilded quivers, paltry compared with the glories of the Moghul court of which I have heard so much, I know, but none the less acceptable, I hope. And now, I have another favour to ask. Will you permit me to present my youngest daughter to you?'

'Of course.'

Mirza Husain whispered something to an attendant. A few minutes later, a short, slight young woman appeared in the great doorway through which two hours earlier Humayun and Hindal had entered. Head erect, she walked slowly towards the dais. Humayun saw dark eyes and a wide-cheekboned, almost feline face. Reaching the dais, she knelt before it, eyes to the ground.

'This is Khanam.'

At Mirza Husain's words, Khanam raised her head and looked straight into Humayun's eyes.

'My daughter is a skilled musician. Will you allow her to play for you?'

'Of course. It would be a pleasure to hear her.'

At a signal from her father, Khanam stepped back a few paces and taking a round-bellied, long-necked stringed instrument from an attendant sat down on a wooden stool another brought for her. Mirza Husain had not exaggerated his daughter's talent. As she plucked the strings, haunting, soaring notes filled the chamber. Closing his eyes for a moment, Humayun saw his mother Maham, head bent over the lute that had once belonged to his great-grandmother Esan Dawlat who had preserved it throughout his family's dangerous, often desperate days in search of a throne.

'Khanam's a beauty, isn't she? The pick of all my daughters. Her mother was Persian.' Mirza Husain's voice cut into his thoughts.

'Your daughter is very beautiful,' Humayun replied dutifully though for his taste she was a little too thin and certainly nothing to compare with Salima's voluptuous charms. Her death – the cruel and sudden extinction of so much beauty and vitality – still haunted him. It seemed a symbol of how much he had lost these past months.

Mirza Husain bent nearer, reducing his voice to a whisper that only Humayun could hear. 'And she is ripe for marriage. I am wealthy. Her dowry will be considerable . . . almost imperial . . .' He smiled, the implication of his words unmistakable.

Humayun looked at Khanam, long hair reddened with henna falling round her as she continued to play. Why not? he thought. Babur had made several dynastic marriages to secure his position. Though Khanam didn't stir him particularly, her looks were well enough. She shared his blood and her father would be a useful friend in the struggle against Sher Shah. Why not form an alliance to be consummated one day in the marriage bed? It seemed that for once Kasim's information had been wrong – Mirza Husain was willing to help him. But of one thing Humayun was certain. Before he could think of taking a wife he must defeat his enemies and be sure of his throne. The time had come for plain speaking.

'Mirza Husain, I would be glad one day to consider Khanam as a wife. She is a fine-looking, accomplished young woman. First, though, my thoughts must be on war and the recovery of my lost lands, not on marriage, and I want your help. You have been generous with your hospitality and your gifts but I need your armies. Let us proclaim our alliance to the world.'

Humayun sat back against the cushions, expecting Mirza Husain's gratitude, even joy. The prospect of marriage with the Moghul emperor was beyond anything the sultan could have hoped for his daughter. But he saw that his host's smile was no longer so good-natured. The curve of his lips seemed to harden and his eyes to grow cold. 'Khanam, enough! Leave us now.' His tone was sharp.

Khanam looked up in surprise and at once stopped playing. Rising, with a swish of her long, dark blue robes she hurried from the chamber.

'Cousin, let us understand one another.' Mirza Husain spoke quietly. 'I did not invite you here. You came. I received you out of duty. Sher Shah is in Lahore, barely six hundred miles away – perhaps nearer for all we know – with armies far outnumbering yours and mine combined. For the present I dare not antagonise him. I can give you money and I will willingly give you my daughter if you will promise to protect and honour her but no more than that. Take Khanam with my blessing, as my gift to absolve me with honour of further obligations to you in your present troubles, but leave my lands before you bring disaster upon me and my people.'

Mirza Husain's voice had risen so all could hear and Humayun saw Hindal looking at him with astonishment. Hot anger flooded through him. Kasim had been right after all. 'Mirza Husain, the blood of Timur – of the *amirzada* – runs through your veins yet you speak like a merchant not a warrior . . .'

Mirza Husain flushed. The taunt had bitten home, Humayun saw with satisfaction. No man liked to hear such words – even less to hear them under his own roof.

'Your ambition is dangerous,' said Mirza Husain. 'Accept your setback. Leave Hindustan. Go back to Kabul, to your homelands there. They are a sufficient kingdom. You cannot flourish where you do not belong.'

'You forget yourself. My father conquered Hindustan and founded an empire which he bequeathed to me. I do belong there. You should not be trying to buy me off with a bag of gold and your daughter . . . Instead, you and I should be planning how to recapture my lands. Immediately we have won our first victories, others will rally once more to my banner. Yet you refuse to recognise this. You have grown so fat on trade you seem to have forgotten our warrior code and the obligations and ambitions it carries with it . . .'

In his anger, Humayun had forgotten that others as well as his brother were close by. Several of Mirza Husain's nobles were seated round low tables beneath the dais and suddenly he became aware of the silence that had fallen and of their startled glances. This was no time to provoke a fight or even an open breach. Humayun forced a smile to his lips though he felt like taking his host's plump throat in his hands. 'But I forget myself. I am your guest. I speak my mind too plainly. This is neither the time nor the place for such a discussion, Mirza Husain. Forgive me. We will talk again tomorrow when we can be alone and when we have both had a chance to reflect.'

But the look on Mirza Husain's face told Humayun that he had little to hope for from the ruler of Sind.

Chapter 11

Hamida

Four hours after Humayun had led his column out through the gatehouse on which the green Moghul banners no longer fluttered, the fortress palace of Sarkar finally faded from view. As he rode slowly northeastwards, Humayun was locked in his thoughts. Though Mirza Husain's hospitality had remained ostentatiously lavish, there had been no point staying any longer in Sind. With so few men to back him, Humayun had no power to coerce Mirza Husain to help him and every day that passed had seemed a humiliation to him.

It felt good to be on the move again and at least he had exacted a high price from Mirza Husain for the four cannon he had decided to leave behind in case they slowed his progress. Eager to be rid of his unwanted guest, the sultan had paid handsomely. He had also given Humayun grain and other supplies to feed his men and fresh pack animals to carry them. If all went well, in two months' time Humayun would be entering the desert kingdom of Marwar whose Rajput ruler, Raja Maldeo, seemed more ready to assist him than his cousin. The raja's ambassador, a tall, thin man in brightly coloured robes with his long hair bound in the Rajput fashion, had reached Sarkar two weeks before. He had spoken eloquently to Humayun of Raja Maldeo's contempt for Sher Shah and his enmity towards him.

'The interloper Sher Shah has demanded the raja's allegiance in his fight against the Moghuls. He has insulted my master's honour by daring to threaten the kingdom of Marwar if he refuses to join him. But my master will never unite with a mongrel dog from the marshes of Bengal. Instead, he extends his hand to you, Majesty. He invites you to Marwar as his honoured guest so that you and he may discuss how to combine against the interloper. With your approval he will also summon other Rajput rulers who, like him, have been affronted by Sher Shah's impudence.'

The screeching of a flock of green parakeets flying low overhead recalled Humayun to the present. He glanced at Hindal, riding by his side on the long-necked, powerfully built chestnut stallion he had purchased from an Arab horse-dealer in Sind.

'In another ten miles we'll make camp for the night,' Humayun said.

'We should. The women will be tired . . .'

'I'll order some sheep to be killed and roasted. Tonight you and I and the women of our households will feast in my tent together with our chief commanders and courtiers. And I will have tables set up outside for our soldiers. It will raise the spirits of us all . . .'

'Do you really think the Raja of Marwar will help us?'

'Why not? I often heard our father speak of Rajput pride. If Maldeo truly believes Sher Shah has insulted him, he'll not rest until he has avenged the slight and what better way than to ride at our side with his Rajput warriors to destroy Sher Shah? Of course the raja will expect favours in return but the courage of the Rajputs is legendary. Maldeo will be a worthy ally and when I sit on my throne in Agra once more I will reward him.'

'You still have faith in our dynasty and its destiny, after all that has happened . . . ?'

'Yes. Even in my bleakest moments when I think of all the blood that has been shed and of Kamran's and Askari's treachery, I don't doubt it. I believe that fate summoned the Moghuls to Hindustan. Don't you feel it too?'

Hindal, though, said nothing.

'Our father endured many setbacks and he never gave up,' Humayun persisted. 'If you doubt me, read his diaries or talk to our aunt. Khanzada is growing old but our father's passion, the passion of our ancestors, lives on undimmed in her. She was the one who tore me from my opium dreams and made me see that a sense of greatness isn't enough – that we must be prepared to fight and struggle and sweat blood for what is ours.'

'Ours?'

'Of course. Though our father named me emperor, we are all Babur's sons, all part of the Moghul destiny – you, me and even Kamran and Askari. We bear the same responsibilities. Our dynasty is young, the roots barely finding a purchase in this alien soil, but we can – we will – be great so long as we do not lose our self-belief or tear our dynasty apart by fighting one another.'

'Perhaps you are right. Sometimes, though, it all seems such a burden that I wish I were back in Kabul, that our father had never heard of Hindustan . . .' The expression in Hindal's tawny eyes was unconvinced and his tall, thick-set body seemed to slump despondently in the saddle.

Humayun reached out and touched his brother's muscular shoulder. 'I understand,' he said quietly, 'but it was not our choice to be born who we are.'

Three hours later, the camp fires were being lit in the lee of a low, stony hill that Ahmed Khan – riding ahead with his scouts – had found. Humayun's large scarlet tent was pitched in the centre with Hindal's next to it. Fifty yards away were tents for Khanzada and Gulbadan and their attendants and for the small group of women in Hindal's entourage, all enclosed by baggage wagons drawn up around them in a protective circle with their traces knotted.

Men squatted on the ground, slapping a mixture of flour and water into flat loaves to bake on hot clay tiles in the fire. Soon the aroma of lamb was mingling with the smell of wood smoke as the cooks' boys slowly rotated the sharpened stakes on which chunks of new-slain sheep, salted and rubbed with herbs, had been spitted. The fires hissed as the fat ran into the leaping flames. Humayun's stomach growled as, inside his tent, he drew off his gauntlets and Jauhar unclipped his sword belt.

'Jauhar, this is the first feast I've held since we left Lahore. Though it will be poor compared with the celebrations I once held in my palaces, we must put on a good display. All must eat and drink their fill . . . For those eating in my tent, have the silver and gold dishes unpacked . . . and I wish you to play your flute for us. It is a long time since I have heard you.'

Later that night, dressed in a dark green tunic over buckskin trousers and jewelled dagger tucked into his yellow sash, Humayun looked around him with satisfaction. To his left, Hindal and the senior officers were sitting in a semicircle on the ground, laughing and talking. Zahid Beg was gnawing on a lamb bone. Despite his leanness, he could easily out-eat any of Humayun's other commanders and took pride in his gigantic appetite. Humayun smiled to see him discard the bone and hack off a fresh hunk of roasted flesh with his dagger.

On the far side of the tent, encircled by high screens that concealed them from view, a small group of women including Khanzada and Gulbadan were seated. Their conversation sounded decorously muted and their laughter was more restrained than the men's but almost as frequent. Humayun hoped they had everything they wanted and decided to see for himself. Looking round the edge of the screen he saw Gulbadan talking to a young woman seated close beside her, feet gracefully curled beneath her. The woman's face was in shadow but as she leaned forward to take a sweetmeat from a dish, candle-light illuminated her features.

Humayun felt a tightening in his stomach as he took in the graceful set of her small head on her long slender neck, the pale oval of her face, the shining dark hair pulled back and secured with jewelled combs and the luminous eyes which, suddenly aware of his scrutiny, she turned towards him. Her gaze was open and appraising – no trace of nervousness that she was looking at the emperor – and it sent an almost visceral shock through him. As Humayun continued to stare, the young woman dropped her gaze and turned back to Gulbadan. Her profile – they were sharing some joke by the way she was smiling – showed a small nose and delicate chin. Then, leaning back, she was once more lost to the shadows.

Humayun returned to his place with the men, his polite interest in the women's well-being completely forgotten. As the feast continued he found it hard to concentrate, so haunted was he by that glimpse of an unknown face. He tapped his brother on the shoulder.

'Hindal, there's a young woman sitting by your sister whom I don't recognise – take a look and tell me if you know her.' Hindal rose, went across to the screen and peered round. Then slowly he returned to Humayun's side.

'Well?'

It seemed to Humayun that Hindal hesitated before answering. 'Her name is Hamida. She's the daughter of my vizier, Shaikh Ali Akbar . . .'

'How old is she?'

'About fourteen or fifteen . . .'

'To which of the clans does Shaikh Ali Akbar belong?'

'His family is of Persian descent but were long settled in Samarkand until, in our father's time, the Uzbeks drove them out. Shaikh Ali Akbar fled as a young man and eventually found his way to my province of Alwar. I made him my chief counsellor there.'

'Is he a good counsellor?'

'Yes. And something more than that, perhaps. The blood of a famous mystic runs in his veins – Ahmad of Jam, who had the ability to foretell events. In his lifetime he was known as *Zinda-fil*, "the Terrible Elephant", because of his powers.'

'Tomorrow morning before we march send Shaikh Ali Akbar to me. I wish to talk to him.'

Humayun barely slept that night. Though in Sarkar he had told Mirza Husain he would not take a wife until he had won back his throne, he knew in his very soul that he must marry Hamida. There was no thought, no logic to it, just an overwhelming attraction. A feeling which, despite his many previous lovers, he had never experienced with such overpowering intensity before, not even when he had chosen Salima. It was not simply the desire to possess Hamida physically – though that was certainly a part of it. Instinctively he sensed within her a beauty of mind, a strength of spirit radiating out towards him. He knew that not only would she make him happy but that with her by his side he would also be a better ruler, more able to achieve his ambitions. However hard he tried to dismiss such

171

thoughts as irrational and better fitted to a blushing adolescent, they returned with renewed vigour. Was this what the poets described as falling in love?

Even before it was light, Humayun washed, dressed and then, dismissing his attendants, waited impatiently. At last his men began to stir, kicking the smouldering embers of last night's fires into new life and starting to pack up their tents and possessions ready for the day's ride. Then he heard footsteps outside his tent and Jauhar held back the flap as Shaikh Ali Akbar ducked inside.

'Majesty, you wished to see me.' Shaikh Ali Akbar was tall and, like his daughter, fine-boned. He made graceful obeisance to Humayun and waited.

'I saw your daughter, Hamida, at the feast last night. I want to make her my wife. She will be my empress and the mother of emperors . . .' Humayun burst out.

Shaikh Ali Akbar looked astonished.

'Well, Shaikh Ali Akbar?' Humayun persisted impatiently.

'She is so young . . .'

'Many are married at her age. I will treat her with great honour, I promise you . . .'

'But my family is not worthy . . .'

'You are nobles of Samarkand . . . Why object if I wish to raise your daughter further as my father did my own mother? Her father – my grandfather Baisanghar – was a nobleman of Samarkand like yourself.'

Shaikh Ali Akbar said nothing. Puzzled, Humayun stepped closer. From the man's troubled face something was wrong. 'What is it? Most fathers would rejoice.'

'It is a great, an unimaginable honour, Majesty. But I believe . . . no, I know . . . that your half-brother Prince Hindal cares for Hamida. He has known her since she was a child. I serve him and it would be disloyal of me to give her to another, even you, Majesty, without telling you this.'

'Are they yet betrothed?'

'No, Majesty.'

'And Hamida. What are her wishes?'

172

'I do not know, Majesty. I've never spoken to her of such things and I have no wife who could have done so . . . Hamida's mother died of a fever soon after she was born.'

'You have been honest. I respect that but I repeat that I wish to wed your daughter. Give me your answer within a week from now. And Shaikh Ali . . . my brother told me that the blood of a great seer who could foretell events runs through your veins . . . If you, like him, have the power to see into the future, use it. You will see that greatness – and happiness – await your daughter if you will give her to me.'

'Majesty.' But Shaikh Ali Akbar's face still looked anxious and unhappy as he turned to leave. Shafts of sunlight came pouring into the tent, dazzling Humayun for a moment, as Shaikh Ali Akbar pushed the entrance flap aside and vanished.

That day, needing space to think, Humayun decided to leave the main column and gallop alone. As the rhythmic thud of his horse's hooves filled his ears, he was still trying to come to terms with these feelings so unexpected, so overpowering, so sudden. No other woman had roused such sensations in him. Something darker was also lurking in his heart – guilt that he wanted to take a woman loved by his half-brother. But he could not get Hamida's exquisite face, her shining personality, out of his mind. He would make her his empress however much he bruised Hindal's feelings.

That evening, Humayun was splashing his face with cold water brought to him in a brass ewer by Jauhar when he heard raised voices outside his tent. Then Hindal burst in, still in his riding clothes, soiled and dusty after the day's journey.

'Is it true?' Hindal's voice was quiet but his eyes were burning.

'Is what true?' Humayun gestured to Jauhar to withdraw.

'Shaikh Ali Akbar tells me you wish to marry Hamida.'

'Yes. I want her for my wife.'

'She . . . she is the daughter of my vizier. I watched her grow up . . . My claim to her is stronger than yours . . .' Hindal seemed almost hysterical.

'I did not want to cause you pain, but it will pass. You will find another woman to please you . . .'

'These last few months I thought we had come to understand one another. I trusted you. I gave you my support when – like Kamran and Askari – I could have sought my fortune elsewhere and perhaps fared better. What reward have I had for following you? Nothing! We fled Lahore with our tails between our legs. In Sind we fared little better – fed like little lap dogs by Mirza Husain until we took ourselves off. Still I remained loyal and worked to keep my force of men together in the hopes that soon you and I would be fighting shoulder to shoulder against Sher Shah. Instead, like a thief in the night, without a moment's thought, you have decided to abuse your position as head of our family to steal the woman I love . . .'

'Believe me, I didn't know that you cared for her until I spoke to her father.'

'But it didn't stop you when you found out, did it?' Hindal came closer. 'Kamran and Askari were right. You are the self-appointed centre of your own universe. For years you ignored us, leaving us to fester in our provinces while you played the great emperor. It was only because you needed us against Sher Shah that you began to speak of fraternal duty, of bonding together against a common enemy.'

Hindal's voice was rising to a shout and he was shaking with pent-up fury. Instinctively, Humayun glanced to the chest on which a few minutes earlier Jauhar had placed Alamgir in its jewelled scabbard. He still had his dagger and could feel its hard metal hilt pressing against his ribs beneath his sash.

'Be careful what you say, brother . . .'

'Half-brother only.'

'You forget why I sent you and the others away. You plotted against me. I could have had you executed . . . I gave you back your life.'

'I was just a youth, easily led. If you'd shown any interest in me it would never have happened. But all you ever wanted to do was stare at the stars . . . You still have no desire to know what I'm really like, what my hopes and aspirations are. You just want my unquestioning loyalty and obedience so you can realise your own ambitions . . .'

Humayun had never seen or heard his half-brother so animated. He was breathing heavily. His face was flushed, his nostrils were dilated and a vein throbbed at his temple.

174

'We must not quarrel over this, Hindal. Believe me, this isn't just some whim or momentary lust for a new woman. I didn't plan it – it happened. When I saw her at the feast I knew . . .'

But Hindal didn't seem to be listening. Without warning he launched himself at Humayun who, taken off guard, didn't move quickly enough. Hindal's powerful hands grabbed him by the shoulders and the next thing Humayun knew, he was crashing into a tall iron incense burner.

Hearing the noise, Humayun's guards rushed into the tent. 'No!' he shouted, waving them back. Hindal was closing in on him again and Humayun felt his half-brother's leather-booted foot slam into his ribs, knocking the breath from him. But from the days of his youth Humayun had been a good wrestler – quick and strong – and the skills hadn't deserted him. Instinctively he grabbed at Hindal's foot as his brother tried to kick him again and twisted it sharply. Thrown off balance, Hindal's heavy body tumbled sideways and he hit his head on the edge of the metal-bound chest where Humayun kept his most valued possessions – the Koh-i-Nur and his father's diaries.

With blood trickling from his temple and looking dazed, Hindal hauled himself to his feet. Before he could steady himself, Humayun ducked forward, pitting his speed and momentum against Hindal's bulk. Hooking his right foot behind Hindal's left leg, he succeeded in pushing him backwards, falling with him and landing on top. He seized Hindal's head with both hands, raised it up then brought it smashing down on the ground. Hindal writhed beneath him, trying to dislodge him, but Humayun's fingers were pressing on his windpipe. Hindal's breath was coming in great, rasping sobs as he thrashed wildly, almost sending Humayun flying. However, gripping as hard as he could with his thighs, Humayun stayed uppermost and pressed harder on his brother's throat.

He felt Hindal slacken beneath him and looked down at his face – it might be a trick, one that he'd used many times himself in wrestling contests – but Hindal's eyes were closed and his face was purpling. Humayun relaxed his grip and rose cautiously from his brother's prone body, eyes never for an instant leaving him.

Hindal was taking great gulping mouthfuls of air as he struggled to breathe and his hands were clutching at his neck which Humayun could see was already darkening with bruises. After a few moments, he got shakily to his feet, looking like a great bear that had just been worsted in a fight. The cut on his temple was bleeding even more profusely, so that blood was dripping on to the front of his tunic. But the eyes he turned on Humayun were clear, bright and defiant.

'Take her then. You are the emperor as you never tire of reminding me. But do not expect to see me again. Our alliance is over. Tonight I will take my men and ride from here.'

'I didn't want to hurt you. You forced me to. Don't act rashly . . . I never schemed to take Hamida from you . . . but when I saw her I knew it was meant to be . . .'

A sneer spread across Hindal's bleeding face. 'Meant to be . . . ? You still don't understand the minds of men, do you, not even your own brother's. You inhabit a different world in which you confuse fate or destiny with your own desires and much good may it do you. Goodbye, brother.' Drawing himself up, Hindal spat slowly and deliberately on the carpet, sending a gob of bloody saliva to land just in front of Humayun's right boot. Then, without a backward glance, he walked slowly and painfully but straight-backed towards the entrance of the tent, looking to neither right nor left as Humayun's bodyguards parted to let him pass.

For a moment Humayun was tempted to go after him, but what would be the point? After what had been said, there could be no going back. 'Jauhar,' he called. As soon as Jauhar was by his side, Humayun lowered his voice so they would not be overheard. 'Send my bodyguards immediately to the tents of my brother's women. They are to find Hamida, daughter of Shaikh Ali Akbar, my brother's vizier, and escort her into the care of my aunt. Hurry, and let me know as soon as my orders have been carried out . . .'

Half an hour later, Jauhar returned to report that Hamida had been taken to Khanzada. Outside, Humayun could hear men shouting and running about, oxen bellowing, the jingling of bridles and the neighing of horses. Peering out through the tent flaps he saw by the orange light burning in the braziers that Hindal's men were striking camp. His half-brother's tent had already been collapsed and was being loaded on to a cart. As he continued to watch, Humayun made out a familiar figure hurrying towards his tent through the press.

'Humayun, what have you done? . . . Have you lost your mind?' Khanzada shouted even before she was inside Humayun's tent. 'How can you hope to succeed if Hindal leaves? And all because of a woman you caught a fleeting glimpse of, a woman you've never even spoken to and whom without telling me you've consigned into my care.' He had seen his aunt angry many times before but never with such a look of outraged bafflement in her eyes. 'Forget this madness. Go to Hindal now, before it is too late, and tell him you will give up the girl.'

'I can't, Aunt. It's as if I had no choice . . .'

'Rubbish!' Coming closer, she stared into his eyes. 'Are you taking opium again? Having hallucinations? Is that what is making you act so crazily? I saw Hindal's bruised and bleeding face . . . is that the behaviour of an emperor, to pound your brother into submission and drive him from your camp?'

'He attacked me . . .'

'That's not the point. He was loyal to you at a time when few others are, when our dynasty's fate in Hindustan has never been more uncertain. Your latest madness has left us in desperate straits – how many men do you have left of those who rode with you from Lahore? Eight or nine thousand only. I know because Kasim told me. If Hindal goes, how many will you have then? Five or six thousand at most. And how many of them will stay when they begin to doubt your judgement? Soon you'll barely have enough to defend us from brigands and dacoits let alone get back your throne. And all through unbridled, heedless, selfish desire . . .'

'No. The moment I saw Hamida, I felt something different from mere physical desire, something I'd never experienced . . . I knew love had overwhelmed me and that I wanted her as my wife. I had not thought such things possible but it happened. I promise I'm not fuddled with wine and opium. My mind is clear and I know that what I am doing is right. Aunt . . .' he laid a hand gently on her shoulder, 'trust me and help me in this . . . I beg you . . .'

'I can't. I'm getting old, Humayun. I've seen too much, suffered

177

too much, to have any energy left. Ever since Babur died I've tried to help you as I promised him I would. You have shown you are a fearless fighter but you have so much to learn about being a king and I wonder whether you ever will. You are different from your father. Babur always used his head. His marriages – even to your mother whom he loved – were considered acts. He didn't behave like a selfish boy who must always indulge his lusts and desires without a thought for the consequences. First opium. Now this.'

'But Aunt, as I keep trying to tell you, my feelings for Hamida go far beyond simple desire . . .'

'And what about Hamida's feelings, left here without her father? You know of course that Shaikh Ali Akbar is going with Hindal? He has just been to bid his daughter goodbye.'

'I didn't know.'

'Gulbadan is trying to soothe Hamida but she is distraught. Truth be told, Gulbadan is distressed too, though she has chosen to stay with me rather than go with her brother.'

'I never meant that . . . I . . .'

'No more, Humayun.'

Khanzada turned and left the tent. Humayun waited, hoping she might relent and come back but she didn't. He sat down and for a while just stared into the dancing amber flame of an oil lamp. Was his aunt right as she so often was? Certainly, he had been impulsive – reckless even – and he had hurt Hamida. He had also broken the fragile bonds that been forming between himself and Hindal.

'Majesty.' It was Jauhar and in his hand was a piece of paper which he held out to Humayun. 'Shaikh Ali Akbar asked me to give you this.'

You are the emperor, Humayun read, *if you ask me for my daughter I cannot refuse. I leave her with a heavy heart but I must go with your brother to whom, long ago, I swore to be loyal. Treat Hamida well. I have no power to protect her and must trust you to do so as you have pledged. Shaikh Ali Akbar.*

A fierce happiness filled Humayun, overriding any lurking feelings of doubt or of guilt about his behaviour towards Hindal. 'I will protect her with my life, Shaikh Ali Akbar. I will make her happy. You have no cause to fear,' he whispered to himself.

Next day, riding at the head of his depleted column across a pale landscape baked hard by the sun, Humayun still felt suffused with joy. If only the price had not been his rift with Hindal. An hour ago his heart had quickened at the sight of dust rising from the road ahead. Seized by hope that Hindal had changed his mind and was coming back, he'd despatched scouts to investigate but they'd found only a group of silk merchants with their mules. By now Hindal was probably some miles to the northwest of Humayun's column. According to Kasim, who had spoken briefly to one of Hindal's commanders, his half-brother planned to cross the Indus and head north.

Was Hindal intending to seek out Kamran and Askari? With all three of his half-brothers allied against him once more, his own situation would be perilous. Hindal knew exactly where Humayun was taking his army and what his strategy was. Such information would be useful to Kamran and Askari – and of course to Sher Shah. Humayun rode on oblivious of the bleached landscape as he brooded on this fresh twist in his fortunes. His disappointment that Hindal had not returned was not simply that he had lost an ally and gained an enemy but that over the last months he had grown closer to his youngest half-brother and had valued his companionship.

That night as the camp was being set up and the cooking fires lit, he looked longingly to where the women's tents were being pitched. What was Hamida doing and what was in her mind? Desire to see her again mingled with guilt at the distress he had caused her and he hesitated, uncertain as a youth about what he should do. Then it came to him. Summoning Jauhar, he ordered him to ask Khanzada to come to him. As the minutes passed, Humayun waited anxiously. He would not be surprised if his aunt refused to see him, but when Jauhar finally returned Khanzada was with him.

'Well, nephew, I understand you wish to see me.'

'Thank you, Aunt . . .' Humayun hesitated, seeking the right words. 'Last night we parted in anger. There was much justice in what you said. Though I cannot undo what has happened – and if I speak honestly I would not wish to even if I could – I've reflected upon your words. All my life you have stood by me, helped me. Do not desert me now.'

Khanzada's expression remained stern and she said nothing but a softening in her raisin eyes gave him courage to go on.

'Tell Hamida that I'm sorry for my thoughtlessness, that I never meant to cause her pain.' He stepped a little closer. 'Talk to her of me. Tell her I acted only out of love. Plead my cause . . . She will listen to you. And tell her that after the evening meal I will visit you all – but only if she is willing.'

Two hours later, Humayun followed some of Khanzada's attendants as they guided him with lighted torches through the camp to the women's quarters. Ducking inside Khanzada's tent, he saw his aunt and Gulbadan seated in the centre on low stools in a pool of soft orange light shed by oil lamps and wicks burning in *diyas*. They rose to greet him, and as he came towards them a veiled figure – he knew it was Hamida – moved out of the shadows to stand at Khanzada's side. Unbidden, Hamida dropped the veil covering the lower part of her face and stood before him. He hadn't realised how tall Hamida was – at least three or four inches taller than either Khanzada or Gulbadan. She was also slender, standing there in her dark blue robes, belted with a silver chain set with turquoises.

'Hamida. Thank you for receiving me here. You know why I've come. I want you for my wife . . .'

Hamida said nothing but continued to look directly at him, her black, long-lashed eyes reddened with tears, and it was Humayun who lowered his gaze first.

'What is your answer to me?'

'My father told me I must obey . . .'

'I don't want an unwilling bride . . . What is in your own heart?'

'I don't know. I cannot answer you. Only yesterday I parted from my father. I may never see him again . . .'

'It was your father's choice to go with my brother. Shaikh Ali Akbar is a good man, loyal and honest, and I have no quarrel with him. I will do everything in my power to make sure that one day – God willing – you are reunited with him. And I also promise that I will be a good husband to you. I will love and honour you. And though at present my fortunes are low, my ambitions are high and one day you will be a great empress . . . I swear it on my life.'

Hamida drew herself up but did not reply. She was still so young,

Humayun thought. She was grieving at her sudden separation from her father and the loss of much of what was familiar. 'A lot has happened,' he said softly, 'and you are tired. I will leave you now but think over what I have said.'

'I will think about it.' Hamida was still scrutinising him intently as if trying to divine something. Humayun felt he was being tested and for the first time his confidence wavered. He realised that he had come to her tonight sure of success, believing any woman would be dazzled to be chosen by him as his wife.

• ◆ •

In the event, Humayun had to curb his impatience and wait for longer than he'd expected. He found it hard to stop himself from visiting Khanzada's tent each night to see Hamida but he forced himself not to. He had promised her time to consider and must abide by his promise. Nearly a month passed before finally, on a humid evening with fireflies shining like jewels in the darkness around the encampment, Khanzada at last brought him news.

'Humayun, Hamida has agreed. She will become your wife whenever you wish it.'

A tremendous happiness overwhelmed him and he embraced his aunt. 'What did you say finally to convince her?'

'The same I've been telling her ever since I took her into my care – that she must marry someone and who better than a king – indeed an emperor? I reminded her that many girls of good family are married off to old men but that you are a handsome warrior in his prime with a certain reputation among the women . . .' Khanzada's eyes twinkled.

'You are certain she is willing?'

'Yes. What counted most with her was my promise that you truly love her.'

'I do.'

'I know. I've seen it in your face every time you spoke of her, otherwise I would never have been your ally in this.'

'What about Hindal? Does she ever mention him?'

'No. He may have loved her but I don't think she was aware of it. If you can find your way into her heart, you'll find no rival there . . .'

'Thank you, Aunt. As ever, you have been my benefactress.'

'And as ever, I wish you happiness, Humayun.'

'Wait – I wish you to take Hamida a present from me.' Going to his iron-bound chest he took out a piece of flowered silk and unwrapping it extracted the double-stranded necklace of fiery rubies and uncut dark green emeralds set in gold that had been among the treasures he had seized in Gujarat. The gems glinted richly in the candlelight and would well become Hamida's dark-eyed beauty. 'You once told me to keep this to give to my wife . . . that moment has come . . .'

The next morning, Humayun cancelled the day's march and summoned his astrologer Sharaf to his tent. Together they studied the sky charts, trying to work out from the positions of the planets the most auspicious day for the wedding. It was soon, Sharaf said, putting down his astrolabe – just three weeks away. That decided Humayun. He would halt his advance into Rajasthan until after the wedding so that there would be time to prepare. Though he was landless and throneless, his union with Hamida must not be a mean affair. They were not humble camp followers to be wedded and bedded in between marches but an emperor and his empress.

· ◆ ·

Hamida was sitting motionless beneath layers of shimmering golden gauze, the veils held in place by a chaplet of pearls interwoven with yellow cat's-eyes symbolising Ferghana and emeralds for Samarkand that Gulbadan had fashioned for her. As the mullahs finished intoning their prayers, Humayun took Hamida's hennaed hand in his and felt a responsive tremor. As his vizier Kasim led the cries of 'Hail *Padishah*', Humayun and Hamida rose and he led her from the wedding tent to his own where the marriage feast was spread.

The guests were few – Kasim, Zahid Beg, Ahmed Khan and some other officers and Khanzada, Gulbadan and their women. If he'd still been emperor in Agra, there would have been thousands of guests. Trays of wedding gifts – rare spices, silks and jewels – would have been spread before him. In the courtyard would have been living gifts – bejewelled elephants with gilded tusks and strings of high-spirited, high-stepping horses. Obsequious rajas would have queued to make obeisance and when night fell soft music would have risen over the scented courtyards and brilliant fireworks would have turned the dark sky back to day.

But glancing at Hamida, seated beside him on a red velvet cushion and all but one of her veils thrown back so that he could see her perfect features – the soft curve of her cheek, the rise and fall of her breasts beneath the thin fabric of her robe – Humayun felt close to true happiness. He had made love to many women, taking pleasure in his prowess as a lover, but the emotions welling inside him were new to him. Not even for Salima had he ever felt such tenderness.

As the feast ended, the dishes were cleared and all but their personal attendants left, Humayun felt shy as a boy about to know a woman for the first time. While his own servants undressed him and wrapped a silk robe around him, Hamida's women led her into the bridal bedchamber created by scarlet leather-covered wooden screens interlaced with hide thongs that stretched across the far end of the tent. Humayun paused then ducked beneath the stiff brocade hung over the gap between two of the screens.

Hamida was not yet ready. He found himself half averting his gaze as her smiling women undressed her, combed the long, shining fall of dark hair and then laid her beneath a thin coverlet on the rosewater-scented bed. As the women withdrew, he could hear their soft laughter. He felt awkward, confused. He had been so determined to have Hamida, so certain that this was the woman with whom his future must be linked, but she was virtually a stranger. They'd never even been alone together. The few words they'd exchanged had always been in the presence of others. Unbidden, the thought returned that she'd accepted him only because she'd felt she had no choice. It made him nervous of approaching her.

'Humayun . . .' Hamida's soft voice at last broke the silence. Turning, he saw she had raised herself on her left elbow and was half sitting up. Her right hand was extended towards him. Slowly he came nearer and kneeling by the bed took her hand and touched the fingers to his lips. As she raised the coverlet, he rose and slipped in beside her. Her body felt warm, and slowly, almost reverently, he touched her face then entwined his hands in the spilled mass of her hair. Her

183

eyes, looking up at him, were wide but trusting. Gently pulling her closer, he began to explore her slender body from the delicacy of her small shoulders to the satin curve of her hips. Caressing her breasts with his tongue he felt the hardening of her small, pink nipples and her response gave him courage. A thin sheen of sweat was forming on Hamida's body as his hands gently probed her. Her eyes were closed but her lips were parted and from them came a gasp.

Containing his own impatience, Humayun waited until he judged she was ready then, carefully easing himself on top, began gently to enter her. As he thrust harder he felt the tightness in her yielding and glanced anxiously down but saw pleasure not pain in her half-closed eyes. As he pushed deeper a passionate tenderness for this woman, a desire to protect her at all costs, filled his soul. She was his now and would be as long as they both lived.

They woke, bodies intertwined, as in the half-light of the tent their attendants came to rouse them, bringing ewers of warmed water. It was Hamida who waved them away but once they were alone again, she sat silent and still.

'What is it, Hamida? Have I offended you . . . ?'

She looked at him a little shyly and shook her head.

'What then?'

'These past days I was afraid . . .'

'Of what?'

'That you wanted me for your wife shocked me. I feared I might displease you . . . disappoint you. But last night your tenderness, the joy you brought me, soothed away my anxieties . . .' She was looking at him now with shining eyes. He began to speak but she placed a fingertip on his mouth. 'You know that a seer's blood runs in my veins. But there is something you don't know. Sometimes, I too have the gift to see into the future. Last night, I dreamed that very soon I will conceive a child . . . a son. Do not ask me how I know, only believe me that it is so.'

Humayun took her in his arms again. 'I will rebuild the Moghul empire and we will be great, you and I and our son,' he whispered as slowly, tenderly he began to make love to her again.

Chapter 12

Into the Desert

'Majesty, my scouts have seized a lone traveller in the bazaar of a small mud-walled town a few miles to the south. Clearly a stranger from his dress and his accent, he had been asking the stallholders and anyone else who would listen whether you and your column had passed this way. I had him brought straight to me in case he was a spy,' said Ahmed Khan.

'If he is a spy, he's not a very good one. He wasn't apparently making much attempt to keep his mission secret.'

Ahmed Khan did not share Humayun's smile. 'He claims to have come from Kabul, Majesty, and says he must see you. If his purpose is genuine, I fear from his face he has no good news to relate.'

'Fetch him here at once.'

'Yes, Majesty.'

A shadow of foreboding crept over Humayun. A few minutes later, through the neat rows of tents, he saw Ahmed Khan returning and, behind him, two of his scouts escorting a tall young man. As they drew nearer, Humayun saw how travel-stained the new arrival's clothes were. He was gaunt and the purple shadows beneath his eyes betrayed his exhaustion.

'Majesty.' He prostrated himself on the ground in the formal salute of the *korunush*.

'Rise. Who are you and what is it you wish to tell me?'

185

The newcomer got slowly to his feet. 'I am Darya, the son of Nasir, one of the commanders of your garrison in Kabul.'

Humayun remembered Nasir – a tough old Tajik chieftain who had served him loyally for many years. He had been well known in the camp for his voracious sexual appetite and for the number of children he had had by his four wives – eighteen sons and sixteen daughters – and many others by his numerous concubines. Humayun had not seen Nasir for many years and the only children of his he had met had been just that.

'So that I may know you are who you claim to be, tell me how many children your father has.'

Darya smiled a slightly melancholy smile. 'No one knows, but he had thirty-four of us by his first four wives and after one of them – not my mother, I give thanks – died last year, he married a fifth who bore him a thirty-fifth. However, as a token of my identity I have here in a pouch beneath my garments the wolf-tooth necklace my father wore.' He made to delve beneath his dusty garments.

'No need. I believe you are Nasir's son. What is the news from Kabul? Speak . . .'

'Bad, Majesty, the worst I could bring. Soon after your grandfather reached Kabul he had a sudden seizure. He lost much of the power of speech and could scarcely use his limbs. He appeared to be slowly regaining his strength but . . .'

'What happened?' Humayun broke in, though in his heart he knew.

'He died in his sleep, Majesty, nearly four months ago. His attendants found him in the morning, a peaceful expression on his face.'

Humayun looked down, trying to take in that Baisanghar had gone.

'There is more, Majesty . . . Your half-brothers Kamran and Askari, who had established themselves in Peshawar at the foot of the Khyber Pass, learned of your grandfather's illness and hoped to take advantage of it. They brought troops up through the pass to Kabul. By the time they reached it your grandfather was dead. Without warning, they attacked the citadel and despite all my father and others could do quickly overran it.'

For a moment Humayun forgot his grief for Baisanghar. 'Kabul has fallen to Kamran and Askari?'

'Yes, Majesty.'

'Impossible! How could my half-brothers have raised an army sufficient for such a task so quickly?'

'They had gold, Majesty, from raiding the caravans. We heard that they captured a group of wealthy Persian merchants and used their gold to bribe some of the mountain clans. Pashais, Barakis and Hazaras and members of other lawless breeds came in great numbers to fight for them. But in the event there was little fighting in Kabul. Your half-brothers bribed one of our captains to open the gates of the citadel to them.'

Though the camp was bathed in sunlight, the world seemed suddenly dark and chill to Humayun.

'My father . . .' Darya's voice shook a little, 'my father was hit between the shoulder blades by a Pashai battleaxe as he tried to run up from the gate to warn the defenders that we had been betrayed and that the enemy had gained entrance. He managed to crawl into a doorway where I found him. His last words to me were that I must escape from Kabul . . . that I must take his necklace to establish my identity and find you and tell you what had happened and . . . that he was sorry . . . he had done his best to defend Kabul but he had failed you. I sought you first at Sarkar but you had already left. Since then I have been searching for you. I thought I would be too late, that you would have already heard . . .'

'No, I knew nothing of this.' Humayun struggled to compose himself. 'Your father did not fail me – he gave his life for me and I will not forget it. You have made an epic journey. Now you must rest but we will talk more later. I must learn as much as possible about what has happened.'

As Ahmed Khan's men led Darya away, Humayun gestured to Jauhar that he wished to be alone and entered his tent. As he splashed his face with water he scarcely felt the cold drops trickle down his face. Conflicting emotions – some personal, some political, but none pleasant – jostled in his mind. Initially simple grief, the knowledge that he would never see his grandfather again, was uppermost.

Humayun closed his eyes as he recalled his father's vivid stories of Baisanghar in his youth, of how as a young cavalry captain he had brought Babur Timur's ring, still crusted with the blood of its previous wearer; how Baisanghar had sacrificed his right hand out of loyalty to Babur and opened the gates of Samarkand to him. Humayun's mother Maham too had had her own fund of stories of her father – less violent but even more fond. Now Baisanghar was dead without ever knowing that Humayun had married. But at least he had died before Kamran and Askari had attacked Kabul.

At the thought, another emotion harsher than grief took over – fury with his half-brothers. If they were brought before him now all Babur's urgings of mercy wouldn't deter him from hacking off their traitorous heads and kicking them through the dust. Instinctively, Humayun pulled his dagger from his sash and sent it spinning across the tent to embed itself in a round red cushion that he wished was Kamran's throat.

Kamran had seen his opportunity for a throne and with Askari as his willing accomplice had taken it. While they held Kabul, it would be almost impossible for Humayun to regain Hindustan. It had long been obvious that family unity, pride in the Moghul dynasty, mattered less to them than the chance to enrich themselves and, so it seemed, above all to damage him. Why could they never see how destructive their vindictive jealousy was, what a risk it was to them all?

Humayun paced about, trying to order his thoughts. He must think and behave rationally not only for his own sake but for his wife and their unborn child. The thought of Hamida for a moment lightened his mood. Despite the dangers surrounding them, these past weeks had been among the happiest he had ever known, especially when, a month ago, Hamida had told him, eyes more luminous than ever, that her dream had been correct. She was indeed pregnant. Perhaps the knowledge that he might soon have an heir was what made Kamran and Askari's latest betrayal especially hard to bear. By striking at him, they were also striking at his wife and unborn child – those Humayun loved most in the world.

And if Hamida was indeed carrying a boy, as she believed, the loss of Kabul made the child's future all the more precarious. Even if the baby survived the dangerous times Humayun knew were coming, instead of inheriting a great empire he might be heir to almost nothing – reduced as some of his ancestors had been to the life of a petty warlord constantly feuding with his relations over a few mud-walled villages and a few flocks of sheep while another dynasty ruled Hindustan.

This could not, must not happen. He would not let it. Humayun dropped to his knees and out loud swore an oath.

'Whatever it takes, however long the struggle, I will regain Hindustan. I am ready to spill every drop of blood to do so. I will bequeath my sons and their sons a greater empire than even my father dreamed of. I, Humayun, swear it.'

• ◆ •

The desert heat was growing unbearable as Humayun and his troops drew nearer to Marwar. Every day seemed hotter and the going harder. The sour-breathed camels with their great splayed feet were managing but the horses and pack mules were sinking up to their hocks in the burning drifting sand. Every day, animals collapsed from dehydration and exhaustion, legs feebly twitching and parched tongues lolling through cracked lips. Humayun ordered his men to slit the throats of those too sick to go on and add their meat to the cooking pot, but he also commended them to collect their blood. In Timur's day, warriors had survived out on the steppes by drinking the blood of their animals.

Glancing over his shoulder, he watched the enclosed litter bearing Hamida appear out of the silvery, shimmering haze, carried on the shoulders of six of his strongest men. Khanzada, Gulbadan and the other women were on ponies but he was doing everything possible to help the pregnant Hamida travel as smoothly as possible. Grass and aromatic herbs and roots had been stuffed into the sides of the litter's bamboo frame and every hour or so attendants dampened it with a little of the precious water to provide her with some fragrant relief from the heat. Even so, her face was very thin and the dark circles in the almost translucent skin beneath her eyes showed that pregnancy had not come easily to her. Often she felt nauseous and found it hard to eat.

Watching her litter draw nearer, the fear he might lose her gripped Humayun anew. He was doing all he could to protect her and bring her to safety but hazards were all around. Snakes and scorpions lurked. They were even vulnerable to the bands of brigands who infested the desert, now that he had so few troops left – barely one thousand. At the news of the fall of Kabul, many of his men had simply melted away.

God willing, soon they should reach the outskirts of the kingdom of Marwar and find sanctuary there. Raja Maldeo's messages of support – brought on the most recent occasion by the same ambassador who had sought Humayun out in Sarkar – were growing ever more fervent the nearer Humayun and his column approached. Nevertheless he wished Maldeo would send practical help – food, water and fresh horses would be more welcome than fine promises. But Humayun hesitated to ask for such things. He was coming to Marwar as the raja's guest and ally, not as a beggar.

According to the red leather-bound volume in which Kasim dutifully recorded daily the diminution of their supplies, just as he had done when Babur had been besieged in Samarkand, they still had enough corn, dates and other dried fruit to sustain them. However, it was many days since they'd tasted fresh food other than that from the carcasses of the exhausted or diseased animals, if that could indeed be called fresh. At first they'd bought produce from the villages along the way. It was the mango season and the flesh of the delicate, orange, sweet-scented fruits hanging in clusters among the glossy, dark green leaves was one of the few things Hamida could be tempted to eat. But six days ago they had passed the last settlement – a tangle of mud-brick houses clustered around a well – and the desert had engulfed them. Ahmed Khan's scouts, riding ahead in the cool of the moonlit nights, had reported no signs of further habitation.

The worst problem, though, was lack of water, which his officers now rationed carefully. Three nights ago, two of his men had drunk strong spirits instead. Then, with their thirsts heightened and their passions unleashed, they had fought for possession of a waterskin containing a few mouthfuls of fetid liquid and one had died, slashed across the throat by the other's dagger. Humayun had ordered the survivor to be beheaded, but he had seen the sullen challenge in the eyes of the soldiers drawn up to witness the punishment. Indiscipline and insubordination were as dangerous as any attacks from desert raiders . . .

His own horse was suffering badly. Its once glossy coat was flecked with dried sweat and sand and it stumbled frequently. Humayun squinted around him. The glare from the orange ball of the sun deadened the landscape, flattening out the rolling dunes and reducing everything to a dispiriting, eye-searing monotony with nothing to catch the mind's attention or freshen the spirit. To spare his horse for a while, Humayun slipped down, and taking the reins in his left hand, plodded by its side.

Suddenly Humayun heard shouts somewhere up ahead. Shading his eyes, he tried to see what was happening towards the front of the column some three or four hundred yards away but the sun dazzle made it impossible. 'Find out what's going on,' he shouted to Jauhar. But before Jauhar could kick his mount forward, a general stampede began. Pack animals that had been trailing listlessly behind were suddenly rushing frenziedly past, no longer finding the sand an obstacle in their headlong charge. It could only be water, Humayun realised, and his heart soared.

Remounting his own horse which was now whinnying with excitement, he rode forward. He would bring Hamida a cup of cool water with his own hands. But as he drew nearer, chaos met his eyes. At first it was hard to see what was happening in the midst of so many flailing, pushing bodies – human and animal – half hidden by a few squat dusty-looking palm trees. Then he saw the raised mud-brick sides of what looked like a cluster of small wells and to one side, a small spring seeping out in rivulets over pebbles into the sand. Men were already fighting over the hide buckets that they'd hauled out of the wells, spilling the precious water.

The pack animals they should have been tending were also acting half crazed. Camels were spitting and frenziedly lashing out with their feet. One man was kicked so hard in the guts that he fell to the ground and was instantly trampled. Humayun saw his head crushed, brains and blood spilling sickeningly out on to the sand where camp dogs at once began to lick them up. Mules were baring their yellow teeth and biting at one another as they all struggled, regardless of the loads on their backs, to get to the spring.

Humayun was beside himself with fury. What were his officers thinking of . . . ? But as he kicked his horse forward, determined to restore order, he saw that officers as well as men were in that tangled, heaving mêlée. He shouted to them but they didn't hear. Forcing his way further into the crush, waving Alamgir above his head and roaring rebukes, he at last made his presence felt. Shame-faced, his officers gave up their own fight for water and began trying to control their men.

Humayun's thoughts now were for Hamida and the other women towards the back of the column. Turning his horse, he galloped back over the hot sand but was relieved to find them still quietly making their way, protected by his guards. They had been so far to the back of the line that they had not become caught up in the stampede. Riding up to Hamida's litter he opened the curtains and peered inside. Her smile, radiant in the shadowy interior, told him all was well and he breathed more easily.

It took over an hour to restore calm but by then half a dozen men were dead, trampled in the crush or slain by others determined to get to the water first. Others were writhing on the ground, clutching bellies swollen with water and screaming for relief. Several were vomiting water and bile and babbling incoherently. It was like a vision from hell and Humayun turned his gaze away. He could only be grateful that his enemy Sher Shah was too far away to know the depths to which he and his little band had fallen.

His spirits didn't rise again until three days later when, across the pale orange drifts of sand, the jagged shape of a high, rocky outcrop emerged from the hazy horizon. Atop it, perched like an eagle's nest, was a fortress – the stronghold of the Raja of Marwar. It must still be some fifteen or twenty miles away, Humayun reckoned, but soon he would be able to bring Hamida, Khanzada and Gulbadan within the safety of its walls. It would be a welcome return to sanity and safety after their precarious desert journey. He despatched a scout at once bearing his greetings to Maldeo.

The distance must have been shorter than Humayun had calculated because the scout returned next day, bringing a detachment of the raja's special guard in orange robes and steel breastplates, splendidly mounted on matching black stallions. The warriors' flowing black hair was knotted on the back of their heads almost like women's but there was nothing feminine about these lean, hawk-nosed muscular men with their gleaming spears.

With Kasim and Zahid Beg by his side, Humayun rode forward. The Rajput leader dismounted and kneeling before Humayun touched his forehead briefly to the hot sand. 'Maldeo, Raja of Marwar sends his greetings, Majesty. He has been waiting for you for many days and has sent me and my men to escort you over the last miles of your journey.'

'I am grateful to the raja for his care. The sooner we reach Marwar the better – my men are weary.'

'Of course, Majesty. If we ride now, we can reach the fortress by sunset where my master will make you and your entourage comfortable.'

As Humayun watched the Rajput ride back to his men, he wondered what impression his ragged little army had made. Looking at his men through a stranger's eyes he saw not a proud Moghul army but a small band of grimy men riding broken beasts, the once-bright blades of the weapons slung from their saddles – the swords and double-headed axes – dull from disuse. Many had thrown their round, metal-bound shields away rather than be burdened with them in the heat and their arrow cases were nearly empty. There had been no time or opportunity to find wood and fletch new arrows since they had ridden into the desert. Only Humayun's musketeers – well drilled by Zahid Beg – looked capable of putting up a fight. But all that would change when he reached Marwar. He still had some money left to re-equip his men and recruit more, and the raja himself would supply him with troops.

That night, beneath a sky flushed a vibrant pinky-orange as the sun went down, Humayun led his small column through the winding streets of Marwar towards Raja Maldeo's massive fortress on top of the steep promontory rising behind the town. Between the last of the wood and mud-brick houses and the outcrop – which looked perhaps a hundred and fifty feet high – was an area of open land with a small spring over to the right. Beyond the spring were rows of tents and brushwood piled ready for burning.

'The camp that has been prepared for your men, Majesty,' said the Rajput commander.

Riding on, Humayun approached an arched gatehouse close to the foot of the outcrop. Drums of welcome beaten by unseen hands boomed as, with his bodyguards, senior commanders and courtiers and the women, he passed through. On the other side of the gate, a steep but wide ramp-like road twisted sharply to the left and, following the rock's natural contours, ascended the outcrop. Slowly Humayun's tired horse plodded up the ramp, snorting with the effort, emerging at the top on to a wide stone plateau. Ahead was a girdle of crenellated walls that enclosed much of the top of the outcrop. The only entrance was through a two-storey gatehouse beyond which Humayun could see further walls.

The gatehouse, with a carving of a Rajput warrior on a rearing horse above the lintel, looked ancient – far older than the Agra fort or even the citadel of Kabul, Humayun thought as he rode beneath the raised metal grille. How many generations of Rajput warriors had swept though it and down the steep ramp to do battle in furtherance of their warrior code? Of all the peoples in Hindustan, these Rajputs were surely closest to the Moghuls themselves – a warrior breed for whom fighting, honour, glory, conquest were as natural as the warm milk they had sucked at their mothers' breasts. But then his curious eyes fell on something he didn't understand. Along each side of the gatehouse's deep inner walls was a series of small blood-red handprints.

'What are those?'

The Rajput commander replied with what seemed to Humayun a deep pride. 'Those are the handprints of the royal women of Marwar made by them on their way to their deaths. When a Rajput woman's husband dies or is killed in battle it is her duty to renounce life and join him on his funeral pyre. These marks that you see here are the last living acts of these women on their way to be consumed in the flames.'

Humayun had heard similar stories before. Babur had told him that his Hindu subjects called this practice *sati* and that the women were not always willing. Babur had witnessed a young widow – barely more than sixteen – struggling and being drenched in oil and thrown bodily into the flames. Her screams had been terrible and she had died before Babur's men could intervene.

As if he could read Humayun's mind, the Rajput continued, 'It is a point of honour for our women . . . And if ever we suffer such terrible defeat in battle that it seems our women might be seized by our enemy, the most senior Rajput princess leads the other noblewomen – dressed in their finery and best jewels as if for a wedding – in the ceremony of *jauhar*. A great fire is lit and the women leap joyfully into the flames rather than face dishonour.' The man was smiling as if at a vision of something wonderful.

Humayun turned his eyes from those red imprints, whether made in ecstasy or despair. Instinctively, he felt that however devoted to her husband, however dire the circumstances, a woman had her own existence to think of, her own obligations – to herself, to her children if she was a mother, and to those around her. Khanzada's experiences had shown that an indomitable spirit could endure and emerge, not unscathed, but stronger. The thought of Hamida being burned alive if he died chilled his blood. Perhaps the difference was that the Rajputs as Hindus believed in reincarnation and that to die with honour meant being reborn with greater status, whereas he believed that one must make the most of the single life one had on earth.

Directly ahead, in the centre of a fresh curtain of walls was a passageway about six foot wide with a near right-angled bend at its centre – no doubt designed to prevent an enemy storming through in great numbers. It gave on to a large parade ground where a group of war elephants were being drilled. Opposite was yet another set of walls, again with only one narrow gateway. These concentric walls, so different from the design of a Moghul fortress, reminded Humayun of the intricate boxes within boxes that the slant-eyed merchants from Kashgar sold in the markets of Kabul.

But this third set of walls was the last. Passing through, Humayun entered a large rectangular courtyard – the heart of Maldeo's fortress. In the centre stood an imposing building more solid than beautiful. It was impossible to tell how many storeys it had – small arched windows pierced its walls seemingly at random. Attached to one side was a wide, sturdily built tower with, on the very top, an elegant stone pavilion.

Humayun reined in his horse and looked critically around him. His host should have been there to welcome him. But just then came a blast from an unseen trumpeter and a procession of orange-clad Rajput warriors filed out of the palace's carved central doorway and formed up in two lines on either side of Humayun. Raja Maldeo followed, a tall, powerfully built man in belted orange robes that swept the ground, dark hair tightly bound beneath a turban of cloth of gold flashing with diamonds. Hand on breast, he advanced towards Humayun and bowed his head.

'Greetings, Majesty. Welcome to Marwar.'

'I thank you for your hospitality, Raja Maldeo.'

'Your ladies will be given apartments near those of the royal women of my house as is our Rajput custom. Rooms for yourself and your courtiers and commanders have been prepared in the *Hawa Mahal* – the Palace of the Winds.' Maldeo gestured towards the tower. 'Yours will be in the pavilion at the very top where the breezes blow through.'

'Again, I thank you. And tomorrow we will talk, Maldeo.'

'Of course.'

• ◆ •

Humayun woke next day to feel a warm breeze stirring the gauze curtains around the soft bed on which, exhausted, he had collapsed into a long dreamless sleep. For a few moments he just lay there, giving himself up to relief and satisfaction that he had brought his family and his men to a safe haven. For a while at least they could all rest, and most important of all Hamida would have the care and

196

comfort she needed. Humayun got up and stepping out on to the wide balcony found himself gazing down the sweep of cliff that fell sheer to the sandy plain below. The sun, already high in the sky, seemed tinged with crimson around the edges, like the flesh of the blood orange.

After the hardships of the past few weeks' journey, the desert held no charms for Humayun. Turning away, he summoned Jauhar to fetch Kasim, Zahid Beg and his other commanders. Word of this must have reached Maldeo because even before Humayun's men arrived, the raja's servants brought great brass trays piled with fruit, nuts and gilded sweetmeats, and golden ewers of chilled sherbet. They were still eating and drinking when Maldeo himself appeared. He was more soberly dressed today in pantaloons and tunic of dark purple and a curved dagger hanging in a plain leather scabbard from the thin metal chain around his lean waist.

'I trust you slept well, Majesty.'

'Better than for many weeks. Join us, please.' Humayun gestured to the orange silk cushion next to him.

Maldeo made himself comfortable and helped himself to a gilded almond. For the sake of politeness, Humayun decided he must wait a while before raising the subject of Sher Shah, but his host was less squeamish.

'You have not made this long and arduous journey simply to drink sherbet with me.' Maldeo leaned forward. 'Let us be frank. We face a common enemy. If left unchecked Sher Shah could destroy us both. He must be defeated. You already know that he has insulted me by threatening to invade Marwar, but in recent weeks he has given me yet further cause to wish to see his head in the dust.'

'How so?'

'He has dared to ask for my daughter in marriage. The blood of thirty kings of Rajasthan runs in her veins – I'll not give her to the thieving offspring of a common horse trader.' Maldeo's eyes were narrow slits and his tone was laced with venom.

'I have few men left but if you will give me an army and ride with me, others will take heart and follow. Like the Moghuls, your people are of warrior blood. Together we can sweep Sher Shah and his dregs into the gutters. And I promise you this, Maldeo – when I am again on my throne in Agra, you will be the first I shall recompense.'

'Whatever is in my power I will do – not for reward but from respect and honour, both for my own heritage and for yours.'

'I know, Maldeo.' Humayun took the raja by the shoulders and embraced him.

· ◆ ·

Eight weeks later, Humayun watched the raja and his escort ride out of the fortress, disappearing across the dry plains in the direction of the desert city of Jaisalmer where Maldeo planned to raise more troops for the campaign against Sher Shah. In the gathering dusk, the shrill cries of the raja's pet peacocks pierced the cooling air as they sought a roost for the night on the battlements. As he contemplated the future Humayun felt more relaxed than for many months. Maldeo was an attentive host. A day seldom passed without either some entertainment – camel races, elephant fights or displays of fire-eating and martial Rajput dances – or the presentation of a gift. Only yesterday, Maldeo had sent him a jewelled bridle and Hamida a necklace of translucent amber beads. Pleasing though this was as a sign of Maldeo's friendship, far more important was that he and the raja had nearly finished planning their campaign against Sher Shah. Soon Humayun would be riding at the head of an army again.

'Majesty . . .' He turned to see one of Hamida's attendants, Zainab, kneeling before him. The girl was badly disfigured by a birthmark that covered the right half of her thin little face and when her mother had died of a fever during the harsh journey to Marwar, her father, a foot soldier with other children to feed, had left her to fend for herself. Touched by her misfortunes, Hamida had taken her as her attendant.

'What is it?'

Still kneeling, Zainab spoke rapidly. 'Majesty, her imperial highness asks you to come to her as soon as possible.'

Humayun smiled. He had been planning to visit Hamida tonight.

Now that they were in comfort and safety and Hamida was feeling well again, his mind turned frequently to the joys of love-making, although with Hamida's rapidly swelling belly he must soon learn to curb his passion for her. Nothing must damage the child. But when, finally, Zainab lifted her eyes to his, they looked troubled and he knew something was wrong.

Without stopping to question Zainab, Humayun swiftly descended two floors to the passage connecting the *Hawa Mahal* to where Hamida and her women had been given apartments adjoining those of Maldeo's women. Ignoring the members of his bodyguard posted by the sandalwood doors leading to Hamida's rooms, Humayun himself pushed them open and strode in.

'Humayun . . .' Hamida ran to him and putting her arms round his neck clung to him. Her body was trembling and he could feel her hectic, shuddering heartbeat beneath her thin silk tunic.

'What is it? The child . . .'

Hamida said nothing but waited until the doors had closed and they were alone. Stepping back from Humayun, she folded her hands protectively over her belly. 'Our son is safe inside me . . . for the moment at least. But if we're not careful we may all soon be dead.' Her voice was low and as she spoke she glanced around as if eavesdroppers might be concealed behind the fluttering hangings.

'What do you mean?'

Hamida came close to Humayun again. 'I have learned that the raja has never been our friend. He has always planned to betray us. Even now he is riding to a secret meeting with envoys sent by Sher Shah from Agra at a fortress deep in the desert. His story about going to raise troops in Jaisalmer was just a blind to conceal his true purpose.'

'But he is my ally and my host and has treated us with honour. We've been in his power these past two months. He could have killed us a hundred times . . .' Humayun stared at Hamida, worried that her pregnancy had addled her wits.

'All that has saved us so far is the raja's greed – he has been negotiating his price. Now he has gone in person to question Sher Shah's envoys to satisfy himself that all his demands will be met. As soon as he returns ... sooner if he sends a messenger ahead of him ... he will have us murdered.'

Hamida's face was taut with fear though her voice was calm. He took her hand, feeling its marble coldness.

'How do you know all this?'

'A woman – her name is Sultana – came to me from the raja's *haram*. She is one of our people – an Afridi from the mountains of Kabul. After her father was killed at Panipat, she and her mother joined a caravan returning to Kabul but as they were attempting to cross the Indus brigands attacked them. Sultana and the other young women were taken to be sold in the bazaars. She was a great beauty. One of the raja's nobles bought her and sent her to Maldeo as a gift.'

'What else did this woman tell you?'

'That in his heart he despises the Moghuls. He thinks us barbarian raiders with no right to Hindustan. The story about Sher Shah wishing to marry the raja's daughter is a lie. As soon as Maldeo knew we were definitely on our way here, he wrote to Sher Shah gloating that he would soon have us in his power and asking what Sher Shah would give him in return for us. For some time there was silence. But finally – two days ago according to Sultana – envoys from Sher Shah reached the outskirts of the kingdom of Marwar and sent a message to Maldeo telling him of Sher Shah's response. What Sher Shah said ... it was terrible ...' For the first time her voice seemed to fail her.

Humayun caught her against him and held her close. 'Hamida, go on. You must tell me everything ...'

After a moment Hamida continued, face against his chest, voice muffled. 'Sher Shah has promised Maldeo that if the raja sends him your head ... and the unborn child I am carrying ... he will reward him not only with money and jewels but with new lands and cities that he will hold independent of Sher Shah. When Sultana told me this I was sick ... for a while I couldn't think, but I knew I must be strong ... for us and for the son I carry ...'

As he thought of Maldeo's smiling face, of all his smooth-tongued lies, such anger and disgust took hold of Humayun that he felt he might choke with rage. 'Does Maldeo meant to accept Sher Shah's offer?' he managed to ask.

'Sultana says the raja is cautious. That is why he has summoned the envoys to meet him in the fortress in the desert – so he can question them himself. But if he believes Sher Shah means what he says, Maldeo will not hesitate to have us killed. That is why as soon as he left this evening, Sultana found a way to come to me . . .'

'Are you sure this Sultana is to be trusted? Why should she run such a risk for us?'

'She hates Maldeo for his callous treatment of her . . . He calls her his savage from the steppes. But her reasons go deeper than that. I saw her distress as she laid her hand on my belly . . . She told me that when she bore Maldeo a son, he said the child was not worthy to be reared in the palace and he sent it away. She does not even know if he is alive. She came to me for the sake of our unborn child and for mine as a mother, I'm sure of it. She called herself my blood-sister and I believed her.'

Humayun gently released Hamida. With her anxious eyes upon him, a cold determination was replacing the heat of his rage at Maldeo's treachery and violation of all the rules of honour and hospitality at the heart of the Rajput code. If he was to save the lives of his family and his men he must push emotion aside and focus his mind on one thing only – survival.

'I promise you this – no harm will come to you or our child. I married you to make you my empress and that is what you will be. And our son will be emperor after me. Maldeo's wickedness will not alter this.'

At Humayun's words, Hamida drew herself up. 'What must we do?'

'Have you talked about this to anyone? Khanzada or Gulbadan?'

'Not to anyone.'

'What does your waiting woman Zainab know?'

'Only that my meeting with Sultana had upset me . . .'

'Can you summon Sultana again?'

'Yes. Her rooms are close by and she is free to move about the palace.'

'I must leave you for a while for appearance's sake. Some of Maldeo's commanders are to eat with me and my officers to discuss the campaign against Sher Shah. I must do nothing to arouse suspicion. But summon Sultana two hours from now and I will join you as soon as I can. I must see this woman for myself.' Bending, he kissed Hamida's full soft lips. 'Courage,' he whispered, 'all will be well . . .'

As soon as he was able but a little later than he'd hoped, Humayun hurried again to his wife's apartments. The light from hundreds of wicks burning in brass *diyas* and the torches in sconces on the walls softened the harsh stone outlines of the place Humayun had thought of as a refuge but – if Sultana was speaking the truth – was not only a prison but a place of execution. All during the meal – though appearing polite and attentive to Maldeo's men – he had been turning over and over in his mind what he should do and he had formed a plan, bold and desperate . . .

'Majesty.' The woman knelt before him as he entered Hamida's chamber.

'Rise.' Humayun appraised her closely as she stood up and waited, hands folded, before him. Sultana was about thirty years old but – with her pale, high-cheekboned face, typical of the Afridi people – still beautiful and her black hair was untouched by silver. Her clear, hazel eyes were fixed anxiously on his face as if wondering whether she was standing up to his scrutiny.

'The empress has told me your story. If it is true we owe you a great debt . . .'

'It is true, Majesty. I swear it.'

'Why should the raja have confided his plans in you?'

'He has spoken openly of them in the *haram* – out of conceit and a desire to gloat. Even as you were approaching over the desert, Majesty, when he knew you had little food or water left, he said he was tempted to attack you. But it pleased him better to lure you on with soft words and fine promises. He is a master of deceit and enjoys spinning a complex web . . . he wanted to make sure he had you fully in his power.' Sultana's voice trembled, 'Truly, Majesty, he is a monster . . .'

202

The horror and revulsion that he read in Sultana's eyes told Humayun that she was no liar.

'God sent you here to save us,' he said as Sultana fell silent.

'I hope so, Majesty. I will do all I can to help you.'

'Then let me tell you my plan . . . Since I have been Maldeo's guest I have been out hawking several times. What could be more natural than that I should wish to do so again? Tomorrow, just as dawn is breaking, I and my courtiers and commanders lodged here in the palace will dress as if for a day's chase. I will order litters prepared for our women, saying that I wish them too to enjoy a day's sport. They have accompanied me before so there should be nothing strange in this. Once we have descended from the fortress we will head east into the desert.

'But of course, I also need to get my forces away. Tonight I will send my attendant Jauhar to Zahid Beg, who commands our camp outside the town below. Jauhar often carries messages from me to Zahid Beg, so again there should be nothing to rouse suspicion. He will tell Zahid Beg to say nothing to the men at present but that early tomorrow morning he must lead them out westward, making it look as if they are going on a military exercise. They will have to leave much of the camp equipment – including our cannon – behind but that cannot be helped. Once out of sight of Marwar, they are to circle round and re-join the rest of us.' Humayun paused. 'What do you think, Sultana? Will the guards permit me and my entourage to ride from the fortress in Maldeo's absence?'

'If it looks as if you are going hunting, they can have no reason to prevent you. As far as I know, Maldeo has given no orders for you to be kept within the fortress – he would not wish to do anything to make you suspect.'

'But you, Sultana?' Hamida touched the woman's arm. 'You must come with us . . . it would be dangerous for you to remain. Maldeo will guess what you have done . . .'

To Humayun's surprise, Sultana shook her head.

'But this is your chance to re-join your own people . . .'

'After what has happened to me here at the hands of Maldeo, I can never go back . . . That part of my life is over. But when I see

203

his ambition, his greed thwarted, that will be my reward . . .' A sad but also triumphant smile briefly lit her face. 'And I doubt he will suspect me . . . he does not think I have the brains or the courage to do what I have done . . .'

'I will never forget you, my blood-sister. And when I am empress in Agra, I will send for you . . . and if you wish to come you will be treated with the greatest honour.' Hamida kissed Sultana's cheek. 'May God protect you.'

• ◆ •

The sky was only just paling to the east when Humayun, dressed in hunting clothes like those around him, rode slowly through the concentric walls towards the gatehouse that was the only exit from the fortress. A fine black hawk given him by Maldeo was on his wrist, bright eyes concealed beneath a jewelled and tufted cap of yellow leather. Behind him, surrounded by Kasim and his other courtiers and commanders, were the litters carrying Hamida, Khanzada, Gulbadan and the rest of the women. After leaving Hamida last night he had gone straight to his aunt and his sister to tell them of the peril and of what they must do. True Moghul princesses, they had at once grasped the situation and obeyed him calmly and unquestioningly.

Humayun's blood was pumping as hard as if he was riding into battle as he led his party nearer to the gatehouse. In the soft morning light he could see that the metal grille was still lowered. His eyes flicked left and right, seeking any sign of an ambush. Though he had believed every word Sultana had said, he had been deceived before in this place. Also, Sultana herself might have been betrayed, perhaps by an enemy within the *haram* curious about her meetings with the Moghul empress. But all seemed as it should be. No arrow tip, no musket protruding from a slit in the gatehouse. Just the usual guards. With seeming casualness, Humayun gestured to Jauhar who called out in ringing tones, 'Raise the gate. His Imperial Majesty wishes to go hawking.' The captain of the guard, a tall man in orange tunic and turban, hesitated. Humayun felt sweat trickle down between his shoulder blades and glanced down at Alamgir, hanging at his side. Across his back was a full arrow case. But there was no need for force. After barely a second or two, the Rajput captain shouted, 'Raise the grille.'

The men above the gate began turning the windlass to draw up the thick black chains from which the grille was suspended. Agonisingly slowly – or so it seemed to Humayun – creaking and shuddering the heavy iron grille rose. With every foot, so too did Humayun's hopes, though he kept his expression distant and slightly bored.

Even when the grille was fully up, Humayun did not hurry but spent a moment or two adjusting the hawk's leather hood. Then, with a wave of his hand, he and his little entourage trotted forward. Slowly, so as still not to rouse suspicion, they rode down the steep ramp curving along the side of the outcrop that only a few weeks ago they had ridden up with such high hopes, out of the ceremonial arched gatehouse at its foot and then through the quiet streets of the town where the people still slept. Soon they were heading eastward, the seeping golden light of the rising sun before them, and into the sandy wastes that though so hostile were their best protection.

Chapter 13

Demon of the Sands

Humayun signalled the small scouting party with whom he had ridden ahead of his main column to halt. He swallowed a single mouthful of the precious water in the leather bottle at his side then patted his horse's neck, which was flecked with creamy patches of sweat. Around him, the blistering, shimmering desert stretched away, silent, endless and all-engulfing.

'Over there, look!' shouted one of the scouts – no more than a youth – hands cupped around his eyes against the glare. 'To the left!'

Humayun scanned the horizon and caught his breath as he made out the indistinct shape of first one and then two palm trees emerging from the heat haze and then, a little further along, what might just be the glint of sunlight on water. 'I see palm trees and what could be a river. How about you, Ahmed Khan?'

'Yes. Perhaps that patch of trees shelters the settlement of Balotra we've heard about. That water could be the Luni river flowing down to the Rann of Kutch.'

'How much do we know about Balotra?'

'Very little. By the look of it, it's still fifteen miles or so off. I'll send some of these scouts ahead, Majesty, if you wish, while we wait for the main party and make camp here for the night.'

'Do so, and have the scouts make sure there are none of Maldeo's men waiting in ambush in the settlement.'

Luck had so far been on Humayun's side. Despite many anxious glances over his shoulder, during these past weeks there had been no sign of pursuers from Marwar. After rendezvousing with his main force, Humayun had turned north for a while in a calculated bid to deceive Maldeo. Over four days' hard march, with everyone's nerves on edge, pickets posted all around the column, scouts ranging even further afield and deliberately abandoning detritus – old equipment and even wagons – to convince any of Maldeo's scouts who came that way that he really was heading north, Humayun had circled eastward. Then he had turned south, parties of men following on foot in the early stages to disguise their tracks by sweeping the sand with bundles of brushwood.

Only once had Humayun thought he could see riders on the horizon, but they'd proved nothing more threatening than a herd of goats that must have wandered from their village looking for the small, bitter berries that grew on the few scrubby bushes. He had tried to picture Maldeo's consternation on returning from his secret meeting with Sher Shah's emissaries to find his 'guests' gone, but his thoughts had quickly turned to how best to find a refuge for his family and his men. They could not meander endlessly through the desert. The suffocating heat and shortage of fresh food and clean water could kill just as easily as Rajput arrows and musket balls.

And all the time he had been worrying about Hamida. At night he heard her tossing and turning, unable to sleep, perhaps tormented by images of their capture by Maldeo and the murder of herself and her unborn child. But she never complained and brushed off his enquiries with the simple comment that it was indigestion – something she was told all pregnant women suffered from. Last night she had said to him, 'We will tell our son what it was like – how we protected him in even the worst of places – and he will take strength from the story of how we, and he, survived, won't he?' Humayun had pulled her close and hugged her in admiration of her bravery and stoicism.

'Majesty.' Ahmed Khan approached Humayun as, next day, outside his tent he took his morning meal – a small cup of water, a piece of unleavened bread and some dried apricots so hardened by the sun that they threatened to crack his teeth. 'My scouts have just returned. It is Balotra, about twenty miles ahead.'

'They saw no sign of Maldeo or his men?'

'No.'

'How many people live there?'

'Perhaps two hundred, just herdsmen and farmers.'

'You have done well, Ahmed Khan. Lead us there.' Humayun finished his meagre meal with greater appetite than he had begun it. If Balotra was indeed what it seemed, they could find refuge there while he planned his next move.

As he and his men approached the settlement later that day, Humayun saw that it was no more than a few dozen mud-brick houses clustered on the flat banks of the river whose orange-brown waters were very low and flowing sluggishly, as was to be expected during the hot season. But there was water enough for the villagers to grow crops whose green shoots poked through the soil in the cultivated strips along the riverbank.

'Jauhar. Go ahead and find the headman. Tell him we are travellers who mean his people no harm and that we wish to pitch our camp along the riverbank beyond their fields. Also, say that we need food and fuel for which we will pay – and a house where our women can find shade and rest.'

• ◆ •

Standing on the roof of a single-storey mud-brick house, Humayun gazed down towards the river. It was September now and the heat was no longer quite so relentless. Balotra had been a good place to halt – a safe place – tucked away in this sparsely inhabited region. According to Simbu, the elderly, almost blind village headman, Balotra and the handful of other settlements sprinkled along the Luni river were of little interest to the regional rulers or warlords, who left them in peace. Only the seasons governed the villagers' quiet lives.

Humayun had not told Simbu who he was and the headman, filmy eyes turned on him, had not asked. In fact, he'd asked few questions and seemed to have accepted Humayun's story that he was a commander a long way from his own lands whose column needed rest and water. Nevertheless, Humayun had sensed Simbu's anxiety that, despite his assurances and his money, he and his soldiers might bring trouble on his people. The old man would clearly be relieved when they rode away.

Humayun was also anxious to be gone – it was too dangerous to stay in one place for long, however remote – but where should he go? He couldn't afford a false move. All his instincts – now that he seemed to have shaken off Maldeo – were to go northward to the Khyber Pass and on towards Kabul to raise the mountain clans who owed him their loyalty and attempt to take back the city before Kamran and Askari became even more entrenched there. Until he had re-established his authority in Kabul and removed the threat to his rear he could not even think of challenging Sher Shah.

Going north would, of course, take him close to Marwar again but his other options were also risky without the benefit of returning him swiftly to Kabul. If he ventured east, he soon would enter the Rajput kingdoms of Mewar and Amber whose rulers, for all he knew, might have joined forces with Maldeo. Though the Rajputs were notorious for warring with one another they might well unite against a man they believed was their common enemy – or if the bribe from Sher Shah was great enough.

If Humayun went south he would enter Gujarat, now in Sher Shah's hands, while the way due west also had its hazards. According to Simbu, across the Luni river lay a further desert, stretching nearly three hundred miles westward all the way to Sind – a treacherous place of wild winds and quick sands that could bring death to the unwary. It had been known to swallow up whole caravans making for Umarkot, the ancient oasis at its heart. Several of Balotra's villagers had made the journey to trade in Umarkot and knew a safe route but, Simbu had cautioned Humayun with a grave shake of his old head, it was not a journey to be undertaken lightly.

Humayun's ignorance of events in the wider world made it even harder to take a decision. He knew nothing of what Sher Shah was doing or Maldeo or indeed his half-brothers. Where was Hindal now? With Kamran and Askari? And were his elder half-brothers attempting further conquests to add to the lands they had already stolen? Knowing the extent of Kamran's ambition he would not be surprised. His half-brother must know that at some point Humayun would come after him and he would be strengthening his position as much as he could. Neither wise old Kasim nor his aunt Khanzada with all her experience had anything to suggest and even his elderly astrologer Sharaf seemed baffled. The stars that shone with such clear and piercing beauty in the night skies offered Humayun no illumination. He knew that, just as his father Babur had done when the world turned its back on him, he would have to rely on his own inner resources to find his answers.

The sound of a woman singing distracted Humayun from his thoughts. Low and sweet, it was a voice he knew well – Hamida's. At least she was healthy, thriving even, belly round as a watermelon. The child would be big, she would tell Humayun, placing his hand on her stomach so that he could feel the vigorous kicks. Descending the narrow, wooden ladder down from the roof he went in search of her.

She was sitting in the shade of a fig tree spinning woollen thread on a wheel she had borrowed from the headman's wife, with her waiting woman Zainab holding the skein beside her. Seeing Humayun, Hamida smiled but went on with her song, matching her movements to the rhythm of the music.

'Where are Khanzada and Gulbadan?' Humayun asked when the song was ended.

'Gulbadan has found a quiet place to write that diary she's started keeping but Khanzada is sleeping. The heat tires her.'

'But it doesn't tire you?'

Hamida shrugged. 'I must keep active and cheerful. It is important for our child and when I think of him nothing seems to matter except that he is born healthy. Gulbadan told me something amusing today – that the mountain clans around Kabul have a way of predicting the sex of a child. They take two scraps of paper and on one they write a boy's name and on the other a girl's. Next they wrap the papers in thin sheets of clay which they plunge into a basin of water. Then they wait to see which sheet of clay opens first . . . I have no need of such tricks. I know it's a boy . . .'

211

She looked so happy, Humayun thought, despite everything. But he still felt guilty. If he hadn't chosen her — insisted on her — as his wife she would still be with her father. Now, instead of living as an empress, waited on by hundreds of attendants, dressing in gleaming silks and dining off jewelled plates as he had promised her father, he had reduced her to living like the wife of a poor peasant. And far worse than that he had exposed her to danger. He ran a finger along the curve of Hamida's cheek. 'As soon as it grows cooler this evening, I will go hunting with Zahid Beg. We might find some ducks amongst the reeds that would make good eating.'

But as Humayun walked along the riverbank to the camp to find Zahid Beg, a rider came galloping into the settlement. Humayun recognised Darya, who had joined Ahmed Khan's scouts. His grey horse was foamy with sweat and his own clothes were dark with it. He looked only a little less anxious and exhausted than when he had brought the news of Kabul's fall.

'Majesty!' Darya slid from the saddle.

'What is it?'

'A column of Rajput cavalry about fifteen miles from here.'

'How many?'

'At least three hundred, well mounted and some armed with muskets. They are travelling light and fast — we saw no baggage train.'

'From which direction are they coming?'

'From the northwest.'

'So they could be soldiers from Marwar . . .' Why had he assumed Maldeo had given up the hunt when the prize was so great? 'Where is Ahmed Khan?'

'Still trying to discover whose men they are and where they might be heading. He sent me to warn you but promised he would not be far behind.'

Ten minutes later, Humayun addressed his commanders. Darya's news had ended his uncertainties. He knew with absolute clarity what he must do.

'Our scouts have sighted a detachment of Rajput cavalry only fifteen miles away. Whether fate has brought them this close to us or whether they know we are here, I don't know. But what I am certain of is that we cannot fight here.' He gestured towards the mud-built dwellings outside which women in cotton saris with brass bangles gleaming on their wrists and ankles were squatting, trying to coax fires of cattle dung into life so they could start cooking the evening meal.

'But where will we go, Majesty?' asked Zahid Beg.

'Over the Luni. The ford a mile upriver from here is easy to cross – no more than a couple of feet deep. I was there yesterday. Then we will head due west across the desert. The headman has told me of a remote place called Umarkot where we should be safe.'

Humayun saw his commanders exchange glances. They too had heard of the desert's dangers. 'The desert has an evil reputation, I know. But that is why our enemies will hesitate to follow us, even if they discover that is where we have gone. But don't fear – we will take a guide from here to lead us . . . He will make sure that . . .'

Distracted by the beat of fast-approaching hooves, Humayun looked round to see Ahmed Khan career into the camp raising plumes of dust and scattering hens.

'Majesty, they are soldiers of the Raja of Jaisalmer. He has allied himself with Maldeo. I learned this from a herdsman who'd sold them some sheep. They boasted to him that they were hunting an emperor, that the scent was warm and that soon they'd be moving in for the kill. But their conceit is greater than their skill. I don't think they've yet discovered exactly where we are . . . I watched them ride off to the south . . .'

'Even so, we have little time. Ahmed Khan, we must quickly strike camp, cross the river and head westward. Summon the headman and ask him to provide us with a guide to lead us through the desert to Umarkot. Tell him I will reward him well – that he will have gold.'

As – watched by startled villagers – his men rushed to douse fires, collapse tents, collect their weapons and fill saddlebags, Humayun returned to Hamida. She had put her spinning aside. Gulbadan was with her now and they were laughing about something, but seeing Humayun's expression both fell silent.

213

'Ahmed Khan reports Rajput soldiers not far from here.'

Gulbadan gasped and Hamida instinctively put her hand on her stomach. Humayun took her face in his hands, feeling the warm smoothness of her skin. Bending his head, he kissed her lips. 'Courage. No one will harm you, I promise. Pack up what you can. We leave within the hour. Gulbadan – find Khanzada and tell her what has happened.'

· ◆ ·

'What's that?' Humayun stared at the cloud swirling and dancing along the distant horizon. Surely it hadn't been there a few moments ago. The sky too had changed – no longer a bright almost turquoise blue but a lowering, steely grey. Humayun's horse whinnied and tossed its head uneasily. Anil – Simbu's eighteen-year-old grandson who was acting as guide and was walking by the side of Humayun's horse – was also peering hard at the rolling billowing shape that even as they watched seemed to grow larger.

'I saw it only once before, when I was child. Desert travellers call it "the Demon of the Sands" . . . it is terrible . . . It's a great sandstorm with whirlwinds in its midst.' Anil rubbed a hand over his eyes as if, by that gesture, he might make the terrible sight bearing down on them disappear. But as Humayun looked, the great tawny cloud was rushing towards them, blotting out the sun. Suddenly he saw one of the whirlwinds at its centre. It looked as if it was sucking up the guts of the earth and spewing them out.

'Quickly . . . Tell us what to do.' Humayun leaned down and shook Anil's thin shoulder.

'We must make hollows for ourselves and the animals in the sand and lie in them with our backs to the storm until it has passed over.'

'How long have we got?'

The youth stared again at the advancing turmoil. 'Only a few minutes . . .'

'Tell the men to dig themselves into the sand and pull their horses down behind them as extra protection,' yelled Humayun to Jauhar and Zahid Beg, who had overheard his conversation with Anil. Dismounting and leading his own nervous, skittering horse by the reins, Humayun stumbled across to the bullock carts containing Hamida, Gulbadan, Khanzada and their retainers.

'Dig places in the sand for the women to shelter in – they must help you – and for yourselves,' Humayun shouted to the bodyguards who'd been escorting them. 'Quickly! Make your horses lie down by you but unyoke the bullocks – they must fend for themselves.'

Even before he had finished speaking, Humayun saw that despite her many years Khanzada was out of her bullock cart and bending to tear at the ground with her hands. Gulbadan was close beside her. 'Aunt, when the storm breaks over us, you and Gulbadan must lie down together, backs towards it, and hold on to each other, do you understand?'

Without stopping her digging, Khanzada nodded but his half-sister looked ashen and he saw she was shaking. 'Dig!' Khanzada shouted at her.

With figures frantically burrowing all around, Humayun hobbled his horse then lifted Hamida from the bullock cart and carried her a few yards away to where the sand looked softer and easier to dig.

'Let me help . . .' Despite her bulk, Hamida knelt beside him and began clawing at the ground. They worked frantically, hollowing out a place as best they could with bare hands. Hamida's nails were soon bleeding. Glancing over his shoulder Humayun saw the storm was much closer now, the sand and dirt within it darkening the sky. A roaring filled the air and though he could see Hamida was saying something he couldn't hear her. Frantically he redoubled his efforts and, as the wind and sand overwhelmed them, grabbed Hamida and pulled her down into the space they'd dug. Her face was against his chest as he held her tightly to him, arms wrapped around her, trying to shield her with his body.

Hamida was almost torn from his arms but he clung tightly on to her, his face feeling as if it was being skinned and his hair as if it was being ripped from his scalp. Sand clogged his nostrils and mouth and as he struggled for breath his burning lungs felt ready to burst. He was choking and as he fought for life felt his grip on Hamida slacken.

With an enormous effort he willed himself to keep hold of her.

What mattered above all was that she and their child should survive. He understood now how his father must have felt when, believing Humayun was dying, he had run into the mosque of the Agra fort to offer God his life for his son's. Let her live, he prayed, and let our child live. Take my life for theirs if that is your will . . .

As he continued to pray he realised that the dust and tumult were receding. He felt his tortured lungs expand as, at last, he managed to take in air. Every gasp hurt – lips, mouth, throat, windpipe felt raw and his nostrils were still full of sand. As for his eyes, sand had got under the lids and he felt as if red-hot needles had pricked his eyeballs. He tried to force them open and through streaming tears to look down at Hamida but everything seemed blurred and he closed them again.

He could feel her lying very still in his arms. Gently releasing her, he pulled himself up into a half-sitting position. 'My love . . .' he tried to say but no words came. 'Hamida,' he managed at last and reaching forward tried to pull her up too. Finding her shoulders, he ran his hands up her neck to take her face between his palms. She felt so limp. It was like holding a dead bird in his hands . . .

Stifled groans were rising from all around but Humayun had no thought for anyone but Hamida. Gently he pulled her face against his chest once more and began to stroke the hair that was once so silken and soft but was now gritty and tangled. He began rocking gently back and forward, as if he were holding a child. The motion comforted him, delaying the moment when he must face the pain of losing the person he loved above all others.

But after what seemed an age but could only have been a few moments, he felt Hamida move. Then she started to cough, spitting out a dirty orange-coloured mixture of saliva and sand. Joy that she was alive surged through Humayun. Helping her to sit up, he heard her taking in great, greedy gulps of air, just as he had done.

'It's all right,' he said gruffly, 'everything's all right . . .'

After a moment he felt Hamida take his hand and place it on her domed belly. As he felt the child within kicking strongly, fresh tears ran down his sand-covered face but this time they were of joy not pain.

Slowly, people and animals were hauling themselves to their feet, though some lay ominously still. Standing up, Humayun saw the feebly twitching body of a horse lying nearby beneath a thick layer of sand. Staggering over, he knelt beside it and brushing the sand from its face recognised his stallion. In the last terrifying moments before the whirlwind ripped over them he'd forgotten the animal completely. It must have tried to gallop off but hobbled had crashed to the ground. Running his hands over its fetlocks, Humayun felt the fracture in the bone. Whispering softly into its ear and stroking its neck with one hand, with the other he drew his dagger and swiftly severed the jugular, warm blood spurting over him and staining the sandy ground.

Looking round he saw that Zainab had brought Hamida some water to drink. But another female figure was stumbling towards him – Gulbadan, hair wild, clothes crusted with sand and glistening tracks on her filthy face from the tears she was crying. He tried to take her in his arms to comfort her but she pulled away from him.

'It's Khanzada . . .' Gulbadan led him over to where a body was lying and Humayun looked down on his aunt's sand-streaked face. Her eyes were closed and from the angle of her head – he who had seen so many dead bodies on the battlefield – knew she was dead. Mechanically, he put a hand against her neck but there was no pulse. She must have suffocated – her nostrils and mouth looked choked with sand and her hands were clenched as if she'd engaged in a mighty struggle with death, fighting until the last.

'She behaved like the mother she had become to me since the death of my own. She shielded me with her body. She knew how afraid I was . . .' Gulbadan whispered.

Humayun was silent, unable to conjure any words even to comfort Gulbadan. Khanzada – the woman who had shared Babur's tragedies and triumphs and guided his own first steps as emperor, forcing him to fight opium and face his destiny – was gone. That she should die like this, snuffed out in a sandstorm, after all that she had seen and endured in her lifetime seemed cruel and terrible. Never would he forget her courage or her selfless love for him and unflinching devotion to their dynasty. A deep sadness crept over him, extinguishing

217

the joy of a few moments ago. Khanzada's final resting place should have been a flower-filled garden on the banks of the Jumna in Agra, or on the hillside above Kabul next to her brother Babur. But that couldn't be. He bent and lifted his aunt's body and cradling her tenderly in his arms spoke. 'Though this is a wild and desolate place, we must bury her here. I myself will dig her grave.'

· ◆ ·

At last, ten long hot days later, the walls of Umarkot appeared on the horizon before Humayun's exhausted column. He saw Kasim and Zahid Beg exchange glances of relief. Ten of Humayun's men had been killed in the storm – two struck by pieces of flying timber from bullock carts that had been smashed by one of the whirlwinds. Many, like Jauhar, had been badly grazed and cut, some had broken bones and one of his best musketeers had lost the sight of an eye to a piece of sharp stone.

So many horses had been killed or scattered that most of the men were on foot, Humayun amongst them. Much of their equipment including many muskets had also been destroyed or buried. Even if it hadn't, without carts and with only a few pack animals left – ten mules and six camels – they would have had to abandon most of it anyway. As it was, they'd loaded what they could on to the few beasts they had. Humayun's one remaining treasure chest had survived intact but had now been emptied and the contents transferred into saddlebags. The Koh-i-Nur was still safely in its pouch around his neck.

Humayun was trudging by the side of a moth-eaten camel that spat balls of malodorous phlegm into the sand and groaned as it made its splay-footed way. Hardly a suitable conveyance for his empress, Humayun thought, glancing up at Hamida who was riding in a pannier suspended against one of the camel's bony sides, balanced by Gulbadan in another pannier on the other side. Hamida's eyes were closed and she seemed to be dozing. With luck they should reach Umarkot by nightfall, Humayun thought, then he could find Hamida somewhere better to rest.

But Umarkot must have been farther away than he'd reckoned.

Distance could be deceptive in the desert. When the western skies turned blood-red as the disc of the sun slipped below the horizon, the low outline of the oasis still looked to be several miles off. With night falling, it might be unwise to go on. Humayun shouted the command for the column to halt and was looking around for Anil to ask his advice when suddenly he heard Hamida give a sharp cry, then another.

'What is it?'

'The baby . . . I think it's coming.'

Tapping the camel on its legs so that it collapsed grunting on to its knees, Humayun lifted Hamida out of the pannier and carried her over to a clump of low, spiny-leaved bushes where he gently laid her down. By now Gulbadan had climbed out of her pannier and was squatting down on the other side of Hamida, stroking her hot face and smoothing back her hair.

'Stay with her, Gulbadan. I will send Zainab and the other women to you. I must try to get help from Umarkot.'

As he ran towards where his men had halted, Humayun's heart was pounding. Never had he known fear quite like this – not even during the worst, most bloody battle. The baby should not be coming now. Hamida had been certain there was at least another month to go . . . what if something went wrong, if she should die out here in this hostile wilderness which had already claimed Khanzada?

'Jauhar,' he shouted as soon as he was within earshot. 'The empress is in labour. Take the best of the horses we have left and ride for Umarkot as hard as you can. Tell the people there who I am and that I ask for shelter for my wife. Under the customs of hospitality they cannot refuse. Even if the people fear me and my soldiers they will surely help Hamida – there will be *hakims* and midwives there. Hurry!'

Jauhar rode off into the gathering gloom on a small roan mare which still had a little life in her wasted legs. Hurrying back to Hamida, Humayun found her surrounded by a small huddle of women who parted as he approached. She was lying on her back, eyes closed and breathing heavily. Her face was slippery with sweat.

'Her waters have broken, Majesty,' said Zainab. 'I know – I watched my sisters give birth many times. And her pains are becoming more frequent . . . it won't be long . . .' As if to bear out Zainab's words, Hamida moaned and tears welled from beneath her eyelids, mingling with the sweat that was pouring off her now. As another spasm racked her, she arched her back then drew her knees up and rolled over on to her side.

Humayun could hardly bear to watch. As the hours passed and Hamida's groans grew louder and more frequent, he paced helplessly about, returning to Hamida's side every few minutes or so only to go off again. The sounds of the night – the occasional rasping shriek of a peacock, the bark of a jackal – increased his sense of powerlessness. Where was Jauhar? Perhaps he should have gone himself – or sent Timur's ring with Jauhar as proof of who he was . . .

Another half-smothered cry from Hamida made him wince as if he was feeling the pain as well. That she should be giving birth in this desperate, desolate place beneath a bush . . .

'Majesty.' Humayun had been so lost in his private agony that he had not seen or heard Jauhar approaching out of the darkness at the head of a small group of riders who were leading some spare horses, between two of which was suspended a litter.

'Majesty,' Jauhar said again. 'The ruler of Umarkot welcomes you. He has sent a *hakim* and a midwife and soldiers to bring you, the empress and your personal entourage to his dwelling.'

Humayun bowed his head in relief.

Pale moonlight silvered the crude mud walls of Umarkot as Humayun and his small party, including half a dozen of his bodyguards, rode in, leaving the rest of the column to make its way under Zahid Beg. The midwife had already given Hamida a potion of herbs which seemed to have eased her pains.

In the torchlight it was hard for Humayun to take in his surroundings and his eyes were anyway on Hamida as the soldiers gently detached her litter from the horses and bore it through the doorway of a large building lit on either side by torches burning in sconces. He followed the litter down a corridor at the end of which he saw a pair of carved wooden doors with attendants stationed by them. As the party drew near, the attendants swung the doors open.

Hamida, with the *hakim* and the midwife close behind, was carried in. Humayun was about to follow when a man he hadn't noticed in long dark green robes stepped forward and bowed.

'Majesty, I am the Rana of Umarkot's vizier, whom he has sent to welcome you. This is the way to the women's apartments. The only man apart from the rana who is allowed to enter is the *hakim*. But you will have apartments close by and news will be brought to you at once.'

What could he could do but agree, Humayun thought, and nodded. The hours passed very slowly that night, or so it seemed to him. Just as dawn was breaking – he had been watching the slow lightening to the east through the casement – he must have drifted into a light sleep. Feeling a hand on his shoulder, he immediately leaped up, feeling instinctively for his dagger, then saw that it was full daylight and that it was Gulbadan who had roused him. She was smiling in a way he had not seen for many days.

'Humayun, you have a son, lusty and sturdy and already bawling his head off. The midwife will bring him to you in a few minutes, as soon as she has cleaned him.'

'And Hamida?'

'The labour was very hard for her. She needed all the midwife's skill. But she is well and is sleeping now.'

For a moment Humayun bowed his head, as joy and relief flooded through him in equal measure. Then from his pocket he drew a pod of precious musk that he had been saving for this moment and handed it to Gulbadan. 'Take it to the birth chamber. Break it open in celebration and let the fragrance fill the room – let it be one of the first things my son smells on this earth. Tell Hamida that though it is all I can give her just now it carries not only my love but the scent of our family's greatness to come.'

Chapter 14

Akbar

'I name you Akbar – it means "great" and great you will be.' As he spoke Humayun picked up a cream-coloured jade dish – a gift from the Rana of Umarkot – and gently showered Akbar's head with the contents, *shahrukhys* – tiny golden coins – to symbolise his future prosperity. Akbar, lying naked on a velvet cushion in Kasim's arms, flailed his arms and legs in surprise but did not cry. Taking him gently from the cushion, Humayun lifted him high so that all his assembled commanders could see him and cried out, 'I present to you my son, seventh in descent from the great Timur. Be as loyal to him as you have been to me.' Clashing their swords on their shields, Humayun's men roared the traditional greeting to a new prince of the blood of Timur, 'Mirza Akbar! Mirza Akbar!' until Humayun raised his arms for calm.

Now it was time for Hamida's part in the ceremony. Propped on a divan she still looked exhausted – skin pale as ivory and deep shadows under her dark, luminous eyes. Though Humayun had suggested waiting until she felt stronger, she had said no. 'Your men have been through so much for you. You owe it to them to show them your heir as soon as possible. It will bind them to you even more strongly.' Carrying the squirming Akbar over to her, Humayun placed him in her arms. Simulating putting the child to her breast, she recited the words that had come down to the Moghuls from before even Timur, from the days of the Oceanic Ruler himself, Genghis Khan: 'Drink, my son. Put your honeyed lips to my benign breasts and sweeten your mouth with the life-giving fluid.'

Discovering that he was not, after all, about to be fed, Akbar began to yell. As Hamida tried to quiet him, Humayun addressed his men once more. 'With my astrologer Sharaf, I have cast my son's horoscope. The date of his birth – 15 October 1542, with the moon in Leo – could not be more auspicious. A child so born will be fortunate and long-lived. We have suffered hardship and reverses. There are perhaps more dark times to come before we can reclaim what is ours but a glorious future beckons to Akbar and to us. Tonight we will feast and celebrate the victories to come.' Again his men clashed their weapons. This time their chant was 'Mirza Humayun' but he turned away, heart too full for any more words.

Later, when they were alone again, Humayun watched Hamida pull down the neck of her robe and give Akbar her breast, looking tenderly down on his head with its soft fuzz of black hair as he sucked vigorously. The knowledge that he had a son filled him with unspeakable pride. In the days before Hamida, none of his concubines had, as far as he knew, borne him a child. Now, at thirty-four years old, he realised how much a son would satisfy his craving for some deeper purpose to his life.

'Hamida . . .' He paused, searching for words to express his feelings. 'For the first time I feel I truly understand the depth of a father's love . . . how far it exceeds even that of a child for its parent. I have tried to be true to my own father's love and trust in bestowing my inheritance on me but now, as a father myself, I promise you I will recapture and enlarge my empire so that I leave a worthy legacy to our son.'

Hamida nodded but said nothing. But there was something he had to talk to her about – something important for Akbar's future. He must tell her that soon another woman would feed her son. They must appoint a wet-nurse. It was the most important position that could be given to a woman at the Moghul court. She became his 'milk-mother', establishing a bond that would endure her whole life through. Any son of her own automatically became the prince's *kukaldash*, his 'milk-brother', bound to protect him and in turn to receive favour. Her husband, too, enjoyed great status. Senior courtiers and commanders coveted the position for their wives as keenly as any political or military rank for themselves. If handled badly, the choice would provoke jealousy and envy.

'Hamida, there is something we must decide. In these difficult times, I have few ways to reward my commanders but I do have one thing to give. As is the Timurid way, we must choose a wet-nurse for Akbar, a woman who is worthy and whom we can trust but also a woman whose husband deserves my favour and will consider himself honoured by our choice.'

Hamida raised her head and looked at him. She had not been brought up as a member of the royal house, of course. She could not know all the old royal customs. Though noblewomen often employed nurses to suckle their children, they were only servants who could easily be dispensed with and had no lasting role in the child's life. He was asking something very different of Hamida – to share her child with another woman.

For a while she was silent, then she spoke. 'Don't look so anxious. I've known about the custom for a long time – Khanzada told me. I think she wanted to help prepare me, not just for becoming a mother but for being the mother of a future emperor. At first I was upset. But since Khanzada's death, I've reflected on her words – that by choosing the right wet-nurse I would not be giving up my child but helping to protect him. Though it still makes me sad, I can see that she was right . . . Let us be practical. Whom should we choose? There are so few women with us now, even fewer with babies.'

'Zahid Beg's wife is too old to have milk in her breasts or I would have chosen her in recognition of his loyalty and bravery. But there is another commander I would like to reward – Nadim Khwaja, a chieftain from near Kandahar whose wife is with him. Shortly after we fled from Marwar she bore him a son.'

'I know her, of course. A tall, handsome woman called Maham Anga. Her son's name is Adham Khan.'

'You would accept Maham Anga? If there is another you would prefer . . .'

'I am content. Maham Anga is strong and healthy, as well as honest and full of good common sense. Her son is a sturdy vigorous baby. She is the one I would have chosen.' Gently detaching Akbar from one breast, Hamida moved him across to the other. How beautiful she looked, Humayun thought, despite all the recent hardships and the ordeal of childbirth. And though still so young, nearly twenty years his junior, how strong. It must be hard for her to think of Akbar in another woman's arms yet she hid her pain as courageously as a warrior concealed his fear. He had chosen her out of love but even here in this remote, mud-walled oasis, far from home and safety, she had the bearing of an empress. Approaching the divan, he bent and kissed Hamida's lips and then the downy crown of his son's head.

'What came of your meeting with the rana? Do you believe we are safe here?' Hamida asked.

'I think so. Though the rana is himself a Rajput, there seems no love lost between him and Maldeo. Last year, Maldeo's men raided caravans from Umarkot as they crossed the Rajasthani desert. As the merchants were formally under the rana's protection he took it as a great insult. Of course, Maldeo is far too powerful for the rana to think of revenge, but he has no wish for any dealings with him. He will not betray us to Maldeo, I am certain of it, though we cannot linger here too long. Inaccessible though Umarkot is, we will eventually be pursued here. As soon as we can – as soon as you are strong enough – we will leave.'

'But where to?'

'The only direction it makes sense to go is northwest to Kabul. Until I have re-taken it and punished Kamran and Askari for their treachery I have no chance of dislodging Sher Shah from Hindustan . . .' Humayun hesitated. 'It will be a hard, dangerous journey. Should I find some safe place to leave you and Akbar until it is safe for you to join me . . . ?'

'No. You already know I can endure harsh conditions as long as we are together. I told you I'd learned much from Khanzada. She would never have agreed to be left behind and neither will I . . .'

◆

226

The walls of dusty Umarkot faded into the pale apricot haze as Humayun led his men once more out into the desert a week later. Their destination was the fortress of Bhakkar, an outpost belonging to his cousin Mirza Husain, the ruler of Sind, two hundred miles away on the northern borders of Sind on the banks of the Indus. Since the two of them had parted on ostensibly cordial terms Humayun hoped to find temporary shelter there. And at Bhakkar, remote though it was, he might also finally learn what had been happening in the outside world.

Knowing that each mile was taking them further from the risk of being overtaken, Humayun pushed the pace. Every morning the column set out as the first rays of the sun seeped over the horizon and, apart from a brief break at midday to rest the animals and to eat a simple meal of bread, dried meat and a few raisins, did not halt until dusk. Within just two weeks, they were entering a land of villages and fields so startlingly fresh and green after their long desert journey that it was obvious the Indus could not be far. Soon Bhakkar's sturdy sandstone walls rose before them while westward, across the Indus, Humayun saw distant purple shadows – the mountains of Baluchistan. They were so like the mountains of Kabul, he felt his heart contract.

'Jauhar, ride to Bhakkar. Ask entry in the name of Humayun, Moghul Emperor of Hindustan and blood-kin of Mirza Husain of Sind.'

An hour later Humayun led his column into the fortress where the officer in command was waiting to receive him. 'Greetings, Majesty, on behalf of my master you are welcome. My name is Sayyid Ali.' As the commander touched his hand to his breast, Humayun saw that he was quite elderly with thin grey hair and a white scar on his left temple.

That night, Humayun sat with Kasim and Zahid Beg by Sayyid Ali's side around a brazier of smouldering applewood whose warmth was just enough to take the chill off the air rising from the river. 'I have had little news since a messenger brought word that Kabul had fallen to my half-brothers, Kamran and Askari. Can you tell me any more?'

Sayyid Ali cast him what seemed a slightly puzzled look. 'Indeed, Majesty, there is much more that you should know, even if the knowledge will displease you. Travellers from Kandahar who passed by on their way downriver told us that your half-brother Hindal had seized their city.'

Humayun stood up so abruptly that the wooden stool he'd been sitting on tipped over, falling against the brazier. 'How did it happen?'

'I heard that it fell to him without a struggle. The governor believed he was still your ally and admitted him and his forces.'

So that was what Hindal had been doing. Not heading for Kabul and an alliance with Kamran and Askari as Humayun had suspected but veering westward to set up his own kingdom in Kandahar. Humayun stared into the glowing embers of the fire as he remembered the last time he'd seen Hindal, blood-spattered and spitting defiance because Humayun wanted Hamida and would not be denied.

'So Hindal rules in Kandahar . . .' he said at last.

'No, Majesty.'

'But you said . . .'

'Something else happened, Majesty. Learning that Hindal was in Kandahar, your half-brother Kamran ordered him to acknowledge him as his overlord and to hold Kandahar only as his governor. When he refused, Kamran and Askari rode there with a large army, captured the city and took Hindal prisoner. No one knows what happened to him . . .'

Humayun's heart was beating very fast. Kamran and Askari were so much nearer than he'd believed . . . Kandahar was no more than three hundred miles away, far closer than Kabul. Perhaps fate had guided him to Bhakkar. Though he had so few men – barely two hundred – they were from the Moghul clans, his most trusted warriors – his *ichkis*. And more would join him if they thought there might be booty. The mountain tribesmen of Baluchistan had a well-deserved reputation for selling their swords for gold. If he was quick he could move on Kandahar, take it and capture his brothers before they had any warning. Yet there was something else he must know before he could contemplate such a move.

'What of Sher Shah, Sayyid Ali? Where is he?'

'In Bengal, where there has been a revolt against him. But more than that I do not know ... except that they say his rule over Hindustan is like iron – hard and unbending.'

Excellent, thought Humayun. With Sher Shah far away and preoccupied, he need fear no pursuit by him.

'I am grateful to you, Sayyid Ali, for your hospitality but even more for what you have told me. I wish to take my people across the Indus as soon as possible . . . The currents are swift and treacherous but you will know the safest place for us to cross . . .'

◆

Humayun shivered as the cold wind seemed to renew its strength and snowflakes fluttered around him. His head felt frozen solid and he pulled his long sheepskin jacket more tightly around him. Ahead rode the two Baluchi tribesmen Ahmed Khan had hired to guide them, who had just assured him that the party had covered nearly half the journey and were now ascending the snowy Bolan Pass, only a hundred and thirty or so miles from Kandahar. The guides seemed to expect praise but to Humayun progress had grown painfully slow the thicker the ice and snow had become. But at least his goal – the city Babur himself had captured for the Moghuls twenty years before – would soon be in sight.

Hamida and Gulbadan, wearing fur-lined cloaks with voluminous hoods over their thick woollen robes, were close behind him on ponies. The oxen had been unable to struggle up the narrow, slippery tracks and been killed for food many days ago and their carts chopped up for fuel. Maham Anga – with Akbar and her own son, both well swaddled against the cold – was in a deep pannier hanging on one side of a camel with Zainab in another pannier together with some cooking utensils to balance the weight on the other. The icy path was so treacherous that Humayun had ordered men to walk beside the three animals to lead them. But in these temperatures even the camel seemed subdued, trudging head down, ice crystals forming on the spikes of its thick fur.

Behind came the bodyguards, then the meagre baggage train – a few camels and mules wheezing beneath their loads – and finally

229

the rest of his men, saddlebags bulging, shields slung across their backs, battleaxes and muskets tied to their saddles. Like his, their faces were half concealed by face cloths and their heads huddled low into their shoulders against the biting, scouring winds. Also like him, tonight they would dine on the flesh of an old mule that had collapsed under its load, which would at least give some variety to their monotonous diet of rice or barley broth and flat-baked bread.

They looked a motley lot – more like one of his father's raiding parties than an emperor's army, reflected Humayun. The spectacle of his small force trudging through this snowy wilderness reminded him sharply how low he had fallen. It was equally sobering that, now he had crossed the Indus to ascend into the mountains of Baluchistan, not one of Babur's four sons remained in Hindustan. It was as if Babur's invasion had never happened and perhaps, though he'd never acknowledged it before, he – Babur's favoured and favourite son – must bear some of the blame. He hadn't understood the extent of the danger posed by the rivalries within his family. In particular, he had underestimated the depths of Kamran's enmity. Far too late he had begun to understand that Kamran would rather see the Moghuls fail than abandon his own ambitions and allow him, Humayun, to sit on the Moghul throne.

Humayun's horse slipped and almost fell, jolting him out of his reverie. He threw his weight back in the saddle, trying to help the animal stay upright, and murmuring encouragement as, snorting in misty spirals, it managed to right itself. He would be glad to get clear of these mountains, he thought, and sank his head deeper into his shoulders as the bitter wind nipped at him. Before long his thoughts returned to his brothers as they so often did during these long days of plodding, this time to Hindal. Now that he had time to reflect, he realised his anger with his youngest half-brother for so guilefully taking Kandahar was less than his concern for his safety at the hands of Kamran and Askari. Though he had reassured an anxious Gulbadan that they would not harm her brother, he was not so sure. Kamran at least might welcome an opportunity to rid himself of a rival.

A distant howling, eerie and desolate, chilling as the wind which carried it, made Humayun's horse skitter in fright. Wolves infested these wild, lonely mountains. At night they sometimes came so close to the camp that Humayun had seen their narrow yellow eyes gleaming out of the darkness and in the morning the ground around their tents had been patterned with paw prints. The snow was falling more heavily now and whirling flakes veiled the steep path ahead.

'Ahmed Khan,' Humayun called over his shoulder.

'Majesty?'

'A blizzard's coming. We'll camp here for the night. That overhanging rock shelf over there should provide some shelter.' Humayun pointed to a great slab of grey rock facing away from the prevailing wind which should keep off the worst of the wind and snow, and there looked to be enough space beneath it for their tents.

Humayun's men tethered their horses and began unloading equipment and erecting the tents beneath the overhang. Though it was still day, the light was getting poorer by the minute as the snow began tumbling in earnest. Keeping their backs bowed against the wind and struggling with numbed fingers to strike sparks from their tinder boxes, two of the men managed to get a fire going with some of the brushwood the mules had been carrying. As soon as it had caught, they made a giant torch from cloths dipped in oil and wound round a tall stick, and drove it into the ground outside Humayun's tent.

Within they set up a brazier, filled it with some of the precious charcoal brought from Bhakkar and coaxed it alight – not for Humayun and Hamida but for Akbar who would be sharing the tent with them that night. In these wild places Hamida insisted that the baby should sleep close by her. Maham Anga would sleep with her son, as she had on previous nights during the journey, in an adjoining alcove screened by saddle blankets. Inspecting the rest of his camp, Humayun saw that his men had erected fewer tents than usual. They'd be cramming in close, using each other's body heat to keep warm.

'Majesty,' came a deep voice. It was Ahmed Khan, cloaked head mantled with snow. 'Zahid Beg and I will post guards around the perimeter of the camp. Four of your bodyguards will also be on duty outside your tent.'

Humayun looked around him. Driven by the rising wind, the

snow was now whirling so thickly he could barely see his commander's face. The previous night one of his pickets had suffered frostbite and the *hakim* feared his blackened toes would need to be amputated. Ahmed Khan himself had been coughing all day from a chill he had caught on a midnight tour of the sentries. 'Thank you, Ahmed Khan, but I don't think we need to worry in this wild place. The men are tired and the weather's bitter. Let them rest tonight. You too – it might help that cough of yours.'

Despite the gusting winds howling around the camp and buffeting his tent, sleep came easily to Humayun that night, lying with Hamida in his arms, her fur-lined cloak spread on top of the sheepskins that covered them. A brief wail from Akbar penetrated his dreams but only for a moment. Humayun moved closer to Hamida, drawing her warm body in against his as he sank back into slumber. Then, suddenly, he felt cold, sharp steel against his throat. He looked up into a familiar pair of eyes, glinting in the light of a flaring rag torch that another man was holding. It couldn't be – he was in Kandahar many miles away beyond the icy passes. Yet there was no mistaking those triumphant eyes – green as their father Babur's had been – above that narrow, hawk-like nose. Kamran!

Humayun half opened his mouth to shout for help but felt the tip of Kamran's dagger prick his throat and a trickle of blood run slowly down. In the shadows beyond the bed he could make out other figures, presumably Kamran's henchmen, watching in silence, weapons drawn.

'One sound and I will cut your throat,' Kamran said. 'You know I mean it.'

Softly as Kamran had spoken, his words woke Hamida, who sleepily pushed her hair back from her face. As she opened her eyes, Humayun gently put a restraining hand on her arm. Taking in what was happening she didn't scream or cry out but immediately looked to where Akbar lay close by her in his basket.

'You have been lax, brother. I never thought to slip into your camp so easily,' Kamran said. 'My men have been observing your progress towards the pass for some days. The blizzard gave me my opportunity. You must have forgotten what our father taught us in the mountains around Kabul – how snow is the raider's friend, how it deadens sound. Your men never heard a thing. We found them packed tight in their tents like dumb beasts in a byre.'

'What have you done with them and the women?'

Kamran smiled but did not answer.

'How did you know I was coming this way?'

'I guessed that at some point you would try to come north. I have had all the approaches out of Hindustan watched for months.'

'Where is Askari?'

'In Kabul.'

'And Hindal, what have you done with him?'

'I haven't killed him, if that's what you mean. He's a captive in Jalalabad for his disrespect to me.'

'How can you speak of "disrespect" after how you betrayed me – offering alliance to Sher Shah to fight against your own blood? Sneaking like a thief into Kabul?'

'You are in no position to criticise. This beauty by your side – I heard you stole her from Hindal.' Kamran leaned closer to Hamida. 'But I can see she's worth it. I wouldn't have let brotherly love, brotherly loyalty, stand in my way either.'

Humayun felt Hamida tauten and he increased his pressure on her arm. 'What do you want, Kamran? If you intended to kill me I'd be dead already.'

'True. I don't share your sentimentality about blood bonds and so-called brotherly love. For me, it's always been *taktya takhta* – "throne or coffin".'

'Then what's stopping you?'

'The only reason I haven't drawn my blade across your jugular – tempted as I am – is that it would stir up blood feuds among the clans. But if I am seen to have defeated you and acted with mercy, chiefs once loyal to you will give me their support. You are more useful to me alive and humiliated than dead.'

'So what do you want?'

'Your promise to leave Hindustan and our ancestral homelands and go so far away that I can forget you ever existed.'

'Go where?'

'Persia has a pleasant climate and you'll find the soft living there to your taste – plenty of opium and plenty of beautiful women.'

'And if I refuse?'

'I will kill you here and now and face the difficulties with the clans. I will enjoy feeling your warm blood on my hands.'

'I've never understood why you hate me. It wasn't my fault our father chose me.'

'Wasn't it? It was your fault he seldom gave me a thought. You played the perfect warrior, the shining emblem of what he hoped to achieve. I've despised your vainglorious conceit ever since we were boys and you assumed I was happy to trail admiringly in your wake. When we became men you assumed you could continue to patronise me . . . But my ambition is as great as yours . . . I want the empire our father forged with his blood and sweat and I deserve it more than any of Babur's sons. Askari already accepts this and will do what I say. Hindal will learn to, if he's wise. When I am ready I will take on Sher Shah and drive him out. The *khutba* will be read in my name in Delhi and Agra and I and my sons – not yours – will sit on the Moghul throne. You had your chance and you failed.'

'Our father knew what you were like, that you were devious, self-serving and my enemy . . . that you were a traitor . . . he tried to warn me.'

'Shut up.' Kamran's voice had risen and Akbar began to cry.

'Your son sounds strong and lusty.' Kamran's green eyes flicked across to the basket on Hamida's side of the bed. 'Let me see my nephew,' he ordered Hamida.

She glanced anxiously at Humayun, who nodded. Gathering her robes around her, she slipped from the bed, lifted Akbar from his basket and carried him slowly towards Kamran.

'Watch my brother. If he moves so much as a muscle, kill him,' Kamran said to his men, three of whom stepped forward from the shadows towards Humayun. Meanwhile, Kamran withdrew his dagger from Humayun's throat, slid it into its scabbard and moved towards Hamida.

If only Hamida and Akbar had not been with him, he could have taken Kamran now, Humayun thought, calculating the distance between himself, his brother and his brother's men. He knew he could leap up and grab Kamran as a shield before one of his men had time to fire an arrow or throw a dagger. But as it was he could do nothing but watch as Kamran pulled back the thick sheepskin in which Akbar was wrapped and inspected the small, bawling face.

'Give him to me.'

Again Hamida looked across at Humayun and again he nodded. Kamran took hold of Akbar, who seemed to like the change and suddenly stopped his crying. For a moment Kamran scrutinised his face. 'Well, do you accept my terms, Humayun?' As he spoke Kamran took one of Akbar's tiny hands in his, but his eyes as he looked across at Humayun were as unconcerned and cold as if he were handling a piece of meat.

'I accept, but only because I have no choice. But I tell you this. One day I will make you pay for what you have done.'

'Remember, I hold your heir in my hands. Provoke me further and I'll order my men to take him outside and lay him naked in the snow. How long do you think he will last before the cold or the wolves kill him?'

Hamida gasped and Humayun watched helpless as Kamran chucked a laughing Akbar under the chin.

'No words, my silver-tongued half-brother, not even of farewell? It's not like you, the great emperor, to be so discourteous.' Their eyes locked but Humayun remained grimly silent. With a contemptuous shrug, Kamran stepped towards the entrance of the tent, still cradling Akbar.

'Give me back my child!' Hamida cried out.

Kamran turned back to her. 'I don't trust Humayun, even though he's so fond of boasting about how honourable he is. I need a guarantee that he will do what he has promised and go to Persia. My nephew is that guarantee . . .'

Before he'd finished speaking, Hamida flew at him, trying to pull Akbar away. As Akbar started screaming again, Kamran pushed Hamida hard. As she fell back, catching her head against the edge of a wooden chest, Kamran handed Akbar to one of his men. 'Take the child outside,' he ordered.

But Hamida hadn't finished with Kamran. Though dazed, she struggled up and launched herself at him again, raking his face with her nails and drawing blood. Kamran took her by the shoulders and pushed her off him. 'It's a shame. With so much fighting spirit you would have made a better empress than your husband has been an emperor.'

At that moment there was a movement behind the curtained-off alcove and the tall figure of Maham Anga appeared. In the shock and confusion Humayun had forgotten all about her. Similarly taken by surprise, Kamran released Hamida and drew his dagger. 'Who are you?' Blood was running down his cheek where Hamida had scratched him.

Maham Anga ignored Kamran but addressed herself to Hamida. 'Majesty, I heard everything. As Akbar's milk-mother, I should go with him. I swear to you that I will protect him with my life.' The expression on her handsome, high-cheekboned face was stubborn.

Hamida's eyes were shining with tears but she controlled herself as she turned to Kamran. 'This is Maham Anga, my son's wet-nurse. I ask that you take her with you to care for my son.'

'She may come.' Kamran looked again at Humayun. 'Your women are braver than your warriors. We captured your men as they slept – they are tied up in their tents like chickens for market. The only blood shed tonight was drawn by your wife. Make haste, Maham Anga. We ride in five minutes.' Turning, he ducked out of the tent.

As the two women embraced, Humayun saw Maham Anga whisper something in Hamida's ear. Then, under the watchful eye of Kamran's soldiers, the wet-nurse hurriedly collected her own son and a few of his and Akbar's things as well as her own and was escorted from the tent. Moments later, Hamida and Humayun heard the muffled sound of hooves on snow and then all went quiet. Leaping up, Humayun rushed outside. The blizzard was over and the snow that had fallen had softened the harsh landscape. So pure and still, it was a scene of almost perfect beauty.

Part III

Farewell the Koh-i-Nur

Chapter 15

Shah Tahmasp

At daybreak, Humayun gathered his men around him in the snow, their breath rising in spirals in the bitterly cold air. None had been seriously injured. They had been pinioned and bound with leather thongs before they realised they were under attack. But their mood was as subdued as his own and he understood why – their warrior code had been violated. In his heart, every man wished he had had the chance to fight. The shame of being taken unawares was a greater hurt than a wound to the flesh. At least a scar was a badge of honour. Where was the glory in being caught asleep in a tent?

'None of you is responsible for what happened last night. It was I who decided not to post guards.'

'Should we ride in pursuit?' asked Zahid Beg.

'No.'

'But why, Majesty? They've no more than an hour or two's start on us . . .'

'I gave my promise, Zahid Beg, and even if Kamran is not, I am a man of my word. Besides, he has taken my son. He threatened to kill Akbar before my very eyes and I believed him.'

'But the lives of young Timurid princes are sacred. That has always been our way . . .'

'But it is not my half-brother's. Ambition possesses him and he won't let anything stand in the way of his dreams of glory. If I give him the excuse, he will murder my son.'

Humayun grimaced. Hadn't he just said exactly the same thing to Hamida, weeping in the arms of Gulbadan who, with the other women, he had found tied up and gagged? Though badly shaken, Gulbadan had managed to recover her composure but Hamida remained not just inconsolable but hysterical. 'Rescue our son!' she had screamed at him. 'If you have a man's blood in your veins, how can you think about doing anything else?'

But for the first time since their marriage he had ignored her. Something dark lurked in his half-brother's soul. He had seen it as their eyes had met over Akbar's innocent head. To achieve what he wanted Kamran would do anything . . . That was why, Humayun had told Hamida as he held her tightly in his arms, they must not, dare not pursue Kamran. At least Maham Anga was with Akbar, he had said, stroking Hamida's hair, and, for the moment, they must trust in her. It seemed that confidence was not misplaced. Between her sobs, Hamida had told him what Maham Anga had whispered in those final moments before leaving – that she was carrying a knife whose blade had been treated with poison. Anyone attempting to hurt Akbar would die for it.

Pulling himself back to the present Humayun continued his address. 'My men, there is something else I must tell you. I also promised my half-brother to leave these lands and go to Persia. I do not think Shah Tahmasp who rules there will deny me sanctuary but the journey will be hard, across hundreds of miles of harsh and icy terrain. Before it is ended we may meet danger and deprivation beyond anything we have yet known. I do not order you to ride with me . . . if you wish to return home, do so with honour . . . but if you come with me, I pledge in the name of my father Babur and my ancestor Timur that once I have fulfilled my promise to go to Persia our stay there will be short. I will reclaim every inch of my usurped lands and those who ride with me – my *ichkis* – will share the glory of events that their descendants will speak of with pride a hundred years hence.'

Humayun paused. The expressions on his men's faces told him

that his words – and the steely determination behind them – had found their mark. Few would abandon him, not yet anyway. He must find ways to live up to their trust.

• ◆ •

The diamond-bright tips of the mountains all around shone with a brilliant, almost magical beauty – towers of ice from a fable. Yet the sight did not move Humayun as, a month later, he rode at the head of his column as it edged slowly upwards through a narrow pass. On the advice of the Baluchi guides who had agreed to take them to the border with Persia, Humayun had ordered his men to make as little noise as possible. Yet as, shading his eyes, he looked up at the glistening snow and ice fields above, he knew – as they all did – that at any moment an avalanche might roll down and obliterate them.

Danger was all around. Only yesterday – and even though Humayun had sent men ahead to probe the trackless, icy ground with the shafts of their spears to make sure it was solid – he had nearly lost a man down a crevasse concealed by a fall of fresh snow. Though the mule he had been leading had tumbled into the icy void, by an extraordinary stroke of good fortune the man had managed to grip on to a rock ledge some ten feet below. Two of Ahmed Khan's scouts had hauled him back up on a rope.

Nature was not the sole threat to their survival. Travellers only passed through this wild, desolate region from necessity. Brigands – 'ghouls of the wastes' the Baluchi guides called them, spitting on the ground – lurked in these high places. Some even said they did not baulk at eating human flesh. More than once Humayun had thought he detected movement among the snow-covered rocks above them but though he had looked hard he had seen nothing. All the same, the sense of watching eyes stayed with him and he knew that Ahmed Khan felt it too. It would be typically devious of Kamran – knowing which way Humayun was likely to go and that he had fewer than two hundred men – to have bribed bandits to attack him. Humayun's death, if seen to be at the hands of others, would be more than convenient for Kamran. Whatever the weather, Humayun posted sentries every night.

But he knew that the greatest risk of all was their growing physical weakness because with weakness came carelessness. Almost all their food – the grain, the dried fruit – was gone. The last three nights' meals had consisted of the fibrous flesh of a horse boiled in a helmet over a small fire. Soon they'd be unable to cook anything – their wood and charcoal were almost exhausted.

As Humayun shivered with cold – his very bones aching with it – he recalled his father Babur's stories of crossing the Hindu Kush, of men being dashed to pieces by sudden falls of ice, of drifts so deep that he and his men had taken it in turns to be 'snow tramplers', beating it down to force a way through. Babur had, by sheer determination, overcome the obstacles and so must he.

Later that afternoon, as they made camp on a saddle of land that seemed safe from avalanches, Humayun had another reason to remember Babur's tales of survival in the cold. Ahmed Khan, muffled in thick sheepskin robes, a flat-brimmed woollen Baluchi cap pulled low and almost all his face concealed by his face cloth so that only his amber-brown eyes were visible, came stumbling over, leather boots slipping on the icy ground.

'Majesty, it was so bitterly cold these past nights that two of my men got badly frozen feet on picket duty. The *hakim* is with them now . . .'

'What does he say?'

'That he must amputate – in one case three toes must come off, but in the other the whole foot . . .'

'I will come.'

The *hakim* and the two soldiers were inside a small tent where a pitiful little fire burned in a brazier. Humayun saw that one of the men who were lying with their pantaloons slit and bare legs exposed was Darya. The young man was looking very pale as he watched the *hakim* pass the blade of his knife through the feeble flame to cleanse it. Another broader blade was stuck into the heart of the fire, no doubt being heated to red-hot to cauterise the wounds. Humayun squatted by Darya and examined his right leg. The foot was black, puffy and swollen to well above his ankle while an evil-smelling greenish pus oozed from beneath the few remaining toenails.

'The *hakim* has told you what he must do?' Darya nodded but Humayun could see terror in his eyes. 'Courage. The *hakim* is skilled. God willing, this will save your life.'

The other soldier – a Badakhshani – looked even younger than Darya. Three of his toes were swollen and discoloured and he seemed unable to withdraw his gaze from the *hakim's* blade, which would soon be cutting through his flesh and bone.

'Ahmed Khan and I will help you, *hakim*,' said Humayun. 'Which one is first?'

The *hakim* gestured to the Badakhshani. While Ahmed Khan took the young man by the shoulders to hold him down, Humayun knelt by his leg which he grasped with both hands just above the knee. It took all his strength to hold the leg steady as the *hakim* went to work and the Badakhshani, trying hard not to cry out, arced in agony. But the *hakim* was quick. With just three precise motions he severed the blackened toes, then he cauterised the bleeding wounds and bandaged them tightly.

Now it was Darya's turn. The *hakim* looked grave as once again he passed his knife through the flames. 'This will take much longer, Majesty. I wish I had opium to give him to deaden the pain . . . I have seen stronger warriors than him die of shock during such an operation.'

Humayun glanced over his shoulder to where Darya was lying very still, pale face covered with a sheen of sweat.

'If he were unconscious, would that help?'

The *hakim* nodded.

Humayun went over to Darya. 'All will be well,' he said, kneeling down beside him. 'Try to sit up a moment, there is something I must tell you . . .' As a puzzled-looking Darya raised himself on his elbows, without warning Humayun swung his balled fist at him, catching him hard on the point of the chin. The young man instantly fell back. Pulling back his eyelids – as he had done many a time to both friend and foe on the battlefield – Humayun saw he was out cold. His aim had been good . . .

'*Hakim*, do what you must.' As Humayun ducked out of the tent into the freezing air, leaving Ahmed Khan to assist the doctor, he caught the rasping sound of metal sawing through bone and his spirits sank yet lower. How was he going to justify his men's confidence and repay their sacrifices? He looked up into the darkening sky and for a moment longed for a draught of Gulrukh's opium-laced wine to wash away his cares and responsibilities and waft him through the heavens. Then the image of Khanzada's face seemed to coalesce in the stars, silently reminding him that it was not his destiny to be carefree and that with it came burdens and obligations. He pulled his cloak tighter about him and determined to do a round of the sentries, warning them to keep moving and stamping their feet to avoid frostbite.

But three days later it seemed that, perhaps, the worst might be over. As they snaked down a narrow winding track the biting wind suddenly abated, and looking down through drifting wisps of cloud Humayun made out a circle of snow-covered houses and smoke rising from what he guessed must be a caravanserai. Muffled figures were grouped in its courtyard and he could see animals wandering about. 'Is that one of the settlements you spoke of?' he asked one of the Baluchi guides.

'Yes, Majesty. We are descending to what we call the *gamsir* – the mountain meadowlands where farmers and herdsmen have their winter habitations. We will be able to purchase provisions and fuel there . . . and even rest for a few days before travelling on.'

The prospect of supplies gladdened Humayun but he wouldn't delay a moment longer than necessary. The pain in Hamida's eyes every time he looked at her matched his own at the thought of Akbar so many miles away and in Kamran's hands. The sooner they reached Persia, the sooner he could begin to make plans again.

'How far from here to the border?'

'The Persian province of Seistan lies just over the Helmand river about eighty miles from here, Majesty.'

'Over what kind of terrain?'

'Mostly downhill from now on. As we near the Helmand it flattens into desert.'

'How many days before we reach the river?'

'No more than ten to twelve to reach the ford I know of.'

That night, after they had reached the settlement and eaten their fill for the first time in many days, Humayun joined Hamida in their tent. 'Now that we are getting close to his lands, I must write to Shah Tahmasp asking him to receive us. If we approach his territory unannounced, the Persian troops guarding his borders may think our intentions hostile. I will entrust the letter to Jauhar as my envoy. He will carry it over the Helmand river and seek out the governor or some other high-ranking official to explain why we have come and to request to be allowed to carry my letter to the shah without delay.'

As he spoke, Humayun settled himself cross-legged at a low table where, by the light of an oil lamp, he began mixing his ink. He knew how much depended on his choice of words. During the journey he had weighed carefully what he must say and now began to write fluidly and without hesitation, speaking the words out loud to Hamida. It was fortunate that Persian was a familiar language to the Moghuls so that he had no need of a translator.

First came a paragraph of graceful courtesies, including repeated hopes for the shah's prolonged good health and the success of his reign. Then Humayun reminded Tahmasp that many years earlier his father Shah Ismail had not only assisted Humayun's father Babur against his enemies but rescued Babur's sister Khanzada from captivity in the *haram* of the Moghuls' implacable enemy, the Uzbek chieftain Shaibani Khan. Humayun did not mention that – as Shah Tahmasp would very well know – the alliance between Babur and Ismail had not lasted long. Instead, he eulogised the fact that these two great rulers had once joined forces to destroy a common enemy.

Next, Humayun decided to make a direct plea: 'I have suffered many reverses. An impostor from Bengal, Sher Shah, rules in my place in Hindustan while my half-brothers have stolen Kabul and Kandahar from me and hold my infant son hostage. You too are an emperor – a very great one – and you will, I am certain, understand and sympathise with my plight. I ask you to be gracious enough to receive me, my family and my small force into Persia.'

'What do you think?' Humayun asked Hamida as, having rounded off the letter with a few last formal courtesies, he laid down his pen.

For a few moments Hamida thought. 'It is eloquent, open and frank. It should sway the shah, but whether it will who can say. So often we've raised our hopes and expectations, only to have them dashed.'

• ◆ •

'Majesty, there is the ford.'

Shading his eyes, Humayun followed the guide's pointing finger and saw across the flat, grey ground the glint of a watercourse – the Helmand river. A squat tower with a long banner streaming from its roof stood on the opposite bank – presumably a Persian fortress guarding the crossing. It must be three or four days at least since Jauhar had passed through this way, so the commander of the fort should be expecting Humayun's arrival. All the same, it was as well to be cautious.

'Ahmed Khan, send scouts closer to the fort to see what they can find out while the rest of us halt here.'

'I will go myself, Majesty.' Summoning two of his men, Ahmed Khan cantered off, raising a cloud of powdery grey dust.

Humayun rode slowly back to the covered wooden cart – one of several he had purchased at the settlement to transport the women and the sick – in which Hamida and Gulbadan were travelling. Pushing his head inside the wool hangings, he saw that Hamida was asleep and that Gulbadan was writing – doubtless that diary of hers. They both looked pale and thin.

'We have reached the river,' he said quietly so as not to wake Hamida. 'If Ahmed Khan reports that all is well and the Persians do not object, we will cross and make camp. How is Hamida?'

'She still says so very little . . . She seldom shares her feelings or her thoughts, even with me.'

'Try to make her understand, as I have, that I won't rest until we have our son again. Everything I am doing . . . will have to do over the months ahead . . . will above all be for Akbar.'

'She knows that she must be strong for you but she worries how the shah will receive us . . . and how Kamran is treating Akbar.'

As Hamida stirred, Humayun turned away and pulling back the hangings returned to the front of the column. He didn't have to wait long for news. Barely an hour after Ahmed Khan and his men had ridden away, Humayun saw them returning. Close behind them were two other riders. As they drew closer Humayun made out that, though one was a stranger, the other was the tall figure of Jauhar. Why wasn't he on his way to the shah? Had the shah denied them entry to Persia? Had Kamran somehow won his favour? Full of anxiety, he kicked his horse forward to meet them.

'Majesty.' Ahmed Khan was smiling. 'All is well. This,' he indicated the stranger, 'is Abbas Beg, the governor of Seistan, who has come to escort you into Persia.'

Abbas Beg, a tall, black-bearded man of about forty, magnificently dressed in dark purple velvet and with a white egret's feather secured by a jewelled clasp to his tall cap, dismounted and bowed before Humayun. 'Majesty, I have despatched your letter to the shah. Our swift post riders can cover eighty miles a day. I requested your envoy to remain behind to advise me how best to receive you. Everything is ready. You only have to cross the ford.'

A tremendous weight lifted from Humayun. For the first time in months he need not worry where his family and his men were to sleep, whether there was food, whether they were safe from attack. For a moment he closed his eyes and bowed his head in gratitude, then drawing himself up said, 'I thank you, Abbas Beg. Your words are very welcome.'

'Then, in the name Shah Tahmasp, Lord of the World, I welcome you to Persia.'

• ◆ •

One hundred attendants were sweeping the road ahead and sprinkling it with rosewater to subdue the dust. Ahead of Humayun and his party trotted one thousand gorgeously caparisoned horsemen whom the shah had sent to escort them to his capital, Kazvin, seven hundred miles to the northwest. Humayun's own party was no less magnificently mounted on Persian horses – sable black with gold-mounted bridle and saddle for Humayun. Hamida and Gulbadan were in a gilded, velvet-lined wagon drawn by white oxen, horns adorned with ribbons of Moghul green.

Shah Tahmasp's response to his letter had reached Humayun just three weeks after he had crossed into Persia. Three pages of extravagant compliments had ended with the words: *You are my brother, a precious jewel of sovereignty whose bright magnificence makes dim the world-illuminating sun. My days will seem empty until I have the happiness of receiving you at my court in Kazvin.*

The shah had issued *firmans*, written orders, to the governor of every town and province through which Humayun would be passing giving the most minute instructions for his comfort and pleasure. Humayun knew this because the shah had sent him copies of these *firmans* – written on thick gold-bordered paper – in an ivory casket *so that my brother may know that I have spared no effort to welcome him.*

The shah had decreed exactly where the column should halt each night so that, as they rode in, tents of fine embroidered white cloth with awnings of velvet and silk were already erected and waiting. Every night brought another exquisite feast – golden platters of sweet white bread baked with milk and butter and sprinkled with poppy and fennel seeds, five hundred different savoury dishes – duck simmered in a walnut sauce, lamb stewed with quinces and dried limes – nuts of every kind covered in gold and silver leaf, dried apricots stuffed with chopped nuts and honey and pyramids of sweetmeats scented with rosewater and sprinkled with jewel-like pomegranate seeds.

Every day saw the arrival of fresh gifts – jewelled daggers and coats cut from cloth of gold and flowered brocades for Humayun and amber and exquisite perfumes sent by the shah's sister, Shahzada Sultanam, to Hamida and Gulbadan. The rest of Humayun's retinue was not forgotten – Shah Tahmasp sent daggers and swords made by the finest armourers for his men. Everyone had new clothes. The ragged, weary band that had crossed the Helmand river had been transformed.

But as the weeks passed and they were drawing nearer to Kazvin, passing through orchards of peach and apricot trees and along riverbanks lined with drooping willows, Humayun had still not found an answer to the question that kept troubling him. Why had

Shah Tahmasp gone to such extravagant lengths? Was it simply to impress Humayun? Did it flatter his ego to have the Moghul emperor seeking his protection, or was there something deeper?

Though Humayun shared his unease with Kasim and Zahid Beg, he knew he could not discuss it with Hamida. Every sign of the shah's goodwill seemed to revive her – in her eyes it spelled hope that Tahmasp would assist Humayun against his half-brothers and help him win back Akbar. Of course, in a way Hamida was right. Whatever the shah's true motives – and just possibly they might be entirely benevolent – he must make an ally of him . . .

At last on an early summer's day, the moment Humayun had been so keenly anticipating arrived. In a meadow bright with flowers near Kazvin, Shah Tahmasp, accompanied by ten thousand of his cavalrymen, was waiting to greet the Moghul emperor. As Humayun had come to expect of the shah, every last detail had been thought of – the exact spot where Humayun was to dismount, where his men were to wait, the path of thick, dark-red rugs sprinkled with dried rose buds leading to the centre of the meadow where a vast, circular, golden carpet – silken threads gleaming in the sun – had been spread.

Standing alone in the very centre of the carpet, his troops drawn up some fifty yards behind, was the shah, dressed in crimson velvet and on his head a tall, pointed jewelled cap of crimson silk embroidered with gold thread. Humayun knew what the hat signified. It was the *taj* – the symbol of the Islamic Shia faith. As Humayun approached the edge of the carpet, Tahmasp stepped towards him and taking him by the shoulders smilingly embraced him. Then he led Humayun to a large bolster and seating Humayun to his right, sat down beside him.

'You are welcome, my brother.' Humayun saw that Tahmasp was about his own age, strong-featured, pale-skinned and with luminous black eyes beneath thick brows.

'I am grateful for your hospitality. I had heard of the glories of Persia and now I have seen them for myself.'

Tahmasp smiled. 'What little I could provide while you were on the road was, I am sure, poor compared with the magnificence of the Moghuls of which I, in turn, have heard.'

Humayun looked sharply at his host. Tahmasp knew very well there had been nothing magnificent about his flight to Persia. Had there been a barb in those flattering words? Conscious of the thousands of watching eyes – eyes that would see what he was about to do – Humayun made a sudden decision. He must show them that he had not come to Persia a beggar. He would make a gesture so splendid that even in fabulous Persia it would be spoken of down the ages – a gesture so unmatchable that it would place Persia's ruler in his debt.

'Shah Tahmasp, I have brought you a gift from Hindustan.' Reaching inside the neck of his robe, Humayun pulled out the flowered silk pouch in which, through all the hard and hazardous times, he had kept his greatest treasure close to his heart. Slowly, deliberately, Humayun extracted the Koh-i-Nur and raised it high in the air to catch the sunlight. It shone bright as a star and Humayun heard Shah Tahmasp gasp.

'Had I not been on the road so long, I might have found something yet more worthy of you. But I hope this bauble pleases you. It is named the Koh-i-Nur, the Mountain of Light. May its light shine on you, Shah Tahmasp, and on our enduring friendship.'

Chapter 16

Kandahar

'That you turned to me in your distress touched my heart. The world will see that when the Moghul emperor sought my help, I answered him. I will give you an army and one of my best generals so that you may reclaim what has been taken from you.' Shah Tahmasp clasped Humayun by the shoulder. 'As our fathers were once allies, so we will be . . .' They were sitting on silk cushions on a marble platform constructed over the intersection of two water channels flowing north to south and east to west through the shah's private gardens. The four quarters of the garden created by the channels were planted with fruit trees – quince, cherry, apple, apricot, peach and the shah's favourite, apple trees – on whose branches small golden fruit were already forming. Song birds with jewelled collars hopped among the branches.

When Tahmasp had summoned him to this audience in what the shah called his 'paradise garden', Humayun had allowed himself to hope. But the shah's offer went beyond anything he'd anticipated. The sacrifice of the Koh-i-Nur had been worth it and he struggled to control his elation. 'You are gracious,' he replied. 'With your men fighting beside mine, I have no doubt of victory . . .'

'You may wonder why I am so ready to assist you. It is not just out of sentiment. I have many reasons. Treachery within royal dynasties such as ours is dangerous. You were not the only Moghul to write to me. Your half-brother Kamran also sent me a message – that you were fleeing into Persia, that if I imprisoned you he would give me many things – gold, gemstones and even the city of Kandahar.' Tahmasp's black eyes glittered. 'He sought to bargain with me as if I were a merchant in the bazaar. His arrogance angered me. But more than that, I asked myself, how can I trust a prince eager to shed his own brother's blood? If I wished I could squash him like a fly but I prefer to help you do so.'

He leaned forward. 'I have little interest in expanding my lands eastwards. What I want is stability on my borders as there was in your father's day. While Babur – may his soul rest in Paradise – ruled, he kept the tribes – the Pashais, Kafirs and others – in check. Persia's merchants travelled safely without let or hindrance all the way from Meshed, Isfahan and Shiraz to Kashgar beyond the mountains of Ferghana. But since your half-brother seized Kabul there has been anarchy and my people are suffering. With my help you can restore order.'

As the shah was talking, Humayun recalled Darya's account of how Kamran had used gold plundered from Persian merchants to raise and fund the army with which he had taken Kabul and wondered whether Tahmasp knew of this.

'Winter comes early to my homelands, and gracious as is your hospitality I am eager to begin the campaign as soon as possible. I would like to move first against Kandahar and then on to Kabul before the first snows. When do you think your troops might be ready to accompany me?'

'I began assembling a force weeks before you reached Kazvin. I can give you ten thousand men, including mounted archers, musketeers, and artillerymen as well as cavalry. They – and their commander Rustum Beg – can be ready with their cannon, other weapons and baggage train in two weeks' time. Do the ladies of your family wish to remain here in Kazvin? My sister will take great care of them.'

Humayun shook his head. 'Danger and hardship are nothing to them. They will want to go with me. My wife is tormented by anxiety over the fate of our son. If she had her way we would leave today.'

'Her feelings do her honour as a mother and as an empress. I've heard much of the courage of Moghul women. My father held your aunt Khanzada Begam in high esteem.'

'She had reason to be very grateful to Shah Ismail . . .'

Tahmasp acknowledged the compliment with a graceful gesture of his bejewelled hand. 'But before we speak further of going to war, there is something I must ask you. You are a true believer but it grieves me that you follow the Sunni path and not that of the Shias, like myself. Show me that you are indeed my brother, that the bonds between us are as strong as those of blood. Embrace the Shia sect so that you and I can worship side by side to ask God's blessing for our enterprise.' Tahmasp's dark eyes, fixed on Humayun's face, were fervent and glowing.

Humayun struggled to contain his surprise and dismay. Tahmasp had chosen his moment well – offering Humayun everything he could wish for before making his demand. It was easier to deal with a man hungry for the material things of life – lands and gold, Humayun reflected. Such a man was usually prepared to compromise. A man hungry for another's soul was not. He must be very careful how he handled Tahmasp.

'You seek this only of me, not of my commanders and my men?' he asked after a moment.

'Only of you, but of course where an emperor leads, others often wish to follow.'

'I must think over what you have said.'

'Do not take too long, my brother. As you yourself said, you wish to campaign before the winter snows become an extra enemy . . .' Shah Tahmasp rose from the silk cushions and summoning his guards, who had been waiting at a discreet distance while the two rulers talked, stepped down from the platform and walked away through the garden, pausing to examine the crimson blooms on a rose bush.

Humayun went straight to Hamida. As he entered her apartments, her hopeful, expectant expression made him feel his predicament even more keenly.

'What did he say? Will he help us?' she asked, as soon as they were alone.

253

'The shah is no friend to Kamran and will give me an army to defeat him, but there is a price . . .'

'What price? He has the Koh-i-Nur. What more do we have to give?'

'He wants me to become a Shia Muslim . . .'

'Is that all?' Hamida came closer and took his face between her hands.

'It's a great deal. Shah Ismail tried to force my father Babur to become a Shia – it nearly cost him his life and it certainly cost him Samarkand. Our people hated him for it – they turned to Shaibani Khan, preferring to be ruled by a murderous Sunni Uzbek than a Timurid prince they suspected of converting to Shiism . . .'

Hamida released him and stared up at him incredulously. 'But those were different times. We're not in Samarkand now. Most important, we have lost our son. We must do everything in our power to save him . . . it is our duty . . . our sacred duty above anything else. You must accept this, just as I accepted your arguments not to pursue Kamran when he took Akbar.'

'But this explains why Shah Tahmasp was so welcoming . . . this is what he really wants . . . to convert the Moghuls to Shiism. I saw it in his face as he spoke to me . . .'

'Are you sure he doesn't just want you to convert as some kind of token recognition of his authority?'

'I don't think even his mind is subtle enough for that. And don't you see? That would be even more repugnant. You don't understand how it would affect my troops.'

'No, you are the one who doesn't understand. Swallow your pride, if not for my sake then for our son's!'

'My pride is one of the few things left to me and you ask me to sacrifice it?'

'You have no choice. Our situation is too perilous to be over-scrupulous. Go through the outward ceremonies. Think what you will in your heart. True pride is internal, not external. Remember how much outward pride it must have cost your father to surrender Khanzada to Shaibani Khan, but he kept his inner spirit strong.'

Humayun said nothing and Hamida continued more softly, 'In

any case, don't Shias and Sunnis worship the same God? Their divisions are of human not divine manufacture. They stem from quarrels in the Prophet's family, just like those that have split your own . . .'

Humayun bowed his head. She was right, he didn't have a choice if he wanted to regain his throne and recover his son. His decision was made. Whatever his commanders and their men might think, at least temporarily he must don the crimson silk *taj* of the Shia monarch and kneel at Shah Tahmasp's side in the mosque to call down God's blessing on his campaign. Sunni or Shia, his cause was just and God – the one God – would still be on his side . . .

• ◆ •

They were making good progress, Humayun thought with satisfaction – much swifter than on the journey to Kazvin that had been at the stately pace dictated by the shah. Ahead of Humayun rode the Persian archers and musketeers and directly behind him were Hamida and Gulbadan and their women in their wagons, surrounded by his bodyguard. Next came the rest of his soldiers, then the baggage train including the cannon loaded on bullock carts and finally the Persian cavalry, the tips of their spears – broader-bladed than Moghul ones but no less sharp – catching the early morning sun.

Zahid Beg was to Humayun's left but at his right shoulder was Rustum Beg, the Persian commander. He was a thin-faced, delicate-boned elderly man, a cousin of the shah's, fond of quoting from the Persian poets to Humayun's war council but content to leave the day-to-day command of his force to his deputy, Bairam Khan. The latter was still quite young – no more than about thirty-four or five – but his thick-set build and the scar at the right corner of his mouth made him look older. His eyes were an unusual colour for a Persian – deep, almost indigo blue – and his long dark hair protruded in a plait from beneath a pointed steel helmet hung with chain mail to protect the neck and the sides of the face and surmounted by a peacock feather.

In the first days after leaving Kazvin, Bairam Khan had spoken little, beyond responding to Humayun's questions. However, as the weeks passed he had become more expansive. Everything he said was well considered and he listened to Humayun's commanders with courtesy and tact. That was good. Had Rustum Beg pushed himself forward more and had Bairam Khan been over-haughty, it might have caused dissension between Humayun's men and the far more numerous Persians. As it was, they co-existed well. Humayun was also relieved that his men seemed to have accepted his conversion to Shiism as the pragmatic decision it was. They had watched the public ceremony at which the shah himself had placed the scarlet *taj* on his head without protest, understanding, as he did, that it was necessary to secure the future of them all.

Humayun looked up to see a small group of horsemen galloping towards him, dust dancing in the air around them. It was Ahmed Khan with two of his scouts and two Persian cavalrymen Rustum Beg had sent as guides.

'Majesty, the Helmand river lies only fifteen miles away.'

'Excellent.' Humayun smiled. In two days – perhaps even tomorrow – he would again cross the cold waters of the Helmand and this time he would cross it with a great army at his back.

· ◆ ·

The fortress of Kandahar with its thick stone walls and slit-windowed towers looked grimly impregnable against a backdrop of jagged, purple-brown mountains. Though it was only September, the chill wind made Humayun and his commanders shiver as they looked towards the fortress from their vantage point on the downward slope of a wooded hill about half a mile away.

Where in that fortress was Akbar? Humayun knew that his son's fate depended on the decisions he was about to take. Kamran was no fool. His spies would have been observing Humayun's progress and he must know that Humayun – backed as he was by crack Persian troops – had the stronger hand. Eventually, whether by siege or assault, Kandahar would fall. So what would Kamran do? Threaten to harm Akbar if Humayun did not withdraw? Kamran was capable of it. On the other hand, Humayun tried to comfort himself, his half-brother would know that if he killed Akbar he would lose his best bargaining counter . . .

Bairam Khan and Zahid Beg were staring at the fortress and discussing its strengths and potential weak spots. Nadim Khwaja too was gazing at it intently. As a chieftain from the mountains above Kandahar the fortress would be a familiar sight to him but his thoughts, like Humayun's, would be for his family. His wife Maham Anga and their own son Adham Khan were, like Akbar, prisoners within those walls. Briefly, Humayun put his hand on Nadim Khwaja's shoulder, and as their eyes met he knew that they shared the same inner emotions. They were both warriors whose natural instinct was to storm into the fortress and rescue their loved ones. But understandable as such hot-blooded impulses were, they were not the way . . .

An idea was beginning to form in Humayun's mind. He must find a means of opening a dialogue with Kamran. Repugnant though he found the idea of negotiation, he knew it was what his father would have done. Hadn't Babur swallowed his pride and negotiated with Shaibani Khan to save the dynasty? It was also what Khanzada would have counselled. She above everyone had understood the value of patience, of making short-term sacrifices in order to win the ultimate prize.

But who could speak on his behalf? He couldn't do it himself. Even if Kamran agreed to see him, if they came face to face there would be blows, not words, such was their mutual hatred. Yet he could not send Kasim or one of his commanders. This was a family matter. Kamran must be made to understand how he had violated every principle of honour and loyalty in the Moghul code, how his ambition had split and weakened Babur's legacy.

There was only one person travelling with Humayun who could speak to Kamran of such things, who shared both his blood and Akbar's blood. Gulbadan. Moghul women often played the role of peacemakers between the clans and her sharp intelligence was the equal of any of his counsellors'.

Dishonourable as he had shown himself, not even Kamran would harm his half-sister and he might even listen – if not to her personal pleas at least to the offer she would carry to him from Humayun. If Kamran would return Akbar unharmed, he could depart freely with Askari and their men and their weapons and Humayun's solemn vow – in the name of their father Babur – not to pursue them.

Only one question remained. Would Gulbadan be willing to undertake such a mission? But as Humayun signalled to his commanders to turn their horses back up the hill to re-join their forces, he was confident he knew the answer.

• ◆ •

'Majesty, Gulbadan Begam is returning.'

Hearing the shout from outside his command tent, Humayun leaped up from the stool on which he'd been sitting and, pushing aside the tent flaps, ducked out into the swiftly falling dusk. On the floor of the valley that lay between Humayun's camp and the fortress, a line of flickering lights was drawing slowly nearer – torches borne by the detachment of guards he had sent with Jauhar to escort Gulbadan, who were riding before and behind the wagon in which she was travelling.

It was seven hours since she had set out under a flag of truce. Straining his eyes into the darkness, Humayun allowed himself to hope for just a moment that Akbar might be in Gulbadan's arms but common sense quickly overcame such wishful thinking. Kamran was not a man to be moved by sentiment. He would not release Akbar until the very last moment, when he was certain Humayun would keep his word.

Nevertheless, unable to contain his impatience, Humayun ran to the roped-off enclosure where his horse was tethered. Without waiting for a saddle and using the halter in place of reins, he urged it to leap the rope and galloped off down to the valley. His heart was jumping so fast that for a moment he imagined the thudding of hooves on the soft turf was the sound it was making. For so much of the time he had to suppress his feelings – to show himself a cool, dispassionate leader to his men, to turn a calm, confident face to Hamida. But out here in the enshrouding darkness he could admit that he was as vulnerable as any man to fears and anxieties, particularly over the fate of those he loved and whom it was his duty to protect.

'It is the emperor!' he heard Jauhar cry out. Swerving to a standstill just a few yards from where Gulbadan's wagon had halted, Humayun slid from his horse. Jauhar had also dismounted and without words led Humayun to Gulbadan's cart. Taking the torch Jauhar was holding, Humayun drew aside the curtains and peered in at his half-sister.

'I am glad to see you safely returned. What did Kamran say? Will he accept my terms?'

Gulbadan leaned further forward into the light, her young face very tired. 'Humayun, I'm sorry. Kamran wasn't there – only Askari. Hearing of your advance, some weeks ago Kamran rode to Kabul which he means to defend against you.'

'And Akbar?'

'Kamran took him with him to Kabul. But Humayun – there is still hope. Askari assured me Akbar is in good health and that Maham Anga is with him . . .'

'How can I trust a word Askari says when he follows a man prepared to use a child as a weapon against me?'

'Askari does feel the shame of it, I think. Also, from what he says I believe he thinks that, by ordering him to remain behind in Kandahar, Kamran has left him to bear the brunt of your anger.'

'Will Askari surrender Kandahar to me?'

'He will – on the promise that you will spare his life and those of his men.'

Humayun smiled grimly. 'He can keep his miserable life and so may his men, but my offer of free passage was conditional on the safe return of Akbar. Askari, at least, will stay in my custody until I have found my son and dealt with Kamran. What of Hindal? Did you learn anything of his fate?'

'My brother is often in my thoughts and I pressed Askari about what had happened to him . . . He told me that Kamran ordered Hindal to be taken to the fort at Jalalabad and held prisoner there. But somehow on the way there he managed to escape. That was many months ago and Askari does not know where he has gone . . . I hope my brother is safe.'

'So do I. Though we had our differences I was not blameless and he was more of a brother to me than either of the others. But you,

Gulbadan, you are a true sister to me and a true friend to Hamida. What you did today was hard and I'm grateful.'

It was a bitter thing that Babur's sons should be so divided. Humayun was locked in gloom as he walked slowly back to his horse. Arriving back at the camp, he went straight to Hamida. She was waiting inside the women's tent and at his sombre look the light of hope in her dark eyes faded. 'So Kamran has refused your offer.'

'Not even that. He wasn't there. Hamida – he has taken Akbar to Kabul . . .'

As tears welled in her eyes, Humayun caught her to him. 'Listen to me. We mustn't despair. Askari is still in Kandahar and he promised Gulbadan that Akbar is in good health. That at least is good news.'

'But Kabul is so far away . . .'

'It's three hundred miles away and I'd go three thousand miles to recover our son. You know that . . .'

'I do, but it's so hard. I think constantly about Akbar and what might be happening to him, even when I try to sleep. When I was pregnant and we were fleeing Maldeo, I couldn't help imagining how it would feel to have him cut living from my womb. I felt the cold blade in my flesh. This worry is as bad . . . it's like a physical pain. I'm not sure how much more of it I can bear.'

'Be strong for a little longer . . . be strong for our son, just as you were when Maldeo plotted our destruction. Askari has offered to surrender Kandahar to me. As soon as I have secured it, we ride for Kabul.' He felt her body relax a little and she stepped back from him.

'You're right – disappointment made me speak as I did. I had convinced myself I would get Akbar back within a day or two. It was foolish to build up my hopes.'

'It was only natural. I'd let myself hope too. I also must learn patience and persistence. Taking strength from each other we will endure and succeed.'

A few minutes later, Humayun entered his command tent, sat down, took a piece of paper and scratched a few sentences on it. Then, though it was growing late, he summoned his war council.

'Ahmed Khan, I want you to send a detachment of your men to Kandahar tonight taking this letter to my half-brother Askari. My message to him is simple. "Tomorrow I will ride at the head of my forces to your gates. If you open them to me, as you promised our sister, you will keep your life though you will be my prisoner. If you attempt in any way to deceive me, your life – and the lives of your men – are forfeit. The choice is yours."'

As Ahmed Khan hurried off, Humayun addressed the rest of his commanders.

'Tomorrow, if my half-brother keeps his word, we will occupy Kandahar. Bairam Khan, I ask you to select two thousand of your men under the leadership of your most trustworthy senior officers to garrison the fortress.'

Bairam Khan nodded. 'I will choose from among my archers and musketeers and, if you agree, Majesty, I will also detail a detachment of cavalry to remain to patrol the surrounding country.'

'An excellent suggestion, Bairam Khan. Once our garrison is in place in Kandahar, we set out for Kabul. Though it is a long journey through difficult mountain terrain, we must travel hard and fast. Every day that passes gives my half-brother more time to buy allies and strengthen his position there.'

'What about our baggage train? That will slow us,' asked Zahid Beg.

'We will carry what we can with us and designate a small force to protect the baggage train, including our cannon, which must follow at the best pace it can. But the hour grows late. We will meet again an hour before dawn to prepare for our advance on Kabul.'

◆

The long valley, framed to north and south by sweeping grey mountains, was filled with tents radiating out in lines from the centre where Humayun's scarlet command tent stood. To its right were the tents of his senior officers, a bright scarlet banner streaming from the roof of Bairam Khan's. To the left, enclosed by wooden screens fastened together by leather thongs, were the *haram* tents where the women had their private accommodation. Hamida and Gulbadan

261

had insisted on travelling with Humayun rather than with the slower baggage column and neither had murmured a word of complaint about the forced marches of fourteen hours a day.

But despite their efforts Kabul still lay nearly a hundred and fifty miles away to the northeast and there was little Humayun could do to increase their pace. All the time it was growing colder. Though it was only early October, the gusting winds already carried a few flakes of snow. Before too long it would be full winter.

At least as he advanced his army was swelling with new recruits. Ahmed Khan had just told him that another group of deserters from Kamran had ridden into the camp offering him their allegiance. Humayun had ordered the leader to be brought to him for questioning.

Half an hour later, Humayun looked down at the man lying at his feet, arms outstretched, in the formal obeisance of the *korunush*. From his black boots embroidered with red stars, an emblem of their clan, Humayun guessed he was a chieftain of the Kafirs who dwelled in the *kotals*, the high, narrow passes around Kabul. The Kafirs were notorious turncoats. When Humayun was just a boy, his father had made an example of the men of one Kafir village who had murdered his envoys by having them impaled before the walls of Kabul so that the earth had been stained red with their blood.

'Get up. You are a Kafir, are you not?'

'Yes, Majesty.' The man, weather-beaten, squat and bandy-legged, looked gaunt and his sheepskin jerkin was torn.

'Why have you and your men come here?'

'To offer to serve you, Majesty.'

'But you served my half-brother Kamran, didn't you?'

The Kafir nodded.

'Why did you desert him?'

'He broke his word. He promised us gold but he gave us nothing. When two of my men complained he had them flung from the walls of the citadel of Kabul.'

'When was this?'

'Three weeks ago. A few days later, when your brother sent us foraging into the mountains, we did not return but came in search of your army.'

'What was happening in Kabul before you left?'

'Your brother was fortifying the citadel and laying in supplies ready for a siege – that was why he sent parties like ours out foraging. He fears you, Majesty. He knows, as does the whole of Kabul, that you are advancing with a great army . . . that you have Persian troops under your command and that in the eyes of the world you, not he, is *padishah* . . .'

Humayun ignored the man's ingratiating smile. 'Do you know anything about my infant son? Did you see him in Kabul?'

The man looked blank. 'No, Majesty. I did not even know he was there . . .'

'You are sure – you heard nothing of a royal child brought with his wet-nurse from Kandahar?'

'No, Majesty, nothing.'

Humayun studied the Kafir chieftain for a few moments. The man had no allegiance to anyone or anything. All he cared about was who had the fattest purse. And he had been in Kamran's service. Humayun's instinct was to have him and his men ejected from the camp. But that would send out a bad message to other clans thinking of joining him. The struggle ahead would be long and hard and he would need every soldier he could get. His own father had made good use of the wild mountain tribes' ferocious fighting skills, though he had kept a tight rein on them.

'You and your men may join my army, but understand this. Any disobedience, any disloyalty will be punished by death. If you serve me well, once Kabul has fallen you will be generously rewarded. Do you accept?'

'Yes, Majesty.'

Humayun turned to his guards. 'Take this man to Zahid Beg so he can decide what use to make of him and his companions.'

As the setting sun cast purple shadows over the valley and dusk came tumbling down, Humayun once more felt the need for solitude, the need to escape if only for a little while from the burden of his responsibilities. Dismissing his guards and wrapping his cloak around him, he set off northwards through the lines of tents, intending to walk the perimeter of the encampment. Instead, when he reached the edge of the camp he continued beyond it, past the pickets, drawn by the outlines of the mountains beyond as they folded away into the greater darkness.

For a while, he followed a goat track as it climbed steeply upwards. Below him he could see the orange lights of a hundred camp fires as his men cooked their evening meal. In a few minutes he must return to eat with Hamida and Gulbadan in the *haram* tent, but there was something compelling about the absolute stillness out on the mountainside. Glancing up, Humayun looked at the stars. Low on the horizon was Canopus – that brightest, most auspicious of stars that his father had seen on his way to Kabul and that had given him such hope. Now he hoped it was shining for him too.

Chapter 17

Flesh and Blood

Winter descended quickly in the mountains. Three weeks ago, the fluttering snowflakes had barely settled but now the wind was driving them almost horizontally down a narrow defile through the icy mountains to the northwest of Kabul as Humayun led his army onwards. With the worsening conditions compounding the difficulties of travelling over the many passes, Humayun had thought it wise to wait for his main baggage train to catch up. Though it had cost him some days, he had not dared risk being separated from his cannon and other heavy equipment for a long period by the winter weather.

Ice crystals stung Humayun's face as he raised his head to scan the twisting track ahead. Even with eyes scrunched to slits against the blizzard's frozen bite, he could see almost nothing, certainly not the tips of the jagged snow-covered peaks nor the summit of the pass of which the defile formed a part and which he guessed could be no more than three-quarters of a mile in front of them.

Ahmed Khan should soon return. He had sent him ahead with some of his men to confirm that the pass could be negotiated by an army such as his in weather as severe as this and also to identify a spot – probably on the downward slope – where they could camp protected from the wind.

Suddenly, despite the howling of the blizzard and the muffling effect of the red woollen cloth wound round the lower part of his

265

face, Humayun thought he heard a cry from out of the snow ahead. Perhaps it was just a trick of the wind, or even a wolf, he thought, as he looked up again and pulled his face cloth down to hear better. As he did so, he heard another cry nearer and definitely human – 'The enemy are ahead!'

Then he saw a shadowy rider appear through the whirling snow, galloping down the snowy track towards him, oblivious of the risks of the rocks and the ice. As the horseman drew closer, Humayun saw that it was Ahmed Khan, frantically kicking and urging his horse on while repeatedly yelling, 'The enemy are ahead! The enemy are ahead!' Two of his scouts were close behind him. Suddenly, one pitched forward over his horse's head, two arrows protruding from his back as he rolled over and over in the white snow, staining it crimson with his blood. Moments later, the second scout's chestnut horse stumbled and collapsed with several arrows in its rump. The rider slid from the saddle and stumbled on through the deep snow, only to fall himself within ten yards, transfixed by a black-feathered arrow.

Then Humayun saw emerging through the snow the dark shapes of unknown horsemen charging towards him, some crouching low over their horses' necks, swords and lances extended in front of them, and others with bows in their hands. Humayun yelled to Bairam Khan through the wind, 'Have the wagons drawn into the best defensive position you can – put those carrying the women right in the centre. Leave sufficient good men to guard them properly then follow me with the rest.'

Humayun kicked his horse forward to face the threat and as he did so shouted as loudly as he could to a company of mounted archers riding just behind him, 'Fire!' The men, who already had their double bows unslung and the strings tightened in case of just such an ambush, stood in their stirrups and loosed a volley of arrows through the driving snow towards Kamran's men. Several horses staggered and fell, throwing their riders. One lost his domed helmet in his fall and hit his shaven head hard against a rock protruding through the snow, smashing his skull and spattering the ground with blood and brains.

However, the rest of Kamran's cavalrymen came on, the downward slope of the defile giving added impetus to their charge as they crashed into Humayun's front line of horsemen, who opened gaps in their ranks to receive them before trying to surround them. One of Kamran's men, wearing a bulky sheepskin jacket and whirling a spiked flail around his head, made for Humayun. Senses heightened by the prospect of action, Humayun noticed as he pulled his own horse's head round how the mane of his opponent's mount was encrusted with icicles. The spiked balls at the end of the man's flail swung harmlessly past Humayun as he thrust at his enemy, but his sword swipe did no more than make a deep slash in the man's thick sheepskin jacket.

Both men turned and rode at each other again, their horses' hot breath steaming in the frozen air. Again both struck at each other but again both missed. As Humayun's opponent tugged hard on the reins to make a third attempt on Humayun, his horse slipped on ice. As the man struggled to stay in the saddle, Humayun turned his own mount sharply and was on him before he could regain sufficient control to swing his flail properly.

Humayun slashed with his sword and, although the man jerked his upper body out of the way, the sword cut deep into his attacker's lower thigh just above the knee, severing sinew and biting into the bone. Instinctively the man dropped his flail and clutched at the wound. As he did so, Humayun struck him again, this time across his throat. Fine droplets of blood spurted into the cold air and the man fell.

All around Humayun his troops were struggling with their opponents, whom they seemed to outnumber. However, Humayun noticed that three of the enemy had surrounded Bairam Khan, who had become isolated from the rest of his men. Humayun kicked his horse towards them. Bairam Khan had lost his helmet and the blizzard was blowing his long black hair out behind him. He was defending himself as best as he could, wheeling his tall black horse expertly to confront each of his attackers in turn. Nevertheless he was being hard pressed and was already bleeding from a deep sword cut which extended from his left ear down his neck to the top of his breastplate.

The first that Bairam Khan's assailants knew of Humayun's arrival was the sword stroke which knocked one of their number from his saddle and the second was the blow which almost severed the sword arm of another who was poised to thrust his weapon deep into Bairam Khan's exposed side. The third man turned to flee but Bairam Khan cut at him as he went, leaving him trailing blood on the snow as he made good his escape. He was followed by all of Kamran's men who were able to disengage themselves. The attack had ceased as suddenly as it had begun. The whole thing had lasted less than half an hour.

'Pursue them,' shouted Humayun to Zahid Beg. 'Kill and capture as many as you can but take care – others may be waiting in further ambushes ahead.' Dismounting, he ran over towards Bairam Khan, who was slumped in his saddle. He was just in time to catch the Persian as he fell sideways. Humayun lowered him to the ground and began to staunch his wound with his own red face cloth. 'Thank you, Majesty. I owe you my life ... I will repay you,' mumbled Bairam Khan, grimacing with pain.

By the time Zahid Beg and his men rode back down the defile, the snow had stopped and the pale winter sun was disappearing behind the western peaks, throwing long shadows across the battlefield where Humayun was supervising the tending of Bairam Khan and the other wounded. Among the riders Humayun noticed a number of captives, bouncing uncomfortably on their saddles, hands tied behind their backs and their ankles roped beneath their horses' bellies.

'Zahid Beg, are any of the prisoners ready to talk? What do they say?'

'That they were a raiding party – no more than fifteen hundred in number and mostly local tribesmen. Your half-brother had promised them large bounties if they achieved success – and in particular if they brought him your head.'

'We must remain alert against further attack. Post more pickets. Kamran will now know we're coming – and from what direction and when.'

●◆●

For the first time since he had ridden out with his father on their conquest of Hindustan twenty-one years ago, Humayun gazed at the place of his birth. The walls and gates of the city of Kabul, just half a mile away, were mantled in snow. Above them he could just make out the tops of the high arched entrances of the caravanserais that accommodated the thousands of merchants who passed through with their trade goods of sugar, cloth, horses, spices and gems, bringing much wealth to Kabul.

On a rocky ridge overlooking the town was the citadel. Though it held so many good memories, Humayun pushed them aside, assessing its thick mud-brick walls and squat towers with a dispassionate, appraising eye. This was no longer the boyhood home beneath whose walls he'd raced his pony and gone hawking but his enemy's stronghold and his son's prison. And the same dilemma faced him as at Kandahar. How could he overcome his enemy and rescue Akbar without putting his son in greater peril than he already was? Even though Humayun's scouts had sometimes seen riders shadowing their column who could only be Kamran's men and chased them off, Kamran had launched no further attacks. He must feel that Kabul was well stocked and prepared to withstand a siege.

Little though Kamran had shown himself susceptible to either, Humayun decided he would again try persuasion and reason. Tonight in their encampment sprawling across the frozen plain outside Kabul he would once again write a letter for his half-sister to carry. And once again, his offer would be simple. If Kamran would release Akbar and hand over Kabul, he and his men could depart with a promise of safe passage. At least his position was stronger than when Gulbadan had delivered his ultimatum to Askari at Kandahar, Humayun reflected. As he had drawn closer to Kabul, more and more tribesmen had joined him. Though his own forces did not yet match the Persians, they now numbered nearly eight thousand men.

Slapping his gauntleted hands against his sides for warmth, Humayun made his way to his scarlet command tent where his war council was awaiting him. 'My sister is courageous. She will again be my envoy. But if Kamran rejects my proposal, we must be ready for an immediate attack on the citadel. Let him hear our cannon roar.'

269

'What about the city itself, Majesty?' asked Bairam Khan. He was making a good recovery from his wound, although he could still scarcely turn his neck which remained heavily bandaged. He would doubtless have gained another fine scar.

'Your Majesty's half-brother will have garrisoned it, of course,' said Zahid Beg. 'The soldiers defending it may fire at us from the walls so we must keep out of range and guard and entrench our camp well.'

'But the city's garrison would be foolish to consider sallying out to attack an army as large as this,' added Bairam Khan.

Humayun now spoke. 'Also, the citizens may not be behind them. The people of Kabul have grown rich on trade. They want peace and prosperity, not war. Although they may feel no especial loyalty to me, if they think I – not Kamran – will be the eventual victor, they might even rise against his troops to gain my favour as they once did for my father against his enemies. Take the necessary measures for the encirclement of the city. But as far as the citadel goes, where should we position our cannon so they are ready for immediate action if my half-brother rejects our surrender terms?'

Zahid Beg answered. 'Take them up the road to the citadel to the most advanced position we can locate for them which will not expose our artillerymen to direct musket and arrow fire from the citadel walls as they go about their work.'

'I agree.' Humayun nodded. 'That rocky outcrop where the road makes its final turn before the gates would make a suitable position, I think. Also, if our men establish themselves there, Kamran's own gunners will find it difficult to depress their cannon far enough to fire on them. Our target should be the main gates themselves. Though metal-bound and protected by a heavy iron grille, they will not withstand a sustained bombardment. We should also aim at the outer walls directly to their right. As I recall, that stretch is older and not quite so thick as the rest.'

'Our main problem will be whether the shot will carry with sufficient force from the position you suggest,' said Zahid Beg.

'What do you think, Rustum Beg?' asked Humayun. 'Can your gunners wreak sufficient destruction from that range?'

The elderly Persian looked at his second-in-command for an answer. 'There should be no problem, Majesty,' said Bairam Khan, dark blue eyes thoughtful. 'The only pity is that our cannon are small. If we'd been able to bring bigger guns from Kazvin, we could have reduced the walls more quickly. But at least we have plenty of powder and stone shot.'

'Excellent. I know it will take time for the cannon to have their effect, but immediately we see that we have made a sufficient breach I want troops ready to charge in waves up the ramp under cover of our archers and musketeers to gain entrance to the citadel. Bairam Khan and Zahid Beg, I leave it to you to select the detachments to train to make the assault and the men to lead them. Most important, keep units of cavalry ready at all times to pursue any who try to flee the citadel. My half-brother must not be allowed to escape or try to spirit my son out of my reach.'

• ◆ •

'If Kamran had dismissed her appeal out of hand, she would be back by now, wouldn't she?' asked Hamida. Despite the bitter cold and occasional flurries of snow, she had been standing in front of the women's tent staring towards the main gate of the citadel of Kabul ever since Gulbadan had climbed into a closed, curtained wagon pulled by two mules and, preceded by Jauhar with a flag of truce, made her way up the ramp to the citadel. After five minutes one of the gates had opened and she had disappeared inside.

'Not necessarily. Kamran is malicious enough to be amused by keeping her and us waiting for a reply even if he has decided to release Akbar,' answered Humayun.

'Yes. If he is evil enough to rob a woman of her small child to further his ambitions, he is evil enough for anything.'

'But they may be assembling Akbar's things.' Humayun offered a suggestion of comfort he could not believe in himself.

'Look, the gate is opening again,' gasped Hamida, shielding her eyes from the glare reflected off the snow by the sun which had just broken through the clouds. 'Perhaps the sunlight is a good omen.'

'Perhaps,' Humayun replied. Jauhar on his grey horse was the first

271

to emerge through the gate followed a minute later by Gulbadan's cart, which began to make its way slowly down the ramp.

'The curtains are still closed. Perhaps Akbar is inside,' said Hamida.

'Maybe,' Humayun replied. As he spoke the sun went behind the clouds again.

Ten minutes later, the small procession reached the women's tent. Even before the wagon came to a full stop Gulbadan pulled back the curtains and prepared to descend. She had no need to speak. From her unsmiling face and grim expression both Humayun and Hamida knew that Akbar was not in the cart and, even worse, that Kamran's answer had extinguished any hopes they had cherished of his early recovery. Hamida dropped to her knees in the cold, wet snow weeping uncontrollably. Humayun raised her gently and held her in his arms.

'I know what you are feeling.'

'No, you cannot,' sobbed Hamida. 'Only a mother can.' Twisting herself away she ran into the snow-covered women's tent. Humayun watched her go then, shaking with anger and disappointment, he walked over to Gulbadan and led her into the tent. Once inside he dismissed all their attendants. 'What did he say?' he asked when they were alone.

'Very little. Kamran kept me waiting for a long time . . . When he did finally admit me he was alone, seated on our father Babur's gilded throne – the throne of Kabul. He made no effort to rise to greet me. I passed him your letter and he scanned it briefly. Then, smiling to himself, he scribbled this.' She handed Humayun a folded piece of paper. 'He tossed it to me, saying simply, "Give him this and tell him to be off." I persisted and begged him to release Akbar, if not for your sake then for mine and his mother's. His only response was, "What kind of fool do you think I am? If you've nothing worthwhile to say, go." I turned and left. I would not give him the satisfaction of humiliating myself further by begging more or by weeping.'

'You did right,' said Hamida, embracing Gulbadan who in turn succumbed to tears. 'I will weep no more, and no more must you. Humayun, what does Kamran's letter say? We must be sure it contains no new treachery.'

Humayun unfolded the note and read out the contents, written in the impatient spiky hand that Humayun remembered from their boyhood.

"'You gave me your word to leave these lands for Persia but you have broken it and returned with a foreign army at your back to threaten me. You dare to offer me safe conduct out of a kingdom I have made my own – you, who failed to hold the lands our father won beyond the Khyber Pass, you, who have lost everything our father created. I sit on his throne now. You are the interloper here, not me. Get on your way back to Persia and exile.'"

Hamida broke the silence first. 'He will not listen to soft women's pleas or to your merciful and reasoned offer. Make him pay in blood for his callousness and cruelty.'

'I will,' replied Humayun and strode to the entrance of the tent. Pulling back one of the flaps he called to Jauhar who was warming his hands over a brazier of glowing coals. 'Jauhar, we have our answer from my brother. It is war. Summon my council. We attack at dawn.'

• ◆ •

The snow that had been falling through most of the previous day and night and had helped shield Humayun's Persian gunners as they had manoeuvred their cannon into position was easing as they fired their first shots. From his command position sheltered behind another rocky outcrop about fifty yards behind the gunners, Humayun watched the teams of men – five per gun – in their leather jerkins, trousers and pointed steel helmets as they went to work, grunting with effort as they heaved linen bags filled with gunpowder and then the stone shot into the bronze barrels, ramming them down hard. Next they inserted the sharp metal spikes of their awls into the touch-holes to puncture the powder bags and carefully sprinkled a little extra loose powder around the holes. Finally, as the rest stood well back, one man from each team approached his gun. In his hands was a long forked staff to which was attached a taper of oil-soaked cord, the tip lit and smouldering orange-red, which he applied to the touch-hole before leaping back.

Though physically gruelling – Humayun could see sweat rising from them in the cold air like steam – the men made the process look smooth and quick, from the thuds as the powder and shot were loaded to the brilliant flash as the charge ignited. Humayun watched as they fired shot after shot. The first few fell several yards short and a little too far to the west, but Bairam Khan's men quickly made the necessary adjustments to the angle of the barrels – by driving wedges under the cannon's front wheels – and to the amount of powder they were using. Now the majority of shots were finding their mark, pounding the gates and the mud-brick walls from which a plume of red-brown dust was soon rising steadily.

Several of Kamran's musketeers were firing at the artillerymen from the walls of the citadel, but to avoid hitting the rocks protecting the cannon they had to bend over the wall and show themselves fully. Although they had at first had some success in wounding a few of Humayun's gunners, his own musketeers had now managed to get into advanced positions where they were, in turn, firing at any of Kamran's men who exposed themselves over the battlements. They hit two of them who, dropping their weapons, toppled from the walls clawing at the air to smash themselves on the rocks below. The rest were now keeping under cover and any shots they fired were hasty, wild and wide.

Humayun saw Zahid Beg galloping up on a broad-chested white horse. 'All seems quiet in the city, Majesty,' he yelled above the booming of the guns. 'Soldiers are watching our bombardment of the citadel from the walls but none has fired on our troops encircling the city or made any attempt to ride out to attack us in the rear. It is as you predicted – they've no stomach for a fight against such odds. But the city walls behind which they are hiding and in particular the citadel walls are strong. We will need time and persistence to conquer.'

◆

'Majesty, they've made a breach in the citadel wall.' Zainab shook Humayun awake as he lay next to Hamida. 'Bairam Khan is outside.' As he struggled to consciousness, Humayun could not help feeling a sudden rush of joy. Now surely Kabul would be his and Akbar would be rescued. He dressed himself quickly and carelessly and stumbled outside into the night cold. 'Where is the breach, Bairam Khan?'

'To the right of the gate where you suggested that the wall was weakest.'

'How big?'

'Not large but big enough, I think, if we act now. I've given orders already to our musketeers and archers as well as to our artillerymen to keep up a heavy fire to dissuade the defenders from attempting to repair it. Dawn is in an hour and a half and I can have a force ready to attack then if you give the order.'

'Do it.'

Low dark clouds obscured the winter sun and a bitter wind was blowing as the day dawned and Humayun, now dressed for battle, spoke to the assault force gathered around him at the bottom of the ramp leading up to the citadel.

'I know the bravery and loyalty of each man here and am proud to go into battle with you. It is a bitter thing to have to fight against one's own blood, but not content with usurping my throne my treacherous half-brother Kamran has betrayed every code of kinship and honour by stealing my son, an innocent child. In doing so he sullies the proud honour of the Moghuls. But together we can wipe clean the insult and punish the usurper. No more words – to battle!'

Humayun charged forward at the head of his men with Bairam Khan at his side. Both were breathing hard as, sometimes skidding on patches of ice, they ran as best they could up the frozen ramp through the white cannon smoke towards the citadel's gate. The sound of his own musket and cannon shot was partly deafening him but through a gap in the smoke Humayun saw there was indeed a jagged breach in the right-hand wall by the gate. His spirits soared. Then, to his surprise, he realised there was scarcely any return fire from the walls of the citadel.

Suddenly, as he watched, he saw through another gap in the billowing smoke some sort of activity on the battlements directly above the gateway. Was Kamran preparing to surrender? He could scarcely believe it. He shouted to his gunners and musketeers to cease fire, then moved forward again to get a better look. As the acrid smoke began to clear, he saw that Kamran's soldiers were erecting what looked like a wooden stake on the battlements. Then more soldiers appeared, pushing in front of them a tall figure with long, flowing hair silhouetted against the grey dawn sky. Humayun ran closer until he could see that the figure was a woman and that she was holding something in her arms. Something that wriggled and writhed – a child.

The blood in Humayun's veins ceased to flow. He watched like a man in a trance as the soldiers bound the woman to the stake, wrapping what looked like a length of rope or chain around her body but leaving her arms free to continue clutching her living burden. That burden, Humayun knew beyond a shadow of a doubt, was his son, held in the arms of his wet-nurse Maham Anga.

A great cry tore from him. 'No!' By now, Zahid Beg and Bairam Khan were by his side, staring as he was at the sight of the woman and child exposed on the walls, living targets of flesh and blood. Wrenching his gaze away at last, Humayun put his head in his hands. Once again he'd underestimated his half-brother. This was what Kamran's response had meant – continue your attack and you will be your son's assassin.

'Bairam Khan, call off the bombardment. I cannot risk my son . . . Zahid Beg, post strong enough detachments to keep the city and the citadel under siege but recall the assault troops to the camp.'

As kettledrums and trumpets sounded and his forces began to pull back across the snow-covered plain to their tents, Humayun turned and without a further word to anyone – neither his commanders nor his bodyguard – made his slow way back. Though the sun was breaking through now, thin, pale shafts lightening the sky, his own world had never seemed so lost in shadow. How was he going to bring his campaign to a successful conclusion? What was he going to say to Hamida?

Chapter 18

A Visitor in the Night

'Rustum Beg, I don't understand. How can you speak of leaving?'
'Majesty, my cousin Shah Tahmasp, the Lord of the World, gave me explicit orders before we left Kazvin that if your campaign faltered – if after six months it seemed to me unlikely that you would succeed – I must lead his troops home. I have been patient but now that time has come. It's over six months since we rode from Persia . . . two months since we ceased the bombardment and began this fruitless siege of Kabul. My men are suffering in the bitter cold and harsh conditions, and to what end? The town and the citadel are well provisioned – your brother's soldiers taunt us from the walls, offering us food . . . I am sorry, Majesty, but I have no choice. The shah can find better employment for his troops elsewhere . . .' Rustum Beg raised his hands, palm up, as if he personally regretted a situation that was beyond his control. But during the past half-hour since he had asked for a private audience with Humayun, though courteous as ever, he had conceded nothing.

By now shock and surprise had given way in Humayun to an anger he was struggling to contain. 'As I've told you, Shah Tahmasp said nothing to me about deadlines or timescales. He called himself my brother and offered me his help to reclaim not only my ancestral homelands but also the throne of Hindustan . . . He understood it would take time. We spoke of it together . . .'

'I'm sorry, Majesty. If I don't take my troops back to Persia I will be disobeying my orders. That I cannot do.'

'Well, when you reach Kazvin tell your cousin this – that I will continue the fight and however long it takes I will crush my enemies so completely they never rise again. And when I once more sit on my throne in Agra I will have the satisfaction of knowing that the glory of the achievement belongs to the Moghuls and the Moghuls alone.'

Rustum Beg's face remained impassive.

'When will you leave?'

'In three or four days, Majesty, as soon as my men are ready. I will leave you the cannon. They were the shah's gift to you.'

If Rustum Beg expected his gratitude he would be disappointed, Humayun thought as he rose to his feet to indicate the interview was over. 'I wish you and your men a safe passage back through the mountains. Tell the shah that I thank him for the assistance he gave me and only regret that it proved so short-lived.'

'I will, Majesty. And may fortune one day shine on you again.'

After Rustum Beg had left, Humayun sat for a while alone. The Persian commander's announcement had come without warning. He needed time to think it through and fathom a way forward. At least his own men nearly matched the Persians in numbers now and these were their own lands they were fighting in. They were hardened to the conditions and would not be deterred by snow, ice and the bitter winds that buffeted the encampment, exposed as it was on the plains. Almost as much as the loss of the Persian forces, what galled Humayun was Rustum Beg's dismissive assessment of his chances. Since the first day of the siege, Humayun had never allowed himself to lose heart, hoping each day to find a way of breaking his enemy . . . of detecting some weakness in Kamran's position. And even if such a breakthrough didn't come, he need only have patience – inevitably Kamran's supplies would run out.

Sometimes, of course, it took as much fortitude to be patient as to ride into battle. The memory of his infant son on the battlements was all that was preventing Humayun from assaulting the citadel with everything he had. Perhaps Rustum Beg had interpreted his feelings for his son – his unwillingness to call Kamran's bluff – as weakness. Well, so be it. If he must, he would – just as he had told Rustum Beg – fight on alone.

Through the tent flap that still hung partially open, Humayun saw the wintry light was fading. Soon he would summon his commanders to tell them what had happened. They might be glad to see the Persians gone. The camaraderie that had existed in the early days when Humayun led his forces out of Persia had ebbed as more and more of the clans around Kabul had come to swell his numbers. Only three days ago, Zahid Beg had told him of a violent incident between his men and the Persians. A Tajik chieftain, believing some Persian soldiers had stolen some of his stores, had called them Shiite dogs. In the ensuing brawl, one of the Tajik's men had been stabbed in the cheek and a Persian badly burned on one side of his body when he was thrown against a brazier of blazing logs. Perhaps it was better that the *Kizil-bashi* – the 'Red-heads', as Humayun's men called the Persians for their conical red caps with strips of scarlet cloth hanging down behind to proclaim their Shiite faith – should depart. He himself would immediately renounce his token adherence to the Shia sect. That too would hearten his men.

The sound of voices outside his command tent interrupted Humayun's thoughts. Then the tent flap was pushed back and Jauhar ducked inside. 'Majesty, Bairam Khan asks to see you.'

'Very well.'

As Bairam Khan entered Humayun noticed that the scar on his neck was pink and puckered and still very new-looking. He was a good fighter and a clever tactician. Though Rustum Beg was overall commander of the Persian forces, it had been obvious to Humayun almost from the start that Bairam Khan was their true leader and general. He would be sorry to lose him.

'What is it, Bairam Khan?'

Bairam Khan hesitated, as if what he wished to say wasn't easy. Then, fixing his indigo eyes on Humayun's face, he began. 'I know what Rustum Beg has told you . . . I am sorry.'

'No blame attaches to you. What I am sorry for is that I will lose you—'

'Majesty,' the usually courteous Bairam Khan broke in, 'hear me out. When we were attacked in the defile on the way to Kabul, you saved me. Never in all the battles I have fought had I felt death so close . . . in my mind's eye I already saw my grave dug in that lonely place. But you gave my life back to me. I have come to ask you to let me repay you.'

'There is no debt, Bairam Khan. I only did what any man on the battlefield would do when he sees a comrade – a friend – in danger.'

'I do not wish to return to Persia with Rustum Beg but to remain with you and do all in my power to further your cause. Will you take me into your service?'

Humayun rose, and stepping forward gripped Bairam Khan's arm. 'There is no man in the entire Persian army I would rather have fighting by my side . . .'

• ◆ •

'Majesties . . . Majesties . . . wake up.' Someone was gently shaking his shoulder . . . or was it just a dream? Humayun moved closer to the soft warmth of Hamida's body lying close beside him. But the shaking grew more insistent. Humayun opened his eyes to see Zainab, an oil lamp in her hand, standing over them. In the flickering light, he saw she looked excited, the birthmark on her face seeming more pronounced than usual.

'What is it?' Beside him, Hamida opened sleepy eyes.

'Half an hour ago a man tried to ride into the camp. When the pickets challenged him, he would not say who he was but asked to be taken to Zahid Beg. After talking to him, Zahid Beg, knowing you were with Her Majesty in the women's tents, sent for me and asked me to summon you.'

'Why the urgency? Can't it wait till sunrise?'

'Zahid Beg told me nothing . . . only to ask that you come at once . . .'

'Very well.' Humayun rose and wrapping a long, sheepskin-lined coat around him stepped out into the chilling wind. Who could it be? Perhaps Kamran had sent a messenger, though why he should do so by dead of night was a mystery. By the light of a brazier of glowing charcoals, he saw Zahid Beg standing beside a tall, square-shouldered man wearing a dark cloak with the hood pulled forward concealing his face. Could it be an assassin sent by Kamran ... or even by the Shah of Persia?

'Is he armed, Zahid Beg?'

'No, Majesty. He volunteered to let us search him.'

As Humayun drew closer, the man pushed the hood back with a slow, deliberate gesture. Even in the shadowy light from the brazier, Humayun knew at once that it was Hindal, thick-set face now heavily bearded but still unmistakably his half-brother. For a moment, the two of them stared at one another in silence. Despite all that had happened since, memories of Hindal were suddenly vivid again in Humayun's mind – of Hindal as a baby in Maham's arms, of how he had taught his younger brother to ride his first pony, of Hindal's joy when he had shot his first rabbit; then later memories of the look on Hindal's face at the time of his rebellion, of how he had loyally accompanied Humayun on his first journey as an exile to Mirza Husain and Maldeo; then above all of their last meeting – how they had pounded each other with their fists over Hamida and how, after spitting at Humayun's feet, a bleeding, bruised but still defiant Hindal had ridden away.

'Leave us, please, and make sure no one disturbs us.' Humayun waited until Zahid Beg had disappeared into the darkness, all the while looking hard at Hindal, then asked, 'Why have you come here? And why alone, placing yourself in my power like this?'

'For some months – since escaping from Kamran – I have been taking refuge with my remaining loyal friends in the high hills of Jagish, northeast of Kabul. But news travels even to such remote regions. I learned what Kamran had done – how he had exposed Akbar on the battlements of the Kabul citadel as your cannon pounded its walls. His actions shocked me – they defy everything noble in our warrior code and stain our family's honour.'

'Fine sentiments, but you still haven't answered my question. Let us be frank with one another. Why have you come?'

'To help get Akbar back.'

Humayun was so astonished that for a few moments he could

281

only stare at the massive figure of his half-brother, calmly warming his large hands over the brazier.

'I know what you're thinking.' Hindal filled the silence. 'You are asking yourself why I should wish to help you. It's simple. Despite the blood ties that will bind us till death, you and I will never be reconciled. That won't change. I have come here tonight for Hamida and Hamida alone . . . to help relieve her agony by offering to bring her child back to her . . . She must be suffering . . .'

Humayun shifted uneasily, uncomfortable about talking to Hindal about Hamida at all and even more so to be talking to him about how he had failed her by being unable to recover her son.

'If you have truly come with thoughts of easing Hamida's grief, I am grateful to you.' He paused again, then made up his mind to swallow his pride. 'To be honest as I said we should be, she has known no true rest or peace of mind since Akbar was taken . . . But when you speak of help, what do you mean? I have been besieging the citadel for nearly four months with no success. What do you think you can do alone that I can't with my army?'

'I can win Kamran's confidence and get into the citadel. Once inside, I can find a way of rescuing Akbar.'

'How? Why should Kamran trust you any more than me?'

'I can do it because I understand him, because I know his weaknesses. He despises you and believes he is the natural head of our family. I will use his conceit, his vanity, to convince him that I have come to my senses and wish to be his ally again . . . to re-unite the rest of Babur's sons behind him against you. But it all depends on creating an illusion . . .'

'Go on.'

'You must raise the siege and make it appear you are leading your forces away from Kabul. That will leave the way clear for me to bring my own men down from the hills and offer Kamran an alliance . . .'

'You are suggesting I abandon the siege after so many weeks, just when I might at last be tightening the screw on Kamran?'

'You must. My plan can't work if you are still encamped anywhere near Kabul. Kamran must believe you've given up.'

'You ask too much. For all I know you've already made your peace with Kamran and he's sent you here to try and trick me.'

'I am ready to swear on our father's memory that this is no subterfuge . . .' Hindal's tawny eyes returned Humayun's gaze unflinchingly.

'Very well – assuming I do as you suggest, what happens then?'

'Kamran will think he's got the better of you. In his elation he will be all the more ready to accept my story – that since not even you have been able to overcome him, I am ready to acknowledge and serve him as our father's true heir.'

'You really think he will believe you?'

'Don't underestimate his conceit. After all, why shouldn't he believe me? Why shouldn't I wish to exchange the life of a renegade in the hills for a share of the reflected glory of a Moghul prince whose star is rising as yours wanes? And he will be glad of the extra men I can bring him. Then once inside the citadel I will find a way of smuggling Akbar out of Kabul . . . but it will take time. Not only must I win Kamran's trust but I must also find the right opportunity . . .'

'What about Kamran's mother Gulrukh? She's as shrewd as – probably shrewder than – her son. If she is with him she won't be easy to deceive.'

Hindal looked surprised. 'Gulrukh's dead. The bullock cart in which she was travelling from Kandahar to Kabul fell into a ravine. I thought you would have heard.'

'No.' Humayun digested the news. He could feel little sorrow for the woman who had tempted him with her potions of opium and wine to further her sons' ambitions. 'Even so, you would be putting yourself at great risk. Just assuming you succeeded, what would you want from me?'

'Nothing. You have taken everything I wanted and you cannot give it back . . .'

For a moment they looked at one another in silence. Now that he was face to face with Hindal again, Humayun realised how much he wanted to say – about his guilt, his regret at having wounded him. But his half-brother wouldn't believe him and anyway nothing could alter the facts – Humayun loved Hamida with a passion he'd never known for any other woman. If he had his time again, he would be just as ruthless in his determination to have her.

All the time Hindal's eyes had never left Humayun's face. 'Well, what is your answer? I must know before I leave your camp – assuming you are prepared to let me go – and I must be gone before it gets light. There are enough men here who know me and there may be spies among them. If word of my presence reached Kamran any chances of my plan succeeding would be over . . .'

'I need time to think. I will ask Zahid Beg to take you to his tent and to stay with you until I come. It is some three hours before dawn. You will have your answer in two.'

After Hindal had gone, Humayun paced up and down, oblivious of the cold. Hindal's plan was bold and brave but if he agreed to it, he must take so much on trust. How many times had his faith in members of his own family been betrayed since he had become emperor? . . . Yet every inflection of Hindal's voice, every gesture, had carried conviction. Whatever his own views, he could not take the decision without talking to Hamida, who would be wondering why he had been gone so long.

He was right. When he returned to their tent he found that she had risen and was waiting for him, her dark hair, still dishevelled by sleep, tumbling around her shoulders and her expression anxious. 'The man who rode into the camp during the night – it was Hindal,' he said before she could speak.

'Hindal?'

'Yes. He offers us his help in rescuing Akbar. If I pretend to raise the siege and march away, he will ride to the citadel and offer Kamran an alliance. Once in Kamran's confidence he will seek a way of smuggling Akbar out of Kabul.'

'Could he really bring back our son to us . . .?'

Humayun could see the hope beginning to take hold of her. 'Well, perhaps . . . but the problem is can we trust Hindal?'

Hamida's hopeful expression faltered. 'Hindal took a big risk riding alone into your encampment in the dark. He might have been killed. And it would have taken courage to face you again too.'

'True, but if he is playing a double game he might have reckoned the possible rewards worth the risk. Though he swears he is not in league with Kamran, this might be a trick either to induce me to abandon the siege or just to enable Hindal and his men to get into Kabul to join Kamran.' The only sound was of the wind beating against the hide walls of the tent as Humayun and Hamida looked at one another. 'If I make the wrong decision, Kamran's position will be strengthened and our chances of defeating him and regaining our son will fade,' Humayun said at last.

Hamida pushed her hair back from her face with a weary gesture. 'You are right to be cautious. After all, why should Hindal want to help us?'

'Exactly what I asked. He says that by threatening a child, Kamran has shamed our family . . .'

'Does family honour really mean so much to him?'

'Perhaps it does. But then he told me of another, perhaps more potent reason. It is you, not me, he wishes to help. He knows that you are suffering and wants to end your pain . . .'

As she took in the implication of Humayun's words, Hamida coloured and looked down. She and Humayun had never spoken openly of Hindal's feelings for her but of course she knew. For a few moments she paced about, just as Humayun had done in the cold night air, but then she turned to him, her face resolute. 'I believe Hindal is sincere. After all, he has no reason to love Kamran who held him captive . . . We should trust him. If he betrays us he would be as guilty as Kamran of exploiting our fears for the life of our child. I believe he is too honourable for that. Please, Humayun, let us seize this chance.'

Humayun took her in his arms and held her close against him, breathing in the familiar sandalwood scent of her. He must not be swayed either by his love for her or by her eagerness to believe in Hindal. This was one of the most important decisions he would ever make. But as he went over and over the arguments in his mind, something deeper, more instinctive than logic told him Hamida was right – Hindal meant what he said and they should trust him. That didn't mean Hindal would succeed. His strategy was a dangerous one, but if everyone played their part it might, just might, work.

'Very well,' Humayun said at last. 'I will tell Hindal we accept his offer – that you are placing the life of your child in his hands.'

'Tell him to bring Maham Anga and her son too. They would be in terrible danger once Kamran found Akbar gone.'

Humayun nodded. 'There are many things I must discuss with him – like how far I should take the army away from Kabul. He must know where to find us when the moment comes.' He bent and kissed her. 'Hamida, tell no one of this. If this plan is to work, our men must truly believe we are abandoning Kabul to Kamran.'

As Humayun stepped once more into the night, some words from his father's memoirs came into his mind.

Caution is a fine and worthy thing in any monarch, but a truly great ruler must also know when to take risks.

Chapter 19

Riders in the Snow

The winter sun was already low on the horizon when Humayun, well swathed in a sheepskin-lined coat against the bite of the cold wind blowing down the steep pass he and his army were descending on their march away from Kabul, saw Ahmed Khan ride towards him.

'Majesty, my scouts have located a place just four miles ahead where we can camp. It's in the lee of a high ridge that will protect us from the prevailing winds, and from the top of the ridge our sentries will have good warning of anyone approaching.'

'Excellent, Ahmed Khan.'

Humayun watched his chief scout ride off ahead of the column again. He had not confided in any of his commanders about the reasons for his sudden withdrawal from Kabul, not because he doubted their loyalty but because even a stray remark by one of them might betray everything. Instead, he had told them he was losing patience with the siege – that he intended to ride east to the mountains of Bajaur where there were other, lesser fortresses garrisoned by Kamran's men to capture and where he hoped to recruit more men. When the snows finally melted, he would return to Kabul to renew his siege.

Zahid Beg, Ahmed Khan and Nadim Khwaja had looked astounded. If Zahid Beg had wondered whether Humayun's decision was connected with Hindal's secret nocturnal visit, he'd not shown it but, like the others, immediately set about the cumbersome business of preparing to strike camp. Only in Bairam Khan's keen-eyed gaze had Humayun thought he detected a hint of speculation as to his motives but, like the others, the Persian had said nothing. Humayun had told the truth to Gulbadan. As Hindal's sister it was her right to know. Just like Hamida, she had been certain Hindal's offer was genuine.

Suddenly behind him Humayun heard shouting and distant cries from the rear of his column. This narrow winding pass with its precipitous drops on one side down to a frozen river would make an ideal ambush spot. Humayun turned in his saddle but could not see round the zigzag bends to where the noise was coming from. What he could see was that some of his men were already turning their horses to head back towards the rearguard. At once the fear that was never far from his thoughts returned. Surely Hindal had not betrayed him and brought Kamran and his men down on him? He hadn't been such a fool as to be deceived again by one of his half-brothers, had he? Humayun wrenched his black horse round and followed by his bodyguard pushed his way back up the pass through the mass of his troops.

Even when he had rounded the first bend he could still see nothing, but the commotion to the rear was louder and increasing. Then, as heart pounding he turned the second corner, he saw the cause. It was not, God be praised, an ambush. Two bullock carts were stuck across the narrow track. One had slewed around entirely. Its back wheels were hanging out over nothingness, while some of his men were hauling at the bullocks' heads, grabbing at the heavy wooden yokes and putting their own shoulders to the front wheels to drag the cart back on to solid ground.

But the greater problem was with the second cart which seemed to have been the originator of the accident. At least half of its bullock team had gone over the edge. Looking down into the gorge, Humayun could see the bodies of three of them lying among the sharp, jumbled rocks of the frozen riverbed, the blood oozing from them colouring the surrounding snow red. Another bullock was dangling, hooves flailing from the traces, over the drop and two of the drivers were leaning out, pulling at the harness in a futile attempt to recover it. Others were trying to stop the cart being dragged over the side by frantically piling rocks in front of its wheels. As Humayun watched, one of the two drivers slipped on the ice and overbalancing plunged head first from the pass. His body struck the rocky side of the gorge twice before hitting the ground by that of one of the oxen.

'Cut the traces. Let the bullock fall,' shouted Humayun. 'It's not worth losing more lives. Let the cart go too if you have to.'

Swiftly, a large, red-turbaned man drew a long dagger from his belt and ran over to the stricken bullock. Within less than two minutes, he had cut through the leather traces and the bullock, bellowing and kicking wildly, had crashed to the rocks with a sickening thud. The cart, which Humayun now saw contained several large copper cauldrons and other cooking equipment, had stayed on the path. Good, thought Humayun; his army needed hot food in this weather. Eventually, too, the men pushing and straining at the other cart, hot breath rising in the winter air, were succeeding in getting its rear wheels on to the track again by dint of lightening its load of tents and piling them on to the icy ground.

Humayun sighed with relief. It could have been much worse. He could have lost more men or some of his few precious baggage elephants. It was time he and his men stopped and he awaited developments, evidence one way or the other of Hindal's sincerity. Tonight, he would announce to his men that, having travelled over forty miles from Kabul and found a good site, they would make camp for some days to rest and overhaul their weapons and equipment. The men should be glad of it, even though their general mood was sombre, sullen even. Some from the clans around Kabul had already drifted away, convinced their hopes of booty were gone, but Humayun had been prepared for that. If Hindal's plan succeeded it wouldn't be long before he returned to Kabul to unleash his full might against the citadel. As his cannon again crashed and boomed, those who had deserted would be quick to return . . .

He had agreed with Hindal in which direction he would take his men and roughly how far. Once they had set up camp he would

289

order Ahmed Khan to ensure his scouts kept watch day and night. They would believe they were watching for signs of pursuit by Kamran's forces. Of course, if Hindal's plan failed, or if Hindal betrayed him, that could still be the case . . .

• ◆ •

Humayun moved restlessly beneath the thick pile of furs and sheepskins, his thoughts and anxieties making sleep impossible. 'We can trust Hindal, can't we?' he asked. 'It's been more than a month and we've heard nothing.'

Hamida was tossing and turning equally sleepless at his side. 'I really do believe so. Everything my father said about him when he served as his counsellor makes me think it. So too does Gulbadan's love and regard for her brother. My worry is not that he will betray us but that he will be betrayed or somehow fail to rescue Akbar. What will Kamran do then? He wouldn't kill Akbar, would he . . . ?'

It was the first time Hamida had asked that question. 'No,' he said with more confidence than he felt. 'He will be even more convinced of Akbar's value as a hostage – though it might go hard with Hindal.'

'You are right,' Hamida said after a moment. 'And there's no reason to think anything has gone wrong yet. Hindal will need time to ingratiate himself sufficiently with Kamran to gain a position of trust so he can rescue our son. We must be patient.'

'Patience and uncertainty have always come hard to me. I long for an end to this gnawing suspense so I can compose myself to the outcome and act.'

'Uncertainty and anxiety are part of all mortal lives. After all, the spotted fever could carry us off at any moment, destroying all our hopes and dreams, but we don't think about it every day. We must learn to accept that sometimes events are beyond our control.'

'I know, but as a leader as well as Akbar's father I have a duty to make things turn out as I would wish and I cannot influence what is happening in Kabul however much I worry.'

'Then you must try not to worry . . . it does no good. We must

290

have faith.' Hamida enfolded Humayun in her arms and at last, clinging to each other in their cocoon of furs, they slept.

This was not the last such conversation Humayun had with Hamida during the long nights when sleep eluded them. Nevertheless, sometimes he could not restrain himself from leaving his tent to stare into the cold stars to see if they held any message for him, but he found no response. Even when he summoned old Sharaf, whose thin mottled hands protruded like gnarled claws from the sleeves of his sheepskin coat, he could find none.

As the days passed little moved over the frozen landscape except trotting foxes and a few rabbits that Humayun's men hunted for the pot. Humayun tried to lose himself in physical activity. Bairam Khan taught him some useful tricks of Persian swordplay including how, by catching the tip of his blade in his opponent's hand guard, he could twist his enemy's wrist and force him to drop his weapon. He also practised his archery, firing at straw targets set up on poles driven into the snowy ground. It was good to find his eye as sharp and his hand as steady as ever, though it made him long for the real action that could only follow news from Hindal. But at last, one afternoon while Humayun was out hawking, watching his bird arcing in light blue skies that hinted at the approach of spring, he saw Ahmed Khan galloping towards him from the direction of the ridge.

'Majesty, my men have seen riders approaching.'

'How many?'

'Just a few, mostly mounted on mules – probably a small caravan of merchants. They are still about two miles away but seem to be heading in this direction.'

'Take me to them.'

Humayun's heart was thumping as, ten minutes later, he galloped out at Ahmed Khan's side. It was probably nothing – just a few merchants as Ahmed Khan had said – yet he couldn't prevent a wild hope from welling up inside him. He strained his eyes into the hazy far distance, impatient for any sign of movement out there on the drear, seemingly empty white landscape. At first there was nothing but then he gasped. What looked like a string of black dots was

291

moving slowly but unmistakably towards them from the west – the direction of Kabul.

Bending low over its neck, Humayun urged his horse on and was soon outstripping Ahmed Khan. All the time the dots were becoming bigger and more distinct – starting to take substance. As he drew yet closer – only some four or five hundred yards away now – he thought he could make out about eight or nine riders; a small party to be out alone in such uncertain times.

They had halted and the foremost had risen in his stirrups and, shading his eyes with one hand, was looking in his direction. Even from this distance, there seemed something achingly familiar about that large figure . . . He wasn't deceiving himself, was he? It could be Hindal, couldn't it? Humayun wheeled his own mount to a halt as he too stared intently ahead. Moments later Ahmed Khan and his guards came galloping up, their horses' hooves flinging up puffs of powdery snow.

'Shall I send men to find out who they are, Majesty?' asked Ahmed Khan.

'No . . . I will go . . . Stay here, all of you!' Ignoring Ahmed Khan's protests, Humayun kicked his horse on. He must be first to know his son's fate if the riders carried that news and he could wait no longer. As he galloped over the frozen ground, the sound of hooves echoing in his ears, he saw that the leading rider was still watching him, motionless. Looking beyond him, Humayun discovered that most of the rest of the group – six men and a slightly smaller figure – a woman by the long plait hanging down from beneath a black shaggy lamb's wool hat – were on mules. The woman was holding the reins of another mule. Drawing nearer he made out that strapped to its back was a wicker basket in which he thought he saw two rolls of bedding – or could it be children, so wrapped in sheepskins they looked almost spherical?

Humayun was just fifty yards away now. For a moment, he felt afraid to go closer in case the people before him on the snowy landscape were just an illusion, conjured by his own hopes and desires. Reining in and not daring to take his eyes from them, Humayun slid from his saddle and made his way on foot over the last few yards, slowly at first but then breaking into a run, feet slipping and sliding.

The leading rider, gazing towards him so intently, was indeed Hindal shrouded in a thick fur cloak. Scarcely aware of what he was doing and with tears of joy already streaming down his face, Humayun ran past Hindal towards the mule carrying the bundles. He heard Maham Anga's cry of 'Majesty!' but then he saw the bundles were indeed children and had thoughts only for Akbar, sitting calmly next to Adham Khan, his milk-brother. As Humayun leaned over him, Akbar gazed at him with friendly interest from within his nest of sheepskins. In the nearly fourteen months since Kamran had taken him he had changed so much, but he was still unmistakably Akbar. As Adham Khan began to wail, Humayun gently lifted Akbar from the basket and held him close against him, breathing in the warm scent of him.

'My son,' he whispered, 'my son.'

An hour later, Humayun rode at the head of the party back into the camp. Reaching the women's tents, he dismounted then carefully took Akbar from his basket. Lulled by the resumed motion of the mule, the child was fast asleep. With Maham Anga by his side, Humayun entered Hamida's tent. She had been reading some of her beloved poetry but the volume had fallen from her hands and she too was sleeping, lying back against some red and gold velvet cushions. How young she looked with her silken hair falling about her and her breast gently rising and falling.

'Hamida,' he whispered, 'Hamida . . . I have something for you – a gift . . .'

As her eyes opened and she saw Akbar, joy such as he had never witnessed before lit up her face. But as Humayun placed him in her arms, Akbar awoke. Looking up at Hamida, he released a bewildered yell and began struggling to get free. Maham Anga darted forward, and as soon as he saw her Akbar's distress vanished. Smilingly he stretched out his chubby arms to his wet-nurse.

◆

All around him, Humayun's officers were reclining against the great bolsters carefully arranged around his scarlet command tent, amid the debris of the celebration feast. Earlier that afternoon he had called an assembly of all his men and announced the rescue of Akbar.

'My loyal men – I present to you my son, the symbol of our future, safely returned to me . . .' Standing on a makeshift wooden dais in the centre of his camp, Humayun had lifted Akbar high above his head. A great cheer accompanied by the clashing of swords on shields had thundered around him. Akbar had still been blinking in surprise at the uproar as Humayun had handed him back to Maham Anga, but he hadn't cried. It was a good omen. Humayun had raised his hands to call for calm.

'It is time to return to Kabul to finish what we started and eject the impostor who hides behind innocent children. Our cause is just and God is with us. Tonight we feast but our feasting will be nothing compared to our celebrations once Kabul is ours. Tomorrow at dawn we ride for the city.'

The cooks had laboured hard on their preparations, spitting and roasting meat over great fires whose smoke billowed into the sky. Now that his son was safe, Humayun didn't care from how many miles his camp was visible.

Some of his commanders were starting to sing – heroic songs of deeds on the battlefield, bawdy songs of even greater feats in the *haram*. Looking around he saw Zahid Beg swaying back and forth, skull-like face glowing with the effects of the strong red wine of Ghazni for which the kingdom of Kabul was famous and which his own father Babur had enjoyed so much. Even Kasim, normally so quiet and reticent, was joining in the singing from the corner of the tent where he had found a comfortable place to rest his old bones.

Humayun had lost no time in telling his inner circle, his *ichkis*, that the abandonment of the siege had been only a ruse. Most had looked genuinely astonished. Only Bairam Khan had shown little surprise and his intense indigo eyes had seemed knowing as gravely he had congratulated Humayun on the return of his son, making Humayun doubly certain he had known all along. More than ever he was glad to have the Persian at his side.

Humayun glanced at Hindal sitting close beside him. Unlike the rest of the revellers, he had said little and looked withdrawn and uncomfortable to be seated with Humayun and his officers. Since their return to the camp the previous evening, Humayun had seen little of his half-brother. Instead, in his relief to be reunited with his son, he'd spent most of his time with Hamida and Akbar. To Hamida's sorrow, their son was still clinging to Maham Anga. Every time Hamida tried to pick him up, he struggled and screamed. But that would pass, Humayun had comforted Hamida, who was torn between relief and exultation at her son's safe return, wonderment at how much he had grown and grief that in the months they had been apart she had become a stranger to him. At least his vigorous wriggling showed that despite his traumatic experiences he was in robust good health, Hamida had said, smiling through her tears. Then she had added, 'Thank Hindal for me, won't you.'

Looking again at Hindal's half-averted face, Humayun guessed this might be a harder task than she had realised.

'Hindal . . .' He waited until he had his half-brother's full attention then continued, lowering his voice so that they would not be overheard. 'I know what you did was not for me, but for Hamida. She asked me to thank you.'

'Tell her there is no need. It was a matter of family honour . . .'

'You may not wish to hear this, but I too will be for ever in your debt. Your reasons for your actions don't absolve me of my obligation to you.'

Hindal gave a slight shrug but said nothing.

'Tell me, did your plan go as you expected? Hamida too is anxious to know what happened . . .'

For the first time a faint smile lightened Hindal's face. 'It went better than I'd dared to hope. Several days after my scouts reported your withdrawal from Kabul, I rode down from the mountains with my men and sent messengers to the citadel to tell Kamran I was ready to pledge my support to him as the true head of our family. As I'd thought, conceited and arrogant as he is and already euphoric at your departure, he ordered me to be admitted. He even threw a feast in celebration and gave me gifts . . .'

'He really had no suspicions?'

'None. Believing he had defeated you, his confidence blinded him.

Even before I'd arrived, he'd ordered the gates of both the town and the citadel to be kept open once more in the hours of daylight. I'd only been there about a week when he began to speak about going south on a hunting expedition in search of wolves and the great-horned sheep forced down from the mountains by hunger and the winter cold. I encouraged him – even offered to go with him. But, as I suspected and hoped he would, he ordered me to stay behind. He'd already found tasks for me like drilling some of his guards. He joked that he'd be leaving plenty of loyal officers behind just in case I'd any thoughts of grabbing Kabul for myself.

'After Kamran left, I just carried out my orders, careful to do nothing to excite comment. I also wanted to be sure that he had really gone for a few days. Then, towards late afternoon on the fourth day – with no sign of Kamran returning that night – I made my move. D'you remember from our boyhood that small courtyard over on the eastern side of the citadel with along one side of it a series of vaulted rooms where grain and wine were stored?'

Humayun nodded. Suddenly, the dusty little courtyard with its row of storerooms that he and his brothers had enjoyed exploring, trying to drive their dagger tips into the casks so they could taste the wine, was so vivid in his mind he could almost smell the mingled aromas of wine and grain.

'Well, I had found out that Kamran had modified some of those storerooms to make apartments where Akbar, together with Maham Anga and her son, was being held under guard. I made my way there quietly with four of my most loyal men. When we reached the courtyard, my men concealed themselves behind some large grain storage jars. Through the spy-hole that had been made in the door, I told the two guards on duty inside that as the boy's uncle, I wished to visit him. Recognising me, they opened the door. As I engaged them in conversation, my men rushed out, overcame them, then bound and gagged them.

'My greatest difficulty was with Maham Anga – she tried to draw a dagger on me and started screaming. I easily took the weapon from her – it was only later that she told me it was poisoned – but it was far harder to quieten her shrieks. I had to place my hand over her mouth and tell her again and again that I meant Akbar no harm . . . that I had come with your knowledge and approval to rescue them all.

'Finally she calmed down, but they were anxious minutes. Though we were in a remote part of the citadel, I knew that at any moment we might easily be discovered. Luckily, no one came, but by now time was running out – I knew that in another half-hour, the gates of the citadel would be closed for the night. We had to get out quickly and in a way that would not attract attention. I'd noticed that towards dusk many of the traders who came each day to transact business in the citadel – there was much reprovisioning to be done now the siege was over – usually left to return to the city. I'd therefore ordered my men to bring robes and turbans so that all of us – including Maham Anga – could disguise ourselves as merchants. We had also brought thick sheepskins in which to wrap the boys to conceal them and a phial of rosewater mixed with opium to make them drowsy so they didn't cry out. I ordered Maham Anga to give a little to each child. When she hesitated, I drank some myself to prove to her it wasn't poison.

'The opium did its work quickly and the children were docile as we wrapped the sheepskins around them. Then, leaving the guards securely locked in the storeroom to conceal Akbar's disappearance for as long as possible, and after quickly pulling on our traders' garb, we hurried through the citadel towards the gates to join the throng of people and beasts pouring down the ramp. No one challenged us. We made our way with the rest towards the town where, just outside the gates, more of my men were waiting with my horse and mules for the rest of the group. I hoped using mules would add to the impression that we were merchants not warriors. As darkness fell, we mounted up and headed north at first to conceal our true direction, just in case we were followed or spotted as we left the city. After riding through the freezing cold of the night, towards dawn we circled round to the east and with the sun rising in our faces began our journey to find you.'

As Hindal had been telling his story, his eyes had shone with an almost boyish excitement and exhilaration at succeeding in a difficult and dangerous task. Now that he had finished, Humayun felt a new and profound respect for his youngest half-brother – for his resourcefulness and coolness, his meticulous planning. Above all, what impressed him was how completely Hindal understood Kamran, exploiting his vanity to slip in under his defences. Hadn't Babur always cautioned them, even as boys, to know their enemy? Hindal had plainly listened, but how well had he himself really understood the need to empathise with others – not just enemies but friends – even family? Had he always striven enough to understand Hindal and to see things from his perspective?

For a brief time the two of them had become close. Perhaps they might yet be so again . . . The red wine he had drunk made his next words easier to say. 'Hindal, you spoke just now of our boyhood in Kabul. We share so much, you and I, not just our blood and our heritage but so much of our past. My mother loved you as her own. Of all my half-brothers, you are the one I feel closest to and would wish to make my friend. I know that unwittingly – selfishly even – I injured you. For that I am truly sorry and ask your forgiveness . . .'

'Humayun . . .'

But determined not to let Hindal speak until he had finished, Humayun pressed on. 'Can't we put our past troubles behind us? Be my ally again and ride by my side to capture Kabul. The future holds so much for us if we are ready to seize it – one day Hindustan will be Moghul again and I will give you a position of power and honour there, I swear it. Hindal . . . won't you forgive me? Won't you share that destiny with me?'

But Hindal was shaking his dark head. 'I told you at our last meeting that we would never be reconciled and it was the truth. I've done what I promised and that's an end of it. Your camp is no home to me. I've only lingered this long to make certain that I hadn't been followed and brought Kamran down on you – and of course to have some time with my sister Gulbadan.'

'Must it be like this?'

'You still don't understand me, do you? Like your mother you are greedy for what you want and do not like to be denied. She took me from my own mother with no concern for anyone's happiness but her own. Now you want me to forget what's passed between us – your unthinking arrogance and utter selfishness – and to play your loyal and loving brother again. I can't do it. It would be a lie and I have too much self-respect.'

'Hindal . . .'

'No, Humayun. You have your wife and your son. Soon perhaps you will have a throne again. Isn't that enough to satisfy you? Tomorrow at first light I will ride from here in search of the remainder of my men, whom I ordered to leave Kabul before Kamran returned. Once I find them, we will go once more into the mountains. I don't know when – or in what circumstances – you and I will meet again. Perhaps never . . .'

Hindal paused. It seemed to Humayun that there was something more he wished to say but after a few moments his half-brother rose and without looking back made his way through the feasters and out through the tent flaps into the night.

Chapter 20

Kabul

'Majesty, they've poisoned the wells.' It was one of Ahmed Khan's scouts, the coat of his chestnut mare steaming in the cold as he rode across the snowy ground up to where Humayun was standing on the crest of a ridge looking towards Kabul. Although the snow was not yet melting, there'd been no fresh falls. That was one reason why he and his men had made such swift progress as they retraced their steps westward. Another was a renewed energy and sense of purpose. He sensed it in his men and felt it deep within himself.

'Tell me more,' he said.

'We found dead and dying wild animals around the streams and wells nearest the citadel walls. The gates of the city and the citadel are closed against us and the walls of both are thick with defenders. They shot down one of our men who ventured too close.'

'Test some of the wells and springs further away. Feed the water to some of those flea-bitten pariah dogs that scavenge around the edges of our camp. Until we find good water we can drink snow melted over our fires.'

By eight o'clock that evening, Humayun's camp again spilled over the plains below Kabul and hundreds of camp fires glowed in the darkness as his men prepared their evening meal. Kamran's troops had not done their work thoroughly. Humayun's men had found supplies of untainted water only a mile from the walls of Kabul.

Standing outside his command tent Humayun could see pinpricks of light high on the battlements of the citadel. Was Kamran perhaps up there, watching and speculating, just as he was? And if so, what was going through his mind at the sight of Humayun's army once more before the gates of Kabul? How would Kamran feel to have been deceived as he had so often deceived others? Having lost his hostage, how did he think he could overcome the avenging Humayun? Was he ruing his arrogant self-confidence in unthinkingly accepting Hindal as a suppliant ally, believing that his natural superiority meant it must be preordained to be so?

Humayun suddenly grimaced. Had he himself been so different from Kamran in expecting, as of right, Hindal's unquestioning loyalty in the past? Perhaps not. He hoped that Kamran was sweating with worry and fear, but this was no time for playing out personal games of revenge. All that mattered was the quickest path to victory and that would not be easy. The citadel was strong and well supplied. Kamran and his men would defend it stoutly, knowing that they could expect little mercy.

In need of her calm comfort and pragmatic commonsense, he wished he had Hamida at his side. However, he knew he had been right to decide that, together with Akbar, Gulbadan and the other women, she should follow behind the main force, heavily protected by a well-armed escort, and then halt at a safe distance from Kabul. He would not risk his wife or his son again. But as soon as the city was his own once more, he could quickly call for her. At last, after so much hardship and heartache she would know the trappings of a queen and soon, he vowed to himself, the glories of being an empress.

◆

A sudden violent explosion just behind him deafened Humayun and a blast of hot air threw him to the ground, hitting his head a glancing blow on a rock as he fell. His eyes and mouth were full of dirt and snow but he eventually managed to re-open his eyes. Slowly he realised that he was surrounded by shards of bronze while what looked like slivers of fresh meat were dotted over the snowy ground.

302

A kite landed and started pecking at one with its curved beak. The silence in his head made the scene even more nightmarish and Humayun put his hands to his ears. As he did so, blood trickled down the fingers of his right hand from a wound to his right temple.

Suddenly there was a crackling in his ears – his hearing was returning . . . He could make out what sounded like frantic cheering from the defenders on the wall of the citadel, together with shouts of mockery. Still dazed and struggling to reassemble his scrambled thoughts, Humayun hauled himself to his feet and looked around. Slowly, he understood what had happened. One of his largest cannon had exploded. It was lying on its side with one of its gunners trapped by the legs beneath it, twisting and screaming in pain. The remains of at least two other men were scattered around, a severed leg here, an arm there, a bloody torso next to the cannon and only a yard from Humayun's foot a singed and mutilated head, its little remaining hair blowing in the breeze. The barrel of the cannon must have cracked, Humayun realised. It had been in daily use since his men had renewed their siege of the city and the citadel three weeks ago. As before, he had made the citadel his main target and his troops had hauled their cannon back to their previous positions, protected by the rocky outcrop where the road to the citadel curved round.

'Majesty, are you all right?' Jauhar appeared, streaked with pale dust and looking more ghost than man.

'Just a graze to my head.' As he spoke, a wave of nausea passed over Humayun and Jauhar caught him as he staggered.

'We will get you to the *hakim*, Majesty.' Jauhar half carried him to where some horses were tethered. As he rode slowly back to the camp with Jauhar holding the reins of his horse as well as his own, the thoughts within Humayun's pounding head were bleak. Even without this latest setback, the truth was that the siege was making little progress. Although the aim of his gunners, sweating in the freezing cold in their leather jerkins as they rammed powder and shot down the bronze barrels of their cannon and placed their glowing tapers to the touch-holes, was good and nearly every shot raised billowing clouds of dust and shards of mud and stone from their main target – the gatehouse and the repaired and reinforced walls around it – they had not yet succeeded in making a breach. Humayun had tried ordering two teams of gunners to fire to the left of the gate to test the strength of the walls there, but the difficult angle meant the only way to fire accurately at that stretch was to move the cannon out from behind the outcrop where an archer or musketeer up on the battlements could easily pick off his gunners. Several had been lost that way and men with their skills were difficult to replace. His supplies of powder too were limited.

He must be patient, Humayun thought, swaying a little in the saddle, just as he had forced himself to be while waiting for news of Hindal's rescue of Akbar. But it was hard knowing Kamran was so close. Sometimes it was all Humayun could do not to gallop up the ramp to the citadel and challenge his brother to single combat. Not that Kamran would ever agree – all Humayun would get would be an arrow in the throat.

Behind him, the cannon began to boom once more. Turning his head painfully Humayun looked back at the citadel. Not for the first time, the fear that Kamran was no longer there seized him. Suppose there was a secret route from the citadel down through the rocks and away. He hadn't known of any in his youth but it was always possible Kamran had located one and fled, leaving others to defend the fortress on his behalf.

He could wait no longer. He would talk to his commanders about storming the citadel. It would be costly in lives but with their overwhelming numbers the outcome would surely not be in doubt. Glancing down, he noticed that the ground beneath his horse's hooves was spongy with moisture from the melting snow. Every day the patches of bare ground were growing bigger. At least the seasons were on his side . . .

• ◆ •

'Nadim Khwaja is wounded. He and his men are being shot down by the musketeers and archers on the battlements even before they can get their scaling ladders into position against the walls,' shouted Bairam Khan to Humayun when the attack on the citadel had been under way for half an hour. 'I'll rush as many musketeers as I can to try to pick off the defenders as they expose themselves by firing at our men.'

'Order the artillerymen to redouble their fire. The smoke from their cannon will at least give some cover,' Humayun commanded. As he watched, some of the defenders fell back from the wall behind its deeply crenellated battlements, seemingly wounded. At least two others pitched head first over them to smash on the rocks below, but the defenders' fire did not slacken and more and more of Humayun's men were falling. 'Sound the retreat, Bairam Khan,' Humayun ordered. 'We are making little progress and we cannot afford to lose so many good men.'

Soon those of Humayun's soldiers who had survived the attack began making their way past his command position, some limping, others bleeding from bandaged wounds. As a litter was carried past by two men, Humayun heard the man on it scream in pain like an animal and saw that his right arm and shoulder had been burned by pitch poured on to the attackers from the battlements. As Humayun looked, his body kicked and twisted and suddenly he was still, free of his torment for ever. Almost the last to pass Humayun and Bairam Khan was Nadim Khwaja, the broken shaft of an arrow protruding from his thigh as he lay on a rough stretcher made of branches and jute cloth. But Nadim Khwaja said, 'It's nothing, Majesty, only a flesh wound. I'll live to serve again.'

It was good he had such loyal supporters, but could he count on the rest of his troops to be ready to take more casualties? He had promised them rewards on victory but that would only mean something to them if they believed they would be victorious in the end. How could he take Kabul? How could he capture Kamran? For the first time he felt truly at a loss.

'What should our next move be, Bairam Khan? I know I can trust you to tell the truth.'

'A frontal attack was as I think we both know a mistake – a mistake born out of frustration. We must once more be patient and keep the siege tight. We can and should send our men out for more supplies but Kamran and his troops cannot. They have no

305

hope of relief. Their morale will decay before ours if we hold our nerve.'

'Wise advice. Give the necessary orders to reinforce the siege.'

· ◆ ·

As he approached one of the picket posts around the perimeter of the camp on a tour of inspection, Humayun heard angry voices. Probably another squabble about ownership of a sheep or a goat, he thought without much interest. As he drew nearer, he saw the cause of the shouting. A man with a stubbly shaved head was standing dagger in hand amidst six of Humayun's soldiers, who had drawn their swords.

Humayun reined in his horse. 'What's going on?'

Recognising him, the soldiers at once touched their hands to their breasts. Humayun saw the man's eyes flicker over his horse's enamelled gold bridle and the jewelled clasps on his sheepskin coat, assessing who he might be.

'I am the emperor. Who are you and why are you causing trouble here?'

The man looked startled but recovered himself. 'I am Javed, a Ghilzai. I didn't start it. Your soldiers thought I was a spy . . .'

'Are you?'

'No. I came to your camp openly. I have information.'

'About what?'

'That depends on the price.'

At Javed's insolent words, a soldier stepped forward and jabbing him in the small of his back with a spear butt pushed him to the ground. 'On your knees before the emperor. Show some respect . . .'

Humayun let the man lie for a moment on the dank ground before saying, 'Get up.' Javed scrambled to his feet and for the first time looked a little nervous.

'I repeat my question. What information do you have? I – not you – will decide whether it's worth paying for. If you don't tell me, my men will force it from you.'

Javed hesitated. Was he simple-minded, Humayun wondered? Only an idiot would ride into a military camp and then seek to bargain with an emperor. But Javed seemed to have made his decision. 'There's sickness in the town. Some two or three hundred have already died and more bodies are piling up in the bazaars . . .'

'When did this start?'

'A few days ago.'

'How do you know?'

'From my brother who is inside the town. He and I are horse and mule dealers. As we do every year, we came to Kabul to sell our animals to the merchants who need them to transport goods when the snows recede and the caravans begin. I was tending our beasts in the hills when the commander of the Kabul garrison ordered the gates to be closed against your advancing army. My brother – who was transacting business in one of the caravanserais – was trapped. Over the weeks since the siege began I of course heard nothing from him. But my hunting dog was with him. Three nights ago it returned to my encampment in the hills, a message tied to its collar. My brother must have found a way to lower the dog over the city walls, though not without injury – one of its sides was badly grazed and bleeding and it was lame in one paw. Nevertheless, it managed to find me.'

'What else did the message say? Why did you think this would be of interest to me?

The cunning returned to Javed's face. 'My brother writes of panic and fear in the town. He says the citizens want the siege to end so they can escape the city and its pestilence. He believes the people may even rise up against the garrison and throw open the gates to you.'

'Show me this message.'

Javed bent and reaching down inside his boot produced a much-folded piece of paper which he handed to Humayun. Humayun unwrapped it and scrutinised the dense lines of badly written Turki. They confirmed everything Javed had said. The last words read: *The disease comes without warning, striking down even the young and healthy. First comes a high fever and vomiting, next uncontrollable diarrhoea, then delirium and death. Every day the stinking piles of bodies grow higher. We are in a trap from which there is no escape. We talk of killing the garrison while we still have strength and opening the gates but perhaps we will not have to. The soldiers are also dying. They too know that unless the siege is lifted or God shows us his mercy, many more will die. But God has turned his face away. What have we done to anger him? I hope this note reaches you, brother, because we may not meet again.*

As Humayun took in the full import of those words, his pulse quickened. This could be the opportunity he was seeking – yet could he trust Javed? He might even be an agent of Kamran. Humayun kept his voice calm and cold. 'You seem more interested in personal gain than in your brother's well-being, but if this information is true you will be rewarded. If it is false I will have you killed.' Humayun turned to his soldiers. 'Keep him closely confined.'

As Javed was led away, Humayun kicked his horse on again and making for his command tent in the centre of the camp allowed himself a smile. If what the message said was indeed the truth, Kabul might soon be his, but only if he knew how to exploit the information to maximum effect.

◆

'Majesty, the citizens of Kabul have sent an envoy. Half an hour ago, the gates opened and a bullock cart carrying an old man came trundling out towards our lines. He is waving some sort of rag as a sign he wishes to speak to us.'

So it had taken only three days. Immediately after receiving Javed's intelligence, Humayun had strengthened the ring of troops he had placed noose-like around the city. He had also withdrawn some of his cannon from the assault on the citadel and, placing them behind makeshift barricades for protection, had ordered his gunners to fire at the city walls to further demoralise the inhabitants and the garrison. Apart from a few half-hearted return salvos on the first day, the guns on the battlements had remained silent and there'd been few signs of defenders on the city walls.

'Bring the envoy to me.'

As he waited outside his tent, Humayun felt the warm sun of an early spring morning on his face. It felt good. So did his growing conviction that victory was almost close enough to reach out and touch. He must not allow it to elude his grasp.

The envoy was indeed old – so ancient in fact that he couldn't walk without the help of a tall, polished wood staff. Reaching Humayun, he attempted to bow low but couldn't. 'Forgive me, Majesty, it isn't lack of respect that prevents me, only my old bones . . . But I have escaped the sickness. That is why I was chosen as the city's messenger.'

'Fetch him a stool.' Humayun waited as the old man lowered himself painfully down, then asked. 'What is your message to me?'

'Many in our city are dying. We do not know the cause – perhaps our water supply became tainted when the soldiers tried to poison the wells and springs outside – but it is especially the young who are suffering. Many mothers in Kabul have reason to mourn a loss. We are all weary of conflict – even the garrison on whose behalf I also speak. We wish for an end to the siege so that those who want can leave the city.'

'I will accept nothing less than total surrender.'

'That is what I told them you would say. Majesty, don't you remember me . . . ?'

Humayun stared at his old face, wrinkled as an apricot left to dry in the sun. Something was familiar.

'I am Yusuf, eldest nephew of Wali Gul who was once your father's treasurer. I remember you and your brother Kamran as boys . . . It is sad that it should have come to this between you . . . it is also hard that ordinary people should suffer because of the ambitions of princes. I have always known that you – the son most beloved by Babur – were the rightful King of Kabul. But men are fickle and these days seem to care more for expedience than honour. When they believed Kamran would defeat you, they gave their allegiance to him.'

'That is why the citizens must submit to me unconditionally. Go back and tell them that if every man – the soldiers of the garrison as well as the ordinary people – lays down his arms I will spare their lives. I want all the weapons from cannon and muskets to swords and bows brought out and piled before the gates. The people themselves cannot leave – not until the disease has run its course. I'll not put my own men at risk. But I will send in *hakims* and supplies of fresh food and water . . . What will be their answer?'

Yusuf's dark brown eyes looked close to tears. 'They will bless you for your mercy, Majesty.'

Slowly Yusuf rose and leaning heavily on his staff made his way back to the bullock cart and climbed in. Soon the cart was on its way back towards the city, whose gates swung open to receive it. Would they open as easily in response to his terms, Humayun wondered, as he paced back and forth in front of his tent, feeling too tense to answer Jauhar's summons to the midday meal. An hour passed, and then another. Then a noise arose within the walls of the city, faint at first but quickly growing in intensity . . . the sound of thousands of voices cheering. It could only mean that the citizens had decided to surrender.

Minutes later, the gates were pulled wide open and a number of bullock carts emerged. When they had gone only halfway into the no-man's-land between the town walls and his encircling forces, they stopped and the drivers and the men sitting beside them began to throw the contents – weapons of all sorts and bows, muskets glinting in the sunlight – unceremoniously down to form rough heaps on the earth.

Humayun smiled. He had judged the surrender terms correctly. The city was his but his task was not even half complete. Kamran's troops still occupied the citadel. Humayun knew that if his half-brother was still with them he would be watching the city's surrender. How would he react now?

The answer was not long in coming. From the battlements Kamran's men fired volleys of arrows towards Humayun's cannon positions. They were accompanied by the discharge of small cannon Kamran had positioned on the citadel walls. Then Humayun heard the drums above the citadel gates boom and trumpets blare and saw the gates inch slowly open. Was Kamran about to surrender? No. Suddenly Humayun saw soldiers wielding long whips drive a dozen or so skinny oxen with bundles of burning straw tied on to their backs through the gates and down the ramp towards Humayun's positions.

Terrified, the animals charged onwards like living torches. 'Shoot them down before they burn the artillerymen's tents or set alight their powder stores,' yelled Humayun.

Soon eleven of the oxen lay on the ramp, arrows protruding from their corpses. Only one in its pain-maddened charge had reached Humayun's position and it had been despatched before it could do any serious damage. However, three of Humayun's archers had been badly wounded, shot down from the battlements of the citadel as they left cover to fire on the oxen.

This response convinced Humayun as could nothing else that Kamran had not fled as he had feared but was still within the citadel. It was so typical of him. When they were young, Kamran had always taken any defeat in play or in sport hard, as a child sticking his tongue out at Humayun and balling his fists and, when they were youths, crying 'foul' and promising all would be different at their next encounter. In those days, Humayun had laughingly ignored Kamran and his gestures and thus increased his half-brother's rage. Now, though, he would test Kamran's resolve and, even more important, that of his confederates. After some minutes' thought, Humayun sat down to compose a letter to Kamran, then sent for Jauhar.

'I wish you to ride to the citadel with this ultimatum for my brother. I will read it to you so you know what words you carry. They are few and they are blunt. "Our sister Gulbadan tried to appeal to your sense of family honour, of duty. You wouldn't listen. Instead to your everlasting shame you threatened the life of a child – your own nephew. The town of Kabul has fallen to me and your position is without hope so I offer you this choice, out of concern not for you but for those who follow you. Surrender the citadel and I swear that I will spare your men. Your own fate, however, will be for me to decide and I can give you no promises. If you will not surrender, I will turn my full might against you. However long it takes, my men will pound your walls to dust and once inside kill every man in the citadel without quarter. You have until sunset to give me your answer. If it is no, I will have archers fire arrows containing this message within your walls under cover of night so that your followers can see how cheap you hold their lives."'

In fact, Jauhar had barely been back from the citadel an hour and the sun was still a spear's length above the horizon when, from where he was standing on the perimeter of the camp talking to Ahmed Khan, Humayun saw a rider slowly descend the steep ramp from the citadel and then set out across the plain towards them. As the man drew nearer, Humayun saw a flag of truce fluttering from the tip of his spear. The minutes seemed to pass impossibly slowly as Humayun waited but at last the rider was just a few yards away – a young man in chain mail, with a falcon's plume in his helmet and a sombre expression. Reining in his horse, he dismounted and raised his arms from his sides to show he wasn't armed.

'Approach,' Humayun said.

When he was some ten paces from Humayun, the young man fell to the ground in the full obeisance of the *korunush*. Then, getting to his feet, he spoke. 'Majesty. The message I bring is short. The citadel of Kabul is yours.'

A fierce joy surged through Humayun. At the same time came a thought. Before he did anything else he would ride to the gardens his father had laid out on the hills overlooking Kabul where Babur's grave lay open to the sun, rain, wind and snow. There, kneeling by the simple marble slab, he would give thanks. Just as Babur had done, he would use Kabul as the stepping stone for his reconquest of Hindustan.

◆

Trumpets sounded as beneath a brilliant blue sky Humayun rode at the head of a picked column of men representing all the clans who had joined in his conquest of Kabul, up past where his cannon had been stationed, past where he had looked up to see to his anguish Akbar exposed as a human shield on the battlements, through the high gate from which the fire-carrying oxen had charged and on into the sunlit courtyard of the citadel itself. As he dismounted from his black horse, an immense pride in what he had achieved since he left Persia washed over him. Most important, of course, he had recovered Akbar, but he had also reasserted his authority over Kamran and Askari and re-occupied the kingdom of Kabul.

Bairam Khan, Nadim Khwaja and others of his generals behind were exultant, waving at the crowds and rejoicing in their victory. But mingling with Humayun's euphoria were more sombre thoughts. Kneeling at his father's grave last night he had vowed never again to become a king without a kingdom. Before he could even think of re-taking Hindustan, just as Babur had done he must make his rule over Kabul and all its lands unassailable. He must force every chief in the surrounding territories who ruled as his vassal to submit totally to his overlordship. Many of those chiefs had supported Kamran and several had friendships and alliances with him going back to the time when as a youth Kamran had remained in Kabul while Humayun had accompanied Babur on his conquest of Hindustan. They would require careful handling. A simple show of force might obtain their allegiance for a while but what would happen when he advanced on Hindustan? They might well rebel.

First, though, he must deal with the half-brother whom he'd last seen face to face two years ago when he'd woken in his tent in a blizzard to find his knife at his throat. 'Where is Kamran?' he demanded of Jauhar, who was as usual at his side.

'I was told he is being held in the cells beneath the citadel.'

'Have him brought before me here in the courtyard now.'

'Yes, Majesty.'

A few minutes later, Humayun saw Kamran emerge through a low door which led up from the cells, blinking at his sudden exposure to sunlight. His legs were tightly shackled and he was followed by two armed guards. However, his hands were free and as he passed three grooms leading some of Humayun's commanders' horses back to the stables at the conclusion of the entry parade, he suddenly grabbed a long riding whip from one of them. Before the guards could react, he had placed it round his neck in the same way that the whip was placed round the neck of common criminals condemned to be flogged as they were led to the punishment frame.

Was Kamran suggesting he was submitting himself to whatever punishment he might impose, Humayun wondered? He motioned to his guards to leave the whip where it was and walked towards

313

his half-brother. As he drew closer, he saw that Kamran looked unkempt and the bags beneath his eyes showed exhaustion, but his green eyes themselves looked straight into Humayun's and betrayed not a hint of submission or repentance, merely arrogance and disdain. There was even a trace of a supercilious smile on his lips.

How can he jest with me? How can he not recognise his guilt for what he has done? How can he not show some signs of remorse for the many lives lost on his account, for all those wasted years when we could have been re-conquering Hindustan, thought Humayun. As he stared at his half-brother the image of Kamran pushing Hamida to the floor as he grabbed Akbar in the tent came unbidden into his mind, quickly followed by that of Akbar exposed on the walls of Kabul as the cannon roared. Suddenly emotion erupted like a volcano within him and he lost all control. He hit Kamran with his clenched fist hard in the mouth, breaking one of his teeth and splitting his lip, yelling 'That is for Hamida' as he did so. Next he brought up his knee with all the force he could muster into Kamran's groin. 'And that is for Akbar!' he screamed, eyes bulging. Then he brought both his arms down on Kamran's neck and Kamran fell to the floor where he lay doubled up, clutching his groin and spitting out bloody bits of tooth but uttering not a single word, not a single groan.

Shaking with fury, Humayun was drawing back his foot, ready to kick his defiant, devious brother hard in the stomach, when a cry of dismay from behind him broke into his rage. He twisted round to see frail old Kasim shuffling towards him as fast as he could propel himself on the two ivory-handled walking sticks that he had long relied on.

'Majesty, this is not the way. If he must die, let him do so with dignity as befits a descendant of Timur. What would your father think?'

His words felt to Humayun like a bucket of cold water poured over him, cooling his temper. Kasim was right. He stepped back from his half-brother. 'I forgot myself, Kamran. I lowered myself to your level. I will decide your fate later and not in the heat of my anger. Guards! Pick him up. Take him back to the cells, but do not ill-treat him.'

· ◆ ·

Humayun surveyed his audience chamber with satisfaction. Hangings of Moghul green shone in the light of hundreds of candles and wicks burning in *diyas* of scented oil. This was truly a victory celebration. It had been such a long time – years – since he had been able to reward his warriors as a Moghul ruler should. The treasuries and armouries of Kabul – though not as full as in his father's time – had yielded enough jewelled daggers and swords, coats of fine mail, finely chased armour, enamelled and gem-encrusted drinking cups and gold and silver coins to reward all his commanders and officers and their men. That Kamran had been so prudent with Kabul's wealth had surprised Humayun.

His officers and commanders were eating now – the sweet, juicy flesh of young lambs, chickens roasted in butter, quails and pheasants stewed with dried fruits and served whole, their tail feathers still attached but gilded, and fragrant flat bread still hot from the bricks on which it had been baked. The luxurious abundance – the exquisite dishes on which the food was served – seemed a dream after all the years of danger and hardship, of betrayal and deceit. Humayun's eyes rested with real affection on the battle-scarred faces of Zahid Beg and Ahmed Khan and on the lined faces of Kasim and Sharaf, who had followed him across blistering deserts and over mountains where the cold was so intense it seemed to freeze a man's heart. When his warriors had numbered less than two hundred – and what tribal leader here tonight had so few? – these loyal men had stayed with him.

Later, as the final course of the meal – sweetmeats of all descriptions including dried apricots stuffed with walnuts and curd cheese mixed with sultanas and pistachios – was brought in on silver platters, Humayun looked around at his commanders, all enjoying the feast and discussing the future and the prospects for the reconquest of Hindustan. He felt content as he had not done for many years. He had never doubted his courage or skill in combat; nor, he suspected, had his followers. But he knew he had gained other perhaps more important strengths as well. He was becoming ever more confident in his authority as a ruler and a leader and in his ability to inspire loyalty in those such as Bairam Khan who had no pre-existing ties to him.

But what about those who had such ties but had not been loyal, among them the nobles and commanders who had supported Kamran and Askari and, of course, his half-brothers themselves? Humayun's mood sobered. Over the past sixty hours since he had entered the citadel he had been pondering their fate, especially Kamran's. He had nearly yielded to a visceral desire to revenge himself on his half-brother with his bare hands for threatening his child.

But as his rage had cooled he had begun to think more calmly. He could never forgive Kamran but did he owe it to the future of his dynasty to try to heal the rifts within it rather than deepening them? His father's face – so like Kamran's with those brilliant green eyes – swam before him. Suddenly the contentment and confidence welling through him coalesced to make his decision. Standing up, Humayun called Jauhar to him. 'Have Kamran and Askari brought before me here, at once, together with those of their leading commanders whom we have also kept prisoner.'

A quarter of an hour later, Jauhar whispered to Humayun that the prisoners were outside the chamber's thick doors. Humayun rose to his feet and clapped his hands to call for quiet. Almost instantly a hush fell on the room as his officers put down their eating implements and goblets, wiped their mouths, sticky from the sweetmeats, and turned all their attention to their emperor.

'My loyal commanders, we have celebrated our victory and rightly rejoiced in our success in overcoming our enemies, but our task is only half complete. Now we must look to the future and the reconquest of Hindustan. However, first I must deal with those who, unlike you, showed me no loyalty and neglected the ties of blood and of ancestral obligations. Bring in the prisoners.'

Two attendants pulled open the doors and Kamran walked into the room. His hands were tied but his legs were free. Straight-backed, head high, and bruised, hawk-nosed face emotionless, he walked forward, looking neither to left nor right until the guards escorting him halted him ten feet in front of Humayun. He was followed by Askari, who had been confined in comfortable private quarters since being brought to the citadel but whose hands were now also bound. Even though he must have known he had less to fear than his brother since Humayun had promised him his life, his demeanour was less assured than Kamran's. He was perspiring a little and looking round and smiling nervously at some of those of Humayun's men he recognised. Behind him came ten of Kamran and Askari's senior commanders. Among them were Hassan Khahil, a burly, wild-haired Uzbek, and Shahi Beg, a diminutive but courageous Tajik with a livid white scar on his left cheek. He had been Kamran's commander in Kabul and was in fact a cousin of Zahid Beg, Humayun's own general. As Shahi Beg entered, Humayun noticed the two men's eyes met but then both looked instantly away.

Once the commanders were lined up behind Kamran and Askari, Humayun began addressing his own troops. 'You see before you the men we have defeated. The men who have shed our blood and killed our friends. Yet the war we have fought was a battle between brothers and relations. I know this only too well, as do many others of you. We have fought those with whom we should have banded together to fight the common enemy who has usurped our lands in Hindustan. Much more − heritage, tradition and ambition − should bind us together than those rivalries and jealousies which have split us apart. Divided among ourselves, we may never reconquer Hindustan. United we should be so powerful we need fear none. The fear would be our enemy's alone − our conquests and ambitions would be without limit.

'For that reason I have preferred reconciliation to punishment, however well deserved. I have decided to forgive these my former enemies you see before you, provided they will join us in regaining and expanding our empire in Hindustan.'

With that, Humayun walked over to Askari and drawing a small dagger cut his brother's bonds and embraced him. As he did so, he felt Askari relax and there were wet tears on his half-brother's cheek as it brushed against his own. Then he moved towards Kamran and severed his bonds too and embraced him. Kamran's body felt rigid but he did not pull back. Nor did he resist as Humayun held his and Askari's arms aloft and yelled to the resounding cheers of all present, 'Onwards to the reconquest of Hindustan.'

An hour later, Humayun made his way to Hamida's apartments in the royal women's quarters. She had arrived with Akbar and Gulbadan the previous evening and in the joy of their reunion they had not spoken of Kamran and his fate. As he entered, he could tell at once from her expression that she knew of his decision.

'How could you!' she burst out. 'You have pardoned Kamran, the man who stole our child and exposed him on the walls of Kabul. Are you mad? Don't you care about our son and my feelings?'

'You know I do. It was a hard decision. A ruler must think about more than his personal emotions. He must think about what's best for his kingdom. If I'd had Kamran executed, I would have made implacable enemies of some of his most loyal followers and relations, not least Askari whom I had already agreed should live as a condition of his surrender of Kandahar. If I'd had Kamran imprisoned, he would have become a focus for discontent and plotting. The same would have been true if I'd punished his commanders. Our family is not the only one riven by the rebellions. Much better that I try to reconcile my enemies than to provoke blood feuds. If I am to reconquer Hindustan, I will need the willing commitment of all my nobles and vassals, not just those who have supported us this far.

'Yes of course I could press others to accompany me or to send levies, but they would soon be plotting or looking for any opportunity to defect or at the very least to return home. That would not help to win back our lands. The wounds that are most difficult to heal are those inflicted by the ones who should be the closest. But if I can heal those from my brothers, our dynasty will be the stronger and Akbar's position in its future the more secure.'

At the mention of Akbar, Hamida's expression softened a little, but it still betrayed scepticism and uncertainty. This was so hard for her. Humayun thought back to his own enraged assault on Kamran. At least he had had an opportunity to vent his feelings . . .

'I loathe Kamran. I can never forgive him.'

318

'Hamida, I'm not asking you to forgive Kamran – that I know you can never do. But I am asking you to trust in me . . . in my judgement. And I have another more personal reason for sparing Kamran . . . loyalty to my father and above all the promise I made to him as he lay dying to follow his wishes and do nothing against my half-brothers, however much they deserved it. Their failure to honour his decision that I should succeed to the throne should not absolve me from keeping my own word to him.'

Humayun looked straight into Hamida's eyes. 'I am truly sorry if my decision hurts you, but you must know nothing can alter my great love for you and our son and my determination that when I die, which God willing will not be yet, I will leave him secure on the throne of Hindustan as my father left me.'

'If you tell me that allowing Kamran to live will make Akbar's future more secure then I must accept it. The future of our son is what matters most. But I cannot lie to you. In my heart I wish Kamran was dead. I would sleep more easily in that knowledge.'

'This is best for Akbar.'

At last, Hamida smiled and stretched out her hand to Humayun. 'Come to bed. It is late.'

• ◆ •

It was nearly ten o'clock the next morning when Humayun emerged from the women's quarters to find Jauhar waiting for him, beaming broadly. 'Majesty, good news . . . wonderful news. Our spies have brought reports that Sher Shah is dead. He was assaulting a fortress in Rajasthan when a missile filled with burning pitch that one of his siege engineers had hurled at the walls rebounded and landed on a gunpowder store. The entire store exploded, dismembering Sher Shah and two of his senior commanders. They say parts of Sher Shah's body were scattered over a hundred yards.'

'Are the reports reliable?'

'The spies say they come from several sources. There is no reason to doubt them.'

Humayun found the news difficult to take in. It seemed to justify his decision to pardon his half-brothers and unite his subjects. They would need to act quickly and together to seize the opportunity to regain the throne of Hindustan.

'Call my commanders to me. Let my half-brothers join us too. Together we will march to fulfil our family's destiny.'

Part IV

Return of the Moghuls

Chapter 21

A Brother's Grief

'Majesty, you must come at once.' Humayun slid back into its embossed black leather scabbard the ivory and steel-hilted sabre – a recent gift from a vassal – that he had been examining. 'What is it, Jauhar?'

Jauhar spread his hands in a helpless gesture and Humayun read such distress in his face that he asked no more questions but simply followed him. Dusk was falling and purple shadows softened the stark outlines of stone and brick as Humayun quickly descended into the courtyard. Just inside the gateway four of Ahmed Khan's men were clustered around a tall chestnut horse. Drawing closer, Humayun noticed that its neck and shoulder were stained with something dark that was attracting flies, and as the men stepped back from the horse to salute him he saw a body slung face down over the saddle, limp as a dead deer. The discolouration on the horse's coat was congealed blood. But it was the body itself that arrested his gaze. Though he didn't want to believe it he thought he recognised that powerful form, whose lifeless arms and legs were so long they dangled down beneath the horse's belly.

With an ever-increasing sense of foreboding Humayun slowly approached and, crouching down, raised the dead man's head. Hindal's tawny eyes stared blankly at him. Unable to bear their unblinking gaze, Humayun closed them. As he did so, the warmth of his brother's dead flesh shocked him, then he realised that Hindal's face had been resting against the horse's flanks. He drew his dagger from his sash and waving back his guards cut through the ropes with which someone had secured Hindal's body to the horse. Then he carefully lifted his brother's corpse and laid it gently, face up, on the flagstones. As he knelt beside it, by the flickering amber light of a torch held aloft in the gathering gloom by one of Ahmed Khan's men he saw a raw wound in Hindal's throat that only an arrowhead could have made.

Grief washed through him. Hindal was the one of his half-brothers he had cared for most. Courageous, honest and principled, and less ambitious than his siblings, perhaps Hindal had been at heart the best of all Babur's sons. 'I wish you godspeed to Paradise, my brother, and that in death you will forgive me the hurt I did you in life,' Humayun whispered. Images of Hindal in his youth and of him proudly recounting his rescue of Akbar filled Humayun's mind, bringing tears to his eyes. It was some minutes before, brushing them away with the back of his hand, he got to his feet and asked, 'Who found the body?'

'I did, Majesty,' said the torchbearer, who, Humayun saw, was no more than a youth.

'Where?'

'His horse was tethered by some juniper bushes half a mile from the town.'

So someone had drawn out the fatal arrow, tied Hindal to his horse and then left him where he would be found. Such an act bore all the hallmarks of Kamran, Humayun thought with a weariness of heart. Far from being grateful for his mercy, within two months of being set free Kamran and Askari had vanished from Kabul. United against him again, they had become raiders, sweeping down from remote strongholds at the head of bands of tribesmen – lawless Kafirs and Chakraks mostly, but whoever they could find; they weren't particular – to attack Humayun's outposts and the caravan trains that were the source of Kabul's prosperity – its life's blood. Kamran would not have forgiven Hindal's betrayal in rescuing Akbar and he certainly had the malice to send Humayun the message of Hindal's slaughtered body.

But what had actually happened? If the murderer was Kamran, had Hindal's death been the result of a chance encounter or had Kamran deliberately hunted Hindal down in the northern mountains which he had made his retreat in the years since he had rescued Akbar? 'Search my brother's body and his saddlebag. Look for anything that might tell us how or why he met his end,' Humayun ordered as he turned away, unable to face the task himself.

A few minutes later, a soldier came up to him where he stood in the gloom, lost in his thoughts and recollections. 'We found nothing of importance, Majesty, except this note in the saddlebag.' Humayun took the scrap of paper and read it by the light of a torch. In a few brief sentences addressed to no one, Hindal asked, if anything should happen to him, to be buried close to his father. He also wrote that he wished Akbar to have his ruby-inlaid dagger that had once belonged to Babur. 'The dagger was still in his sash, Majesty.' The soldier held out a silver scabbard, also inlaid with rubies, that glittered in the torchlight. So whoever had killed Hindal had not been a thief, Humayun thought. It also told him that death had come suddenly and probably unexpectedly to Hindal, who had had no time to draw his dagger. Again he saw Kamran's green-eyed, sneering face . . .

• ◆ •

Three weeks later, the branches of the tall cherry trees brought by Babur as saplings to Kabul stirred in the breeze, shedding blossom that fluttered like pink snowflakes. Spring melt water from the mountains rippled through the two intersecting marble-lined channels that divided the garden into four quarters planted with pomegranate, apple and lemon trees. The scent of honey rose from the lilac clover covering the ground as, walking through the garden Babur had planted, Humayun came to the new grave in the middle of a grove of young willows. The inscription on the marble slab told the onlooker that here lay Mirza Hindal, youngest and beloved son of Babur, Moghul Emperor of Hindustan.

Gulbadan had chosen the delicate tracery of irises and tulips that the masons had carved round the stone's edge and every day, on Hamida's orders, the pale marble was sprinkled with dried rose petals.

She had never forgotten her gratitude to Hindal for saving Akbar – if anything it had grown because Akbar was still their only child. The *hakims* blamed the long and agonising labour she had endured giving birth to him and had predicted that though she was still young – not yet twenty-five – there would be no more children.

Turning away from Hindal's grave, Humayun walked the few paces to Babur's simple tomb. Every time he came here, he sensed his father's presence so keenly he could almost see him standing before him, eyes fixed understandingly upon him. Babur too had taken Kabul only to have his hopes of advancing quickly to invade Hindustan disappointed. Yet there was a profound difference between their circumstances. Babur's problem had been that he lacked an army strong enough to take on Sultan Ibrahim, Hindustan's powerful overlord. That obstacle had been overcome when his friend Baburi had brought him Turkish cannon and matchlocks – weapons then unknown in Hindustan. Humayun's problems were more complex, more corrosive, because they came from within his own family. Because of Kamran and Askari, Humayun had been forced to delay his invasion of Hindustan just when the prospects of victory had seemed so good.

The chaos following Sher Shah's death should have been a perfect opportunity for Humayun to invade – Sher Shah's reign had lasted only five years and many would have returned to the green banners of the Moghuls.

Instead, the threat of Kamran and Askari had made it impossible for him to mount a prolonged expedition. Sher Shah's chiefs had had time to rally and choose a new emperor. Rejecting Sher Shah's elder son – a man better known for his love of luxury than for his military prowess – they had elected his younger son, Islam Shah, whose first act had been to order the murder of his elder brother. The message had not been lost on Humayun. If he had executed Kamran and Askari rather than pardoned them, then he, not Islam Shah, would have been sitting on the throne in Agra.

That his half-brothers should have been able to frustrate his plans for so long hurt as well as enraged Humayun. Where was their gratitude for his mercy? Perhaps he shouldn't be surprised at Kamran, whose hatred and jealousy of him were seemingly implacable, but why had Askari repaid his generosity with such deceit? When Askari had surrendered to him at Kandahar, he had seemed to feel remorse, even shame for his actions. Perhaps those feelings had been genuine but under Kamran's influence hadn't lasted. All his life Askari had been dominated by Kamran . . .

Still brooding, Humayun walked slowly back to where Jauhar was holding the reins of his horse while it grazed the sweet grass beneath an apple tree. Climbing into the saddle, Humayun pushed the horse quickly back towards the citadel. He had made a decision. Hindal's death had been a sign that there must be no more waiting, no more prevaricating, no more sentimental hopes that his half-brothers might still be reconciled. So far his efforts to flush them from their mountain hideaways had been futile. Something more determined was required . . .

That night, as Humayun entered his audience chamber, he found his commanders and his counsellors already waiting. As he surveyed their faces, there was one man he still instinctively looked for – Kasim, whose calm commonsense and absolute loyalty had been one of the few constants of his turbulent reign. But last winter, crossing the icy courtyard Kasim had slipped and shattered his right hip. The *hakims* had sedated him with opium but the shock to his old body had been too great. He had slipped into unconsciousness and two days later passed away as quietly as he had done everything in life. Kasim had been with Babur from the first precarious days of his reign as boy-king of Ferghana, just as he had always been at Humayun's side. Humayun had been so used to his calm, reassuring presence and to listening to his softly spoken and consistently valuable advice. His death had been a true severing from the past.

But it was the future Humayun needed to think about now. Sitting tall on his throne he began. 'My patience with my half-brothers is at an end. They will always be a danger until their forces are destroyed and they are caught.'

'Our troops have been unlucky . . . one day we will succeed in taking them prisoner,' said Zahid Beg. He regarded the failure to defeat Kamran and Askari as a blemish on his honour.

'If we carry on as at present I doubt it – unless we are very lucky. I have long suspected that they have spies among our soldiers as well as in the city. That is why they always elude us, making us waste time and energy that would be better spent elsewhere.'

'But what more can we do?' asked Zahid Beg.

'That is why I have summoned you here. Dealing with Kamran and Askari and their mountain raiders cannot be beyond us. Kabul is wealthy. The merchants who come here to trade and fill our caravanserais are numerous. The taxes they pay fill our treasury. I have been preserving this wealth for my long-postponed invasion of Hindustan but I intend to spend some of it to deal once and for all with the problem of my half-brothers . . .'

'How, Majesty?' asked Zahid Beg.

'I will give my own body weight in gold to any man who captures either of my half-brothers. We will also redouble our own efforts – mobilise all our troops to hunt for them. I will lead them myself. I will also pay large sums to tribesmen to ride with us. They know every ripple and fold of the mountains. I pledge not to rest until my half-brothers are caught.'

◆

'Majesty, one of our patrols reports smoke rising from Karabagh,' Ahmed Khan said, galloping up to Humayun and reining in his white horse so sharply it snorted in protest.

'You think the settlement's under attack?'

'I'm sure of it, Majesty.'

'Then let's ride.' As his horse's hooves beat the sun-hardened earth beneath a glaring orange sun, Humayun allowed himself to hope that at last he was getting close to Kamran and Askari. For the past three weeks he and his men had been following in the wake of a large raiding party through the mountainous valleys north of Kabul, always arriving only in time to find settlements burned, orchards hacked down and bodies already putrefying in the intense summer heat. But Karabagh was only about four miles away. Humayun remembered it well from hunting trips in his youth – a large, prosperous place with almond and apricot orchards irrigated by a willow-fringed stream flowing past the mud walls that enclosed it.

The five hundred troops riding at his back – mounted archers and cavalrymen with bright, steel-tipped spears – should be more than enough to deal with whoever was attacking Karabagh, he thought. As he swept round the side of a hill on which a few young oak trees had taken root, Karabagh and its orchards came into view. It wasn't the peaceful scene Humayun remembered. Fields and orchards had been set alight and through the acrid drifting smoke he saw that the gates into the settlement had been torn down. Even above the thundering of hooves he thought he heard screaming.

'For justice!' Humayun yelled and, circling Alamgir above his head, he urged his horse to a gallop, outstripping his bodyguards. He was the first through the shattered gateway and into the settlement, swerving his mount around the body of an old man from whose bloodied back a battleaxe protruded. To his right, some twenty yards away, Humayun saw two men – Chakraks from their shaggy, spherical sheep wool hats – dragging a terrified girl from a house. One of them was already loosening the drawstring of his baggy pantaloons. Seeing Humayun they gaped. Letting go of the girl, who scrambled out of the way, both men reached for their bows but Humayun was on them. With a sweep of his sword he decapitated the first man, sending his head spinning through the warm air to smash against a stone lintel. Then, pulling hard on his reins and leaning back, he brought his horse up on to its back legs and then urged it forward so its front hooves smashed down on the second Chakrak with a satisfying crunch of bone.

All around, his men who had poured into the settlement behind him were having the best of the fight. The raiders, intent on looting and raping, had been taken completely by surprise. Those who could were running to find cover. But all Humayun's thoughts were now on his half-brothers. Wheeling his horse, he looked around for them among the heaving, struggling mêlée. 'Majesty, get down!' he heard Ahmed Khan yell above the shouts, groans and clashing of weapons, and ducked just in time to avoid a spear hurled at him by a wild-haired giant of a man standing on the flat roof of a house. Humayun pulled his battleaxe from the thongs securing it to his saddle and sent it hurtling through the air. It hit the man in the chest so hard he tumbled backwards off the roof as if struck by a musket ball.

Humayun's blood was pounding in his ears. It felt good to be in the heart of the fight. Brushing the sweat from his face with his green face cloth, he saw what seemed to be the last surviving raiders running towards some horses tethered to the wooden frame above a well. 'Let no one escape,' he yelled as, pulling his own mount round, he bore down on them. Leaning forward, he grabbed one man by the shoulder as he was about to jump on to his horse and with a violent push sent him sprawling to the ground. Reining in, Humayun shouted at the man as he lay in the dust, 'Whose men are you? Answer me at once or I'll put my sword through your throat.' The man was winded and still struggling to speak when Humayun heard a familiar voice behind him.

'They are mine. I surrender. Let's be done with all this.'

Turning, Humayun saw Askari standing about four yards behind him, thin face streaked with blood from a cut above his right eyebrow. At his feet were his curved sword and a throwing dagger. When they saw what their leader had done, Askari's remaining men also dropped their weapons.

By now, Humayun's men were all around. 'Tie them all up,' he ordered. Then, dismounting, he slowly approached Askari. Puzzlement at his brother's behaviour and the knowledge of how close he might have come to death at his hands if Askari had used his weapons rather than discarding them, combined to make him take refuge in a simpler emotion – anger.

'How dare you bring destruction and havoc to my people – our people?'

Askari said nothing.

'You've never had the guts to act alone. Kamran must be nearby. Where is he?'

Askari wiped away the blood that was still leaking from the cut on his face. 'You're wrong. I haven't seen Kamran for over five months. I don't know where he is.' His black eyes met Humayun's.

Humayun came closer and dropped his voice so they could not

330

be overheard. 'I don't understand. You could have attacked me from behind before I even knew you were there.'

'Yes.'

'So what stopped you?'

Askari shrugged and looked away. Humayun gripped his shoulder. 'You don't baulk at attacking innocent people, allowing these vermin' – he gestured at a couple of sullen Chakraks whom his men had trussed up with rope – 'to rape and murder, so why hesitate to attack your own flesh and blood . . . ?'

'Humayun . . .'

'No, now I think about it, I'm not interested. It was probably cowardice. You knew my men would kill you if you attacked me. I don't want to listen to any more of your lies about how sorry you are and how everything that's happened has been Kamran's fault.' Humayun turned away and shouted to his guards, 'Take him away and keep him from my sight until we reach Kabul. Just looking at him shames me.'

• ◆ •

Not until ten days after his return to Kabul, when the trees were turning red and gold as autumn came, did Humayun finally have Askari brought before him again. His words to his men had been the honest truth – he was ashamed of his half-brother, of the depths to which he had fallen and the dishonour it had brought to their family. Pallid and thinner than ever from his confinement in the common dungeons, Askari shuffled slowly into Humayun's private apartments, hands bound, legs shackled and flanked by guards. 'Leave us,' Humayun ordered them, 'but stay within call.' As the double doors of mulberry wood closed behind them, Humayun walked to his gilded chair, sat down, and chin in hand looked Askari in the face.

'There's something I've never understood. Twice I've spared your life though you threatened mine. More than that, I invited you to be not just my brother but my ally in my invasion of Hindustan . . . You must think I've wronged you, yet I offered you everything . . .'

Askari slowly shook his head. 'You didn't,' he said in a low voice.

'All you ever offered me and Kamran was a little of your reflected glory – not power and lands of our own. I see from your face that you don't understand, but for you life's always been about your so-called "great destiny".'

'It's not just my destiny – it belongs to us all.'

'Does it? What about the saying of our people, *taktya, takhta*, "throne or coffin"? That's not about a shared destiny – it's about winner takes all. Humayun, let us speak plainly – perhaps more honestly than we ever have in all these years. I don't like you but I don't hate you ... I never did. I was just looking out for myself as you would have done in my place.'

'You're just making excuses for thwarted ambition and greed.'

Askari looked down at his bound hands. 'That's what you call it. I'd say it was a desire for independence – the freedom I'd have enjoyed if our father had divided his territories fairly between his sons as our ancestors did.' He paused.

'But you didn't have to betray me. Hindal didn't.'

At the mention of Hindal Askari's self-righteous expression altered. 'Hindal was different from any of us. He was as gentle as he was big in stature. He was without guile and so naïve that he expected everyone to be as honourable as he was. You lost a good ally when you stole Hamida from him ...' Suddenly there were tears in Askari's eyes. 'I wish ... but what's the point ...'

'What do you wish?' Humayun rose from his chair and came so close to Askari he could smell the pungent dankness of his skin and clothes after his days of confinement.

'I wish I hadn't killed Hindal.'

'You? I thought it must have been Kamran ...'

'It wasn't. It was me.'

'But why? How had he injured you?'

'I didn't mean to kill him. It was an accident. A cruel coincidence of fate. I was on a raid with some of my men on a moonless night. In the darkness we encountered a small party of fast-moving riders who wouldn't halt or identify themselves. I shot an arrow at their leader who tumbled from his saddle as the rest of his men fled in panic. When I looked at the body I ... I saw it was Hindal ...'

Askari said dully, eyes avoiding Humayun's. 'I ordered my men to leave his body outside the walls of Kabul where it would be found before wild beasts took it so you could give him a decent burial.'

'I did. He lies near our father as he wanted.' Humayun was still adjusting to the genuine remorse he saw on his half-brother's face when a thought struck him like a shaft of light suddenly illuminating a dark corner.

'Hindal was the reason you surrendered when you did, rather than attacked me, wasn't he? You might well have been able to kill me . . .'

'Yes. My guilt weighed on me. Everything felt so futile. I didn't want to add another brother's death to the burden of regret I already carry.'

Humayun felt tears prick his own eyes as he thought over Askari's tale. Why had Hindal put himself at risk by riding south with only a few men into lands where he must have known he might encounter Kamran's and Askari's robber bands? Was it wishful thinking to think Hindal might have been on his way to Kabul to seek a reconciliation with him? Now he would never know . . .

For a few moments, both brothers were silent. Then Askari slowly crossed the room to the window and looked down into the courtyard. As he did so a half-smile crossed his face. 'When we were children, Hindal and I used to stand here sometimes while the guards drilled in the courtyard. At other times we watched you and Kamran learning to fight with dagger and sword. We were very impressed – compared with us you seemed like grown men, warriors . . . We also watched our father ride out on his invasion of Hindustan from here. We'd never seen anything like it – so many thousands of soldiers, so many baggage wagons assembled in the meadows below the citadel, so much noise and excitement in the early morning light. Hindal was yelling with excitement though he didn't really understand what was happening . . . Humayun . . .'

'What?'

'Do you intend to execute me?'

'Probably not.'

Askari closed his eyes for a moment. 'In that case, help me find a way to make peace with myself and with the past . . .'

'How can I do that?'

'Let me make the journey to Mecca, the *haj*. I want to atone for what happened to Hindal . . .'

'You want to make the pilgrimage to Mecca?' Why not, Humayun thought after a moment or two. Making the *haj* would take Askari nearly a thousand miles from Kabul and from Kamran for months – years even. It was a better solution than incarceration or exile and might even provide Askari with the spiritual comfort he seemed in such need of. 'Are you certain this is what you want?'

Askari nodded.

'Then I will send an escort with you under the command of one of my best young officers, Mohamed Azruddin.'

'To spy on me?' Askari smiled bleakly.

'No. To protect you – it is a long and hazardous journey by sea as well as by land . . . You may not believe me but I wish things could have been different between us. It is too late for that now – the past will always lie between us – but I pray that you find the peace you are seeking.'

Chapter 22

Kamran Padishah

O ne clear early spring morning, five months after Askari's departure on his long journey to Mecca, Humayun stood at the stone casement of his apartments in his fortress palace overlooking Kabul and gazed towards the mountains to the south. Although there had been no falls for some weeks, their jagged peaks were still snow-capped. The winds were chill and Humayun pulled his fur-lined cloak tightly round him. Few travellers made the journey up through the passes from Hindustan at this time of year but as Humayun watched, a small caravan appeared round the bend of the road that led south to Hindustan.

As the caravan got closer, Humayun saw that it comprised a few horsemen, no more than twenty – presumably merchants and their attendants – and about twenty or thirty pack camels. The riders were all well protected against the cold by heavy sheepskin jackets and most had scarves wound round their faces. The camels' warm breath hung in the cold air as they plodded slowly up the hill under the burden of heavy panniers crammed with trade goods strapped on either side of their bodies, and headed towards one of the caravanserais that clustered just inside the thick walls of the city. After ten minutes, the caravan disappeared from view through the city gates into the caravanserai. Shortly afterwards, Humayun saw the smoke of extra fires lit to warm and feed the newcomers rise from within its walls.

335

Thinking no more about the caravan, Humayun looked down into the courtyard of the fort where Bairam Khan was teaching the ten-year-old Akbar some of the finer points of swordplay, watched by Akbar's milk-brother Adham Khan. Akbar – a strong, muscular boy for his age – was clearly perfecting a technique for parrying Bairam Khan's thrusts. Dodging beneath his tutor's shield, he stabbed the protective quilted padding worn for such training sessions with his blunted sword.

As Akbar and Bairam Khan paused for breath, Humayun saw a man wearing a heavy sheepskin jacket, his face muffled beneath a red woollen cloth, enter the courtyard. He spoke urgently to one of the numerous guards, who pointed first to the officers' quarters and then to Humayun's own apartments. Ten minutes later, Humayun heard a knock on the door and Jauhar entered. 'Majesty, one of Ahmed Khan's spies has arrived, bringing news from the south. Ahmed Khan seeks your urgent permission to bring him into your presence to report in person. They are outside.'

'Let them come in.'

Moments later, the familiar, straggle-bearded figure of Ahmed Khan appeared. Behind him was the man in the sheepskin Humayun had seen in the courtyard. He had removed his red scarf and headgear to reveal a stubbly beard and thinning dark hair, both of which made him appear older than he probably was. Ahmed Khan and the newcomer bowed low.

'What is it, Ahmed Khan?'

'This is Hussein Kalil – one of our best and most trusted scouts. He has just returned from the south around Khowst.'

'He was with the caravan that I just saw arrive, wasn't he? He clearly brings important news if he has come to us so soon after his arrival, without even stopping for a bowl of soup or to warm himself before the fires just lit in the caravanserai.'

'It is important news – serious too. Your half-brother Kamran is raising yet another rebellion, collecting forces south of Khowst.'

Humayun grimaced. This was news he had half expected to hear but had hoped not to. After Hindal's death and Askari's departure on his pilgrimage, Kamran seemed to have disappeared from the face of the earth despite the most extensive searches by Humayun's troops. Humayun had tried to convince himself that Kamran had decided that he too should abandon the struggle and retreated to some remote area or sought exile, leaving Humayun freer than he had ever been since he had lost the throne of Hindustan to focus all his efforts and all his resources on recovering it.

However, in his heart Humayun had known all along that Kamran had always been the most resolute and determined of his fraternal foes and was unlikely ever to desist from his rebellions and liberate Humayun for the reconquest of Hindustan. There could be no peace, no truce between them. Kamran had never lost a deep-seated resentment fuelled by his belief that Humayun's five-month advantage in age alone had led Babur to give him all. Perhaps he even felt that Babur had loved the unworthy Humayun more than himself – probably his mother Gulrukh had encouraged him in such a belief. Humayun could not be certain of any of this, but he knew he must act against his half-brother once more and this time put an end to his threat for ever. 'Whereabouts exactly is Kamran?'

'On the borders of our Afghan territories and those of the Baluchis,' Ahmed Khan replied. 'The high mountains, secluded valleys and remote caves provide good hiding places for all sorts of rebels and bandits and are almost impregnable to those who do not have local supporters. But may Hussein Kalil tell his own story?'

'Of course.'

Hussein Kalil shuffled from foot to foot and, eyes on the ground, began slightly nervously, gaining in confidence as he went on.

'Under Ahmed Khan's orders I was travelling in the south, in the guise of an itinerant seller of medicine – I have some knowledge of the subject. I was nearing Khowst when I heard rumours that your half-brother had taken refuge in a hill fortress about fifty miles away. I determined to go there and set out along the steep, stony tracks, over the numerous passes and small, twisting, fast-flowing rivers. As I got nearer to my destination, I noticed how full the wayside resting places and the *chai khanas* – the tea houses – were. Nearly all their customers were travelling in the same direction as myself. Most were well armed and strongly built. It took little effort to deduce that they were on their way to join your brother's force and indeed some were ready enough to tell me so. Nevertheless, I decided to see the fortress for myself and to confirm the presence of your brother Kamran and the number of his men before returning.'

'What did you find when you got there?'

'When I reached Kamran's stronghold after a few days more, I discovered it was, in fact, a small fortified village at the head of a narrow valley, high in the hills. Its mud walls were tall and thick and around them was a cluster of felt tents, housing recruits such as those I'd seen along the way. Trusting in my disguise as a medicine seller I entered the iron-studded gates in the walls and made my way to the small market place. Stalls edged its sides, selling vegetables and the like, but in the centre a stout man – clearly an officer – was inspecting a line of potential recruits and their mounts, prodding the men in the walls of their stomachs to check their muscles, testing the sharpness of their weapons and examining the teeth and legs of their horses. Before he had got a third of the way down the line, your half-brother rode up on a tall ginger horse with some of his men and called the recruits to gather around him. As a brief flurry of snow fell, sprinkling everybody and everything with white, he addressed them.'

'What did he say?'

'Forgive me, Majesty. I am not sure I should repeat his harsh words, for they concerned you.'

'Go on. The words will be his not yours, and I will hear them.'

'They went something like this: "My half-brother, the emperor, is a weak, indecisive man, not worthy to rule. Despite his protestations he remains addicted to opium. It makes him sluggish and hesitant. He has had many opportunities to regain the throne of Hindustan but failed to grasp them. I – not he – have the true hunger for land and booty that inspired Babur, my father. Be loyal to me and I will bring you great reward."'

Humayun tensed and clenched his fist. How typical of the devious Kamran to spice his lies with a grain of truth. Yes, he had sometimes again resorted to the solace of opium as relief from the aching disappointment of his failure to make progress in the recovery of

Hindustan. But the cause of that failure was Kamran himself and his constant rebellions. Humayun controlled himself. 'How did the men react?'

'They cheered him and he beckoned to one of those accompanying him, who produced a large green leather purse. Your brother extracted some silver coins and gave five to each man, saying, "These are mere tokens of the rewards you will gain." Eyes shining with greed, they roared out "Kamran Padishah! We will follow you to the death."'

'That will be a short journey. If they and Kamran persist in their rebellion they will surely die. But continue.'

'I remained at the settlement for four days, talking to the recruits and spying on their preparations for war. One white-haired officer who was suffering badly from chilblains for which I prescribed a mustard patch that – I thank God – seemed to help him, told me that they were to begin their march on Kabul in a week. I waited no longer but retraced my steps. Ten days ago, for protection against bandits and lawless tribes, I joined the caravan that arrived today.'

'You have done well, Hussein Kalil. Ahmed Khan, send scouts to check for signs of my brother's approach.'

'I have done so already, Majesty.'

Within half an hour, Humayun was surrounded by his military advisers in an inner room of the citadel warmed by a great log fire. Humayun spoke first, summarising what Hussein Kalil had reported and then went on, anger in his eyes and a steely determination in his voice, 'I will brook no more of my half-brother's disloyalty. Provided the scouts confirm his advance I propose to ride out to confront him before he nears Kabul, perhaps taking him unawares in the passes.' He paused, then asked, 'Bairam Khan, how many men can we muster quickly?'

'Around four thousand, Majesty. It's good that we'd already started recruiting among the tribes around Kabul for the probing campaign towards the Indus you are contemplating.'

'Will the recruits remain loyal? Those tribes are fractious and rent by feuds.'

'We believe so, Majesty. As you know, we gave them a bounty on recruitment and promised more after each victory.'

'Good. We will march in five days.'

Four days later – preparations had taken less time than Humayun had originally thought – he rode on his black horse down the stone ramp of the citadel of Kabul to the parade ground on the plain below where his army of four thousand men had assembled, pennants flying in the stiff chill breeze. As Humayun took his place in the centre of the column, he reflected that although they were many fewer than the troops he had once deployed in Hindustan, they should be more than enough to defeat Kamran. Nearly all his men were mounted and while he had decided, for speed of movement, not to take cannon with him, many of his soldiers had six-foot-long muskets tied to their saddles. Others had bows and quivers full of arrows across their backs.

Ahmed Khan's spies had confirmed that Kamran was indeed on the move and that by now he should be no more than ten days away from Kabul, advancing up the long defile through the Safed mountain range. Because the campaign would be short – they might expect to clash in battle in less than a week – Humayun had ordered the provisions and equipment they carried to be kept to a minimum. Most of it – like the felt tents to keep out the late frosts, the copper cooking pots and the sacks of rice – was loaded in wicker panniers strapped on the backs of camels. The rest was carried by the lines of pack horses and mules waiting, roped together and restive, at the rear of the column.

Once arrived among his officers, Humayun waved to his trumpeters to sound their long brass trumpets and to his drummers to beat out their martial tattoo on the drums slung on either side of their horses. This was the signal for the column to move off, which it did with a jangling of harness and neighing of horses and the foul-breathed snorting of the haughty-looking camels.

Late in the afternoon of the third day, as the sun was dropping low over the jagged mountains lining the valley as it descended to the south, Humayun was discussing with his officers where best to make camp for the night when Ahmed Khan cantered up. A white-haired

340

man with a weather-beaten face was riding by his side. Humayun saw he was guiding his long-haired mountain pony with only one hand and that the bottom of the right sleeve of his brown wool jacket flapped empty. The old man dismounted with surprising agility and bowed to Humayun.

'Majesty,' Ahmed Khan began, 'this is Wazim Pathan. When one of our scouts entered his village he asked to be brought here. He claims he was one of three soldiers you rewarded in front of the whole army before the battle of Kanauj. He had lost his hand and lower arm in a skirmish with Sher Shah's advancing troops and you discharged him to return home with a bag of coin. As proof he showed me this.' Ahmed Khan produced a faded red velvet bag with the mark of the Moghul empire embroidered upon it.

'I remember both the occasion and you, Wazim Pathan, well. The years have been kind to you and I am glad to see you.'

'Majesty, I have told Ahmed Khan that I wish to repay some little portion of the debt of gratitude I owe you. Over the years, I have become the headman of my small village in a side valley off the main track only two miles from here. I was born and brought up in these mountains you see around you and I know all the paths. There is one which climbs up through the scree slopes behind my village and then winds between tumbled rocks to a position high above this main valley road along which your traitorous half-brother must pass. From those heights you could ambush him, shooting his men down and attacking him in the rear.'

Humayun had no doubt that Wazim Pathan was telling the truth. 'We will halt tonight near your village and in the early morning explore the paths you suggest. Now we must hurry if we're to make camp before darkness falls completely.'

· ◆ ·

Wazim Pathan had begged Humayun to use his small windowless flat-roofed mud house, with its central fireplace vented by a hole in the roof, as his temporary headquarters. To honour his old soldier, Humayun had agreed, although he had slept in his usual tent erected under Jauhar's watchful eye within the low walls of Wazim Pathan's

341

compound. Just before first light, Ahmed Khan and some of his men had departed to check the practicality of Wazim Pathan's proposed route for an army the size of theirs. Now, just after the sun had reached its zenith, Humayun could see them returning, their horses zigzagging their way down tracks through the grey scree-strewn slope of the nearest of the mountains.

'Majesty,' reported Ahmed Khan when, three-quarters of an hour later, Humayun and his military commanders sat around the fire in Wazim Pathan's humble home, sometimes coughing as gusts of wind blew smoke back into the room through the hole in the roof, 'it is indeed possible to get armed men along the paths Wazim Pathan has shown us, though not all the army could go that way. The track leads to a position overlooking the valley just where it narrows into a defile. It is ideally suited to ambushing your half-brother's men.'

'What do our scouts who are shadowing Kamran's troops report about their progress?'

'They should pass below the ambush position around midday the day after tomorrow.'

'Then,' said Humayun, putting an end to any further debate, 'my mind is made up. We will take six hundred of our best men including most of our musketeers up into the ambush place. Zahid Beg, you will select who will come. Tell them to take not only their arms but also animals' skins and blankets to keep them warm in the night we must spend up there as well as enough water and cold food for two days. We will light no fires either for warmth or for cooking in case they reveal our position. The rest of our men will remain here under your command, Bairam Khan, to barricade the main road to block the way of any of Kamran's men who are left alive and try to flee north along the road towards Kabul.'

Next morning, beneath a clear blue sky and with Wazim Pathan on his tough pony and Ahmed Khan on his usual brown mare at his side, Humayun rode out from Wazim Pathan's small village towards the nearby mountain and the track leading upward through its scree slopes. After an hour, he and the front of the column had reached the area of jumbled, tumbled boulders and began slowly and in single file picking their way upwards through them and across gullies in which snow had collected and frozen. At the end of another hour and a half, Wazim Pathan pointed to a ridge about half a mile ahead. 'Majesty, over that ridge lies the main road that runs south from Kabul – the one that your brother will come up.'

Humayun and Ahmed Khan followed Wazim Pathan as, with his single hand, he guided his pony through more rocks and boulders towards the crest of the ridge. Once on the top, which still had a thick covering of frozen snow, Humayun could see that it afforded a great vantage point over the road and that the rocks lower down were ideal to conceal musketeers to fire upon any unsuspecting army advancing towards Kabul.

Humayun spoke. 'The musketeers will have to eat and sleep in those rocks just in case Kamran and his men arrive earlier than we expect. Ahmed Khan, give orders for them to take up their positions immediately, carrying with them their bedding and provisions as well as their weapons. But what of the rest of us, Wazim Pathan? Is there any flat ground nearby where we could bivouac before exploring further along the ridge? We need to find a place from which to sally down to take Kamran's men in the rear so we can drive them forward under our musketeers' fire.'

'Yes, Majesty. There is a flat area of land in the lee of the ridge about three-quarters of a mile further on where we could camp. From there I will guide you along a path which descends towards a place where the scree slopes more gently to the road and it would be possible for skilled horsemen to charge straight down rather than having to zigzag.'

In the deep cold of the next morning an hour before dawn, as Humayun was slapping his arms against his sides to warm himself and readying himself for the day ahead, Ahmed Khan reported to him that one of the musketeers who had been stationed in a particularly exposed position overlooking the road had died of cold. 'He deserved to die,' was Ahmed Khan's unsympathetic explanation. 'He brought spirits not water to drink and not enough bedding.'

'Are the other musketeers awake and alert?'

'Yes, Majesty.'

'Are they in position and have they checked their weapons?'

343

'Again yes, Majesty.'

'Good. Now have the remaining men mount up. As soon as it's light enough we'll make our way along the track I explored yesterday afternoon with Wazim Pathan to what is indeed an ideal launching point for our attack on Kamran's rear. The path is narrow and icy with steep drops in places. Tell our men to take care, particularly as the wind is rising.'

An hour later, Humayun, his face numb despite his woollen face cloth from the cold wind blowing from the north, had just traversed the narrowest part of the route, which was less than two feet wide with precipitous drops on both sides, when he heard a cry from behind, followed by a thud and then a second heavier one from below. Turning in his saddle, he saw that one of the riders following him had fallen from the ridge together with his mount, perhaps caught by one of the increasingly frequent heavy gusts of wind. The man's sheepskin-jacketed body was spread-eagled on a ledge only about thirty feet below but the horse had landed much lower down among jagged rocks which had penetrated its body and spilled its intestines.

As Humayun watched, another rider and his horse toppled from the track, crashing down to land among the jagged grey rocks. Humayun spoke urgently. 'Pass the word back. Any man who is uncertain either of himself or of his horse should dismount and lead his animal across the narrowest and most exposed stretch. There is no shame in that.'

After that, all of Humayun's men got over safely, except one whose bay horse stumbled on the ice as he led it across. The animal fell, hooves flailing at thin air, pulling its rider – a small, black-bearded Badakhshani – with it as, desperately trying to steady it, he failed to let go of the reins before he too overbalanced and plunged from the path.

Half an hour later, Humayun and his men had concealed themselves and their horses as best they could among the jumbled rocks at the top of the slope of pewter-grey scree down which they intended to charge to ambush Kamran's men. Humayun knew they would have some hours to wait. The very latest scouting report to reach him indicated that Kamran's troops might not get to this point until two or even three o'clock in the afternoon. It would leave little time to draw any battle to a decisive conclusion before the early sundown.

In fact, it was a little after three when Humayun himself peering, eyes narrowed in concentration, from behind a large boulder, was the first to spot Kamran's vanguard ascending the road. They seemed to have no scouts or pickets posted and not to be keeping any formal order. Clearly, they had no suspicion of ambush. Humayun motioned Ahmed Khan to him. 'Pass the message to the men not to attack until I give the signal. It'll be a little while until enough of the column has passed by for us to be able to charge down on their rear. When we do, it must be hard and fast, leaving Kamran no chance to rally his men.'

For perhaps a quarter of an hour Humayun waited as Kamran's men continued to advance, chatting and laughing as they rode. During that time Humayun thought he saw his half-brother riding a chestnut horse in the centre of the column but at such a distance he could not be sure. When the last element of the rearguard and the straggle of camp followers were making their way beneath his hiding place, Humayun signalled his men to mount. Immediately they had done so, with a wave of his gauntleted hand he set his four hundred riders in motion. Together they charged down the scree slope.

Although less precipitous than elsewhere, the descent was still steep and as Humayun rode down, leaning back in his saddle to help his horse keep its balance, he saw one of his men's horses lose its footing and fall headlong, catapulting its rider over its neck and rolling over and over down through the loose, powdery scree. However, almost instantly, Humayun and his men were among Kamran's rearguard, striking and slashing around them. In the first minute of the attack, Humayun felled a black-turbaned rider from his saddle as he struggled to free his sword from its scabbard beneath his sheepskin. He wounded another in the thigh before he too could raise a weapon and inflicted a deep sword cut on a third's arm.

Kamran's horsemen seemed taken completely by surprise. The hindmost of them surged instinctively forward away from their attackers, crashing into their comrades in front and, as they did so, panicking their horses and in turn propelling them onwards up the valley road. Soon Humayun heard the first musket shots from the boulders high on the hillside where his musketeers were concealed. From his position within the crush and dust of battle, Humayun could not see their direct effect, but he could see confusion and surprise turning to absolute panic and fear around him.

Some of Kamran's men tried to turn their rearing horses and force them back through their attackers, to return south and away from the musket fire. None succeeded; all were either killed or felled from their horses. Others tried to ride up the steep scree slopes. Humayun saw some of these topple from the saddle, presumably shot down by his musketeers. Within twenty minutes, cohesion and discipline in Kamran's ragtag army was evaporating. Pockets of his desperate, frightened men were dismounting, throwing down their weapons and raising their hands above their heads in token of surrender.

Gathering some of his own troops around him, Humayun pushed his black horse through Kamran's disintegrating army in search of his brother, striking left and right as he did so. But he could not find Kamran. Once he thought he saw him on his chestnut horse, but as he swerved closer he realised that the rider was in fact a younger man, probably an officer, who quickly kicked his horse to escape but not quickly enough to prevent Humayun's sword slicing into his helmetless head and splitting it like a ripe watermelon.

Shouts from the north where his main force under Bairam Khan would have engaged Kamran's fleeing men from behind the barricades showed that the fight had been joined there too. Unable to distinguish clearly enough between friend and foe in the mass of fighters below, and with their sight partially obscured by smoke from their weapons, Humayun's musketeers in the rocks above dropped their muskets and drew their swords before charging and sliding their way down through the scree into the chaotic battle.

Humayun, still eager above all to capture his brother, broke away and with a dozen riders made for the barricades. Before he had gone half a mile he was confronted by a band of about twenty of Kamran's men galloping back towards him. Urging his black horse on, Humayun gathered speed. So too did those around him. The two groups met head on. One of Kamran's men cut at Humayun's head with his sword but the blow glanced off his helmet. At the same time, Humayun's sword sliced into his opponent's upper arm. Not expecting an attack, very few of Kamran's men had been wearing chain mail so Humayun's sword bit deep, splintering bone and almost severing the arm.

A second man swung at Humayun with a battle flail. One of the spikes on the ball at the end of its chain nicked Humayun's nose as it whirled, parting the air in front of his face. His nose felt numb and instantly blood ran into his mouth and down the back of his throat. However, turning his horse tightly, he pursued his assailant who swung his flail once more, this time wildly, missing Humayun by a distance. As he passed, Humayun slashed at the back of the man's neck. The stroke deflected off his opponent's helmet, losing some of its force, but still cut into his neck, drawing blood. The man fell forward, losing control of his horse which reared up, throwing him heavily to the ground where he struggled to rise but soon collapsed and lay still.

'Look out, Majesty, behind you!' Humayun turned only just in time as another of Kamran's men rode into the attack with his curved scimitar held high. This time Humayun's response was instant and instinctive – a sword cut over the head of his assailant's horse and into his groin. He fell at once.

As he coughed and spat the salty, metallic-tasting blood from his mouth, Humayun saw that he and his men had killed eight of their twenty assailants and that the rest had lost their appetite for the fight and were fleeing. Within moments Humayun was once more riding hard up the stony track towards the barricades, only, almost immediately, to see Bairam Khan leading a detachment of around five hundred of his own horsemen towards him, his scarlet banner flying.

Reining in his snorting, foam-flecked horse, Bairam Khan said, face creased in a triumphant smile, 'Kamran's men are fleeing in every direction.' Looking around him in the now gathering dusk, Humayun saw that victory was his – but was it really a victory? To his intense disappointment he had failed to capture his half-brother – something he must do before he could safely turn to his great enterprise, the recapture of Hindustan.

'Make sure we pursue and capture as many of Kamran's men as we can before night falls entirely. I'll offer a bag of gold coin to anyone who takes my traitorous half-brother alive or dead.'

Chapter 23

Doing Good to the Evil

Humayun lay back against a red and gold brocade cushion and away from the low gilded table piled with silver plates from which he and Hamida had just eaten their midday meal. Humayun had chosen chicken baked slowly with spices and yoghurt in the tandoor – the clay oven that was essential to any Moghul kitchen and was always taken with them on campaign. He smiled at Hamida who after taking a bite from a sticky orange sweetmeat was daintily rinsing her fingers in a small, engraved copper bowl of rosewater. She smiled back. As he watched a shaft of sunlight fall through the casement on to the small, bubbling marble fountain behind her, Humayun felt content.

He smiled again at Hamida and from the quiver in her lips and the twinkle in her eyes he realized that she knew he was contemplating love-making after the meal and she would welcome it. He was about to stretch his arm out to her when her attendant Zainab entered. Even before she spoke, Humayun saw from the anxiety on her face that his afternoon of warm, languorous love would have to be postponed.

'Majesty. Ahmed Khan begs your urgent presence – they have captured your half-brother Kamran.' As Zainab spoke the words, Humayun saw Hamida's expression suddenly change from that of a warm lover to a triumphant, avenging mother. She had never forgiven

– never mind forgotten – Kamran's treatment of her only son and had often rebuked Humayun for the number of times he had spared Kamran's life. She had frequently quoted to him some lines from her favourite Persian poet: *Bad earth does not produce hyacinths, so don't waste seeds of hope in it. Doing good to the evil is as bad as doing evil to the good.*

Before Humayun could say anything, Hamida burst out, 'Praise God for his capture. This time I hope there'll be no talk of mercy. He's had far more chances than he deserves and each time spurned the opportunity you gave him to reform. His resentment of you runs so deep within him he will never relent. Don't think twice. Have him executed within the hour, if not for my sake, for that of our son whose life he held so cheap.'

Humayun said nothing as he rose to leave the room, pausing only to grab his father's sword Alamgir. Nevertheless, he felt some of the same deep anger so clear in Hamida's words welling up within him. It mingled with an almost ecstatic relief that at last he would be free of Kamran's threat to his rear while he pressed on with his plans for probing raids beyond the Indus to test the strength of Islam Shah's grip on Hindustan.

Ahmed Khan was waiting in the sunlit courtyard as Humayun emerged through the silver-lined doors of the women's quarters.

'Where did you capture him, Ahmed Khan, and how?'

'Two days ago we seized a petty tribal chief who had supported Kamran in his last rebellion. We brought him to the citadel and confined him in the dungeons. Early this morning he asked for me and in a bid to reduce his punishment he hinted that he knew where Kamran might be. I told him I could make no deals without reference to you, Majesty, but he should tell me immediately what he knew. He could be sure that if Kamran were found you would not be ungrateful. He said he believed that Kamran was hiding in a poor quarter of Kabul itself – the area around the tanneries. He admitted when I pressed him that his information was old – at least a week – and that his informant, a petty thief who had been among Kamran's camp followers, was not necessarily reliable. Nevertheless, I thought it worthwhile to send a strong detachment of our men immediately down to the tanneries area to cordon it off and make a house to house search.

'I'm glad I did, Majesty. When the soldiers came to the house of a tanner whose family is from the south, the tanner seemed panic-stricken and tried to prevent them entering, claiming that his wife's mother was lying gravely ill with the spotted fever. My men pushed him aside and searched the house, throwing aside piles of skins and even probing with their spears the deep copper vats of dye and urine used for tanning. They found nothing, but still convinced that the tanner was hiding something – or someone – they entered the curtained-off portion of the top floor where the tanner claimed his sick mother-in-law was lying. Here they found a body hunched beneath some dirty blankets. Pulling the blankets off they saw a large figure with big feet and hands – too big for a woman, they thought – curled up like a baby. The so-called "mother-in-law" was wearing rough women's garments and had a thick black veil of the type worn by Arab women over her face. She was pleading piteously in a high-pitched voice to be left to die in peace. Nevertheless, the officer leading the party reached out to lift up her veil. As he did so, the figure pulled a dagger from the voluminous folds of her grubby brown robe and stabbed him in the forearm. Two of the officer's men quickly restrained her, and without her veil it was clear she was no woman but your stubble-chinned half-brother.

'At first he struggled and screamed that you were a worthless ruler and he the rightful king; that our men were lickspittles of a wastrel and should come to their senses and let him go. However, after a little he grew silent, seemingly resigned to whatever fate had in store for him.'

'Where is my half-brother now?'

'In the dungeons below the citadel, Majesty.'

In his mind's eye, Humayun saw the three-year-old Akbar on the battlements of Kabul and again felt a sudden surge of anger against his half-brother. How easily Akbar could have been killed. How many others had died in Kamran's rebellions? He drew his sword Alamgir from its jewelled scabbard.

'Ahmed Khan, take me to Kamran.'

Swiftly, Ahmed Khan led the way across the courtyard, through a low door with guards on either side, and down a series of steep steps into the damp lower reaches of the citadel. Humayun struggled to adjust his eyes to the darkness of the interior corridors in which only an occasional oil lamp burned in an alcove. As his vision improved he thought he saw a large rat run close along the wall. At least he could stop his rat of a brother living to infect others with the disease of rebellion, he thought, and tightened his grip on his sword hilt. By now they were approaching the door of Kamran's cell, which was guarded by four of Ahmed Khan's men.

'Let me enter alone,' said Humayun. 'I will deal with this obdurate traitor. I alone should spill my family's blood.'

One of the guards pulled back the heavy iron bolts at the top and bottom of the thick wooden door. Humayun entered the small cell and there was Kamran, whom he had not seen for over five years, slumped on the straw-covered floor, his back against the damp stone wall. He was still dressed in the brown women's clothes he'd been wearing when he was captured. They were full of holes, and with the heavy black veil thrown back over his head he looked ridiculous not rebellious.

After a moment, Kamran got slowly to his feet. He avoided Humayun's eye, and it was he who broke the silence first. 'I'm not going to plead with you for my life. So don't think I'm about to fall at your feet and beg for mercy. I see our father's sword in your hand. Use it. Kill me. If I were in your position I wouldn't hesitate . . . There's only one thing I want . . .' and here he raised his green eyes for the first time and looked deep into Humayun's. 'Bury me next to our father.'

Humayun stared unflinchingly back. 'Why should I when you have dishonoured his memory? Why should I when you have broken every promise you ever made to me, thrown back my offers of peace and reconciliation, and worst of all exposed my son to danger?'

'To prove you're better than me, just as you loved to do when we were children. But what do I care about where my body lies. Get it over with. Prove you're not the weakling everyone, including me, knows you are.' Kamran pushed his face into Humayun's and spat a great gob of rancid-smelling spittle into his eye.

But Humayun did not react. Suddenly the real wisdom behind Babur's dying words, *Do nothing against your brothers, however much you think they may deserve it*, had hit him with a new clarity. Babur had been protecting Humayun as much as his brothers. Could he live with himself if he murdered his own brother in anger? By inciting him to kill him now in this squalid cell, Kamran – who knew him so well – was setting one last trap for him, daring him to set honour aside and descend to his level, and in his anger to prove that all his previous gestures of reconciliation had been acts of weakness, not of mercy.

Humayun lowered his sword and wiped away the spittle. 'I am pleased you recognise you deserve death but I'll consult with my counsellors as to your fate. If you die it will be an act of cool justice and not hot vengeance.' As he turned to leave, Humayun thought he saw a brief half-smile cross Kamran's lips. Was he laughing at him for what he saw as his weakness or, after all, was he simply relieved that for the moment he would live?

When he turned back to look at Kamran again, his half-brother's eyes were downcast once more, his face expressionless.

• ◆ •

Humayun scrutinised his counsellors, gathered in his sunlit audience chamber. His own mood was dark. He needed to decide the fate of Kamran. To delay would be to appear weak. His counsellors too seemed grave as he began.

'It is for me to take the decision whether my half-brother Kamran should live or die but I wish to seek your views. Undoubtedly he has been responsible for the death of many men in the rebellions he has raised against me. His opposition has weakened my power, delayed my plans to reconquer Hindustan, as well as exposed my son Akbar to danger. Yet he is my half-brother, my father's son and of the blood of Timur. If I am to spill that blood I must do so only if I am convinced that there is no other course I can take and that his death is for the sake of justice and the benefit of my realm and its people. Give me your views.'

'Majesty,' Bairam Khan stepped forward, his voice firm and clear, 'I think I speak for all of us here. There can be no doubt. Your half-brother should die for the sake of you, your son, your dynasty and us all. Kamran is not your brother, he is your enemy. Put aside any brotherly feelings you have for him. They have no place in a ruler's decisions. If you wish to remain king and to achieve the ambition we all share of regaining the throne of Hindustan for yourself and your son there is only one course to take. Execute him. Am I not right, my fellow commanders?'

Without hesitation and as with one voice they answered, 'Yes!'

'Does none of you advocate any other solution?' Humayun asked.

'No, Majesty.'

'Thank you. I will ponder your advice.' Humayun walked straight from the room, his brow furrowed. The decision was not as easy as his counsellors suggested. They did not share Kamran's blood as he did. Without thinking consciously of what he was doing, Humayun headed for the women's apartments and when he got there went straight to Gulbadan's room. His half-sister was sitting on a low gilt chair wearing a loose purple silk robe as her attendant pulled an ivory comb through her dark hair. As soon as she saw the expression on Humayun's face, Gulbadan dismissed the woman. 'What is the matter?'

'You know they have captured Kamran once more and he is imprisoned in the dungeons?'

'Of course.'

'I am desperately searching my conscience as to what his fate must be. I realise that by all the normal conventions he deserves death for his many misdeeds and my advisers tell me unanimously that this time he must die. Often, when I've anticipated the moment he'd be in my power again, anger at him for his ill-treatment of Akbar alone has made me want to kill him myself, and Hamida – as Akbar's mother – urges this upon me. However, when I become calmer I know I must not act in anger but for what is best for our empire. I remember our father's injunction to do nothing against my brothers and I hesitate.'

'I understand your dilemma,' Gulbadan said, taking Humayun's hand. 'You have always been a man of your word. Remember how you honoured your promise to Nizam the water-seller that he could sit on your throne for an hour or two, despite the mutterings of your courtiers? Because you always keep your word, you sometimes fail to realise that others like Sher Shah who deceived you before the battle of Chausa – or indeed our half-brothers – will not. You have given Kamran so many chances and he has exploited your mercy so often that even I believe that his persistent wickedness negates any promise you ever made to our father . . .' She paused. 'If I am honest I think he should die. It would be best for the dynasty that our father fought so hard to establish. With Kamran gone you will be free to concentrate on the recapture of Hindustan.'

Humayun said nothing for a long time. At last he spoke very deliberately. 'I know that in logic you are right. I know also our father always said I loved solitude too much . . . but I must go to consider alone for a time before taking my final decision.'

'Why not take our father's memoirs with you to see if they offer you any solace or guidance? After all, he wrote them, as he put it, "to give guidance for living and ruling".'

A few minutes later, Humayun climbed the stone stairs to the top of the highest watchtower on the walls of the citadel in Kabul. In his hand were his father's memoirs which, in their ivory binding, he had preserved so carefully throughout all his vicissitudes. He had left Jauhar at the entrance to the watchtower with strict orders that no one should be allowed to enter. As he reached the top of the stairs and emerged on to the flat roof, Humayun felt that the day's heat was dying. It would be dark in an hour. Perhaps he should wait until the stars came out to see what guidance they might offer him, but then he dismissed the idea. He had learned from the many trials and disappointments he had endured during his life that he could not abdicate responsibility for his decisions to the stars any more than he could to his advisers, his wife or his blood relations.

Babur had told him that he had discovered early that a ruler had to rule. This gave the ruler an unparalleled freedom and opportunity to fulfil his ambitions, but it also made his role an intensely lonely one.

He had not only to take the decisions but to live with the consequences both in this life and when called to judgement in the life beyond.

As the light began to fade, Humayun opened his father's memoirs at random. His eyes first fell on a paragraph which described how, during one of his campaigns, Timur had in a rare moment of mercy followed an older tradition among the dwellers on the steppes and had a powerful member of his own family who had been caught plotting an uprising blinded rather than killed to avoid creating a blood feud. Babur had commended this as a way of disarming a rebel and noted that such punishments still continued among many of the tribes and were considered just and proper.

Immediately, Humayun knew that this must be Kamran's fate. His threat would be extinguished with his sight. No rebellious chief could ever again consider Kamran a rival to Humayun. Yet his half-brother would have time to consider and perhaps to repent before he was called to eternal judgement. Such a punishment would be harsh, but Humayun knew that in inflicting it he would be respecting his instinct to show some mercy and also be taking some account of his father's injunction not to be provoked into unthinking violence against his half-brothers.

Closing the ivory covers of Babur's memoirs, Humayun descended the stairs. 'Call my advisers to me straightaway,' he told Jauhar. Within five minutes they were standing around him. 'I have decided that my half-brother Kamran must be blinded, both as a punishment for his consistent misdeeds and to obviate any threat he might continue to pose to my rule here and to our recovery of our possessions in Hindustan. The punishment will be carried out tonight an hour after sunset. I ask you, Zahid Beg, to take charge. I wish the method to be the quickest known to the *hakims* and my half-brother to be given no warning so that he does not have time to fear what is to come. I do not wish to see his agony and suffering. Jauhar, you will be my witness. However, Kamran needs to know that the punishment has been inflicted on my specific orders and I alone take responsibility for it. Therefore, you will bring my half-brother to me a little before the time of evening prayer tomorrow.

• ◆ •

'Majesty,' reported Jauhar an hour and a half later, 'it is done. The whole thing was over within five minutes or less of Zahid Beg's six men entering the cell. Four of them each seized one of your half-brother's limbs and held him to the ground. As he struggled and kicked, the fifth – a bear of a man – took hold of Kamran's head in his great hands and held it still. The sixth took needles he had previously heated red hot in the flame and quickly pierced each of your brother's eyeballs in turn several times. As Kamran screamed like a wild beast in his agony, the man rubbed lemon juice and salt into his eyeballs to ensure all vision was lost. Then he bound your half-brother's eyes with clean, soft cotton bandages and told him that he had no more to endure. Then they left him to contemplate both his punishment and that he was to live – albeit an impaired life . . .'

• ◆ •

The next evening, just before prayers, Kamran was led into Humayun's presence. His eyes were no longer bandaged and on Humayun's orders he had been washed and clothed in garments befitting a Moghul prince of the blood. Humayun dismissed the guards and spoke softly to Kamran.

'It is I, Humayun, your half-brother. I give you my word we are alone.' As Kamran turned his sightless eyes towards him he continued, 'I want you to know that I and I alone am responsible for your blinding. No blame should attach to those who committed the deed. I acted as I did because I had lost faith that any clemency I showed would cause you to repent and I needed to protect my throne and the future of Akbar and of our dynasty.' Humayun stopped and waited, half expecting a stream of invective from Kamran or even an attempt, despite his blindness, to attack him.

But after a short silence Kamran spoke in a subdued voice. 'You have left me with my life but at the same time taken everything I cared about from me – my plans, my ambitions. I congratulate you. You can appear the great and merciful *padishah* while knowing you have destroyed me more completely than if you'd struck off my head . . .'

Humayun said nothing and after a moment Kamran continued. 'I don't blame you. I have often scorned your mercy and know I deserved punishment. As I lay awake last night, praying for the pain in these now useless eyes to ease and reflecting that my life as I have always known it was over, another thought came into my mind. It was strange, but I felt almost a sense of relief . . . the feeling that finally, after all these years, I could shake off the burden of earthly ambitions. I have one thing and one thing only to ask of you and I ask it sincerely.'

'What is that?'

'I do not wish to remain here, an object of contempt or of pity or even of any generosity you may wish to extend to me. Let me, like Askari, make the *haj* – the pilgrimage to Mecca. It may even afford me some spiritual consolation.'

'Go,' said Humayun, 'go with my blessing.' As he spoke he felt tears wet his cheeks. He was, he realised, crying partly from sadness at the loss of the innocent times he and his half-brother had so briefly enjoyed, partly for the years they had wasted in conflict when together they could have been recovering their father's empire, and partly for the pain he had inflicted on Kamran the night before.

However, above all, his tears reflected a profound and transcending relief. He was now free to concentrate on achieving his ambition once more to be *Padishah* of Hindustan and even to enlarge his dominions and to build the great empire of which Babur had dreamed.

Chapter 24

Warm Bread

M ajesty, Islam Shah is dead. The throne of Hindustan is vacant.
While the masseur kneaded the muscles of his upper back and rubbed sweet-smelling coconut oil into them, Humayun smiled as he remembered the first time – six weeks ago – that he had heard these words from an excited Ahmed Khan. Over the subsequent days the rumours had grown stronger, brought by travellers making the journey up through the Khyber Pass from Hindustan. Some had said that Islam Shah had died unexpectedly several months ago and that his supporters had been successful for a time in concealing the fact while they tried to agree on a successor. With each passing day and with each piece of news, renewed energy had pulsed through Humayun. He could feel a great opportunity to recover his throne opening up. Free of anxiety about threats to Kabul from his half-brothers if he left the city, he would grasp it and put an end to his long years of disappointment and exile.

Immediately, he had taken measures to prepare his army for action. At this very minute outside the walls of the citadel, his officers were drilling his musketeers to increase the speed and discipline with which they primed, loaded and fired their weapons. His recruiting agents were busy in the remotest valleys of his kingdom and beyond gathering additional recruits. The masseur now pummelling Humayun's thighs and buttocks was also part of Humayun's mental and physical preparation. To help plan his campaign he had begun to re-read his father's memoirs of his attack on Hindustan and to compare them with his own recollections of the invasion.

He had tried in conversation with his commanders, particularly Ahmed Khan, to understand where he had made mistakes in his own campaigns against Sher Shah and why he had succeeded elsewhere such as in Gujarat. Sitting alone in his apartments late one evening he had summed it up to himself. 'Prepare well, think and act fast and decisively. Make your opponent respond to you and not the other way round.'

Over the years he had allowed himself to indulge once more in the wines of Ghazni and, since he had regained Kabul, just occasionally in the care-numbing relief of the opium pipe. Now, to sharpen his mind and toughen his body for the rigours of warfare, he was, after a great internal struggle and an enormous effort of will, abstaining entirely from both alcohol and opium. He had also taken up wrestling again and the masseur was readying him for his daily training contest. With a quick gesture to the man to cease his work, Humayun rolled over on to his back and stood up. He pulled on a pair of long cotton trousers, his only clothing for the fight, and made his way through some fine yellow muslin curtains into the next room. Here his opponent, a tall, heavily muscled Badakhshani, awaited him, similarly clothed and oiled.

'Don't hold back, Bayzid Khan.' Humayun smiled. 'You have taught me well. There's a bag of coin in it for you if you can overcome me within ten minutes. Now let's get on with it.'

The two men circled each other, waiting to see who made the first move. It was Humayun who darted forward to seize Bayzid Khan's arm and try to throw him. However, Bayzid Khan twisted himself from Humayun's grip and in turn grabbed Humayun's shoulders to pull him off balance. Humayun resisted and the two men struggled, arms on each other's shoulders, testing their strength. Then Bayzid Khan tripped Humayun with a swift kick of his foot to the back of Humayun's knee. Humayun fell and Bayzid Khan launched himself to pinion him against the mat on the floor and end the contest.

But Humayun was too quick and rolled away. As Bayzid Khan landed on the mat, Humayun leaped on him and putting his knee in his back pulled both his arms out behind him. Hard as Bayzid Khan struggled he could not free himself. 'Enough, Majesty. You have got the better of me for the second time.'

'The first, I think. I strongly suspected that previously you let me win, but not on this occasion.'

'Perhaps, Majesty.'

Humayun returned to his robing room and washed himself clean of the mixture of sweat and oil coating his body in the large copper bath of warm, camphor-scented water that his servants had prepared during the contest. As he dried himself with a rough cotton towel and dusted himself with sandalwood-scented chalk powder, he looked at his naked body in a nearby burnished mirror. His muscles were more toned and prominent than a month ago. His looks belied his forty-six years, he thought, and smiled with satisfaction. The exercise seemed to be helping him focus his mind and think more clearly. Certainly too he was making love more frequently.

With the help of his attendants, Humayun quickly dressed, ready to meet his counsellors. Minutes later, wearing a gold-belted navy tunic and a cream turban with a long peacock's feather at its peak, he entered the council chamber.

'What is the latest news from Hindustan, Ahmed Khan? Didn't another caravan come in this morning?'

'Yes, Majesty. It brought confirmation of what is for us good news. There can be no doubt that Islam Shah is dead. What is more, a rich merchant in today's caravan says that fighting has broken out among three contenders for the throne in and around Delhi. With no proper authority dacoits have been robbing with impunity, invading the homes of the wealthy by night, stealing, raping and killing. The merchant concealed some of his treasure and packed the rest and brought his family on the arduous journey north to your realm to be safe until he sees what happens in Hindustan. Other members of the caravan substantiated his news with many circumstantial details of the chaos. One reported that when robbers could not remove valuable rings from the arthritic fingers of a rich old woman, they simply hacked off her fingers and left her to bleed to death.'

'The fighting and lawlessness will give us the opportunity we have looked for to regain the throne and to bring back justice and order to the citizens of our rightful kingdom. What do we know about these three other contenders?'

'One is Adil Shah, the brother of Islam Shah's favourite wife – the mother of his only son, a boy of five years of age. Adil Shah is said to have been so drunk with ambition that oblivious of the ties of blood he entered the *haram* and cut the child's throat in front of his mother with as little concern as a butcher slaughtering a beast for the table. Then he had himself proclaimed emperor.'

Humayun blanched. Not even Kamran had stooped so low. 'And the other two?'

'The most powerful is a cousin of Islam Shah who has had himself proclaimed emperor as Sekunder Shar. He's already defeated Adil Shah once but failed to follow up his victory because of the activities of the third pretender, Tartar Khan, the head of the old Lodi clan we supplanted and who fought against us with the Sultan of Gujarat.'

'We need to obtain as much information as we can about each of them – who their friends and enemies are, their personal strengths and vices, how many men, how much money they have.'

'We will question the recently arrived travellers further. And of course send out more spies and scouts.'

'We will resume our discussion tomorrow to plan our campaign in detail. Now is the time for our evening meal.' Humayun turned to leave the audience chamber. However, as he did so, Ahmed Khan approached him and handed him a small square of paper.

'One of the travellers brought this sealed message which he told our guards was for your eyes only. He said that a member of his family – a sailor who had just returned from Arabia and heard that he was travelling to Kabul – had asked him to bring it to you. It is probably nothing, Majesty, but I thought I should leave it to you to open.'

'Thank you, Ahmed Khan. I will read it shortly.'

A quarter of an hour later, Humayun entered the women's quarters and made his way to Hamida's apartments. Looking up, she said, 'I hear there is good news from Hindustan . . .'

Humayun smiled, but the smile and his eyes were clouded by a look of melancholy. 'The news from Hindustan is indeed good, but I've received other, sadder news today. It's about Askari. As you know, I've long feared that some accident had befallen him since I'd had no news of him after the message eighteen months ago that he had taken ship from Cambay for the holy lands around Mecca. Today I received confirmation of his fate . . .'

Humayun pulled from his pocket the paper which Ahmed Khan had handed him. It had many creases and folds. 'It is from Mohamed Azruddin – the commander of the escort I provided for my brother. It tells briefly how the voyage from Cambay was going well with favourable winds when about twenty miles from the port of Salala on the Arab coast a fleet of three fast pirate vessels overhauled their ship. Askari led the fight against the pirates as they boarded but was overwhelmed and killed, sword in hand. Many others died with him. Mohamed Azruddin was badly wounded and captured with the remainder of the escort and the coin they were carrying. On his recovery he was sold in the great slave market of Muscat to work in the quarries outside the town. He escaped his captors six months ago and his first action was to send this message to me in advance of his return.'

'May God forgive Askari for his misdeeds and may his soul rest in Paradise,' said Hamida. After a few moments she continued, 'Nevertheless, this definite news of his death frees you from any fear that he might have disappeared on purpose to plot in exile against you.'

'True, but he was never so committed an adversary as Kamran and often, I think, acted only from loyalty to his brother and mother. I believed him when, before he left on the *haj*, he said he'd renounced all thoughts of rebellion. His death makes me more conscious that I am the only one left to fulfil the destiny my father saw for his family.'

'For a long time you have been the only one of his sons to be true to his memory.'

'But I have lost much of his empire and failed to recover it, never mind to expand his dominions. I have let myself and you, as well as my father, down. My intentions have been good but I've not been single-minded enough to carry them through.'

'That is changing. Since Askari's departure for the *haj* and that of Kamran too, I have seen a real determination within you. You no longer allow your mind to be distracted by pleasure or idle musing. You've always wanted to recover what is yours, but now you give time and concentration to achieving it.'

'I hope so. I've used bitter memories of how I lost my throne, of your face in our bleakest moment when Akbar was taken from us, of how we passed, frozen and half-starving, into Persia as suppliants to the shah, to act as goads to focus all my energies on recovering Hindustan.'

'You are succeeding. I know you don't think just one step ahead but about how to plan the whole journey.'

'I pray that it will take me back to my throne.'

'Make sure it does, for our son's sake.'

Humayun had never seen Hamida look so determined. He would not fail her.

• ◆ •

In November 1554, Humayun stood straight-backed, a fur-lined robe pulled tight around him against the autumn cold, on the walls of Kabul with the twelve-year-old Akbar at his side as his newly recruited armies marched before him.

'Our emissaries have done well. They have brought in men from all over our own lands. Those pale-skinned men over there are from Ghazni. The ones with the dark turbans and face cloths are from the mountains north of Kandahar. Our vassals in Badakhshan and the lands of the Tajiks have sent soldiers. They are always amongst the bravest and best fighters, and well equipped too. Look how fine their horses are.'

'But who are those men over there under the yellow flag, Father?'

'They are from Ferghana – the land of your grandfather's birth. Hearing rumours of the death of Islam Shah they had started unbidden on the road to Kabul to offer their services to me, knowing I would be sure to attack Hindustan . . .' Here Humayun stopped for a moment, his voice choking with emotion, and then continued, 'I will lead them to victory just as your grandfather did. But see that group of mounted archers? They are from around Samarkand and Bokhara and have fashioned themselves the flag of our great ancestor Timur – see it fluttering now with its orange tiger . . .'

'How many men do we have?'

'Twelve thousand.'

'That's less than when my grandfather invaded Hindustan.'

'True, but we've more cannon, more muskets and additional recruits are joining every day. We have messages that many of Islam Shah's vassals will defect to us once we reach their territories in Hindustan.'

'How can you be sure?'

Humayun smiled wryly. 'Just as when their fathers deserted me so many years ago, they believe they know who the victor will be.'

'So their belief in our success will ensure it happens?'

'Yes – to have the confidence of those around you in your success takes you a great way to victory. Once it abates it is difficult to restore. That is one lesson I have learned. This time we must ensure it does not. Each victory we win will add to the tide of confidence washing away any remaining strength our opponents have.'

'I understand, Father.'

Looking at his son, Humayun realised that Akbar probably did. He had changed a lot in the past year. He was mature for his age, not only in his muscular physique and stature but also in his power of analysis and in a growing astuteness in his judgement of others. Humayun recalled his discussion with Hamida the previous night when he had told her that he intended to take Akbar with him when he set out on his invasion of Hindustan in a few days. He had reminded her that Babur had only been Akbar's age when he became king. To take Akbar with him would inspire confidence in the future of the dynasty, he had told her. It would show that, should he himself fall, unlike Islam Shah he would have a worthy successor.

Humayun had expected Hamida to resist, mindful of the danger to which Akbar would be exposed, but although tears had wetted her cheeks at first, she had choked them back. 'It is right that he should go, I know. It is difficult for a mother to see her son ride to war but he will soon be a man. I must remind myself I was only two years older when I left my family to share your life and the many dangers that accompanied it – a thing I have never regretted.'

As she spoke, Humayun had realised why, despite the many other women he had known, Hamida was the one true love of his life. He had embraced her and together they had made love long and tenderly.

Humayun forced himself back to the present. It was time to tell his son of his decision. 'Akbar, would you wish to accompany me as I go to recover our inheritance?'

Without a moment's hesitation, Akbar answered simply, 'Yes, Father.'

'Aren't you afraid?'

'A little bit, but somehow I know inside myself it is right. It's my destiny . . . Besides,' and a youthful grin lit up his face, 'it will be a great adventure and no adventure is without danger – that I already know. I will make you and my mother proud of me.'

'I know you will.'

By now, musketeers were marching below in disciplined ranks, some on horseback with their long weapons tied to their saddles, others on foot with them over their shoulders.

'How will the men on foot keep up, Father?'

'They will be able to march as fast as the oxen who pull the cannon. Besides, we'll gather more horses as we advance. We'll use rafts on rivers such as the Kabul to speed us on our way and to carry the heavy baggage and cannon. Those on foot can ride on them too. I've already given instructions for rafts to be built for the Kabul river with special mountings constructed for the oars and for the steering rudders.'

Two nights later, Humayun lay with his arm across Hamida's smooth, naked body. They had just made love and Humayun felt that never before had the act made them so truly one. Perhaps it was because of the knowledge they shared that Humayun and Akbar were to set off on their campaign the next morning.

Hamida lifted herself on one elbow and looked fondly into Humayun's dark eyes. 'You will protect yourself and our son as best you can, won't you? It's more difficult than you realise to be a woman, left behind waiting and watching for the next post runner, scrutinising his face and, if it looks drawn, wondering whether it reflects merely fatigue from the journey or bad news. Sometimes you go to bed and try to sleep, attempting to guess what is happening, knowing that any news that comes, good or bad, will be many weeks old and that the loved one you are thinking about may already be dead and you an unknowing widow.'

Humayun touched her lips with his index finger and then kissed them long and hard. 'I know Akbar and I will live and – more than that – that we will be victorious and you will be my empress in the palace at Agra. I feel it deep within me. This is my great chance to redeem my past failures and reclaim my father's throne to make it safe for Akbar, and I will take it.'

Hamida smiled and Humayun pulled her towards him and they began to make love once more, moving slowly at first and then faster and faster in passionate and all-consuming union.

• ◆ •

Humayun sat on his black horse on the south bank of the Indus. A chill wind blowing from the Himalayas in the north ruffled his hair. As he watched, on the north shore – already churned into sticky mud by the passage of many men and horses – twenty or so of his gunners pulled and heaved at the yokes of a team of oxen hauling one of his great bronze cannon. They were using their whips as well as shouts of encouragement to persuade the reluctant beasts to set foot on the bobbing bridge of rafts and boats Humayun and his men had constructed over the river, which at this point was nearly two hundred feet wide.

Humayun had learned from his father's experience and chosen a point just downstream from where a right-angled bend in the river slowed its force. In the six weeks since he had left Kabul, the oared rafts he had had manufactured in advance had speeded him down the Kabul river through the grey, barren mountains even faster than he had anticipated. They had been so useful, in fact, that remembering his father's difficulty in assembling enough boats to cross the great barrier of the Indus and conscious all the time that he must move

367

fast if he were not to lose his opportunity, Humayun had had half the rafts dismantled and put on the backs of pack animals for the journey into Hindustan so that they could be used again for his Indus bridge. He was glad he had done so since, although he had managed to secure some boats, nearly half his makeshift bridge consisted of his rafts or components from them. They had been lashed together through the ingenuity of his engineers during the past three days since he had reached the shores of the river. Humayun had joined in, standing waist-deep in the cold water, encouraging his men, himself twisting and knotting leather thongs with fingers which soon grew blue and numb with cold.

Now he saw with relief that the first pair of grey oxen was moving on to the bridge and that the rest of the team were following. More of his gunners were pushing and heaving at the four large wooden wheels of the cannon's limber to help the oxen propel it through the mud on to the bridge. As they did so, the bridge sank much lower into the water beneath the weight. However, within less than a minute, cannon, men and beasts were across and the next team of oxen was being encouraged down the north bank to begin the whole procedure over again.

All of a sudden Humayun heard a trumpet sound out from one of the circle of pickets he had placed on the low hills bordering the southern banks to warn of anyone drawing near during the crossing. The first call was followed by a second and then a third – the signal he and Ahmed Khan had agreed would warn of the approach of a large body of men.

'Stop any more cannon being transported across the bridge while we investigate what the pickets have seen. Throw out a further screen of horsemen and have our musketeers load and prime their weapons.'

Gesturing to his bodyguard to follow, Humayun urged his black horse into a gallop and soon he was on the low hill from which the trumpeter had sounded the alarm. Humayun immediately saw why he had done so. About three-quarters of a mile away, riding up from the south – the direction of Hindustan – was a large party of mounted men. Even at this distance Humayun could make out the tops of their lances glistening in the sunlight and flags fluttering as the horsemen advanced. The riders, who probably numbered around a hundred, seemed to be cantering rather than galloping as they would if they intended to attack. Humayun, however, was taking no chances.

'Make sure we get musketeers and archers into firing positions quickly,' he shouted to one of his officers. As the horsemen came nearer Humayun could see that they were unhelmeted and that their weapons remained sheathed. When they were about three hundred yards away they halted and after a minute or so one man rode slowly forward alone on his grey horse. He was clearly an ambassador or herald of some kind and Humayun ordered two of his bodyguards to ride out in front of his line to bring the man to him.

Within five minutes, the rider – a tall, slim youth dressed in cream robes and wearing a heavy gold chain round his neck – was brought before Humayun. Seemingly oblivious of the dirt and stones he prostrated himself face down, arms widespread, before Humayun, who was still mounted on his black horse which was restlessly pawing at the stone ground with its front hooves.

'Who are you? What do you want?'

'I am Murad Beg, the eldest son of Uzad Beg, the Sultan of Multan. I come from my father who waits with his bodyguard over there. He seeks your permission to approach and offer you, his overlord, his obeisance. He wishes to pledge his troops to you to assist in the recapture of your rightful throne of Hindustan.'

Hearing the name of Uzad Beg, Humayun smiled. During his descent of the Kabul river and the Khyber Pass, many tribal chieftains had come to submit to him. Some had even followed the old tradition of appearing before Akbar and himself with grass in their mouths to show that they were Humayun's beasts of burden, his oxen, to do with whatever he would. In each case, Humayun had welcomed them and their men as useful additions to his army.

However, Uzad Beg was different. He was no small tribal chieftain but a sophisticated and wily ruler. Fifteen years previously, after the battle of Chausa, Humayun had sent emissaries to him asking for troops to help halt Sher Shah's advance, but Uzad Beg had been one of the most assiduous prevaricators. His repertoire of excuses had varied from personal illnesses through the need to suppress rebellions to a fire in his fortress-palace. Later Humayun had heard he'd been one of the first to recognise Sher Shah as his overlord. That he was now rushing to offer his submission to Humayun once more was a real indication that victory was expected to be his and that soon he would again sit on the imperial throne. Humayun realised that this was no time to settle old scores but rather to conciliate his former vassals and subjects to be sure that peace ruled in his rear as he advanced on Delhi and Agra. Besides, if he recalled correctly, Uzad Beg's men were doughty, well-equipped fighters when their ruler could be persuaded to commit them to battle rather than to sit on the sidelines until the outcome was clear. Nevertheless, thought Humayun, he would make Uzad Beg sweat just a little . . .

'I remember your father well. I am glad that his health, which he used to write to me was such a trouble to him, has improved so much over the years that he is able to visit me in person. You may tell him that I will be delighted to receive him in an hour's time, just before sunset, when my camp will be better equipped for the reception of such an important vassal as he.'

'Majesty, I will tell him so.'

Just over an hour later, Humayun, dressed as befitted an emperor, was sitting beneath the scarlet awning of his command tent on a gilded throne with Akbar seated at his side on a low stool. Humayun's commanders were arranged on either side of his throne, behind which stood two green-turbaned bodyguards with shining steel breastplates. The sunset was colouring the sky pink and purple as Uzad Beg approached, accompanied by his son and flanked by an escort of Humayun's guards. As soon as they reached him, Uzad Beg and his son prostrated themselves full-length. He allowed them to remain face down on the cold, damp ground for just a little longer than he thought they might have anticipated. Then he spoke.

'Rise, both of you.'

As Uzad Beg did so, Humayun saw that his vassal's hair and beard were now white and his shoulders a little stooped, and that a pot belly strained the ties of his green silk under-tunic. Almost unconsciously Humayun pulled in his own already much flatter stomach and began.

'I am glad to see you again after all these years. What brings you before me?'

'I thank God he has preserved Your Majesty and that I have kept my own worthless life long enough to greet you on your journey to recover your rightful throne. I come to offer you, my overlord, my humble submission and that of my people.' Uzad Beg paused and gestured to one of his attendants who had followed him at a distance. 'If I may, Majesty, let this man approach.'

Humayun nodded his assent and the servant came forward to Uzad Beg with a large ivory casket on a gold cushion. Uzad Beg extracted from it a golden drinking cup set with rubies which he held out to Humayun.

'I bring you this gift, Majesty, as a small token of my loyalty.'

'I thank you. I am also pleased that you have come to recognise me as your overlord once more. You were not always so ready to answer my call.'

Uzad Beg flushed. 'Majesty, circumstances alone prevented me for a while, and after that you had left Hindustan.'

'You could have followed me into exile.'

'I had my throne and family to protect,' Uzad Beg stammered.

Humayun decided that enough was enough. 'Circumstances have conspired against us all over the last years. Bygones must be bygones. I am glad that you offer your submission once more and I accept it in the spirit in which it is rendered. How many men can you contribute to my forces?'

'Eight hundred well-equipped cavalry can join you within days on your march south.'

'I would like your son here to come as their commander,' Humayun said, conscious that the presence of Murad Beg with his army would be an effective guarantee of his father's good behaviour.

'I was going to suggest it myself, Majesty.'

•◆•

The early April sun had only been up for three hours when Humayun with Akbar and Bairam Khan at his side breasted the crest of the last of a series of high ridges in the Punjab and saw before him the massive sandstone fortress of Rohtas. It sat on the top of a low rocky outcrop on the plain below, overlooking the junction of roads leading south from the north and east. As he had pushed further into Hindustan, Humayun had still faced no significant opposition. Instead, Uzad Beg had been followed by many other defecting vassals of Islam Shah. So vehement had they been in their denunciation of their former overlord and in their vows of loyalty and support that Humayun had subsequently advised young Akbar never to take such protestations at face value. After all, several had previously shifted their loyalty to Sher Shah from Humayun and, as Akbar had observed to his father, these had been particularly unctuous in their present praise and professions of loyalty. Humayun's army when it crossed the Indus had already nearly doubled in size to twenty thousand since leaving Kabul. Now it numbered nearly thirty-five thousand men with more recruits arriving every day.

'Father, the fortress gates are closed. There are armed men on the walls and I see the smoke from cooking fires. Do we need to take the fortress or can we bypass it?' asked Akbar.

'It's one of the keys to the control of northern Hindustan. We cannot leave it in the hands of an enemy who might sally forth at any time to attack our rear, so take it we must. However, the defenders are rumoured to be only few in number. They have no prospect of any relieving force and will not relish dying in a hopeless cause. I intend to see what an initial show of strength will do. Bairam Khan, have our cannon deployed in front of the fortress just out of musket range but where they can do some damage to the lower walls and the main gateway. Have our horsemen encircle the outcrop and have our musketeers and archers form up behind the cannon so that the defenders may see their number.'

Within two hours, teams of straining oxen had pulled the Moghul cannon into place and the encirclement of Rohtas had been completed by Humayun's horsemen, their green pennants fluttering in the spring breeze. During this time, although there had been much movement on the walls, the defenders made no attempt to make a sortie to disrupt their besiegers. When he saw everything was in place Humayun commanded Bairam Khan, 'Order the cannon to fire at the gates. Once there is enough smoke billowing around, have some of our musketeers advance under its cover to within range and attempt to pick off any who show themselves above those crenellated battlements. In the meantime have our scribes write messages offering the defenders safe passage if they leave within an hour. After we've shown them a little of what we're capable of, we'll have our best archers fire the surrender offers into the city.'

Almost immediately a loud boom echoed across the plains as the gunners pressed their lighted tapers to the firing holes of the bronze cannon. Some of the first shots were too low, crashing into the lower slopes of the outcrop and sending showers of earth and shards of rock into the air rather than damaging the walls and gates. Sweating and stripped to the waist as the day began to warm, the gunners rushed to change the cannons' elevation by packing stones beneath the wheels or manhandling smaller weapons up mounds of earth. As they did so, a few musket shots rang from the towering battlements but the range was, as Humayun had planned, too great for them.

However, some of the arrows the defenders fired from bows pointed high into the air to increase their range did reach the cannon. As they dropped from the cloudless sky, most thudded harmlessly into the ground but several oxen were hit, blood staining their dun-coloured coats, and Humayun saw one of his gunners being helped away, two black-shafted arrows stuck into his back where he had been hit while straining to push a cannon into place. Soon, the cannon were firing again and regularly hitting the stone walls flanking the gate. A pall of white smoke hung over the cannon like the early morning mist that formed in the valleys near Kabul.

Humayun continued to watch as a band of his musketeers ran forward into the smoke, their weapons and firing tripods at the ready. They were followed by some of his archers with their double bows in their hands and full quivers on their backs. A minute or two later, a body fell, arms flailing, from the battlements to crash on to the rocks below. It was followed by another clawing at the air, this time with an arrow clearly visible protruding from its neck. No more puffs of smoke came from the muskets of the defenders on the walls and the number of arrows dwindled while the gates of Rohtas remained firmly shut.

'The defenders clearly have little stomach for the fight, as we suspected. Have those archers with the message offering surrender terms attached to their arrows advance and fire them into the city,' Humayun commanded. Within a few minutes he saw the arrows fly into the air, most of them overtopping the walls and landing within the fort.

Scarcely two hours later, with Akbar at his side, Humayun rode through the tall, iron-studded gates of Rohtas and into the silent, deserted courtyard of the fortress, which was strewn with abandoned weapons and items of heavy equipment. Having seen the strength of Humayun's army, the defenders had immediately appreciated the generosity of the surrender offer. Within a few minutes the great thick wooden gates had creaked open and the garrison had begun to stream through them, some on foot and some on horseback, carrying what valuables they could and all heading south, leaving Humayun master of this gateway to Hindustan.

Humayun ordered some of the officers of his bodyguard to check that all the garrison had indeed departed and that none lurked in ambush. Receiving their swift confirmation, Humayun walked towards the open doors of the fortress's great hall. As he did so, he glanced to his right where he saw that charcoal fires were still glowing beneath some clay tandoor ovens. Looking inside one, he found several loaves of warm, unleavened bread. He took one, bit a small portion from it and then handed it to Akbar.

'Enjoy it. It tastes of victory.'

Chapter 25

Shock and Awe

'Humayun *Padishah*! Long live Emperor Humayun!' The cries of the citizens of Lahore rang out all around as, one warm late February day in 1555, Humayun and Akbar made their triumphal entry into the city in a gilded howdah atop a tall elephant, whose long saddle cloth embroidered with golden thread and set with pearls swept the dust of the city's wide streets. At the head of the procession was a squadron of Humayun's best cavalry, all riding on black horses and all wearing turbans of gold-coloured cloth. The afternoon sun glinted on the steel points of the long lances they held vertically as they rode. Behind them, just in front of Humayun, six mounted trumpeters and six drummers with small kettledrums on either side of their saddlebows played with skill and vigour. Their music, together with the roar of the crowd, made it difficult for Humayun to hear Akbar's words.

'Father, ever since we left Kabul we have fought only skirmishes. All the major fortresses like Rohtas have surrendered at our approach and now this great city of Lahore has too. How much further can we go into Hindustan without a real battle?'

'Not far, I think. We'll soon be entering what were the heartlands of Sher Shah's and Islam Shah's dominions. The three contenders for their throne will have heard of our advance and will know that we – the rightful rulers of Hindustan – are a greater threat than any of their fellow pretenders. One or all of them will turn aside from their squabbles to attack us.'

'D'you think they will unite against us?'

'Possibly, but the amount of death and destruction they have inflicted on each other makes that unlikely. However, each will be a formidable opponent in his own right.'

'How long will we stay in Lahore?'

'Only long enough to have the chief mullah proclaim me emperor once more by reading the *khutba* – the sermon – in my name at the Friday service in the mosque. Look, you can see its two tall minarets over there through the palm trees. We need to keep up the impetus of our advance. Too often I've delayed and let my opponents seize the initiative.'

Two weeks later, as, shrouded in early morning mist, his troops were lighting their cooking fires to prepare their early meal, Humayun sat with his military council around him in his scarlet tent at the centre of his camp. Since leaving Lahore eight days earlier, he and his army had advanced ninety miles southeast, ever deeper into Hindustan across the featureless, red plains.

'You are certain, Ahmed Khan, that the forces of Adil Shah are heading east across our line of march?'

'Yes. Five days ago they had the worst of another encounter with the army of their rival Sekunder Shah and now they are hastening towards their stronghold in the fortress of Sundarnagar to regather their strength.'

'How far away are they?'

'Perhaps eight miles ahead of us, Majesty.'

'How many of them are there?'

'Ten thousand or so, nearly all mounted. They have abandoned most of their cannon and heavy equipment.'

'Do they have pickets and outriders posted?'

'Only a very few, Majesty; they are in too much disorder. They paused merely for a few hours overnight to snatch some sleep and were in the saddle again before dawn. Their minds seem concentrated only on reaching Sundarnagar as speedily as possible.'

'Then let us attack immediately, taking advantage of the cover of the mist while it lasts. Tell the men to douse their cooking fires. There is no time to eat. We will take mounted cavalry and archers. Also, order some of the cavalrymen to take musketeers up behind them on their horses. You, Bairam Khan, will remain with Akbar in charge of the camp. Ensure you establish good defences and post pickets. I expect to win but the camp must be strongly protected in case Adil Shah evades us or for any reason secures a temporary advantage.'

Two hours later, the mist had entirely evaporated. Humayun – who had ridden a mile or so ahead of his advancing main force with Ahmed Khan and a party of his scouts – looked over the low mud wall of a small village inhabited by a few poor farmers and their goats and chickens. Shielding his eyes with his hands against the sun's glare, he saw about three-quarters of a mile away a large cloud of dust billowing as it crossed from right to left in front of him. Within the dust cloud, Humayun could just distinguish the shapes of riders and a few small baggage wagons pulled by mules or oxen. Two large banners fluttered at the head of the column. At this distance and through the dust, Humayun found it difficult to make out their colour, let alone any device on them, but it could only be Adil Shah's forces. They had no scouts posted and appeared as yet oblivious of any danger.

'Send orders back to Nadim Khwaja to take his division of cavalry and attack the rear. Tell Zahid Beg to bring his men here and I will lead them in an attack on the vanguard. Additionally, let those horsemen who have musketeers with them ride straightaway to within a hundred yards of the enemy line of march and there let the musketeers add to our opponents' discomfort.'

Soon, Humayun's musketeers were dismounting to place their long muskets on their firing tripods and Humayun and his troops were almost on Adil Shah's vanguard. At the last moment their opponents had suddenly become aware of them and were turning to face them, unsheathing their weapons as they did so. Officers were shouting orders to close ranks and to prepare to receive the attacks. Almost immediately, Humayun's musketeers fired their first volley, which knocked some of Adil Shah's men from their saddles and wounded and panicked some of their horses.

Moments later, Humayun at the head of his cavalry thudded into their vanguard. His first action was to cut down one of the two banner holders with a sword swipe to the head. As the man fell backwards, he dropped his great banner, which Humayun could now see was orange with a gold sun on it. The long cloth twisted around the legs of Humayun's black horse and it stumbled. Humayun, caught off balance as he leaned from the saddle to aim a sword stroke at the second banner carrier, fell. As he landed on the hard ground, his sword was knocked from his grasp.

Another of Adil Shah's men, a stocky officer wearing a domed helmet with an orange plume, reacted more swiftly than Humayun's bodyguard. He kicked his chestnut horse towards Humayun and attempted to impale him on his long lance. Humayun rolled quickly away, throwing off his gauntlet as he did so and trying to extract his dagger from its jewelled scabbard hanging at his waist. After what seemed an age, he tugged it free and threw the foot-long weapon with all his force at the throat of the horse of his opponent, who was attempting to ride him down once more. The point of the dagger hit its mark and the horse, bleeding profusely, staggered and collapsed, throwing its rider, who hit the earth with a thump.

Humayun was by now on his feet and rushed over to the winded officer, who had lost his helmet in the fall. Humayun grabbed him round his thick neck as he too attempted to stand. For some seconds they fought as the officer tried to extract himself from Humayun's headlock. Then he bit hard into the bare flesh of Humayun's wrist and hand, drawing blood. Humayun relaxed his grip slightly and the officer wrenched his head free.

Half smiling through teeth flecked with Humayun's blood, he immediately kicked out at Humayun's groin. But Humayun leaped back and his opponent missed, throwing himself off balance. Humayun swept the man's trailing leg from beneath him and, as he fell, leaped upon him, landing with his knees on his opponent's chest. The officer, although winded again, in turn succeeded in kneeing Humayun in the back and dislodging him. They rolled over and over in the dust together until Humayun used his superior strength and agility to get both his hands firmly round his opponent's neck. Deliberately he pressed his thumbs into the man's windpipe as hard as he could and twisted his neck sharply. There was a loud crack and slowly the officer's face suffused with purple and his bulging eyes grew unfocused as he ceased to struggle. Throwing the limp body aside, Humayun scrambled to his feet and retrieved his sword. Grimly he realised that without the training of his wrestling bouts with Bayzid Khan he might not have prevailed. It would have been very difficult in the press of the fight for his bodyguard to protect him once he was unhorsed.

These same bodyguards were by now gathering round and Humayun saw that many of Adil Shah's men were already fleeing. Others were surrendering. It was still less than an hour since he had first seen Adil Shah's army, phantoms in the dust, from the shelter of the farmers' village. Now they were in complete confusion and disarray, as were Adil Shah's chances of making good his claim to the throne of Hindustan.

'Pursue our enemies. Capture as many animals and as much equipment as you can. We will need them for the harder fights that surely lie ahead. If you capture Adil Shah show him no mercy, as he showed none to his young nephew.'

Three hours after the battle, some of the troops Humayun had sent in pursuit of his defeated enemy returned. Humayun saw that one of them was leading a horse with a body slung across its back, the arms and legs tied together beneath the animal's belly. The rider leading the group dismounted and bowed low before Humayun. 'It's Adil Shah, Majesty. Members of his bodyguard whom we overtook only two or three miles from here surrendered the body to us. They told us that he had died a short time before from a chest wound inflicted by a musket ball at the beginning of the battle.'

Humayun walked over to the corpse and, pulling the head back, looked into his opponent's face. Beneath the caked blood and dirt, Adil Shah looked ordinary. Humayun could see no outward trace of the wicked depth of his ambition which had led him to slaughter his sister's son. Letting Adil Shah's head drop, he suppressed the temptation welling within him to show his contempt for his enemy by leaving his corpse unburied for the birds and pariah dogs to feed on. Instead, he turned away with a curt instruction, 'Inter him in an unmarked grave.'

That night, in the quiet of his tent, Humayun offered a silent prayer of thanks. He had eliminated one of the three other major contenders for the throne of Hindustan. But he knew he must not relax. He must retain the initiative and the impetus of his victories, pushing himself and his army to the utmost. Otherwise, his chance to recover his throne and to transform himself from failure to victor might be lost and might never arise again.

The next morning Ahmed Khan's scouts brought news of a further opportunity. Travellers coming up the road from the south had told them that a small army led by two of Tartar Khan's generals was about five days' ride away, heading north in their direction. Its apparent aim was to confront Adil Shah of whose defeat they were as yet ignorant. Realising that he had a great chance to inflict a serious blow on the second of the contenders for the throne of Hindustan and in all probability remove him too from contention, Humayun immediately ordered his men to move south to attack Tartar Khan's army.

A week later, Humayun surveyed another battlefield. Riding hard, his troops had come up with their enemy earlier that day and had found that their opponents were travelling in two distinct divisions separated by at least a mile. Neither group numbered more than four thousand men. Humayun had straightaway ordered an attack on the leading division, which had quickly broken under the impact and scattered across the plain. Rather than riding to the aid of their stricken comrades, the second division had retreated and occupied a defensive position on a nearby small hill, which Humayun's troops had swiftly encircled.

At this moment, Humayun could see a group of officers conferring on the hilltop. Turning to Ahmed Khan at his side, he asked, 'Do we know who the general of that division is?'

'Majesty, during the recent battle the commander of a squadron of cavalry surrendered almost immediately and told us that he and his men wished to serve you. We put his men under guard and confined him to one of our tents where he volunteered much information about the make-up of our enemy's army and its morale. He is sure to know.'

'Bring him to me.'

A few minutes later, two of Ahmed Khan's men appeared leading a tall man of about thirty with a neatly trimmed black beard. To forestall any possibility of his attacking Humayun they had shackled his ankles so closely that he could only shuffle forwards. When he was within a few yards of Humayun he threw himself on the ground.

After a moment Humayun spoke. 'Help him up.' Then he asked, 'Who are you?'

'Mustapha Ergun, a Turkish officer in the service of Tartar Khan.'

'I understand you wish to transfer your allegiance to me.'

'My hundred men also.'

'Why?'

'We joined Tartar Khan in search of booty and of position if he became *Padishah* of Hindustan. But we have found he is not serious about pursuing this ambition. While he loitered on the borders of Gujarat in the arms of his concubines, he despatched us on this tentative expedition against the weaker of his fellow contenders, Adil Shah. He didn't even provide us with enough men, weapons or equipment to do our job properly and our pay is three months in arrears. We believe that you are serious in your ambition to regain the imperial throne and that when you succeed you will reward us generously.'

'I remember well the esteem in which my father held his Turkish gunners. I too have been served well by officers from other nations. Bairam Khan here joined me from the army of the Shah of Persia. But how can I be sure of your sincerity?'

'We are prepared to swear our loyalty to you on the Holy Book – or let us lead the attack in your next battle to prove ourselves.'

'I will consider both offers, but I pose you this initial test. Go to the other division of your army who sit surrounded on that hill. Persuade them to surrender. I extend to them the following terms – either to depart unmolested retaining their personal weapons but leaving behind their heavy equipment or – like you – to volunteer to join my forces. If they do not surrender, I may take up your offer to lead the next attack, which will be on them. Do you accept my proposition?'

'Yes, Majesty.'

'Strike off his shackles.'

A quarter of an hour later, Mustapha Ergun rode out from Humayun's camp accompanied by ten of his men. When he reached the hill on which his comrades were drawn up, they opened a gap in their lines to receive him. Humayun could see him and his men ride to the top of the barren hill to talk to the officers congregated there. Soon the knot of men broke up and individual officers seemed to be consulting their men. There were occasional outbursts of cheering before the gap in the front line reopened and Mustapha Ergun with his ten soldiers behind him re-emerged and rode back down to Humayun's position.

Two of Humayun's bodyguards placed themselves on either side of him as, smiling, he approached Humayun, who had Bairam Khan and Akbar at his side. 'What success have you had?'

'No more blood will be spilled, Majesty. The division on the hill is commanded by a Gujarati prince named Selim and two-thirds of his troops are Gujaratis enlisted by Tartar Khan when he first decided to pursue the imperial throne. They're tired of this campaign and wish to return home and are prepared to accept your conditions for doing so.'

'Good. And the other third?'

'A mixed bunch from many places. Some are mere boys who joined our ranks as we passed through their villages from a desire for adventure, most of whom now want nothing more than to preserve their lives. Others are hardened soldiers of fortune like ourselves, including one hundred musketeers from my own country under the command of an old comrade of mine, Kemil Attak, and about the same number of Persians, recruited to man the few small cannon we have with us. Both these two groups wish to join you with their weapons, as we do ourselves.'

'You have done well. I accept your offer of service and that of your men and I will accept those of the other volunteers, provided like you their officers convince me of their sincerity.' Then, turning to Bairam Khan, he said, 'Each victory brings us nearer to our goal. But we cannot falter or all we have achieved so far will be lost. This evening we will feast to celebrate our victory and to welcome our new comrades-in-arms but tomorrow we will march to vanquish the last of the pretenders to my throne, Sekunder Shah. He is the best leader and his army is the largest of the three. His governor occupies Delhi and he himself sits with his army across the road to the capital. Our greatest battle is to come.'

Later that night, as the sounds of merriment and raucous singing echoed around the camp, Humayun left the celebrations. For a moment he stopped and gazed at the stars sprinkling the black velvet of the night but then he walked slowly back to his tent. A waiting guard lifted the flap and Humayun entered and sat at a low table. Taking a pen he dipped it into the jade inkpot and by the light of a flickering oil lamp started to write a letter to Hamida to be handed to a post messenger in the morning to begin its long journey back to Kabul. He wrote that he and Akbar were safe, of his love for her and of his certainty that he would soon sit once more on the throne of Hindustan.

• ◆ •

The air was hot and still and as Humayun looked across from his vantage point on a low sandstone hill he saw that dark clouds were piling up on the far horizon as they always did in the afternoon in early summer as the monsoon approached. It was nearly a month since his defeat of Tartar Khan's generals. In that time he had turned east in pursuit of the forces of Sekunder Shah who, according to his scouts, had a quarter of a million men in his main army – a number which considerably exceeded Humayun's forces even though they had now grown to over a hundred thousand.

Humayun had quickly realised that to be certain of victory he needed to erode his enemies' numerical advantage before taking them on in the open field. Therefore, a fortnight previously he had despatched a raiding force under Bairam Khan to ride hard and light to harass his enemies' outposts and to disrupt their communications with Delhi. Now he could see Bairam Khan's troops returning across the dry plains. Messengers had already reported that they had had some successes, but he needed to hear from Bairam Khan's lips their extent and what more he and his men had learned about their enemies' strength and future plans.

Too eager for news to wait for Bairam Khan to come to him, Humayun called his bodyguard to him and, kicking his black horse into a gallop, set off down the hill towards Bairam Khan's column. An hour later, beneath the limited shade provided by a solitary tree, he and Bairam Khan were sitting on a red and blue carpet spread with cushions.

'Our successes in our raids were hard won, Majesty. Unlike our other opponents, Sekunder Shah's men are disciplined. Even when surprised and outnumbered they did not panic or flee but closed ranks and battled hard, sometimes inflicting heavy casualties on us before we finally prevailed.'

'As we feared, they make powerful opponents. What did you learn of Sekunder Shah's movements?'

'He is concentrating his main forces in the vicinity of a town called Sirhind on the south bank of one of the branches of the Sutlej river before making his next move. According to a despatch some of our men found on one of a party of Sekunder Shah's messengers they captured three days ago, he has called for further reinforcements from Delhi and is expecting a large detachment of them to arrive within the next ten days bringing with them extra money to pay his other troops as well as more equipment.'

'You are sure the message was genuine?'

'It has Sekunder Shah's seal on it, look . . .'

Bairam Khan unfastened the worn brown leather satchel he had looped across his chest, took out a large folded sheet of paper with a red wax seal on it and held it out to Humayun.

'It certainly looks the real thing, but could it have been planted as some kind of ruse?'

'I don't think so, Majesty. The group of our men who captured the messengers were a scouting party operating well away – perhaps forty miles further east from my main force. They said that the messengers were galloping hard when they came upon them rather than loitering as they might have been if looking to be taken. When I spoke to them, Sekunder Shah's men gave a good impression of being surprised and humbled to be captured. If they were acting, they were playing their parts to perfection.'

'In that case, let us strain every sinew to intercept the reinforcements and seize the money and weapons. Send scouts out immediately to cover all possible approach routes.'

• ◆ •

'Majesty, their pickets have warned them of our presence,' a slightly breathless Ahmed Khan told Humayun. 'They have halted and drawn themselves into a defensive position about two miles away over the crest of that ridge, in and around a small village whose inhabitants fled at their approach. They are positioning their men behind the village's mud walls and are overturning their wagons to form extra barricades.'

'How many of them are there?'

'About five thousand, mostly horsemen including some with muskets, protecting a large baggage train. They've also got quite a few small cannon with them.'

'Now we've lost any chance of surprising them, our best hope is to attack before they can complete their preparations. Have Bairam Khan ready our men.'

Ninety minutes later, Humayun stood on the top of the ridge above the village and watched as the first wave of his men led by Bairam Khan himself charged the barricades behind which Sekunder Shah's men were drawn up. There was a loud crash as Sekunder Shah's cannon fired. Several of Bairam Khan's men fell. A crackle of musketry followed which emptied more saddles. More fell from a second wave of cannon fire before they could reach the barricades, but still Bairam Khan's men rode on.

'Look, Father, isn't that Mustapha Ergun at the head of the line over there?' shouted Akbar.

Humayun followed his son's pointing hand and saw through the white smoke drifting across the village his new recruit leaping one of the mud walls on his bay horse, followed closely by some of his men. Elsewhere, Humayun could see that a number of his other cavalry had come under such heavy fire and taken so many casualties that they were retreating, leaving bodies of men and horses strewn in front of the makeshift fortifications thrown up by Sekunder Shah's men.

Then Humayun saw Bairam Khan gesturing to a detachment of his men previously held in reserve. They galloped to the area of the barricades where Mustapha Ergun and his troops had made a breach and swiftly followed them into the enemy camp. Once inside, they began attacking their opponents' positions from the rear. For several minutes the horsemen, locked in combat, swayed back and forth, but slowly Humayun's men were beginning to seize the upper hand as more and more reinforcements poured over the barricades despite suffering continuing casualties from Sekunder Shah's resolute musketeers. Inch by inch the defenders were being herded into a small portion of their original position. Suddenly a group of Sekunder Shah's horsemen broke out from the mass of their closely packed comrades and fought their way to a gap in the barricades before beginning to gallop determinedly in the direction in which Sekunder Shah's main army lay.

'We must stop them,' shouted Humayun. 'Follow me!'

Head bent low over his horse's neck and with Akbar at his side, Humayun galloped after the riders. Led by a thick-set officer wearing a steel breastplate, they were maintaining cohesion and formation, seemingly bent on alerting Sekunder Shah as soon as possible to the fate of their comrades rather than on simply preserving their lives.

Slowly Humayun and his men gained on the group. When they were within arrow shot, Humayun grabbed his bow and quiver from his back. Standing in his stirrups with his reins clenched in his teeth he fired at the officer. He missed by inches, his arrow embedding itself in the man's saddle. However, before he could fit another arrow to his string, the officer slid from his horse, an arrow in his neck. His foot caught in his stirrup and he was dragged for a while – head bumping along the stony ground – behind his frightened, galloping mount before the stirrup broke. Then he rolled over twice and lay still. Humayun realised it was Akbar who had fired the fatal arrow. Others of Sekunder Shah's men had also fallen from their horses.

'Well done!' Humayun shouted to his son, 'but stay back now.'

Humayun kicked his horse into a gallop once more and headed after the remaining dozen or so riders. Soon he was up with the hindmost of them, who was desperately urging his sweat-soaked, blowing pony onwards. Seeing Humayun he half raised his round shield but he was too late. Humayun's sharp sword caught him across the back of his neck beneath his helmet. His blood gushed crimson and he crashed to the hard ground.

Humayun did not look back but galloped after the only one of the riders who had not been overtaken and engaged by one of his men and was still in the saddle riding hard. He was a fine, fluid rider mounted on a speedy black horse whose hooves kicked up pebbles as they pounded the ground. It was all Humayun could do to gain on him even though his horse was fresher. Finally Humayun and three of his bodyguard drew alongside the rider, who aimed a stroke with his scimitar at one of the bodyguards. The man managed to get his arm up to protect his head but received a deep wound to his forearm and fell back from the fight. However, in striking at the bodyguard the horseman exposed himself to a thrust from Humayun which penetrated his thigh and he too fell, leaving his horse to gallop off alone.

Reining in his own horse and turning in his saddle, Humayun saw that all the break-out party were accounted for, and most important of all Akbar was safe. As they rode back towards the main battle around the village, Humayun could see that in most places the combat was over. There was still some fighting going on around a group of mud huts. The thatched roof of one was burning, perhaps set ablaze by a spark from a musket or cannon or perhaps ignited deliberately by his men to flush out their opponents. However, as he came closer Humayun saw that this fight too had ceased and the remaining defenders had thrown down their arms.

Four hours later, dark, almost purple clouds were filling the sky and a hot breeze had sprung up – the monsoon would start any day soon, thought Humayun, perhaps even this very afternoon. Turning to Akbar, who was standing by his side beneath the awning of his scarlet command tent, he put his arm round his son's shoulders. 'I've always prided myself on my skill as an archer, but your shot that brought down the officer was exceptional.'

'Thank you, but it was probably a fluke.'

'I think not – I've seen you practise . . .' Humayun paused and squeezed his son's shoulder. 'Good shot as it was and glad as I was that you made it, I should have ordered you not to accompany me when I chased after those riders. Lucky arrow shots might have killed us both, destroying my hopes for our family's destiny as well as causing your mother immense grief. In future we must remain separated on the battlefield, and I am afraid you must stay in the rear.'

'But Father . . .' Akbar began, then let his words trail away as he saw the determination in his father's eyes and realised the logic in his words.

'Enough of this. Here come our officers, led by Bairam Khan, to discuss our next move.' Humayun turned back into the tent where cushions had been placed in a semicircle round his throne for his commanders and a gilded stool had been set up for Akbar immediately to the right of his place. Once they were all assembled, Humayun asked, 'What were our casualties?'

'Two hundred men killed, at least, and over six hundred injured, many badly, including several of Mustapha Ergun's Turks who first got behind the barricades.'

'Mustapha Ergun and his men did well. When we divide the booty we must double their share, but before we can allocate rewards we must know the extent of our capture.'

'Two large chests of gold coin,' said Bairam Khan, 'and five of silver designed to pay Sekunder Shah's troops. Their loss will disappoint his men and may affect their commitment to his cause.'

'We can only hope it does. What military equipment did we acquire?'

'Two bullock carts loaded with wooden cases of new muskets and their powder and bullets. Two new medium-sized bronze cannon and ten smaller ones. Sekunder Shah's men managed to destroy six more by exploding excess powder in their barrels. There are also boxes of swords and battleaxes as well as three thousand five hundred horses and some oxen and other pack animals. All in all, a welcome and substantial contribution to our supplies and an equally substantial loss for Sekunder Shah.'

'How many of his men did we capture?'

'About four thousand. The rest were killed. What should we do with the prisoners, Majesty?'

'Hold them for forty-eight hours then allow any who are prepared to swear on the Holy Book that they will fight no more to depart south on foot without their weapons. Now let us turn to planning our final victory over Sekunder Shah. What do you think our next move should be, Zahid Beg?'

'The monsoon is imminent. We cannot campaign satisfactorily during it − our baggage trains and artillery will scarcely be able to move. We should encamp while sending scouts south to keep the main routes between Sekunder Shah and Delhi under observation, and then when the monsoon ceases . . .'

'No,' Humayun interrupted, 'I will not let the monsoon stop us. That is what Sekunder Shah will expect. The prize of the throne of Hindustan is too great. It has been lost to me too long. Now is no time to hold back. If we press on to attack him at once we will have the advantage of surprise. Too often in the past I've delayed and lost the initiative. It will not be so this time. Ahmed Khan, how far away is Sekunder Shah's main force? How many days' march will it take us to come up with them?'

'They are still encamped at Sirhind on the Sutlej, about a hundred miles east of here, perhaps ten days' march for the army with its baggage. Our spies report they seem to be well established there and preparing to see out the monsoon in comfort before making their next move.'

'Well, they're in for a shock.'

Chapter 26

Victory

Fat drops of rain were splashing from a leaden sky into the large puddles of water that had already formed outside Humayun's scarlet command tent. As he looked out from beneath its dripping awning while he waited for his commanders to join him for a council of war, he could see that the puddles had already coalesced to form pools in some of the lower-lying and muddier parts of his camp. The water rose over the feet of his soldiers who, heads hunched into their shoulders against the downpour, splashed their way to and from picket duty. In whatever direction he looked there was no sign of a break in the weather.

Humayun turned back into his tent, where his officers were now assembled in a semicircle, some of them still shaking from their clothes the rain which had soaked them as they ran the short distance from their own tents across to his. Humayun took his place in the centre with the young Akbar at his side.

'Ahmed Khan, what are the latest reports of Sekunder Shah's army?'

'He remains six miles away behind his fortified positions at Sirhind, just as he did for the fortnight we were making our way towards him before we set up camp here. We know from the number of his scouts that we've encountered or captured that he has long been aware of our approach, yet he has made no move to confront us.

No doubt he still believes that we will not attack him during the monsoon for fear of being slowed down by all the mud and made into easy targets for his well dug-in cannon and for his archers and musketeers.'

'I have delayed our assault for this last week to encourage Sekunder Shah in that false belief, attempting to convince him that we will be as cautious and conventional in our thinking as he is and that – having come up to his position – we will postpone any combat until the rains have abated and the ground has begun to dry.'

'But doesn't he have a point, Majesty?' asked Zahid Beg, a deeply concerned expression on his thin face. 'We cannot move our cannon at any speed and the powder for our muskets is always getting damp. There have been several accidents when our men have rashly brought it too close to fires in an attempt to dry it out.'

'Of course we will face some problems when we attack,' said Humayun, 'but these will be mere inconveniences compared to the benefits surprise will secure us.'

Bairam Khan was nodding but some others still looked doubtful. Suddenly, Akbar, who usually listened attentively but rarely spoke, rose from the place where he had been sitting and said in a steady, firm voice, 'I believe you are right, Father. Now is the time to seize our destiny and surprise Sekunder Shah before he succeeds in raising more troops. He has a far greater reservoir to draw on than we.'

'Well spoken, Akbar,' Humayun said. 'I will have Ahmed Khan send scouts to test out the firmest approach route to Sekunder Shah's camp. It would seem to lie over that slightly higher ground northeast of here. If we go in that direction we may have to ride a mile or so further but it will be worth it. We will not attempt to move our cannon forward but will take some mounted musketeers. Even if only some of their muskets fire because of the damp it will help.'

'But if we follow that route we will be seen and it will give Sekunder Shah longer to prepare,' interrupted Nadim Khwaja.

'I've thought of that. To add to the surprise and to conceal our movements, I intend to attack under cover of darkness in the hour before dawn tomorrow. We will make our preparations as inconspicuously as we can today and will rouse our troops at three in the morning to begin our advance an hour later. We'll move in separate divisions of five hundred men, each identified by a brightly coloured cloth tied around the arm to reduce the chances of confusion in the dark.'

'Majesty,' said Bairam Khan, 'I understand your plan. I believe our men will be disciplined enough to carry it out, trusting as they do in their leaders.'

'I intend to go amongst the troops towards dusk with Akbar to encourage our soldiers and tell them of our plan and of my faith in it – and in them – to see it through.'

The rain had slackened a little during the day but more dark clouds were gathering on the horizon as, with Akbar, Ahmed Khan and Bairam Khan at his side, Humayun rode up to the cluster of tents occupied by some of Bairam Khan's cavalry – mostly men from Badakhshan. Humayun had decided to keep his address to this group to the last. He dismounted from his tall black horse and, as the men gathered around, began.

'Your fathers served my father well as he won an empire. You have served me well in this campaign to win back the lands clawed away by greedy usurpers. Tomorrow you will join me in the vanguard. Together we will face our greatest battle so far. When we conquer, as I know we will, we will regain Hindustan and secure its rich lands for our sons.'

Humayun paused to put his arm around Akbar's shoulders before continuing. 'I know that your sons – like young Akbar here – will be worthy of the legacy we will win for them. Remember that tomorrow we fight for their future as well as our own. Let us seize our destiny. Let us show such valour and gain such a victory that our grandsons and their children will still talk with awe and gratitude of our deeds, just as we recall the fabled feats of Timur and his men.'

As Humayun finished a burst of cheering rose from the Badakhshanis. His words had hit home, just as they had with all the other men he had spoken to on his tour of the camp.

•◆•

Jauhar quietly entered Humayun's tent at two in the morning to rouse him but found that Humayun was already awake. He had been for some time. While listening to the rain falling steadily on his tent he'd searched his mind, rehearsing his battle plan over and over again to check he had overlooked nothing. Eventually he had convinced himself that he had not.

Then his thoughts had turned involuntarily to the course of his life since he had first left Agra seventeen years ago to confront Sher Shah. At that time – he now realised – he had been immature, too ready to believe that success would be his by right and consequently not sufficiently motivated to apply all his inner resources to achieving it. However, he had never lost his belief in himself and in his destiny, never conceded that a setback, however severe, might be a final defeat. He was immensely grateful that he had been granted a second chance and for that he knew he had deserved his birth name of Humayun, 'Fortunate'. So many – even kings – only received a single opportunity and, if they did not grasp it, disappeared from history as if they had never lived, all their promise, all their hopes and ambitions evaporating into eternal obscurity. He had learned over his reign that a consistently indomitable spirit was as essential to a ruler as bravery in battle. Today, however, was to be a day of battle and he knew he must put his courage to the test once more.

With that thought, he had begun to prepare himself for combat, a task in which Jauhar now started to assist him, helping him draw on his long yellow leather riding boots and – as he had done since they were both young men – strapping on Humayun's jewel-studded, engraved steel breastplate. As Jauhar finally handed him his father's great sword Alamgir, Humayun smiled at him and touching him on the arm said, 'Thank you for your loyal service during all my troubles. Soon we will be back in our fine quarters at Agra.'

'Majesty, I have no doubt of that,' said Jauhar as he held open the tent flaps for Humayun to step out into the wet night air.

Akbar was waiting outside for his father and they embraced. Then Akbar asked, 'May I not join the attack? I envy my milk-brother Adham Khan who will ride in the vanguard. He will be able to boast of his part in the fight when we again meet our tutors while I . . .'

'No, you are the future of our dynasty,' Humayun interrupted. 'If, God forbid, Adham Khan were to fall, Maham Anga would weep but his loss would be a personal one to his family. If you and I fell together our line would be extinguished. I cannot risk that happening so you must remain behind.'

Humayun realised that Akbar had asked more in hope than expectation and could not but admire him for doing so. As he moved away from Akbar towards the place beneath the neem tree where Bairam Khan and his other commanders were waiting, he saw by the ghostly light of one of the frequent flashes of sheet lightning that a few yards away Bairam Khan's young *qorchi* – his squire – was bent over being sick as he held on to the reins of his own horse and that of his master. Humayun turned and walked over to him. Seeing him approach, the young man quickly straightened up and wiped his mouth with a cloth.

'Are you nervous . . . or perhaps a little frightened?' Humayun asked.

'A bit, Majesty,' the youth, whose smooth face showed that he was no older than Akbar, admitted.

'It's normal,' said Humayun. 'But remember something my father told me before the battle of Panipat. True courage is to feel fear but still to mount your horse and head into battle.'

'Yes, Majesty. I will not let you or Bairam Khan down.'

'I know you will not.'

The weather had deteriorated dramatically by the time – an hour later – Humayun and the first division of his Badakhshani cavalry halted. They had reached the point where they would need to turn from the relatively firm but circuitous northeastern approach track Ahmed Khan had successfully identified to begin their final assault on Sekunder Shah's camp. The rain was slanting down harder and heavier than ever, reducing further what little visibility there was in the darkness. Even the flickering sheets of lightning revealed little more than the drenching drops of rain which they turned silver and steel before the peering eyes of Humayun and his men. The occasional rumbles of distant thunder had turned into an almost constant crash and crack overhead. Even the elements were allying themselves to him, thought Humayun with grim satisfaction. From his perspective, the change in the weather was not a worsening but an improvement. There was little prospect that Sekunder Shah's men would see or hear their approach before they were almost on them.

Minutes earlier, Ahmed Khan had ridden up through the downpour. The rat tails of wet hair protruding from beneath his helmet were now flecked with grey and his face was deeply lined, but the smile that lit it was as broad and as vital as when together they had climbed the sheer cliff to assault the Gujarati fortress of Champnir.

'Majesty, we have captured the only outpost of Sekunder Shah's that we picked out in daylight as protecting this approach to his camp. Thirty of my men crept up to and silently climbed a section of its low mud wall which was crumbling away in the rains. Then they rushed the garrison, which numbered a dozen men, and quickly and quietly slit their throats or strangled them with thin cords. None escaped to give the alarm – none even raised a cry.'

'As usual you've done well, Ahmed Khan,' Humayun had said and Ahmed Khan had departed to despatch more of his scouts to advance stealthily towards Sekunder Shah's camp. Their task now was to try as best they could in the conditions to pick out the worst quagmires between Humayun's current position and the camp which lay unseen in the darkness no more than a mile away so that Humayun's assault troops could skirt them, avoiding becoming bogged down.

Impatient as he was to bring on the battle that would decide his destiny, Humayun knew their task was a crucial one and that it would be worth the wait for their report. In any case, the distances were small and they should soon return. After what seemed to Humayun an age but was, in fact, no more than a quarter of an hour, Ahmed Khan reappeared with six of his scouts, all mud-spattered and soaked like himself. Ahmed Khan spoke.

'The mission was so important I went forward myself with these brave men. We were not detected. We used lances to probe the firmness of the ground and the depth of the mud. We found that if we ride directly forward we will indeed come upon great stretches of extremely boggy ground which would impede our advance and might even cause some of the horses to become completely stuck.

However, if as we ride we take a rightward arc we will have a better if still very muddy approach. We will reach the earth barricades that Sekunder Shah has thrown up around his camp at their northern corner. Here they stand higher than a man. We may need to use the ladders that you ordered to be brought with us.'

'Thank you, Ahmed Khan. Jauhar, tell Bairam Khan to choose some pairs of soldiers from among the vanguard, each to carry slung between their horses one of the ladders we have brought this far on the backs of pack animals. Ask him to let me know once he is ready and I will join him in the advance.'

Jauhar rode off and Humayun could just distinguish by the lightning flashes Bairam Khan's horsemen forming up in battle order. Now combat was imminent, Humayun realised that he felt no fear but a general heightening of his senses which made a moment last a minute and a minute an hour and even seemed to sharpen his vision, enabling him to see Bairam Khan beckoning him through the murk before Jauhar appeared to tell him he was ready.

Humayun tugged on his leather gauntlets and instinctively touched his father's sword Alamgir in its jewelled scabbard at his side. Then he repositioned his feet in his stirrups to ensure they would not slip and finally kicked his black horse into motion and rode over to where Bairam Khan was waiting with Ahmed Khan. The latter would lead the advance with his six scouts who had made the reconnaissance. They had each draped white linen sheets around their shoulders to make themselves easier to follow in the gloom.

'May God go with us,' Humayun said. 'Lead off, Ahmed Khan.'

Ahmed Khan simply nodded and rode forward. He was quickly followed by the other six scouts and then by Bairam Khan and his young *qorchi*, now looking fully composed with a stern, concentrated expression on his young face. Humayun turned his horse and headed with them into the murk and falling rain towards Sekunder Shah's camp.

The conditions meant that they could not advance at much more than a canter. Even then, the horses' hooves threw up large amounts of mud and water which splattered those following. After they had ridden for no more than two or three minutes, Ahmed Khan reined in his horse by a small cluster of boulders on a low rise and Humayun rode up to him.

'Majesty,' Ahmed Khan spoke softly, 'these rocks are the last important marker. From here, the walls of Sekunder Shah's camp are about six hundred yards directly in front of us.'

'Summon up the pairs of men with ladders.'

As they rode up, the rough ladders slung between their horses by leather thongs, the rain slackened and almost as if by a miracle the moon appeared, pale and watery, through a gap in the scudding clouds. In the few moments before it disappeared again, Humayun glimpsed the walls of Sekunder Shah's camp. They were as Ahmed Khan had described, about eight feet high and made of earth, some of which appeared to have slipped down in places, making those sections more like steep hillocks.

There was no sign of sentries as moments later the men rode up to the walls and, dismounting quickly, positioned the ladders and scrambled up them on to the walls. There they began pushing the mud down, some kicking at it with their feet, others using spades they had carried strapped across their backs. Soon, about thirty feet of the wall had been reduced to no more than a low mound and Bairam Khan, followed by his *qorchi*, was leading his horsemen quietly into the camp. The rain was falling more heavily again and still there were no signs of alarm as Humayun himself and his bodyguard crossed the remains of the wall.

Suddenly, however, a startled cry rang out from somewhere in front of Humayun. 'The enemy!' Another fainter shout came from along the mud walls, then the much louder blare of a trumpet from the same direction. Perhaps the dozing personnel of a guardhouse had woken to the peril that was flowing all around them and were giving the alarm. There were answering trumpet blasts from towards the centre of the camp.

Now that surprise had been lost, Humayun realised that he and his men needed to advance as quickly as possible to destroy their enemy before they had time to arm and to form up. As he rode over towards Bairam Khan to give him the order to ride for the centre of the camp, a straggling volley of arrows fell, slanting down among the raindrops from the direction of the guard post. One implanted itself in Humayun's saddle. Another struck Bairam Khan's breastplate and bounced harmlessly off but a third caught Bairam Khan's *qorchi* in the thigh. The youth clutched at his leg and as the blood began to run through his fingers stifled a cry.

'Bind his wound tightly,' shouted Humayun. 'Get him back to our camp to the *hakims*. He's young and has been brave. He deserves to live.' One of Humayun's own bodyguards rushed to comply.

Another volley of arrows fell but they were few in number and the only casualty was a cavalryman's bay horse which slipped to the ground, two black-flighted arrows protruding from its neck. Its rider, a squat Tajik, jumped clear as it fell but slipped as he landed heavily in the mud, lying winded for a moment before scrambling to his feet.

'Bairam Khan, send forty men to locate the position those arrows came from and destroy the enemy archers. The rest of you, charge with me to victory.'

As Bairam Khan quickly detached the men to deal with the guard post, Humayun drew Alamgir. Holding the sword straight out in front of him, and with his bodyguard around him and Mustapha Ergun and his Turkish mercenaries close behind, he kicked his black stallion into as near a gallop as it could come to in the mud, riding deeper into the camp. By now there was a slight lightening of the sky on the eastern horizon, the precursor of dawn, but Humayun could still see little through the rain as he rode, head low over his horse's neck. Then, after a minute or so, he managed to distinguish the dark shapes of close-packed lines of tents ahead and at the same time heard the cries of Sekunder Shah's men as they emerged from them, pulling their weapons from their scabbards.

'Push the tents over to trap the enemy beneath. Ride down any who are already outside.' Following his own orders, Humayun leaned down from the saddle and slashed hard at the guy ropes of a large tent, which crumpled to the ground. Then he cut at a shadowy figure who, after emerging from a second tent, was raising his double bow. Humayun felt Alamgir slice deep into the unprotected flesh of the man's chest before biting into his ribs. The archer twisted and fell beneath the hooves of one of Humayun's advancing cavalrymen, who was in turn thrown.

All around other of Humayun's soldiers were jumping from the saddle the better to collapse the tents and to come to close quarters with their enemy. Soon Humayun could make out men rolling in the mud, fighting and stabbing at each other. He recognised one of his warriors, a curly-bearded, muscular Badakhshani who was sitting, smiling broadly, on an opponent's shoulders pulling his head back by the hair. As Humayun watched, he thrust the man's head forward again down into a quagmire of mud and water. He held it there for a couple of minutes before throwing the lifeless body aside.

Another of his men had run to a line of tethered cavalry horses and was slashing at their leg ropes. As he cut their tethers, he whacked each horse on the rump to send it galloping away into the gloom. Good, thought Humayun, it could only add to the panic and confusion among his awakening enemies. Yet another of his soldiers had grabbed a lance from a rack outside one collapsed tent and was stabbing at two figures struggling beneath its folds. Soon the squirming bodies were still and dark stains were spreading into the tent's material.

'Come,' Humayun shouted to Mustapha Ergun, 'it's getting lighter. Now we can see more, let us try to find Sekunder Shah's personal quarters. You too, Bairam Khan, follow me with your men.'

Soon, by the swiftly rising light, Humayun distinguished on a low rise about half a mile away a collection of large tents erected in a hollow rectangle with a big flag hanging wet and limp from a pole outside a single vast tent – surely Sekunder Shah's own – at its centre. As Humayun rode closer, he saw a number of men milling around the tents. Some already had their breastplates and helmets on, others were throwing saddles on their horses, clambering unprotected into them and forming up ready to defend themselves.

Moments later, Humayun heard a crackle of musket fire from beneath the awning of one of the tents – at least some of Sekunder Shah's men had kept their powder dry. Out of the corner of his eye, he saw one of Mustapha Ergun's Turks slide silently from his saddle with a bullet wound in his temple. His frightened horse swerved into the path of Humayun's own mount. Humayun hastily pulled on the reins of his horse but the frightened animal reared up. It took all Humayun's skill to retain his seat as his mount, dropping back on to its four legs, skittered sideways, further disrupting the progress of his other cavalry. They in turn, seeing Humayun's difficulty, almost instinctively began to rein in, presenting an attractive target to Sekunder Shah's men. A flight of arrows rose from another of the tents, which were now becoming veiled in white smoke from the muskets. Several more of Humayun's men were hit. One dropped his sword and, falling headlong into the mud, lay still. Others remained in the saddle but slowly dropped back from their comrades to tend their wounds.

Almost simultaneously, from Humayun's flank came two louder explosions. Turning his head towards the sound, Humayun realised that Sekunder Shah's artillerymen had got two of his larger cannon into action from where they had been dug in, protected from the wet by a rough, timber-planked roof. Each cannon ball found a mark. One hit a black horse in the belly, causing it to collapse. It tried to stagger to its feet, its intestines protruding from the gaping wound, before subsiding back into the mud neighing piteously. The second cannon ball carried away the front leg of another horse which buckled and fell, pitching its rider – another of Mustapha Ergun's men – over its head.

It had all happened very quickly and as Humayun regained full control of his dancing horse a sudden thought chilled him. He might be being drawn into a carefully prepared trap. Sekunder Shah's men might even now be circling round to block the route behind them. Surely the prize of the throne of Hindustan would not be ripped from his grasp once more? No, it could not be . . . He must not falter in his moment of destiny, not let doubt stand in the way of overcoming this momentary disorder.

'Come on, re-group! We mustn't lose impetus,' he yelled. Waving Alamgir he turned directly towards the tents from which the musket men had fired and kicked his horse forward as fast as it would go in the glossy deep mud. He was immediately followed by his bodyguard. Another few musket shots rang out and another rider fell but then Humayun was among the enemy musketeers who were now trying to flee, throwing aside their long weapons and supporting tripods. Humayun cut one down with a slash from Alamgir but then he and his men were in turn charged by some of the riders he had seen mounting up previously. A stout officer on a brown horse with a diamond blaze on its face made directly for Humayun, his lance held in his left hand aimed at Humayun's chest.

Humayun twisted his horse's head and the lance struck a glancing blow against his breastplate, knocking him slightly off balance so that his own sword slash also missed. Both men wheeled their horses round tightly and the officer drew his sword and came at Humayun again. Humayun ducked under his arcing sword cut, hearing a whooshing sound as it parted the air above his head. Then he lunged with Alamgir at his opponent's midriff, which was unprotected by chain mail. The sharp sword cut deep into soft, fatty flesh and, bleeding profusely, the officer collapsed over the neck of the brown horse, which bore him away into the mêlée.

Humayun next attacked an imposing red-turbaned figure he saw directing the fighting a little way off. As he rode closer, he saw the man pull a double-headed battleaxe from its sheath, which was attached to his saddle. He drew back his arm and sent the battleaxe spinning through the air towards Humayun. Humayun got his mail-clad arm up to protect his head but the sharp axe blade caught his arm a glancing blow. It was heavy enough to damage Humayun's chain mail and to reopen the scar tissue of the wound he had suffered all those years ago at the battle of Chausa. Bright scarlet-orange blood started to run down his arm and into the gauntlet on his hand. Humayun ignored it and, still gripping Alamgir tightly, slashed at the man as he rode past him so close that their legs bumped together. Humayun's stroke caught the officer full on his throat, just above his Adam's apple, severing his neck and sending pulses of blood into the air from his torso for the few moments it remained erect before collapsing from the saddle.

Breathing hard, Humayun reined in his horse and looked around. He and his men had won the battle around the command tents. To his left he could see Mustapha Ergun and some of his white-turbaned warriors pursuing a fleeing band of Sekunder Shah's cavalry while to his right Bairam Khan's men, among whom Humayun could identify Akbar's milk-brother Adham Khan, had encircled another large group who, as Humayun watched, flung down their arms.

Bairam Khan rode up to Humayun. 'Majesty, my junior commanders report that twenty of our divisions have entered Sekunder Shah's camp and more and more are doing so by the minute. We have killed many of our opponents before they could arm and captured many others, while yet more have fled in small groups in panic. We have already secured more than three-quarters of the camp. However, our enemies are still resisting strongly and in numbers in the southwest corner. Some of my men claim they saw an important officer, perhaps Sekunder Shah himself, riding in that direction with a bodyguard from the command tents when we first made our attack on them.'

'Let's get ourselves over there to organise the assault and attempt to capture Sekunder Shah if that is where he is. But first, bind this wound of mine with my neck cloth,' said Humayun, pulling off his gauntlet and stretching out his bloody arm to Bairam Khan. Within a few minutes, Bairam Khan had bound Humayun's forearm tightly and the wound, which was not deep, had more or less stopped bleeding.

Humayun and Bairam Khan headed through the rain across the slightly undulating ground towards the southwest corner of the camp, past collapsed tents, overturned cooking pots and the bodies of dead and wounded men and animals lying slumped amid the puddles, some of which were now stained red. As they drew closer, the cries and sounds of battle grew louder, including the occasional crack of muskets when soldiers from one side or the other managed to open their powder horns and prime their muskets sufficiently quickly or under sufficient cover for the powder to remain dry enough to ignite.

By the sombre leaden light of the new day, Humayun could see that Sekunder Shah's men were fighting determinedly. They had managed to overturn a number of baggage wagons around some small hillocks, and archers and musketeers were firing from behind the protection they provided. Several squadrons of cavalry were grouped in the middle of the barricades, whose perimeter stretched for perhaps twelve hundred yards. There appeared to be several thousand of the enemy in total. However, they were completely encircled by his own troops.

'Bairam Khan, order our men to pull back just a little but to keep Sekunder Shah's troops securely surrounded. We will offer them a chance to live if they will lay down their arms and tell us the whereabouts of Sekunder Shah.'

A quarter of an hour later, a gap was opened in Sekunder Shah's barricades and Humayun's emissary, a young officer named Bahadur Khan, re-emerged and galloped over to where Humayun was waiting, seated on his black horse.

'Majesty, they are willing to surrender. They are adamant that Sekunder Shah is not among them and that although it was indeed he who left the command tents with his bodyguard just after we attacked, he did so in flight. They accuse him of deserting them to save himself and it is for that reason that they have agreed to surrender. Several commanders actually volunteered to join our armies.'

Relief and joy swept through Humayun in equal measure. Victory was his. He had surmounted the last obstacle to his regaining Hindustan. Even if, as it seemed, he had failed to capture Sekunder Shah, his victory was complete. Sekunder Shah's vast army had been smashed in less than two hours of combat. Those who remained unwounded had surrendered or fled. Voice shaking with emotion, Humayun spoke.

'I thank you, my commanders. We have won a great victory. Hindustan is firmly within our grasp, but there is still no time to waste. First we must care for our wounded and bury our dead, but then we move on to Delhi to secure that great city.'

• ◆ •

Humayun woke to the sound of birdsong in his scarlet tent at the centre of his camp, just outside the great sandstone walls of Delhi. Later that morning he was due to make his ceremonial entry through the high gateway in them to hear the *khutba* read once more in his name at the service in the Friday Mosque, proclaiming him Padishah of Hindustan. The days since his victory at the battle of Sirhind had been crowded as he and his army had marched as quickly as the monsoon would allow towards Delhi. Local rulers had hastened to offer their obeisance and groups of soldiers formerly loyal to other of the pretenders to the throne had ridden in to surrender and to volunteer their services to Humayun.

Four days ago Humayun had passed the site of the battle of Panipat where he and his father had first won Hindustan. Even now, twenty-nine years later, the white bones of some of Sultan Ibrahim's great war elephants killed by Babur's artillerymen still lay scattered across the plain.

The previous evening, lying in his tent, Humayun had pondered the parallels and paradoxes within his own life and the comparisons with that of his father. He had lost his first great battle with Sher Shah when his enemy had made a surprise night attack during the monsoon and won his last great battle against Sekunder Shah by using those same tactics. On both occasions he had been wounded in his right forearm. His forces had melted away after his defeat by Sher Shah just as they had grown by desertion from Sekunder Shah and the other claimants to Hindustan during his recent campaign. His half-brothers had rebelled against him and threatened his family but Sher Shah's relations had exceeded even this. Not content with fighting his family, Adil Shah had killed his young nephew, the legitimate heir, in front of his mother, his own sister, something at which even Kamran had baulked.

Humayun had gained the Koh-i-Nur for the Moghuls following the great victory at Panipat and sacrificed it at his and the dynasty's nadir to help bring about its renaissance. Like his father, he had known youthful triumph but then suffered great reverses which had tested his resolve. Persian support and the religious compromises it had demanded had proved of less assistance to both than they had hoped. Like Babur, he had spent far more time in Kabul than he'd intended before seizing Hindustan.

Were these real patterns, just as in the movements of the stars?

405

And if they were, how did they come about? Were events inevitable, predestined and laid down by a superior power, ready to be read within the stars by anyone with insight, as he had once believed? Or, on the contrary, were the patterns in men's lives he thought he saw figments of his imagination and its search for structure in a shifting world, and the events themselves caused by coincidence or understandable similarities in circumstances? Weren't family rivalries inherent threats to ruling dynasties? Hadn't Babur's own half-brother rebelled against him and hadn't Timur's sons disputed and dissipated their father's legacy? Weren't defeats always followed by desertions, great victories by swathes of fawning new adherents? Hadn't learning from his father's experience and using it to strengthen his resolve created the similarities between their lives?

In his youth, he had liked to believe in patterns and in predestination. Such beliefs had seemed to absolve him from full responsibility for his actions and their consequences. They had fed his indolence and justified his naive trust that his supreme position was his by right and inviolable. But his experiences had changed him and now, in his maturity, he usually rejected such external explanations – excuses for failure even. Although it was God's will into which station a man was born, it was up to an individual and his use of his abilities to shape his life from there on. He had not regained his empire because it was predestined but because he had striven to do so, mastering his weaknesses and spurning indulgences to focus all his efforts on that single goal. Proud of this thought, Humayun had fallen asleep as he wondered how his renewed reign would evolve in comparison with the few short years Babur had had on the throne after conquering Hindustan.

As he stood up and prepared to call Jauhar, Humayun recollected his thoughts of the previous evening. As he did so, his eyes happened to fall on one of his volumes of star charts. He smiled. Even if he no longer believed that the stars held all the secrets of life, the study of them, their movements and the reasons underlying them, still stimulated his intellect. Stargazing would never lose its fascination for him.

Two hours later, after he had finished dressing him, Jauhar held up a long, burnished mirror for Humayun to inspect himself in his imperial finery. He saw a tall figure as erect and muscular at forty-seven years of age as he had been when he first had come to the throne, even if the hair at his temples was now flecked with grey and there were lines around his eyes and at the corner of his mouth when he smiled.

He was wearing a white surcoat embroidered with suns and stars in gold thread and hemmed with a border of lustrous pearls over a long cream silk tunic and pantaloons of the same colour. His belt was made from fine gold mesh and from it hung Alamgir in its jewelled scabbard. On his feet were short tawny leather boots with curled, pointed toes and a massive gold star embroidered on each side of the ankles. On his head he wore a turban of gold cloth with a peacock plume set at its peak and a circlet of rubies around its middle which matched his heavy ruby and gold necklace. On the index finger of his right hand he wore Timur's tiger ring and his other fingers sparkled emeralds and sapphires.

'Thank you, Jauhar; you have helped me to dress as befits an emperor. I've learned that as well as being powerful and possessing authority it is well to appear so to the people. It adds to their confidence and loyalty . . . but enough of that. Where is my son?'

'Waiting outside.'

'Ask him to come in.'

Moments later, Akbar appeared through the curtains at the entrance to the tent, which were held open by two bodyguards dressed entirely in green. Even though not yet thirteen, Akbar was almost as tall and broad-shouldered as his father. He too was dressed in royal finery, in purple and lilac, colours which only seemed to accentuate his burgeoning, youthful masculinity.

'Father,' said Akbar, for once speaking first and smiling broadly, 'one of the messengers who relays post from Kabul to Hindustan arrived a quarter of an hour ago. He brought a letter to us both from my mother. By now she will already have set out from Kabul to join us as you suggested after the battle of Sirhind. She should reach Delhi in six to eight weeks if the monsoon does not delay her too much.'

Humayun felt a lightness in his heart. Hamida's presence would complete his happiness. The sooner he could keep his promise made on their marriage fourteen years ago to offer her the life of an empress in Delhi and Agra the better. 'This is great news, Akbar. We must send orders immediately for a detachment of troops to meet her and to speed her on her way to us.'

Then Humayun walked slowly with Akbar from the tent towards where two imperial elephants were kneeling about two hundred and fifty yards away. Jauhar and Adham Khan, who were to ride with them, followed a few respectful paces behind. As they walked, attendants held silk canopies over their heads to protect them from the sun since there had been a break in the monsoon. Others waved large peacock-feather fans to cool them and to repel the buzzing mosquitoes which proliferated around the stagnant puddles which still covered the camp.

Once they reached the elephants, Humayun climbed up a small, gilded ladder on to the back of the larger of the two. He was followed by Jauhar and one of the tall green-clad bodyguards, who took their places behind him. The jewels – mostly garnets and amethysts – which encrusted the howdah shone in the sunlight as the first elephant rose to its feet, followed by the second only slightly smaller one which held Akbar, Adham Khan and another bodyguard. Akbar was chatting to his milk-brother as if they were merely going hunting.

Together, the stately elephants plodded slowly over towards a line of their companions. Humayun could see Bairam Khan in one of their howdahs, accoutred in Persian court fashion. Beside him was his *qorchi* who had recovered from his thigh wound, although it had required painful cauterising and he would never walk without a limp again. Zahid Beg was to ride on the elephant immediately following Bairam Khan and Ahmed Khan would ride on the leading elephant on Humayun's orders. 'You have deserved this honour – you always led the way when there was no prestige but much danger,' he had told him.

Mustapha Ergun and his men would be among the leading squadrons of cavalry which would precede the elephants. For a moment Humayun reflected on some of the other humbler people who had played a part in his story. He would have liked one-armed

Wazim Pathan and even Nizam the water-carrier to be present but Wazim Pathan had preferred to stay in his village as headman after Kamran's defeat and there had been no time to search for Nizam. Then, pulling himself back to the present, Humayun spoke. 'Let's get going.'

The order was relayed down the line of elephants through the ranks of cavalry to the riders at the very front of the procession who carried the great fluttering banners of Humayun and the Moghul dynasty as well as that of Timur. As they got underway towards the tall sandstone gateway half a mile ahead of them, the phalanxes of drummers and trumpeters immediately behind the banner bearers began to play, quietly at first and then with increasing vigour as they approached the thronging crowds whom ranks of soldiers had kept back from the camp but who now lined the ceremonial pathway to the gate, which they had strewn with palm branches and even flower petals.

As Humayun's elephant moved forward, he watched the sunlight glinting off the breastplates and harnesses of the cavalry ahead and the gilded howdah in front of him and listened to the sound of the music and the jangling of harnesses and neighing of animals being all but drowned out by the cheering of the crowds. Then, heart bursting with emotion, he looked upwards into the hot, blue sky and saw – or thought he saw – in the shimmering glare two circling eagles, harbingers of Moghul greatness. Hindustan was his. He had recovered the Moghul throne. From now on their dynasty would only go from strength to strength. He – and Akbar – would ensure it was so.

Chapter 27

The Stars Smile Down

Humayun was sitting in his private chambers in the Purana Qila, the red sandstone fortress that early in his reign he had begun building on Delhi's eastern edge but Sher Shah and his son Islam Shah had completed. The fortress's thick, well-buttressed walls, pierced by three gatehouses, snaked for over a mile and it made a fine imperial headquarters. Piled on a table before Humayun were the official imperial ledgers recording the administration of the empire under Sher Shah and his son that Jauhar – whom he had made Comptroller of the Household in thanks for his years of selfless service – had just brought him.

Now that the lush ceremonial and festivities of his entry into Delhi had come to an end, Humayun knew he must discipline himself to learn in earnest about how his empire worked and not simply relax and enjoy once more the indulgences his newly regained territories could offer. As he had told his counsellors, 'Our job is still only half done. Recapturing Hindustan was perhaps the easiest part. We must ensure we keep it and then expand our rule.' He had already questioned those of Sher Shah's and Islam Shah's officials who had remained in Delhi and despatched trusted commanders to inspect and rule the various provinces, among them Ahmed Khan to Agra.

Frowning slightly, he began to read. Despite himself, what the usurpers had achieved impressed him. The ledgers revealed that Sher Shah had been as tough, cunning and effective an organiser as he had been a cold-blooded and calculating warrior. He had reorganised the system of provincial government to prevent any individual governor from becoming too powerful. He had restructured the collection of revenue. Of course, during the recent wars, tax-gathering had been at best spasmodic and chaotic, but Humayun's own officials had already reported that the foundations of Sher Shah's system were still in place and robust enough to be revived. And that was all to Humayun's advantage. What was it his father had written in his diary? . . . *at least this place has plenty of money*. Controlling the wealth of Hindustan would, Humayun knew, be key to retaining and extending his power.

Sher Shah had improved roads, rebuilt the old mud-walled caravanserais along them and constructed new ones so travellers could find shelter every five miles. But the main purpose of the caravanserais was to act as post houses – *dak chauki* – for the messengers and horses that speeded the imperial mail along the new highways and made it possible to know quickly what was happening in the most distant regions of the empire.

To prevent rebellion, Sher Shah had built new forts to control the provinces and stamped hard on lawlessness of any kind. Humayun re-read a passage that had particularly caught his eye: *In his infinite wisdom and unbounded goodness, His Imperial Majesty Sher Shah has decreed that every headman shall protect his village lest any vile thief or murderer should attack a traveller and thus become the instrument of his injury or death*. When Sher Shah had said the headman must be responsible he had meant it. If the perpetrator of a crime was not apprehended, the headman himself had been forced to suffer the punishment.

Putting down the heavy, leather-bound ledger on the inlaid marble table beside him, Humayun smiled to recollect his own early days on the throne. How bored he would have been even thinking of some of the things that had preoccupied Sher Shah. What was heroic about collecting taxes or reorganising provinces or building roads? But now he could see that such things were essential to maintaining power. Had he focused more on them and less on seeking the answers to good government in the stars and in opium, he might not have lost Hindustan.

What mattered now was not to overturn what Sher Shah and Islam Shah had done but to retain the best elements so he could strengthen his own authority over Hindustan . . . But there was one change he would make. Though Delhi had been Sher Shah's capital and the Purana Qila was a palace-fortress fit for an emperor, he yearned to be in Agra once more, the city Babur had made his capital. As soon as he could, he would move his court there. Hamida had never seen Agra, and together they would create a place of such beauty that his court poets would require all their skill to capture it in words. But for the time being Delhi was better placed strategically for the tour of all the provinces of his empire he was planning in the next few months to remind the ordinary people of Hindustan, buffeted as they'd been by the winds of war, who their true emperor was – and that he was powerful . . .

'Majesty, Empress Hamida's caravan is just five miles from the city.' An attendant interrupted Humayun's thoughts and his heart leaped. He knew his wife had been making good progress, but that she was here so soon was a great surprise. He stood, overcome with joy and longing for her. The administration of the empire could wait. 'Bring me my imperial robes. I must look my best for my wife. Even then she will outshine me by far.'

Humayun watched the slow approach of Hamida's procession from the top of the western gate of the Purana Qila. It was the most magnificent of the entrances, with its tall pointed arch inset with white marble stars and two round flanking towers, and it was through this gate that Hamida, Moghul Empress of Hindustan, was making her entrance. The elephant carrying her was clad in plates of beaten gold and even its tusks were gilded. As it passed beneath the western gate, the trumpeters in the gatehouse sounded their instruments and attendants threw fistfuls of rose petals and tiny twists of gold leaf from the roof. Humayun hurried down to an inner courtyard where a vast green velvet tent had been erected, with awnings fringed with green ribbons and the entrance curtains tied

413

back with tasselled golden cords. Within the tent Humayun could see the block of pure white marble placed ready for Hamida to dismount in privacy.

Hamida's elephant was coming into the courtyard now and the *mahout*, seated on the beast's neck, carefully guided it towards the great tent and on through the opening. Then, tapping his metal staff gently against first the right and then the left shoulder of the elephant, he caused it to kneel by the marble block. As soon as the animal had lowered itself, the *mahout* slid down and stood respectfully to one side. Humayun approached the howdah and, stepping on to the block, gently pulled aside the shimmering gold mesh.

As she smiled back at him, Hamida seemed more beautiful than ever in gold-embroidered robes, her long, black, sandalwood-scented hair spilling over her shoulders and, rising and falling on her breast, the necklace of rubies and emeralds that had been his wedding gift to her and they had preserved through so many misfortunes.

'Leave us,' Humayun ordered the *mahouts*. As soon as they were alone, he lifted Hamida from the howdah and held her against him. 'My queen,' he whispered, 'my empress . . .'

That night they made love in the apartments he had had prepared for Hamida overlooking the Jumna river. They had once formed a part of Islam Shah's *haram* and the carved alcoves, set with tiny pieces of mirror glass, sparkled like diamonds in the candlelight. Frankincense glowed in slender-legged golden burners at each corner of the room and scented water bubbled from a marble fountain carved to resemble the petals of a rosebud.

Hamida was naked except for her necklace and Humayun stroked the satin skin of her hip. 'At last I can give you what I promised you. During our flight across the Rajasthan desert sometimes at night when I couldn't sleep I'd watch the stars, wondering what messages they held and finding some comfort there. But you were my greatest solace – so brave, so resolute, so patient, even when all we had to eat was mule flesh boiled in a soldier's helmet over a dung fire . . .'

Hamida smiled. 'I still remember how shocked I was when my father told me you wanted to marry me . . . I'd only seen you from far off . . . you seemed like a god . . . On our wedding night I was still nervous, but when you came to me I saw your love for me burning so bright that I knew you would become a part of me . . . you have . . . you are my life . . .'

'And you are mine . . . but let me prove to you once again that I am indeed a man, not a god.' As Humayun pulled Hamida to him, he saw the answering gleam in her brown eyes.

• ◆ •

'Majesty, a post-rider has arrived with a message from Bairam Khan.'

'Bring him to me immediately.' Humayun paced his apartments as he waited. At last . . . but what news did the man bring? It was nearly three months since Bairam Khan had ridden out at the head of twenty thousand troops to deal with a sudden and serious threat to Humayun's supremacy. Though in the aftermath of the battle at Sirhind Sekunder Shah had fled into the foothills of the Himalayas, he had reappeared on the plains of the Punjab where he had been seeking to rally support. Bairam Khan's early reports had been encouraging, suggesting that he might soon be upon Sekunder Shah and his forces, but then Sekunder Shah had retreated back into the mountains. Bairam Khan's last despatch, received nearly a month ago, reported his plan to pursue him there. Since then there had been silence.

Humayun's greatest fears, as day followed day, had been for Akbar. His son had begged to be allowed to accompany Bairam Khan and Humayun had reluctantly agreed, ordering that Akbar be kept back from the fighting and placing him in the special care of Nadim Khwaja, father of Akbar's milk-brother Adham Khan who was also to go. Though it had filled him with pride, it had been hard to watch his only son ride off cheerfully to war. It had been even more difficult for Hamida and though they had resolutely avoided discussing it he knew how many restless nights she had endured. But now, with luck, the waiting would soon be over.

As he was ushered into Humayun's presence, the post-rider's dusty clothes and stiff-legged gait spoke of many hours in the saddle. Bowing before Humayun, he reached into his leather satchel and extracted a folded letter. 'My orders were to hand this to no one but you, Majesty.' Humayun took the letter eagerly but then felt a sudden reluctance to know its contents. But that was foolish thinking. Slowly he unfolded the letter and saw the lines of Persian written in Bairam Khan's neat, elegant hand.

Rejoice, Majesty. Your armies have defeated the traitor Sekunder Shah who has fled like a coward eastward to Bengal, leaving his men to their fate. We have taken five thousand prisoners and great booty. Within a month, God willing, I hope to lead your troops back into Delhi and have the joy of reporting in detail the story of our campaign. Your son is in good health and begs to send his respects to you and Her Imperial Majesty.

For a moment Humayun bowed his head in silent joy. Then he shouted to his attendants, 'Order the drums to be beaten above the gates of the fortress and on the city walls. We have won a great victory and the world must know.'

• ◆ •

Just as the sky was pinkening in the west, Humayun heard the strident blast of trumpets that announced that Bairam Khan was riding in through the western gate. Moments later, one of Humayun's personal attendants came to help him dress in a coat of dark green brocade with emerald fastenings.

'You have the gift I wish to present to Bairam Khan?'

'Yes, Majesty.'

'Then let us proceed.' Followed by six bodyguards, Humayun made his way to the audience chamber and entered through the arched door to the right of his gilded throne. His courtiers, commanders and officials – Jauhar among them – were already grouped in a semicircle facing the throne. Their robes and tunics of every hue from saffron yellow and red to purple and blue were as brilliant as the rich carpet from Tabriz on which they were standing. Jewels sparkled in their turbans, around their necks and on their fingers. At the sight of Humayun, all bowed low.

His impulse was to stride right past them and on through the open double doors of polished mulberry into the antechamber beyond, where he could see Bairam Khan and Akbar waiting. But he had summoned his courtiers to witness the homecoming of a victorious general and must give them a dignified spectacle. Seating himself on his throne, Humayun raised his hand. 'Let Bairam Khan approach.' He watched as his commander entered the chamber and made his way slowly towards the throne, then halted and bowed.

'Bairam Khan, you are welcome,' said Humayun, then gestured to his attendant who stepped forward with a bag of turquoise velvet. Loosening the cord of twisted silver thread at its neck, Humayun tipped the contents into his left hand and extended it towards Bairam Khan. Those closest to the throne gasped as they saw the dark red glitter of rubies.

'Bairam Khan, you are a soldier to whom such fripperies as this gift of gems mean little. But I have something else to give. You will become my *khan-i-khanan*, commander-in-chief of the imperial Moghul armies.'

'Majesty.' Bairam Khan bowed low once more, but not before Humayun had seen his dark blue eyes flash with surprise. It was a good way to reward the general who had left his Persian homeland for him and served with such distinction. Zahid Beg might also have expected the honour and had certainly deserved it, but he had recently asked leave to return to his ancestral lands near Kabul. He was growing old and stiff, he had told Humayun. His days as a warrior were nearly done, but if ever Humayun had need of him he would come.

Humayun looked over Bairam Khan's head to address his courtiers. 'On the night of the next full moon, we will illuminate the Purana Qila with so many lamps and candles that its radiance will rival the moon itself and we will feast to celebrate this victory.' Humayun turned again to his attendant. 'Now summon my beloved son before me.'

As Akbar entered Humayun saw with love and pride how much he had altered in the months he had been away. He looked even taller and his broad, muscular shoulders strained against the green cloth of his tunic. He was also, Humayun noted, looking more than a little pleased with himself. But as his son drew nearer and touched his right hand to his breast in salute, he saw it was bandaged. Before Humayun could ask the cause, Bairam Khan, who had seen the direction of his glance, spoke.

417

'Majesty, as you instructed I ensured that during major actions the prince was well protected by bodyguards. But late one afternoon, not many days after we had crushed Sekunder Shah, my scouts reported that they had spotted a band of his men in the foothills. I decided to lead a party of a thousand cavalry, together with a few small baggage wagons carrying weapons and supplies, in pursuit and to take Akbar with me to gain experience of such operations. I thought there would be little danger. But as we were riding up a narrow ravine, there was a sudden rockslide and amid the shower of pebbles and scree several heavy boulders came crashing down, killing three of my men and blocking the way.

'Most of the column had already passed beyond that point but the last hundred or so riders and our few wagons were now cut off from the main party. With darkness falling and the risk of further rockslides, I shouted to those who had been separated from us to retreat back the way they'd come. I then moved the rest of the column quickly out of the ravine and returned with some of our strongest men to attempt to clear the debris. But it quickly became obvious we could not complete the task until the light returned . . . My greatest anxiety was for the prince who with his milk-brother was among those we could not reach, but . . .' here Bairam Khan paused, 'I should let him tell his own story . . .'

'I'd heard Bairam Khan ordering us to get out of the ravine,' Akbar continued eagerly, 'but just as we were turning the baggage wagons – which wasn't easy, the defile was narrow – we were suddenly attacked by men swarming about on a rock shelf high above us. From what little we could see of them they didn't look like soldiers of Sekunder Shah. They were poorly armed – no muskets, just arrows and spears. I think they were probably mountain tribesmen who'd been observing our progress and hoped for a chance of plunder. Perhaps they'd even caused the landslip . . . Whoever they were, their arrows and spears were soon falling thickly around us and several of our men were hit.

'I shouted to our troops to take cover behind the wagons and then ordered the few musketeers we had with us to fire at our assailants. They had the sinking orange sun in their eyes but the flash

418

and bang of their guns was enough to frighten our attackers off and we got at least one of them. His body came tumbling down and when we inspected it we found a musket ball in his forehead. Though we remained on guard all that night they didn't return and next morning, after the fallen rock had been cleared, we were reunited with the main column.'

'And your hand?'

'My first battle wound – a graze from an arrow. Adham Khan saw it coming and pushed me to one side or it might have hit me in the body . . .' Akbar's amber-brown eyes – so like Hamida's – had been glowing as he had relived the skirmish.

'You acquitted yourself bravely and well,' said Humayun. Privately he wondered what Hamida, watching and listening behind the grille set high in the wall to the right of his throne, would be thinking. But despite her maternal fears she should be as proud of Akbar as he was. He had shown coolness and resourcefulness – essential survival skills for an emperor and ones that could not be acquired too early.

• ◆ •

That night, Humayun ate with Hamida and Akbar in the *haram*. As he looked at his exquisite wife and handsome, athletic son bursting with confidence and youthful vitality, he felt a deeper content than he had perhaps ever known. The pieces of his fragmented life seemed to have fallen into place at last. The empire that God in his wisdom and mercy had allowed him to take back was secure and with Akbar by his side he would expand it. And one day Akbar in turn would launch his own wars of conquest and extend the Moghul lands from sea to sea.

Hamida too looked happy. Her face had acquired a new bloom and her clinging silk garments showed the supple, fluid outline of her body that, grown a little more voluptuous since the days of her girlhood, was even more beautiful. Tonight ornaments of blue sapphires set with diamonds sparkled in her flowing dark hair, and another sapphire was in her navel left bare by low, wide-cut trousers of duck-egg blue and a short, tight-fitting bodice that revealed the swell of her breasts.

'How is it with my empress?' Humayun asked when Akbar left them and they were alone.

'As I have told you again and again' – she smiled – 'it is very well. So many hundreds of attendants . . . my every desire anticipated . . . My life is everything I could have imagined and more. But what pleases me above everything is that our son has returned safely. He fills me with such joy. It seems so strange to me to remember how – after he was taken from us and Hindal brought him back – Akbar seemed not to know me. I was so envious of Maham Anga when I saw how he stretched out his hands to her and how his smiles were for her, not me. I was so angry with myself, so ashamed of my jealousy, after everything we owed to brave Maham Anga . . . But all that belongs to the past. Now I feel I know every thought running through Akbar's mind, that I understand all his desires and ambitions. The bonds between us could not be stronger . . .'

'I remember what you told me on the morning after our wedding night – that you knew you would bear a son and that he would be a great ruler one day . . . What do you see now when you look into the future?'

'Akbar's birth was the last thing I foresaw clearly. Though as a girl I seemed to have inherited the mystic powers of my ancestor, they left me . . . Perhaps that is for the best. The ability to see into the future may not always bring happiness . . . sometimes it may be better not to know . . .'

Chapter 28

Staircase to Heaven

In his apartments Humayun was studying the plans for a new library that his architects had presented to him earlier that afternoon. The pale clear light of a perfect January afternoon played over drawings of a building of red sandstone patterned with milk-white marble and, on each of its four sides, a tall *iwan* – a recessed entrance arch – on which would be inscribed verses from Humayun's favourite Persian poets. One day, Humayun thought, his library would eclipse even the fabled collections of his Timurid ancestors in their glorious palaces beyond the Oxus. And in pride of place, carefully preserved in an ivory box to match their still beautiful but yellowing ivory covers, would be his father's memoirs.

Babur had constructed a handsome mosque and madrasa in Kabul and laid out several fine gardens, but had not had time to leave any great monument behind him in Hindustan. Humayun felt grateful that he now had that opportunity. At forty-seven years old he was still in his prime. As well as planning a library, he had already commissioned an octagonal floating palace to be built on the Jumna river and surrounded by barges planted with fruit trees – oranges, lemons and pomegranates – and sweet-smelling flowers.

He was equally pleased that the observatory he was installing on the roof of the Sher Mandal – a graceful octagonal pavilion of red sandstone, built by Sher Shah in the grounds of the Purana Qila –

was nearly complete. On the Sher Mandal's open roof was a platform beneath a small open dome – *chattri* his Hindustani subjects called it – supported on slim white pillars which was a perfect place from which to view the stars. The astronomical instruments he had had specially made and the copy he had acquired of the *Zij-i-Gurkani* – the astronomical handbook compiled by Timur's grandson Ulugh Beg that gave the celestial locations of the stars – were all ready and in the care of a new imperial astronomer.

According to the star charts, this evening – Friday 24 January – would be an especially good time to observe the ascent of Venus into the night sky. Glancing out through the casement Humayun could see that the sun was already starting to sink. Putting down the building plans and calling to his attendants that he was going to the observatory and was not to be disturbed there, he quickly descended from his apartments and went out across the flower-filled gardens to the Sher Mandal. Climbing the steep, straight stone stairway to its roof, he found his astronomer already waiting for him beneath the slender-columned *chattri*.

Humayun had seldom seen the sky – flushed pink and gold – look so mesmerising. And there she was – Venus herself – the Evening Star – growing every second more brilliant in the darkening heavens. Moths fluttered around the wicks in *diyas* of oil that the observatory servants were lighting as dusk fell, but Humayun continued to stare upwards, transfixed.

It was the voice of the muezzin calling sonorously from the minaret of the nearby royal mosque that finally jerked Humayun from his reverie. He would far rather stay here but it was Friday – the day when he prayed in public before his courtiers. Dragging his gaze from Venus, Humayun turned and made for the stairs. The muezzin had almost finished – he must hurry . . .

But as he stepped down on to the first step, the toe of his leather boot caught in the fur-edged hem of his long blue robes and he was suddenly pitched forward into nothingness. He put out his hands but there was nothing to grab and he went plunging down head first. A sudden pain sharp as a blade pierced his skull. Stars appeared before his eyes, forming and re-forming in dancing patterns, drawing him onwards to become one with them and merging into a single bright light. Then all was black and still and peace.

• ◆ •

'Is the great *hakim* here yet?'

'He is coming, Bairam Khan.' Jauhar's expression in the dim light of Humayun's sick chamber was as anxious as the Persian's. 'We sent for him at once, of course, but unluckily for us he had left Delhi a week ago to attend a family wedding in his home village a day's ride from the city. It took my messengers time to discover this and then to go there. However, word reached me just an hour ago that he has been found and is being brought to the Purana Qila.'

'I pray God that he is in time and that his skill is as great as his reputation . . .' Bairam Khan broke off as he heard voices outside in the corridor. Then the doors swung open to admit a tall, smooth-shaven man in dark robes, a large, battered leather bag on his shoulder.

Bairam Khan stepped forward. 'I am His Majesty's *khan-i-khanan*. I sent messengers to find you. You are the most respected *hakim* in Delhi and our last hope. Our own doctors have been able to do nothing but one of them told us of you – that you once saved Islam Shah when he was close to death after a fall from his horse.'

The *hakim* nodded.

'I trust that your past service to Islam Shah doesn't make you unwilling to treat his successor?'

'A doctor's duty is to save lives.' The *hakim* glanced at the bed where Humayun was lying, head heavily bandaged, eyes closed and utterly still. 'Before I examine His Majesty, tell me exactly what happened and how he has been. I must know everything.'

'I fear there is little to tell. Three days ago he fell down a stone staircase. He must have smashed the side of his head against the bottom step – the edge is hard and sharp. His attendants found him with his head covered with blood and carried him unconscious to his apartments. Our *hakims* examined him and found a gash and a huge swelling on his right temple. He was also bleeding from the mouth and from his right ear. Since then he has been drifting in and out of consciousness. Even in his more lucid moments, which

423

are becoming fewer, he recognises no one – not even the empress or his son.'

The *hakim* nodded thoughtfully then moved towards the bed and gently pulled the coverlet back from Humayun, who made no movement. Bending his head, the doctor listened for a few moments to Humayun's heartbeat, then lifted first one of his eyelids then the other. His expression was grave as, covering his patient again, he raised Humayun's head a few inches and, unwinding the bandage of fine wool around the top of his head, revealed his cut, swollen and discoloured temple. Humayun stirred briefly as the doctor's fingers probed gently but made no sound.

The *hakim* was still examining the wound when Akbar returned to the sickroom from the women's quarters where he had been comforting Hamida. He had hardly been able to bear the sight of his father lying so helpless but at the same time couldn't stay away. For most of the seventy-two hours since the accident he had been at Humayun's bedside hoping in vain for some sign of improvement. 'Please,' he whispered to the *hakim*, 'you must save him. Return my father to life.'

'I will try, but his life is in God's hands.'

The *hakim* slid his bag from his shoulder and opening it took out a bunch of herbs whose pungent bitter smell filled the air. 'Build up the fire,' he ordered the attendants. 'I need to infuse these herbs in boiling water to make a poultice to reduce the swelling.' As the attendants added more charcoals to the brazier burning at the foot of Humayun's bed, the *hakim* took out a small brass bowl and a bundle fastened with a strap. Undoing it, he unrolled the bundle to reveal a selection of medical instruments from which he took a small sharp-bladed knife. 'I will try bleeding His Majesty. It may help relieve the pressure on his brain that I believe his injury has caused. I need someone to hold the cup.'

'I will,' Akbar said at once. The *hakim* carefully took Humayun's right arm from beneath the coverlet, turned it wrist side up, picked up his knife and drawing the blade over Humayun's waxen skin made a small incision just beneath the elbow. As the blood flowed, Akbar carefully caught it in the brass bowl. The sight of the vital red fluid brought him hope. It was proof that the inert figure still lived. His father was so strong, he thought. He had already survived so much. Surely he could overcome this . . .

As the *hakim* gestured to Akbar to remove the bowl and pressed a pad of white cotton against the cut to staunch the flow, Humayun murmured something. Akbar put his head nearer to his lips, trying to catch what he was saying, but he couldn't. 'I am here, Father, I am here,' he said, hoping that somehow Humayun would hear him and understand. Suddenly tears ran down his face and splashed on to Humayun's.

'Majesty, we must leave the *hakim* space to do his work.' Bairam Khan touched Akbar gently on the shoulder.

'You are right.' With one final glance at his father, Akbar rose and walked slowly from the sick chamber. As the doors closed behind him, he didn't see the *hakim*'s slow shake of the head as he turned to Bairam Khan and Jauhar.

◆

'Majesty, I am sorry to intrude upon your grief so soon after your husband's death, but I have no choice. If you value your son's life you must listen to me . . .'

Hamida lifted her pale, strained face from her hands and looked towards Bairam Khan. Above the veil she had pulled across the lower portion of her face her eyes were red with weeping. But at the suggestion that Akbar might be in danger, something in Hamida changed. She drew herself up and her voice was calm as she said, 'What do you mean, Bairam Khan?'

'God saw fit to call His Majesty your husband to Paradise when he had been back on the throne of Hindustan for only six months. Although Akbar is his undisputed heir, the prince is only thirteen years old. If we are not careful, ambitious men will try to take the throne from him. Men who had been supporters of Kamran or Askari but would have remained loyal to your husband for years if he had lived may see his sudden death as their opportunity, even though Askari is dead and Kamran blinded and in Mecca. We must also think of the rulers of subject kingdoms such as the smooth-tongued and slippery Uzad Beg, the Sultan of Multan, who have only resubmitted to Moghul authority during our invasion and may try to break free again. And of course the news may encourage Sekunder Shah to emerge from the jungles of Bengal to attempt to raise armies once more. There are also our external enemies such as the Sultan of Gujarat . . .'

'Bairam Khan, enough,' Hamida interrupted. 'My husband chose you as *khan-i-khanan* because he trusted you. I trust you too – tell me what we should do.'

'We must keep His Majesty's death a secret for a few days to give us time to summon from the provinces those we know to be loyal – men like Ahmed Khan from Agra. When enough of our faithful supporters are here with their men, we can have the *khutba* read in the prince's name in the mosque without fear of challenge. I wish Zahid Beg were not so far away. I've already sent riders to inform him of His Majesty's death and to ask him to secure Kabul and the territories beyond the Khyber for Akbar.'

'But how can we keep my husband's death from becoming known?'

'By acting quickly and decisively. Although here in the Purana Qila and outside in the city people know that the emperor has had an accident, at present only a very few – the *hakims*, Jauhar, your husband's personal attendants – know of his death. All must be sworn to secrecy and as soon as I have despatched messengers to the provinces – which I will do within the hour – I will order that no one is to enter or leave the fortress. I will say that there has been an outbreak of disease in the Purana Qila and that I am taking measures to prevent its spreading to the city.'

'But my husband showed himself to the people every day from the balcony of the Purana Qila that overlooks the river. What will they say when he doesn't appear?'

'We must choose someone of similar height and build to dress in imperial robes and impersonate the emperor. From across the river no one will be able to distinguish his features.'

'What of Akbar during these next days?'

'He should stay within the *haram*. I will post extra guards – my most trusted men – around your apartments. All his food, everything he drinks – even water – must be tasted first.'

'You think the situation so dangerous?'

426

'Yes, Majesty, beyond a doubt. Remember how the newly dead Islam Shah's eldest son was murdered before his mother's eyes here in Delhi, scarcely three years ago.'

'Then we will do exactly what you say. It is what my husband would have wished.'

• ◆ •

That night, with only moonlight and starlight for illumination, Akbar was standing in the small garden within the walls of the Purana Qila that Humayun had begun laying out just three months earlier. Behind him stood Jauhar, Bairam Khan and a few others who could be trusted to witness the secret burial of Humayun, Moghul Emperor of Hindustan. Since women did not attend funerals – even clandestine ones – Hamida and Gulbadan were watching from a casement above. Humayun's body, washed in fragrant water and shrouded in soft linen, lay inside a plain wooden casket beneath the freshly turned earth. The mullah had just finished intoning the prayers for the dead and Humayun's funeral – such as it was – was over.

Tears welled in Akbar's eyes as he thought of the father he'd never see again. He also felt apprehensive. A few days ago his life had seemed happy and secure but now everything had changed. He sensed tension all around him. Though his mother and Bairam Khan had said little, he knew from their every look and gesture that they were concerned and that their concern was for him.

But he wouldn't be afraid. He was of Timur's blood. Like his grandfather Babur before him, he wouldn't allow a cruel mischance to deprive him of what was his. Closing his eyes, Akbar began silently to address his dead father. 'I promise that you won't lie long in this simple grave, hidden from the eyes of men. As soon as I am able, here in Delhi, I will build for you the most magnificent tomb the world has ever seen. I, Akbar, the new Moghul emperor, swear it on my heart and on my soul . . . My beloved father, you named me "Great" and great I will be – not only in memory of you but in fulfilment of the destiny I feel within me.'

Historical Note

I was fortunate that the story of Humayun — warrior, star-gazer and second Moghul emperor — is quite well documented, better than that of his father Babur, the subject of the previous book in the Empire of the Moghul quintet, *Raiders from the North*. The adventures, tragedies, contradictions and eventual triumphs of Humayun's extraordinary life were captured by his half-sister Gulbadan, 'Princess Rosebody', in her detailed and affectionate account of his life — the *Humayunnama*. Humayun's attendant Jauhar also wrote a record of his master's life — the *Tadhkirat al-Waqiat* — while Abul Fazl, friend and adviser of Humayun's son Akbar, chronicled Humayun's reign in the first volume of his *Akbarnama*.

Despite the elaborate language and flowery hyperbole and certain gaps and inconsistencies in the accounts, Humayun emerges as brave, ambitious, charismatic — and at times more than a little eccentric. He indeed believed that messages were written in the stars and early in his reign organised the administration of his empire into departments based on the four elements of earth, fire, air and water. He dressed in certain colours on certain days — woe betide any miscreant brought before him on Tuesdays, the day of wrath and vengeance, when Humayun dressed in blood-red robes — and ordered the weaving of a vast astrological carpet. An early and well-documented addiction to opium probably explains some of the excesses of his early years but they were also the product of an enquiring, restless, mystical mind.

The main military, political and personal events described in *Brothers at War* all happened. Humayun was pushed out of Hindustan by Sher Shah, the ambitious son of a horse-trader from Bengal, and after one battle against Sher Shah was saved by a young water-seller called Nizam whom he allowed to sit on his throne. Humayun's flight with Hamida across the Rajasthani desert, Akbar's birth in lonely Umarkot, and the journey to find sanctuary in Persia, reduced to eating horsemeat boiled in a helmet, are true. So was Humayun's happiness at eventually regaining his lost empire in Hindustan. His death just six months later after falling down a steep staircase from the roof of his observatory where he had been watching his beloved stars seems as poignant as anything a novelist could invent. It left his distraught widow Hamida with a young son to protect and the Moghul Empire again in the balance.

The treachery of Humayun's half-brothers – especially Kamran and Askari – indeed tainted and dominated nearly his entire reign. Humayun really did pardon his brothers several times when his courtiers expected him to have them executed and argued for it. Humayun did alienate Hindal because of his determination to marry Hamida, whom Hindal is also said to have loved. Finally running out of patience, Humayun did have Kamran blinded and sent him, like Askari, on the *haj* to Mecca. However, I have sometimes condensed or simplified the action and omitted some incidents as well as compressing the timescales. I have also obviously used the novelist's freedom to invent other incidents while remaining true to the overall framework of Humayun's life.

Nearly all the main characters in the book existed in addition to his three half-brothers – his son Akbar, mother Maham, wife Hamida, half-sister Gulbadan, aunt Khanzada, Akbar's milk-mother Maham Anga and milk-brother Adham Khan, Sher Shah, Islam Shah, Sekunder Shah, Shah Tahmasp of Persia, Bahadur Shah of Gujarat, Husain of Sind, Maldeo of Marwar and Bairam Khan. A very few like Baisanghar, Humayun's grandfather, Ahmed Khan, his chief scout, Kasim, his vizier, and Baba Yasaval his general are composite characters.

As part of my research for this book over a number of years, I visited most of the places described – where they still exist – not only in India but in Afghanistan, Iran and Pakistan. I remember in particular the red sandstone pavilion – the Sher Mandal in Delhi on the banks of the River Jumna – where I descended the stairs down which Humayun tumbled. I could picture the charismatic star-gazer hurrying towards those narrow stone steps, so full of energy and confidence, with so much he still wanted to accomplish, just seconds before his light was extinguished for ever.

Additional Notes

Chapter 1

Humayun came to the throne in December 1530.

Humayun was born to Maham in 1508.

Kamran was born to Gulrukh during a period not covered in the *Baburnama*, Babur's memoirs. The precise date is unknown but he was clearly very close to Humayun in age.

Askari was born to Gulrukh in 1516. Hindal was born to Dildar three years later in 1519. Maham did beg Babur – even before Hindal was born – to let her adopt Dildar's child and he agreed.

Of course Humayun would have used the Muslim lunar calendar, but I have converted dates into the conventional solar, Christian, calendar we use in the west.

Timur, a chieftain of the nomadic Barlas Turks, is better known in the west as Tamburlaine, a corruption of 'Timur the Lame'. Christopher Marlowe's play portrays him as 'the scourge of God'.

Khanzada's abduction and the circumstances surrounding Babur's death are described in the first volume of this quintet, *Raiders from the North*.

Chapter 2
Humayun's conquest of Gujarat took place in 1535–6.

Chapter 6
The battle of Chausa took place in June 1539. Jauhar tells the story of Nizam.

Chapter 8
The battle of Kanauj was fought in June 1540.

Chapter 9
Both Humayun and Kamran did indeed write offering terms to Sher Shah which he rejected.

Chapter 10
Gulbadan described the flight from Lahore as 'like the day of resurrection, people left their decorated palaces and their furniture just as they were'.

Chapter 11
Hamida and Humayun were married at midday on 21 August 1541.

Chapter 13
Khanzada died some years later and in different circumstances from those described here.
Akbar was born in Umarkot on 15 October 1542.

Chapter 14
The circumstances of Akbar being handed over to Kamran are fictionalised.

Chapter 15
Gulbadan described the vicious mountain tribes with their propensity for cannibalism as 'ghouls of the wastes'.
Humayun crossed into Persia in December 1543.
The once magnificent city of Kazvin was destroyed by an earthquake. It lies in the northwest of Iran, south of the Caspian Sea.

Shah Tahmasp's luscious reception of Humayun – and the tensions – are described by both Jauhar and Gulbadan. The nearer Humayun drew to Kazvin, the more the journey resembled a triumphal progress. Kettledrums boomed as they rode. In the towns and villages people were ordered to put on their best clothes and cheer the column as it passed by.

Abul Fazl wrote that the Koh-i-Nur diamond reimbursed all Shah Tahmasp's expenditure on Humayun 'more than four times over'. The Koh-i-Nur later made its way back to India where a French jeweller saw it in the collection of Humayun's great-grandson, Shah Jahan. It is now among the British Crown Jewels.

Chapter 16

The Safawid dynasty had made the Shia practice of Islam the state religion of Persia in 1501. The distinction between Shia and Sunni derived from the first century of Islam and originally related to who was Muhammad's legitimate successor and whether the office should be an elected one or restricted, as the Shias claimed, to the descendants of the prophet through his cousin and son-in-law, Ali. 'Shia' is the word for 'party' and comes from the phrase 'the party of Ali'. 'Sunni' means 'those who follow the custom (sunna) of Muhammad'. By the sixteenth century further differences had grown between the two sects, such as the nature of required daily prayer. Humayun did indeed convert to Shiism temporarily.

Chapter 17

Kamran did expose Akbar on the walls of Kabul to forestall one of Humayun's attacks on the city of which historically there were several. The city changed hands between the two brothers more than once.

Chapter 20

Sher Shah died in May 1545.

Chapter 21

Hindal died fighting Askari in 1551 in somewhat different circumstances from those described here.

Chapter 23

Jauhar describes the blinding of Kamran. Unlike Askari, Kamran made it to Mecca. He died in Arabia in 1557.

Chapter 24

Islam Shah died in October 1553.

Chapter 26

The battle of Sirhind was fought in June 1555.
Humayun entered Delhi at the end of July 1555.

Chapter 27

Sekunder Shah died in 1559.

Chapter 28

Humayun died on 24 January 1556. His vast sandstone mausoleum inlaid with white marble still stands in Delhi, an architectural gem and an obvious precursor of the Taj Mahal.